FRASER VALLEY REGIONAL LIBRARY

Praise for Curt Le\

D0499001

Kafka's Son

"By following a labyrinthian circuit—under the sign of Calvino and Perec—Curt Leviant takes us along the trail of Kafka. Breathtaking! … As to whether or not Kafka had an heir, the answer is obvious. His name is Curt Leviant."
—*LIRE Magazine*

"A true literary success. Here Prague reveals itself as a magical, bewitching, mysterious, perplexing city. *Kafka's Son* is a fascinating novel that tempts you to take the first plane to Prague carrying a pile of Kafka's books."
—*Art Press*

"*Kafka's Son* is a realistic fantasy, a captivating maze, a detective novel, a love story, with multiple layers that never ceases to delight."
—*Magazine Litteraire*

"*Kafka's Son* is a work of genius."
—France 2 TV

"Leviant likes to captivate his readers, to dazzle them, to shake them off as he leads them deep into the recesses of his labyrinth, only to find them again unexpectedly."
—*Le Monde*

"With the genius of a Salman Rushdie, Leviant takes his readers into a kind of cinematic journey. He grabs the reader's attention and keeps him in suspense until the final page."
—*Soundbeat Magazine*

Diary of an Adulterous Woman

"Astute character studies drive this sexy, witty, philosophically complex novel. Without sacrificing humor or character development, Leviant manages to write an ingenious romantic farce in the tradition of Vargas Llosa's *Notebooks of Don Rigoberto.*"
—*Publishers Weekly*

"Lots of fun. Leviant wanders into Harold Pinter's dressing room and ends up hanging out with James Joyce.... A comedy of errors as well as a bedroom farce—and much more."

—*Kirkus Reviews*

"Curt Leviant is a leading candidate for the title of best unknown American novelist....Compulsively readable and entertaining."

—*Sun-Sentinel*

"If Milan Kundera lived on Long Island, he might have written this novel, a meditation on love and intimacy. Like David Foster Wallace's *Infinite Jest* or Martin Amis's *The Information*, Leviant has put a post-modernist strategy in service of a character-driven novel with good results."

—*Library Journal*

The Yemenite Girl

"I read straight through without a stop. I don't often read so quickly and with so much interest. I enjoyed every turn of the story.... Shultish is a man with a life of his own...and the celebrity [the Israel Nobel Laureate, one of the heroes of the novel] too is marvelously drawn. *The Yemenite Girl* is done with great tact, feeling, and skill."

—Saul Bellow, Nobel Prize–winning author of *Humboldt's Gift*

"A passionate story...a true fiction.... The tension between the charm of the text and the intensity of the subtext is what keeps the pages turning."

—*New York Times Book Review*

"The best novel I've had the luck to review this year, and it may be the best novel many people will have the luck to read. In his first book, Curt Leviant has put together depth, delicacy, full-fleshed characters and gloriana.... The writing is rich and luxurious."

—*The Boston Globe*

Katz or Cats

—or—

How Jesus Became My Rival in Love

Other Fiction by Curt Leviant

The Yemenite Girl

The Man Who Thought He Was Messiah

Partita in Venice

Diary of an Adulterous Woman

Ladies and Gentlemen, the Original Music of the Hebrew Alphabet

Weekend in Mustara

A Novel of Klass

Zix Zexy Ztories

King of Yiddish

Kafka's Son

Katz or Cats

— or —

How Jesus Became My Rival in Love

Curt Leviant

5220 Dexter Ann Arbor Rd.
Ann Arbor, MI 48103
www.dzancbooks.org

Katz or Cats. Copyright © 2018, text by Curt Leviant. All rights reserved, except for brief quotations in critical articles or reviews. No part of this book may be reproduced in any manner without prior written permission from the publisher: Dzanc Books, 5220 Dexter Ann Arbor Rd., Ann Arbor, MI 48103.

Library of Congress Cataloging-in-Publication Data

Names: Leviant, Curt, author.
Title: Katz or cats : or how Jesus became my rival in love : a novel / by Curt Leviant.
Description: Ann Arbor, MI : Dzanc Books, [2017]
Identifiers: LCCN 2017026274 | ISBN 9781945814457
Subjects: LCSH: Storytelling--Fiction.
Classification: LCC PS3562.E8883 K38 2017 | DDC 813/.54--dc23
LC record available at https://lccn.loc.gov/2017026274

First US Edition: December 2018
Jacket design by Steven Seighman
Interior design by Leslie Vedder

This work was supported by a writer's residency offered by the Emily Harvey Foundation in Venice, whose assistance is gratefully acknowledged.

This is a work of fiction. Characters and names appearing in this work are a product of the author's imagination, and any similarity to real persons, living or dead, is coincidental and not intended by the author.

Printed in the United States of America

10 9 8 7 6 5 4 3 2 1

for

Erika

The Beginning

1

OPENING

I STILL SEE KATZ making his way down the up escalator, shouting to me in the waiting train:

= John! Wait. I want to confess something—his words tailing away behind him.

But let's backtrack—a fitting, inadvertent pun in the Katz style—a bit.

Katz, my months-long seatmate on the New York-bound train, had bade me goodbye and left our car. Here, in Newark, the train waited, as it usually did at 8:40 a.m., for another train on a different line, before continuing on to New York. I saw Katz ascending the escalator, and then he disappeared. In installments. First his head. Then his torso. His briefcase. His legs. His cuffed trousers.

Then came a bizarre sight. A figure was struggling, trying to force his way down against the push of the upcoming throng. A couple of people moved to the left, opening a path for the man. I saw who it was. It was Katz, a wild look on his face, determined to descend as more and more people funneled into the up escalator. The scene reminded me of a Chaplin comedy, for—zhoop!—Katz again was back up at the top of the stairs. Now once more he has to elbow his way down, battling not only crowds but gravity and the inexorable laws of physics. For a man to go down an up escalator, his descent velocity has to exceed the machine's up speed, in conjunction of course with the resistant force of the crowd that keeps ascending, impeding his dogged downward path.

At times Katz seemingly stood still, since the speed of his descent equaled that of his involuntary ascent. And facing the wrong way too. Going up backward. Imagine being in transit, yet motionless, or seeming to stand still while in obvious kinesis. And then, like a quarterback finding an opening and rushing for the one-yard line, Katz finally finds a gap and leaps and lands on the platform. He dashes to the now closing door in my car, can't get his foot in quickly enough stop it from shutting but shouts as the door slides shut—

= I have a confession to make, John…I'm…—he says as the door slams shut in his face, cutting off whatever he wanted to say.

My train began to move. He ran alongside. Anyone who can run down a crowded up escalator can run with a New Jersey Transit train. He ran with it, looking for an open window to shout his words in at me. But a Jersey train isn't like a European railroad car. The windows don't open. For some reason Katz pointed to himself; he poked his index finger into his chest. I saw him mouthing his name: Katz. Katz. Katz. Then he opened his mouth wide as though he were meowing. The Katz meow. What was he trying to tell me?

And then the train, my train, gathering speed, now really zooming, entered a tunnel and Katz—Katz vanished.

Again.

•

But let's begin at the beginning, since what I've told you is almost the end.

I'm aware that some people—I'm an editor, a careful observer of readers' habits, so I should know—have the annoying habit of opening a book and reading the last page first. For those of you who do this, please note that you've just read the (almost) last page.

But I assure you, you won't have lost anything—or gained anything, for that matter—by reading this, for there's lots and lots to learn as you keep turning the pages, and lots and lots to turn as you keep learning the pages.

So relax and enjoy this—

his

their,

our,

my,

your,

story.

2

RE: TOMMY MANNING

Remember Thomas Manning, hero of that touching, sometimes comic novel, *Partita in Venice*, a kind of antipode to Mann's *Death in Venice*? Sorry, I forget the author. I should remember but I don't. Since the title was unusual, I remember it. But not the author. Tommy was actually my neighbor in a little town outside of Manchester, New Hampshire. We went to Old Manchester High together. Not much formal religion in his house, but raised with strict New England, old-fashioned Puritan ethics. Old-fashioned, yes, but tinged with twentieth-century modernism, liberalism. Not with Cotton Mather's mouth-foaming madness. I don't want you to get me wrong. But we did have values.

That's why Katz's story is a problem for me. What would Manning have done? Can I ethically arrogate another writer's tale even if I made variations, or am I just retelling it, transcribing it as Katz, a reteller himself, told it to me? Remember Duchamp's *Mona Lisa* with the mustache? Was that theft of intellectual property, or an honest-to-goodness original variation? Whom am I kidding? Honest-to-goodness original variation is a first-class oxymoron.

On the other hand, maybe I'm just reporting on what I heard. If a journalist quotes a famous writer's words in an interview, is that plagiarism? What will a sharp lawyer say? After all, under my by-line I'm writing down word for word what the writer said. His words—under my byline. Is that technically plagiarism? Tommy, come help me out with your New England ethical stance.

Never mind. I'll just put down what Katz told me and what I experienced with the girl I met. Then you can put our two stories together and have a double matinee. And maybe I'll use someone else's name.

And if there's a problem, well then—

Like one of the chaps in *Guys and Dolls* says:

So sue me!

3

FIRST MEETING WITH KATZ ON THE TRAIN

For a moment I raised my eyes from the manuscript I was editing and looked out the streaked plate glass (New Jersey Transit doesn't do windows either) at the drab towns racing by, on their way to some unknown western destination. A man sat next to me. I didn't look at him but I saw his well-pressed, superbly tailored trousers and Gucci loafers on his stretched-out feet. I'm tempted to say that he looked like a man who would comb his hair before making an important phone call. I sensed him watching me work. Another nosy guy, I thought. Any minute, I imagined, I'd hear him say: My brother is a writer; or, my niece wants to write; or, isn't that interesting, I always wondered, what does an editor *do*? Pretty soon, from his sleeve, like a magician, he would draw a manuscript and present it to me. Although I had been deeply immersed in my work since I boarded the train in Trenton, I felt this man had slipped in next to me for a reason. And since such nosiness, or, to be generous, curiosity, annoys me, I try to tilt the pages toward me to show they're mine.

But he still hadn't said a word, which completely disarmed me. From his briefcase he took out a *Wall Street Journal* and began reading. He's an analyst for a brokerage house, I thought, or perhaps a compliance officer at a hedge fund. What links do these guys have to literature?

Finally, I turned to him. He gave me a fetching smile, this well-dressed, handsome man in his mid-fifties, but he said nothing. Now I was about to speak. This later amazed me, for when I'm working on the train I don't initiate small talk. But this quiet chap was turning the tables on me. Even without speaking he radiated energy, magnetism, drawing the iron filings of my attention. I felt I was in an inside-out conversation, in a mirror-image, effect-and-cause world. While praying my seatmate wouldn't talk to me, I was half expecting him to. Change that to expecting him to. His surprising silence hexed me into talking to him. I opened my mouth and was about to say, "I sense you're interested in writing," but caught myself at the last minute.

What's the matter with you? I asked myself. Soon you'll ask him to favor you with one of his manuscripts. Come on, just pull it from your sleeve and I'll start reading it now. Or maybe, even more absurdly, I would proclaim, I've got this great manuscript for you to read, and he would respond, using my favorite line, I'm so sorry, our publishing house doesn't accept unsolicited manuscripts. We deal only with accredited literary agents.

But the fact is I didn't tilt my manuscript toward me. Didn't use it as a place of refuge. I turned to him and he uttered a curt, = Hi.

I waited for him to continue. But, again to my surprise, he said nothing more. He was frustrating me, my taciturn seatmate.

Then, finally, he said, = Looks like you're either an editor or—

I was about to respond amicably, but he stopped in mid-sentence. I don't know if he picked up his *Wall Street Journal*, for I turned from him and looked out the window.

Then softly, so seductively I had to face him, he continued:

= What a fortuitous meeting! I'm a writer. And I have an unusual love story I'd like to show you. You see—

Another love story, I thought. Everyone has a love story.

= Forgive me for interrupting you, I said, looking him in the eye, = but I get this all the time.

His face reddened, which immediately made me feel bad. What could I do now with this seemingly gentle man with thick black curly hair with a bald spot on the top of his head and a few strands of gray threading here and there? It's always hard to say no, especially in person.

= I don't want to be mean or sound abrupt, but the small publishing house I work for—you guessed right, by the way, I am an editor, but I could be an author too, you know, correcting my own manuscript—doesn't do fiction. We used to, but not anymore.

The man nodded, absorbing the disappointing news. And, in any case, how could I afford to read a manuscript by an unknown? Take any ten people in a room, twelve of them claim they are, used to be, or want to be writers. Most people assume writing is calligraphy: take a pen in hand and start writing. But it's not handwriting; it's think-writing, for which the hand is only an instrument, a faithful intermediary, sometimes a less-than-willing amanuensis.

I looked out the window at the Jersey swampland. Just a few minutes earlier, trees in their June green were whizzing by. And now the swamp. I imagined I was a tourist in some Asian country. It looked rather appealing in the early morning sun, as does most anything in sunlight. I felt my seatmate's tension and dashed hopes, vivid and palpable, stirring in the small space between us.

= But I didn't finish my sentence, he said.

= Sorry. What were you going to say?

= That this isn't a run-of-the-mill, dime-a-dozen love story. Did you ever hear of a love affair where a guy's rival is not the fellow next door, but Jesus?

It took me a moment to absorb that.

= Well, that *is* interesting, I said. = You mean the girl has an infatuation with Jesus.

= You'll see how it plays out.

= All right, I'll make a deal with you, I suddenly said.

The man brightened. = You won't be disappointed, I assure you. And I'll make a deal with *you*. If it isn't worth your while, I'll buy you a yearly pass.

I laughed. = I admire your confidence. And thanks for your generous offer. But that won't be necessary. Do you take this train every day?

= Well, almost.

= I take this one Monday, Wednesday, and Friday. On Tuesday and Thursday I take an earlier one. How far do you go?

= Penn Station, the man said.

= Me too. My name is John.

= So what's the deal? the man asked.

= I'll be frank with you. I won't be able to read the manuscript, but you'll narrate the story for me. And by the way, telling a story is the best way to fine-tune it, to make it clearer and sharper. But you still didn't tell me your name.

= Call me Katz, he said. = Katz is how I like to be called. Okay, I'll narrate the story, but would you mind if once in a while I read from the manuscript?

= That's fine with me.

= Okay, it begins like this. My hero, who is separated, but maybe not, we're not sure…

= We? I interrupted. = Who's the "we?"

Katz raised his index finger, requesting patience. = I'll tell you in a minute. The hero, also named Katz, met this girl about twenty years ago, almost the same way I met you, on a train. Actually, a waiting room in Boston's T, the trolley car line that goes in to the city from the western suburbs. And she tells me, I mean him, my hero, her name. Wait! Why should I break my tongue, like the Italians say, and keep saying "him" and "he," when I'm writing the story in the first person? Though it didn't happen to me.

= To be sure, I said. = It's just a narrative device. And I thought to myself: I haven't yet met a writer who will honestly say, Yes, that first-person hero, that's me.

= Exactly, a narrative device, Katz was quick, too quick in my estimation, to reply. Then he added, = Actually, to be perfectly honest…

At that I shut my ears. Whenever I hear that phrase it sounds discordant, like two elbows on a keyboard. Hearing it I immediately brand the speaker an inveterate liar.

= Actually, it's not my book. It's my brother's fiction, I heard Katz say.

= Ah, I said. = There's that "we."

= Yes, John. It's his work. My brother's. I must accent this. Please understand that the Katz who is the protagonist of the novel should in no way be confused with Katz the author, and certainly not with his brother, me, Katz the reteller. I'm just retelling his fiction. I told you I'm a writer because everyone probably begins his spiel to you by saying, my brother is a writer. But in this case, my brother *is* the writer... Okay, although I have a good memory—my brother says I have total recall—I still won't be able to repeat word for word what's he's written, but I'll look over the pages the night before and try my best.

= Fine.

= You'll see, he's a terrific writer with great imagination. I too wanted to become a man of letters, Katz said wistfully, = but it didn't work out. My brother became the writer, but of course he has a day job, and I ended up in business. Still, I wish I could write.

And, at once, blindsided, I fell into his neatly baited trap.

= What would you write?

= Wrongs, he said, and again gave me that wicked, engaging smile.

It took a while for that wordplay to sink in.

Then I admitted to Katz that one of my ambitions too had been to become a novelist or short story writer, but I wasn't good enough. But since I had a good literary sensibility, I got a job as an editor.

= How long you been at it?

= About twenty years.

Then I panicked, fearing the question Katz might ask me. But to his credit, he was discreet enough not to ask the name of my firm.

= Got my first job soon after I graduated college. And since I did so well, I capped the flame of my ambition to write fiction.

To which Katz responded, = That's why Balzac said, "It is as easy to dream up a book as it is difficult to put it on paper." And the American novelist C. L. Eviant once wrote: "Fiction is like dreams, imagining and vivifying the impossible." And me, I have dreams, can't write them down. So I admire my brother for his determination. Sometimes, when I read his book, I feel I'm entering a magical world, where the page splits and two new, previously unseen pages appear, and you enter a dream world…

Then I added:

= And the great Argentinian short story writer, Jorge Luis Borges, who never wrote a novel, once said something similar. "To imagine the plot of a novel is a happy task. To actually write it is an exaggeration." You've read Borges, right?

= Read him? Katz said indignantly. = I wrote most of his stories, including "Pierre Menard, Author of *Don Quixote*."

= Mmm, I said, not really knowing what to say. At times I felt I was talking to him in foreign tongues.

I didn't want to ask Katz what he did. That is, I *did* want to ask him, but the protocol of train friendships forbade it. Like giving your last name. But perhaps my silence spurred Katz on.

= So I became a surveyor. I'm principal of a land surveying company.

= Well, well. K the Land Surveyor. How interesting!

= I never thought of the similarity of initials. So you know *The Castle.*

Katz didn't phrase it as an interrogative, but I sensed the question lurking.

= Why do you ask? You can see I'm making reference to Kafka's famous novel.

= Not necessarily, he said. = Some people read reviews or dust jacket flaps and think they've read the book.

= Did you major in land surveying, if there's such a thing?

= I majored in comp lit but sort of sidled into land surveying, but let's get back to my brother's novel. The hero doesn't usually give his name because he's a very private person. Quite shy. Just like my brother. But for some reason he can't quite explain, maybe because the girl is so appealing, after she introduces herself, he gives her his name right away.

= That's amazing, I said.

= What's amazing, John?

= I don't like to give my name either, I said. = On planes, when a stranger starts talking to me and asks my name, I give the guy a card that a previous nudnick had given me and which I keep for just such an occasion.

= What a terrific idea! Katz said. = I'm going to remember that. Only problem is now both of us will be suspicious that we've given each other false aliases.

= Fear not. It will be all right.

= So as soon as I tell her my name, she says: The author of *Travels in Bessarabia*. And I say, That book was published more than fifteen years ago. How do you remember that one? And she says she used it for her trip to Romania after a Jewish friend gave her that book...one of the best-written travel books she ever read. Soon as she said, 'a Jewish friend of mine,' I knew for sure Maria was Christian. That's not her real name, by the way. That's what my brother calls the heroine to protect her privacy.

Katz pronounced the word the British way, with the short "i," as in 'privilege.' I couldn't tell if it was an affectation. Then he stopped and gazed out the window.

= I wonder, Katz continued, where she is now, after all these years. Probably back in Romania, helping the poor gypsies again, for her goal was to help poor people in Seventh World countries perfect their shop-lifting and wallet-snatching skills.

= What's the novel about? I asked.

= What's it about, you ask? It's about a guy named Katz and a girl named Maria. They get to know each other, but she's a deeply devout off-the-wall Protestant, and how this love affair of hers with Jesus, which complic—but I don't want to get ahead of myself.

= You said you had a brother.

= Had? Why had? He's still alive. The author of the book.

= Okay. So what do people call him?

= Katz. He doesn't like first names either.

= So how do you, or your mother, or anyone else distinguish you from him?

= By the pronunciation.

And Katz, that rascal, didn't even smile. I decided to drop it. He was either being purposely obtuse or didn't know when to stop teasing. But Katz continued as though our conversation had not taken an untoward turn.

= So we hope this book, with its unusual theme and plot, will work for him. My brother wants to see this book published so badly.

= Then he should come to our house. We publish all our books badly.

Katz disregarded my joke.

= He doesn't want it to be part of that ever-growing library of imaginary books, in the uncatalogued collection of the Universal Library of Non-existent Books of which Borges is the Honorary Head Librarian…Oops, here we are. My stop.

= But it's only Newark. I thought you were going to Penn Station.

= Newark has a Penn Station too. You New Yorkers, with your transito-geographic chauvinism! If we both make it through the night alive and well, I'll see you Wednesday for another installment of My Love Story Which Jesus Elbowed Into, which, by the way, is not the title of my brother's book. Which station do you get on?

= Trenton. And you?

= Princeton. Save me a seat, okay? See you tomorrow morning, Katz said.

4

FIRST MEETING WITH MARIA ON THE T

= THANKS FOR SAVING me a seat, John, Katz said as he slid in next to me. = Shall we begin? And before I even had a chance to nod, he began his narrative.

•

How did we meet? In the Boston T waiting room in Newton while I was on the line to buy tickets. She sort of stood outside the line. But I could see she wanted to get to the clerk. I motioned her ahead of me. She was a tall, fairly good-looking girl, I'd say in her mid-thirties, with an open, innocent, sort of longish face.

"It's okay," she said. "I just want to say hello to the ticket agent."

"Go ahead," I said. "I have my ticket. I just need a timetable."

She went up to the clerk and wished him a happy new year. She apologized for the belated greeting but she'd been away for three weeks.

I watched them speaking. You should have seen the shy smile on that overweight clerk's shiny moonface. Every pore in his cheeks was beaming. Every hair of his little black Charlie Chaplin mustache shone.

When she finished talking to him, she handed me a timetable.

I was impressed by her demeanor and commended her gentilesse. I said we don't see such considerate behavior toward our inferiors anymore. She smiled a hesitant smile, wondering if I was serious or not. We began chatting, and as the tram pulled in I asked her:

"How far are you going?"

"To the last stop." I had expected her to say: *All the way*, and then blush.

"Me too," I said. "Let's sit together."

"Do you like the window seat?"

"Makes no difference to me," I said, studying her green eyes. "I surely won't be looking at the scenery."

At once she told me her name: Maria Christian—but I was unsure if the last syllable was "sen" or "son."

"Sen," she said. "Danish descent. Here's how I spell it." And from her colorful bag that looked like it was knitted in Africa, she pulled out her card and gave it to me. Then she took out a little white leather-bound book and placed it on her lap, the sort that looked like a pocket Bible or a Siddur that Bar Mitzva boys get as a present and which is never ever opened.

"What's that, your Bat Mitzva present?"

"Close. It's my Bible." And she opened the well-worn book to Luke. In the margin were small, handwritten annotations. "It's my daily tram reading. I hardly read anything else."

"Do you know what language the book you call the Old Testament is written in?"

"English?" she said, wide-eyed. "Just kidding. It's *Ivrit*," she said, using the Hebrew word for Hebrew.

"Very impressive," I said. "So go ahead. Read. I don't want to disturb you."

"No no no. It's fine. Let's talk."

Within a couple of minutes, we learned that we both lived in Waltham and drove to Newton to catch the T. We had both gone to Brandeis, she some years before me, and had majored in comparative literature; her minor was labor arbitration, mine psychology.

"And now," she said, smiling at me, "now you have to tell me your name, you know."

Although I don't usually give strangers my real name, I told her, "My name is Katz. It's a Hebrew acronym for *kohen tzedek*, or, righteous priest."

"No first name?"

"Katz is what my friends call me. Ever since I was a kid, I've always been called Katz."

"Okay. Katz." She brightened. "A great name. Katz. I love it. Would your first name by any chance be—?"

I was hoping, I was praying, she wouldn't say "pussy." If she says "pussy," I thought, she's finished for me.

"...by any chance be M? The only Katz I know is M. Katz, the author of *Travels in Bessarabia,* a book that was so useful when I was traveling there."

The coincidence, the serendipity, astounded me. But, instead of exclaiming, all I could say was: "You must love travel to remember that book that came out, oh, let's see, about twenty years ago."

•

= Excuse me for interrupting, Katz, but didn't you say fifteen years ago the other day?

= I may have. But these aren't my changes, John. They're my brother's. He's constantly revising.

•

"I do like to travel," Maria said, "but I remember the book because the writer is, you know, knowledgeable, witty, detailed, with a very personal approach to travel. That combination made me remember the book."

"What did you do in Bessarabia?"

"I volunteered, as part of my desire to make real Jesus's teaching, to help poor gypsy children..."

"...improve their pickpocketing skills. And I must say you did a great job. They nabbed my wallet in Bucharest."

Maria assumed I was joking. I asked her where else she had traveled; she said Israel. I looked at this Christiansen girl. Did I tell you she had long brown hair with a reddish tinge? And a face as goyish as a face could be.

"And what did you see there?"

"I spent two weeks touring the Christian holy sites. I loved it. Seeing the sites where Jesus walked was thrilling."

"Thrilling?" I couldn't imagine being thrilled by that. Would I be thrilled walking where Moses walked? Where David danced? "Thrilling? How thrilling?"

But Maria did not get my dig.

"Because it made Jesus come alive for me. I saw him more clearly than ever. That's what those two beautiful weeks did. And I can't wait to go back."

"Two weeks for that? I thought one could see the Christian sites in two days."

"But of course I saw the Jewish sites too....But you still haven't told me if you're M. Katz, author of that marvelous book."

Once I heard praise like that, I couldn't help myself. Despite her longish chin, this girl was appealing, although she did have an ungainly way of walking: sort of self-conscious, and high-shouldered, which contradicted her pleasant face. She loved the book. I couldn't resist the deception. Sometimes deception comes as naturally as breathing. And so I passed off my brother's book as my own. Then I had a moment of fear. I couldn't recall if his book had an author photo. I had misplaced my copy years ago. And I think to myself: Maria goes home, looks for the book, sees the photo of my brother, and...Then I relaxed. Even if the book did have a photo, it was a picture taken years ago. And, anyway, my brother and I resemble each other. It's a family trait. My father and his brother also looked almost alike, and they weren't even related. Even my mother and father looked alike; if my father put on lipstick, you couldn't tell my parents apart.

Here's a cute story. My brother and I went to different schools, but once I played hooky and attended my brother's class. We had cooked up a trick. We both wore white shirts and brown pants. We sat in the back. We must have been eight or nine. The teacher, an old man with glasses, called on my brother. We both stood up. The teacher says, I see two of you. No, my brother says. There's only one of me here. You're seeing double. The befuddled teacher sat down, took off his thick specs, and covered his eyes. That gave me time to run out...But that's neither here nor there.

"So then, are you M. Katz?" Maria insisted.

I looked down modestly.

"My, what a memory you have," I told Maria. " My book came out years ago. I still can't understand how you remembered the author. The book's title I can understand. I read a book and as soon as I finish it, the author's name slips away from me."

"Well, if your name had been Jones, you know, I might have forgotten it. But Katz is such an unusual family name. How could I forget Katz? You'll have to, you know, autograph that book for me."

"Sure. Gladly."

"If I can find it."

"I'll sign it anyway," I said.

She didn't even react to my absurd remark. I saw her staring at the slightly open door between the two joined streetcars. She looked ill at ease. What was bothering her?

Suddenly, she jumped up. "I'm sorry. I can't stand open doors." And she went and shut it.

"Me neither." I smiled with satisfaction."

"Wow!" Maria said. "Me too. Amazing."

"I don't believe it. I never thought I would find another loon like you and me."

And then, without even thinking, I put my arm around her shoulder and drew her to me. She didn't resist. On the contrary, with a happy looked she pressed even closer.

"I just had to hug you for that consanguinity of ours."

"I love that word, 'consanguinity.' I love words altogether."

"So you must love the dictionary."

"Are you kidding? It's my second-favorite book." Maria looked pensive. "Do you know what words in a dictionary do at night when you don't consult it, them?"

"No. I never gave it a thought. At night I'm too busy shutting doors."

"The words get together, you know," she said, "and conspire to bring in new words from botany that hadn't been included before. Botany words are my pet peeve. They should be in an encyclopedia. Not a dictionary. From week to week my unabridged dictionary gets fatter and weightier from the totally unnecessary botanical words stuffed into it."

"Do you leave your unabridged open?"

"Yes. Of course. Always. That way it's, you know, available when I want it. Why?"

"You see, that's the problem. Make believe it's a door. Close it. If it's open, then the dictionary is bridged. The invasive botany words use the pages as a bridge to get in. If it's closed, then it's un-a-bridged and the words can't get in."

"What an idea!" she said and nodded, seriously considering my suggestion.

"Have you ever been in a library after midnight?"

"No."

"You told me what words in a dictionary do at night. Now I'll ask you, do you know what books do late at night?"

"Gossip about who has run off with an overdue book?"

"No, but good try. They read each other. They socialize. They copulate."

"Populate? Populate what? The shelves?"

"You misheard. But you're not too far off. They copulate and, in their own mysterious way, create more books. Just like your dictionary secretes more words, libraries make their own books. Endlessly."

"The Good Book knew that thousands of years ago." Maria pointed to her little white Bible. "That's why Ecclesiastes 12:12 says: 'Of making books there is no end.' He witnessed it himself."

"I'd substitute 'love' for 'books' in that verse," I said.

That was the tenor of our talk during our first meeting. We played with, sparred with, words. We flirted with words as if they were love darts. It was the beginning of what would become for us a continuing game with words, sending us deeper into that zone we lovingly call "same wavelength."

I have to put the story in reverse to make an observation. I think it's an important one. When I told her I knew why she shut closet doors, she asked me, "You do? Why?" As she said this, I think I noticed a slight—the very slightest—tremor in her voice, a faint vibrato in the vowels of those three words, like a shudder through thin glass, indicating nervousness, insecurity, perhaps even fear. She probably didn't notice it. It came deep from within. Maybe I'm imputing this vocal tremolo to her at this time in light of what I was to discover later. But in any case, that closing of doors sealed our friendship. It was as if we had known each other for years.

•

= Excuse me, Katz, I interrupted his narration. = Closing doors? That seals a friendship?

= No no no. Please understand. I'm exaggerating. It was just a touch of symbolism. An affinity for closed doors cannot seal a friendship. Still, a certain warmth flowed between us as we agreed on this arcane point. We were on the same wavelength. With words. With dislikes. With jokes. Even for something so minute as closing doors.

And, of course, my book that I didn't write that she read. It compressed a lot of things for me. Us. Do you understand?

= I'm trying, I said. And as I said this, I looked at the open door at the end of our car, which Katz didn't jump up to close. Of course, I remembered it after a moment. It's his brother's quirk, his brother's story, not his.

= Let me give you an example, John. Think of music lovers. Let's say two people love classical music. Okay. Nothing special in that. But let's say two people meet and they discover they both love the string quartet of Arriaga, a Spanish contemporary of Mozart, who died at eighteen. Don't you think a special bond would form between them?

•

"Even the English language itself supports the closing of closet doors," Maria announced.

"How's that?"

"The word 'closet' has the word 'close' in it, and if a European is pronouncing it, you know, it sounds like 'close it.'"

I liked Maria's humor. I loved it. She made me laugh. Not many people can make me laugh. Not even me. I make others laugh, but she—she made me laugh. What a delicious ride this has been, I thought. I could have hugged her again, but this time I restrained myself.

And then she said some words I'll never forget. But before I tell you what she said, did I mention that her long hair had a reddish tinge? And that I liked the awkward way she walked. If you can imagine a happy walk, she had a happy walk. I said happy, not graceful. A little high-shouldered, the left shoulder slightly higher. But that walk made her human. She moved as if programmed by some manager of a mannequin agency. And I don't mean the runway model mannequins; I mean the unpaid plastic ones that hang around in the show windows.

Let me expand what I said about her walk. But first let me say how she didn't walk. She didn't wiggle or sashay. She didn't swing or sway. Her amble was sans music or ballet. If there were mirrors at the tram station, she didn't check herself along the way. If you walked behind her, her left hip didn't swing up provocatively when her right foot strode forward. She didn't sail. She didn't float. She walked like she wanted to part water. I saw this the first day she walked in Penn Station.

•

= Penn Station? I interrupted. = I thought you're in Boston.

= Of course, John. Boston, Katz corrected himself. = What am I talking about? Riding now with you to Penn Station, that's the mixup. That's what happens when I narrate by heart and don't use my brother's text.

•

I saw the way she walked at the tram terminus. She told me she couldn't stand crowds, couldn't bear people pressing up and around her during rush hours, would rather work three-four more hours and come home late rather than being near foul people who "smelled to high heaven and exhaled into the air everything rotten they'd eaten during the day." End quote.

That's why when she walked, she had an in and out weave, not a straight line, practicing to avoid a humanity that reeked of sweat, tobacco, and beer.

As I got to know her, I noticed she walked like a sack of potatoes gliding across a dance floor. No, that's not fair. First of all, sacks of potatoes do not glide. And certainly not Yukon Gold. More precisely, she walked as if she were *carrying* a sack of potatoes. Totally oblivious to her body. She just wasn't conscious of her movement. Although I did not witness it, I am confident that in walking through a woman's clothing section in a department store, probably every leap year, her quadriannual shopping spree, she did not even glance at herself each time she passed a mirror. I don't know which planet she was on when she walked. Certainly she wasn't here with us. Maybe she felt she had too much meat on her thighs and that held her walk back. No sense parading what you ain't got.

Okay, so she didn't hold herself like a queen, but you don't fall in love with posture. I saw at once she had a rare personality.

For instance, her way with words. We bantered; we exchanged big words like 'propinquity'—you'll see that one coming up in a minute—and little ones like 'prolix.' We tried to outdo each other. She liked "q" words so we played with "querulous," "quotidian," and "quondam."

"All right," I said. "Use 'quondam' in a sentence."

"The quondam president of Argentina was arrested at the airport as he tried to flee the country."

"Bravo," I said. "Perfect. Now I'll use that word in a sentence. The fat friars in Boccaccio's *The Decameron* rarely used quondams."

Maria laughed hysterically, then said: "Now you go. Use 'querulous'."

"Okay. Let's see. At my mother's house the other day, I was very querulous and broke a beautiful wine goblet...Now you do 'quotidian.'"

"I can't top that puny pun, even though it's not your run-of-the-mill quotidian jest."

After forty minutes, near the end of the tram ride, we pulled words out of our mental dictionaries for each other. She used words like "rebarbative," "ancillary," and "eidetic."

"Where do you get that vocabulary from?"

"Reading," Maria said. "I hardly go out, you know, so I come home and read. I've devoured books since I've been a kid. I know it's such a banal expression, but that's what I do."

She pronounced it "bay-nal," with the accent on the "bay." I told her it was buh-nahl, stress on last syllable.

"We'll look it up when we get home," she said.

Did I hear that right? I replayed those words.

"Why, do you have a pronouncing dictionary?" I said aloud to cover my rattled thoughts.

Wow! A lot said with that sentence of hers. A mouthful, I would say, if I were prone to clichés. To banalities. First, she invited me to her house so elegantly, so unobtrusively, so naturally, without standing on ceremony, without even inviting me, without even asking me if I wanted to come.

And the warmth of that "we" and "home," whether intended or not, whether innocent or calculating—I must tell you those two words sit in my imagination like glowing logs in a fireplace, shedding radiant warmth, those two words that told me there was indeed a spark between us. She had snagged the humming electrons. Now it was a two-way street.

"When we get home..."—it was like an old married couple talking.

And more. Despite her very forward invitation, Maria wasn't coquettish. She didn't have any of those tricks, moues, motions a girl has to get you to admire her. She didn't fiddle with her hair, flicking a wave back, running her fingers down a long strand, calling attention to herself in the instinctive mating game all females play. She didn't have pouting lips, a tease in her voice, a fetching smile. She did—had—none of that.

It doesn't often happen that you feel a sense of ease and familiarity with a girl within minutes. I'll give you an example. Quite often as she spoke, instead of looking at me, she looked straight ahead. As if I wasn't there. I didn't like that. I like people who talk to me to look at me just as I look at them. But after that indirect invitation and the warm, friendly chatter, I felt I had known her long enough. Funny how with guys and girls time becomes compressed in unusual ways. I felt as if we'd established a bond of some kind, as if we were kin. So I didn't feel I was crossing boundaries when with four fingers of each hand I touched her cheeks and turned her face toward me.

"Look at me when you talk to me…"

With a smile she said, "Sure. Sorry." She looked straight at me. "Like this?"

I gave her a thumbs up, told her I felt a propinquity with her, and asked:

"Are you propinquity or against it?"

"I'm all for, you know, kinship." And Maria's sly smile said: you can't fool me with that polysyllabic word.

Then, since I felt perfectly at home with her, I took the next step. Hearing this bright, articulate girl inserting that dumb, low-class "you know" into almost every sentence for forty-five minutes became annoying. So since she accepted my first suggestion so graciously, each time she said, "You know," I squeezed her hand. She soon got the point and stopped using that empty phrase.

Too bad, I thought. I rather liked holding her hand. If I were a romantic or a sentimentalist, I would say I fell for her by the time the T arrived in Boston.

•

During that forty-five minute ride, we didn't talk about books or music or politics. But I did ask Maria what she didn't like. She gave me an entire list.

Later I thought that when two people are drawn to each other, it's not so important that they share likes. What's more important is that you share dislikes. So in those few minutes we understood that there was a pull between us, an instant affinity, a kind of unsigned common consent.

Soon we didn't have to use words. We measured, assessed, took stock of each other in nanoseconds. You know the old rule of thumb. A guy decides if he likes a girl in ten seconds, maybe less. It's true. Folk wisdom, street smarts—the former village, the latter urban—had it that it took those seconds for a guy to assess if he liked a girl. Dead wrong. I could do it in one second. Even less. How long does it take to run your glance down from a girl's face, using the Song of Songs descriptive north to south template, to neck, breasts, waist, hips/ass, and legs in one tidal swoop? Never mind the hair. Just see if she has the classic Parisian ass where both cheeks are grabbable with one palm. One time in Paris I assessed the provenance of a girl by the size of her tush. If too broad-beamed, she was obviously a tourist, likely an American. A Parisian ass was a cinch to identify.

King Solomon, the reputed author of the Song of Songs, also took about ten seconds to take in his beloved, even adding a few poetic touches to each inventoried part of the girl's body: your eyes are like doves, your hair like a flock of goats, your lips like a thread of scarlet, your neck like the Tower of David (I wonder if Modigliani, who was a Jew, got the inspiration for his long-necked women from this image), your breasts like two fawns. Okay, maybe twelve seconds. A girl, however, takes five weeks to assess if she likes a guy.

But with me, Maria broke the rule. I sensed she liked me at once—but as you will learn later; well, you'll find out later what I wanted to say.

We read each other quick as a one-word headline. Maybe I exaggerate. But language is exaggeration. The only thing that is not exaggeration is silence—and even that's exaggeration. Can we ever isolate that discrete point in time when two people begin to like each other? With us it happened instantaneously; something clicked in a flash. We sensed it right away. At once. That's why I—I mean, I wouldn't have done this with anyone else after forty-five minutes—that's why I hugged her when we parted in Boston as if we were old friends. I was just a hair away from kissing her cheek. I told her I don't have the time to shake her hand, nor the inclination, but I promised I would give her a more meaningful hug next time I saw her. And she must have felt the same closeness. Remember how she invited me to her house in that loop-de-loop, ass-backwards, *moyshe-kapoyr* fashion, when she said, "We'll look it up when we get home" and "When you come to my house, I'll show you...." I forget now what she wanted or promised to show me. Maybe it was photos she took in Romania. Taken during one of her private how-to-pickpocket-better gypsy seminars. Or maybe it was something else. But me coming to her house was a given.

In that T station in Boston, we saw, the both of us, a light, a green light if you will, a green light that gave us both leave to go, move, press down on the gas pedal, get moving and cut out all the time-consuming, turtle-slow, conventional, lugubrious, evolutionary cortesia that makes people go from zero to ten in a pre-ordained, paced time. We, Maria and I, did time-frame photography, where a movie camera snaps a picture daily of a budding plant over a period of several weeks. When the film is played, the plant blooms in seconds.

Same with us. We rushed time, compressed it gladly. We went through the wormhole into unexplored dimensions. Mind you, we did not fall into each other's arms and kiss. But the scaffolding, the architecture, was there. In place. All prepared.

As we walked out of the tram, she surprised me by suddenly saying, "Wanna see how I do my hair?"

I nodded.

She stopped, made a deep bow, and, with a quick forward snap of her head, her long, slightly curly mane flew forward until it covered her face, became a curtain over her face; it hung there like a still Niagara perpendicular to the pavement. Then she rose and cast her head back swiftly and her hair became a long arc like a coat flying until it returned to its previous position.

"That's how I do my hair."

I still see that arc of reddish hair like a peacock's feathers in full bloom making its way from her back over her head and then back again.

Boy, did I enjoy that tram ride with Maria! It was nearly an hour but felt like minutes. With her time flew by so swiftly. Time flew by so swiftly I couldn't believe we were almost in town. And then that invitation to come to her house.

Imagine! Without me saying I want to see her, without a call from me, without me going through that elaborate boy-girl ballet of asking her for a date, without Maria even inviting me directly, in her mind my visit was all set.

Maria had a crooked smile and a sometime rapid speech, her words flying through kissable lips, which, from the first meeting, I dreamt of kissing. "*Andante, andante, per favore.* Slow down, for goodness sake," I said, with no qualms about putting my fingers on her lips. "I want to hear every word you're saying."

I think I can say on that day we exchanged hearts. From the first day I met Maria. It didn't take long. How long? As long as the tram ride from Newton to Boston. But maybe it wasn't an exchange; maybe it was only my heart to hers, not hers to mine. You know the old expression, I lost my heart.... Well, I lost mine. I felt at once that closeness, that bond, those buzzing electrons. Otherwise, I wouldn't have behaved as I did. Wouldn't have been as bold. A person can gauge if the electrons hovering between two people are floating one way or two. Well, maybe she lost her heart just a little—let's say a ventricle or part of it, a cubicle, a tentacle, or whatever those appurtenances are called.

In Boston when we parted, I hugged her and she hugged me, and I joked, "Next time I'll shake hands," the absurdity of which made her laugh.

From her bag she removed a piece of paper and was about to jot down her phone number. I reminded her that she had given me her card. We made up to meet after work and take the same tram back to Newton.

Before we parted at the station, I held her shoulders and said:

"It still amazes me how you remembered the name of the author of *Travels in Bessarabia*."

"Well, for me Katz has a special resonance. And it's also such an unusual name, you know...oops!" And she covered her mouth. "Delete that....Have you published anything else?"

"No. I didn't devote myself to literature."

"Okay, Katz," she said. "Gotta run. See you later, right? And you'll autograph your book?"

I noticed a tremor in her voice, as if taken by a fear I might say no.

Then she turned and, with a determined stride, wove and dodged her way energetically through the morning rush hour Boston crowds. I watched her until she disappeared.

•

Then Katz looked out the window, jumped up, and said hastily:

= Uh-oh, my stop. Talk to you next time.

5

FIRST VISIT TO MARIA'S APARTMENT (VERSION A)

"Hi," Maria said, sort of shyly, when I came to see her for the first time.

I stretched my hands out to embrace her. "Here's the hug I promised you," I said. "But first shut the door. The hallway doesn't have to bear witness to your promiscuity."

She closed the door with a laugh. There was an intimacy to that laugh. A familiarity. I could have reached out and touched that laugh. I hugged her and she pressed close to me, her arms around my waist. Let's not forget those sizable breasts chugging into my chest. Boy, was I tempted to kiss her. I sensed the vibes were in place. But, my God, I was but one minute into her apartment. I wouldn't, couldn't, do that. Shouldn't? Perhaps that too. I spotted her little white Bible and remembered her affinity to Jesus. Still, as in a flash forward, I saw her responding to me. No doubt about it, she would kiss me, eyes closed, a sweet and sleepy smile on her lips. I bet if I asked her about it she would confirm every word, even the commas.

Over her shoulder I noticed her dictionary, which we had discussed during our beautiful tram ride to Boston. Her massive, seven-inch-thick *Webster's Unabridged* reposed on an antique, nicely carved dictionary stand.

"I see you closed your dictionary. Did it work?"

"Absolutely. No new words have infiltrated. On the other hand, no extraneous synonyms have been able to escape."

Then I saw the electric Hanuka menora on her windowsill. A quick thought ran through my mind: maybe she *is* Jewish—but how could that be, with all that Jesus stuff?

So I asked her, "What's with the menora?"

"Oh, I light it in my window during Hanuka to show my identification with the Jews during their victory over their oppressors…"

There was a moment of silence. I didn't know what to say next. I looked around. Her little white Bible, open to Luke, lay on the easy chair armrest. On the wall hung a framed print of a gypsy caravan, probably from Romania. No other art. A house without art is like a head without music, I thought of saying but didn't. Since the print was slightly atilt, I straightened it.

"My God!" Maria cried. "You too? That's exactly what I do. I go to someone else's house and I see a crooked frame on the wall, I can't help myself and I straighten it right away."

"So how come you missed this one?"

"This isn't someone else's house."

Again she smiled that wry, crooked, endearing smile that was a kind of parallel to the offbeat way she walked. I think I mentioned that she also talked quickly, so fast the words seemed to fly from the side of her mouth.

"What else do you do," I asked her, "that's persnickety, fussy, pointed, precious, or otherwise obsessive and eye-catching? Memorable enough to get tongues wagging at the office water cooler?"

"Hmm." Maria put her finger to her lips and thought. "I can't stand open doors, open drawers, closet doors, tram doors, cabinet doors. I see 'em, I close 'em."

I admired her for her cleverness, for her willingness to recreate a fun dialogue we'd had as though we were rehearsing it for a show, going into it so naturally to accent our instant rapport.

"Even sliding doors?" I asked.

"Especially."

Again a moment of silence. I looked around for something to say. "I see you don't have a TV. I admire that."

"And I didn't grow up with one," she replied. "My parents didn't let us have television. We had something else with a wide screen that my parents said was TV. On Monday nights they'd let us watch the Chicken Rotisserie Show. In color. The heating element of our rotisserie would slowly start to glow red. That caught our attention. But the exciting part came later, when the chicken was in. The motor had a quirk. It would not turn smoothly. It would rotate slowly, then, at one point—we would never know when, that was the suspense and comic part of the Chicken Rotisserie Show—it would suddenly plop forward quickly, and then resume its slow turning. If we were good, we would watch this sudden fall of the roasting chicken three times. We would laugh and clap when this happened. None of the other kids had this channel and it was commercial free. But we were puzzled why no one else in school ever watched our program and why our set had the only program you could eat when the show was over."

"That's absolutely delightful," I said. And then I didn't know what else to say.

Maria put her hand to her mouth, thinking. "Would you mind if I asked you a question?" she said, again sort of shyly.

"Not at all."

"I used the word 'Jews' before when I spoke of the Hanuka victory...and I always wondered if it's polite to say 'Jews,' or if it's better to say 'Jewish people,' because sometimes anti-Ṣemites hiss the word 'Jews.' So I'm wondering if it's okay."

"I can't say I'm the final arbiter on that, but it seems okay to me. And, by the way, that menora lighting is a lovely gesture."

Again a period of silence, a silence that, if extended long enough, could become uncomfortable. The sort of silence between a man and a woman I wasn't used to. Had we run out of things to say?

•

= Katz. Do you mean a woman you weren't used to or a silence you weren't used to? English modifiers are sometimes two-faced.

= Silence, Katz replied.

•

"What do we do now?" Maria asked to overcome, sidestep, undermine the silence.

Well, I knew what we could do now, but I didn't know if she (or me) was quite ready for that yet.

"I like that question," I told her, and then added without the slightest hesitation, "but it betrays a certain awkwardness regarding male visitors. When was the last time you had a man here?"

"Not counting you as a man, 1865."

"Unbelievable! Wow! Lincoln? Here?"

"No. He couldn't make it. He had a theater engagement that night. He sent in Ulysses S. Grant as a pinch swinger."

"I think you mean pinch hitter."

"No. I mean swinger."

"Was he good?"

"His beard tickled," she said, to her—and my—delighted laughter.

But still, once more, the awkward silence. Had we been onstage, at that moment both of us would have come out at the same time with a nervous torrent of words, paused, and then again spoken at the same time.

"To break the silence at Appomattox," I said, "I'll tell you what we should do now. How about making me a cup of tea?"

"You read my mind. I was just about to offer that. Here you are, my first male visitor since the War Between the States, and I haven't offered you anything yet. Would you like to have a cup of tea?"

"No, thanks," I said.

She said, "You're funny," and went to her little kitchen. I tagged along.

"But you're funnier...looking."

When the water was boiling, she opened a drawer and took out two teaspoons. That's all the drawer had in it: two teaspoons.

"No forks, knives, tablespoons?"

"Nope. Why keep silverware? I don't give dinner parties. I eat out or order in. And since I only make tea, all I need is a teaspoon. That's why I don't have knives or forks. Come to think of it, since I don't take sugar, I don't even need the teaspoons. I think I'm going to throw them out. Do you take sugar?"

"No."

"Then out they go," and she threw the two teaspoons into the garbage basket.

"Please, not on my account." I retrieved them. "Maybe someday Grant and Lee will return. It's a historical fact that Grant loved sugar. At the surrender ceremony, Lee gave him a huge loaf. In appreciation Grant let the South have Florida." I washed the two teaspoons and put them on her counter. "And now show me the pictures you allegedly lured me into your apartment for. And the book I was supposed to sign."

"Well, the book I haven't been able to find yet, but the slides of my trip are here in the box on the table. I'll show them to you in a minute. But first sit down on the sofa and tell me about your interesting name. Katz. I just love that name."

It took months for me to finally discover another reason she loved that name.

I sat on the sofa. I thought she would join me. But no. She sat down in her big, overstuffed easy chair. I patted the cushion next to me.

"If you can sit next to me on the tram, you can certainly sit here with me now."

Maria rose and sat next to me.

"Okay, my name. I'll begin with an anecdote. When I say Katz over the phone, especially outside of New York, the receptionist at the other end usually says, "Is that spelled the usual way?

'Yes,' I tease her.

'C...A...T...S, right?'

'No,' I say. 'Substitute K for C and Z for S and you've got it.'"

I turned to Maria, the same desirable girl whom I felt so at home with during that first tram ride to Boston. And here I was sitting alone with her in her apartment—the apartment she had invited me to so cleverly and indirectly—and now, now the hesitancy vanished, now I wanted to put my arms around her and press my lips to those kissable lips of hers, but instead of doing that, here I was, my hands tied, my will tied, my lips paralyzed, talking nonsense about my name.

The electricity, I could swear it hovered in the air. All I had to do was be man enough to take that live wire in my hand and share the voltage with her, who hadn't been kissed in this room since the night Lincoln was shot. But Katz was mewing, woe to me, ow to me, me ow to me, sitting on my will instead of letting it run free.

"I'm glad you're interested in my name," was the moronic monotone that bubbled, babbled, out of me.

And then I thought, maybe she was waiting for me to make a move. That's why she sat next to me. Maybe she also felt the electric tension in the air. But the next move would not come from her. This she would not do. Not in a million years. It was enough she invited me to her house after just meeting me. Nevertheless, I sensed that if I moved she would be ready. All I had to do was put my arm around her shoulder and draw her close and she would kiss me, and those lips I had been thinking of kissing in my daydreams, those lips, and of course the rest of her, would open up for me.

But kissing has to be initiated by someone. It doesn't come about by itself, like sunrise or moonset. Even gravity doesn't come about by itself. You have to throw something for the item to go down. But a kiss, well, that has to be my move, and I wasn't making it. I was looking at that metaphysical kiss, those lips that were absent of a kiss, those lips waiting to be kissed, and instead I started speaking about my name. I say Katz, Katz, Katz, and I think to myself: kiss, kiss, kiss.

"Would you believe that through the generations in America our original family name kept changing? You'll never guess what it once was."

"Katzenjammer."

"How'd you come up with that?"

"Wild guess...just kidding...I peeked into the manuscript."

"Katzenjammer is pretty good. Quite close, in fact. Actually, it was Katzenellenbogen. And it went through several permutations. You know what it means?"

"Of course I know what permutation means."

"I mean, do you know what Katzenellenbogen means?"

"How should I know? I don't even know one syllable of German."

"Then how did you know it was German?"

"Any word that long has to be German."

"If you love Katz, you'll go crazy over Katzenellenbogen. Strange for a family name but that's what you goyim..."

"It wasn't me," Maria said, hurt.

"I know. I'm just teasing you. But that's the sort of ridiculous name the goyim foisted on the Jews in the eighteenth century. Katzenellenbogen. The elbows of cats."

"Delicious!" Maria exclaimed. "I'd love to have a name like that instead of that prosaic, mundane, banal Christiansen."

"Take it, it's yours." And then I thought, she isn't proposing, is she? In that ass-backwards way she invited me to her house? To get that name, she'd have to marry me, or my great-great-grandfather. But if she married me now, she would only have the first syllable.

"But wait," she said. "Cats don't have elbows."

"Not any more. That's why, over the centuries, we kept paring off final syllables. We kept reducing and reducing until almost nothing was left. The first generation was Katzenellenbogen. The next, Katzenellenbog. Then, Katzenellen. Followed by Katzenell. Then Katzen. Then, me, Katz. The next generation will be Kaye, then Kay. Then, finally, the ultimate last name: K, the shortest in the Western world, even shorter than former UN Secretary General U Nu."

"Okay," she said, pleased with her little pun.

I looked at her lonely, widowed lips, lips that should have had my lips on them to seal that instant closeness we felt that day on the tram to Boston. But I knew I would go home today without kissing her, and at night replay my stay with her and interrupt the mental movie with freeze frames pinpointing the spot where I should have turned to her, oh so easily, and kissed her. I knew I was living in two time zones at once: the now and the memory of it later, with cinematic touches that changed the screenplay.

In those two zones, there were two different mes. In one me, the physical; in the other, the mental. In the physical, I'm talking like a parrot, mechanically, about the Katz name, not knowing what I'm saying. In the mental zone, at exactly the same time, I'm thinking what would I think later, at home, how easy it would have been to tell this engaging, moderately pretty, thirty-five, thirty-six-year-old, Close your eyes. She closes her eyes. I'm going to shut the door, I say. She smiles, wondering what I mean. In my fantasy, I put my arms around her shoulders and draw her close. Her lips are slightly open. I kiss her and shut the portal of her lips. "The door is shut." And she says "Hmm" and presses closer to me.

"I like the name Katz," says Maria, with the very goyish family name, Christiansen.

While she says Katz, I think of another word that begins with "k."

6

FIRST VISIT TO MARIA'S APARTMENT (VERSION B)

= John, I've got to tell you that, according to my brother's manuscript, this chapter, just like the one before it, also deals with the protagonist's first visit to Maria's apartment. He's including them both. At least, that's his thinking now. I suppose he's leaving it up to the reader to decide which one is really first. It's his choice, of course. I don't interfere. I'm no editor. You are. I'm just retelling what's in the manuscript. Maybe he wrote one chapter and forgot about it. Then, another time, he wrote another version, then found the first and realized he had two chapters about Katz's first visit to Maria. So, out of an error, my brother is creating an aesthetic construct. In any case, it seems to me a fascinating device. Two different chapters on the same first visit. Stretching, bending, reality. I think my brother Katz is a genius.

= What's his first name? I asked.

= Katz. I told you first day we met that, like me, he only goes by the name Katz.

= So what did your mother call him when she wanted him, not you?

= But you asked me this the other day.

= But you didn't give me a straight answer.

= She yelled: Katz, come over here.

= And what if you were there too?

= And I usually was. But no problem. None of us came. We didn't pay any attention to her.

= Stop fooling around, Katz.

= My mother's exact words!

= Will you please give me a straight answer? You're a nice guy, but you test my patience. How did she call you? And don't tell me, By raising her voice.

= All right. I'll give you an example. And by the way, she did raise her voice. When she shouted, Katz! she wanted him. And when she yelled, Katz! it's me she wanted.

= I can't hear the difference.

= But he and I could. I told you last time it was the pronunciation, the slight nuance in pitch that separated him and me.

= You know what, Katz?

= What?

= I'm beginning to suspect you don't even have a brother.

= You know what, John? Let's go back to his book.

= Just one more question, Katz, before you begin. What year was your travel book published?

= Why do you ask?

=Because I looked for *Travels in Bessarabia.* Looked it up. Couldn't find it. Why are you laughing?

= Why? Because, John. Because, Mister Editor, you're coming out of the screen.

= What does that mean?

= You're coming out of the silver screen into reality. You're mixing up fiction and memoir. You have to remember that my brother's manuscript is a novel and that that travel book is also part of the fiction. That book is no more real than is the Thai novelist Truc T. Naivel's comic masterpiece, *Daily Journal of an Adulteress,* or L. E. Viant's novel, *Partying in Venezia.* And, by the way, if that book were real, it's my brother's book, not mine.

I thought a moment and lifted my index finger to protest.

= Not so fast, Katz. If you're narrating your brother's book and he, the author, says it's really his brother's book—remember you said the hero passes off his brother's travel book as his own?

= Yes.

= Then you, his brother, in the fiction of course, are the author of *Travels in Bessarabia.*

= If your convoluted thinking is right, then I too must say: I see. But the onus is on you, editor John, to separate the two. Keep the borders apart. Memoir on one side, fiction on the other...

•

So, okay, I come to Maria's house for the first time. She welcomes me with a big smile.

"Now for the promise," I said.

"What promise?"

"You forgot already? My promise when we got off the T?"

"To sign your book?" Maria asked.

"No," I said. "That's what I said I would do. But that's not a promise."

"But you did say you'll sign the book. Isn't that a promise?"

"Maybe so, but I didn't use the word 'promise.' Don't you remember what I said, did, when we parted?"

"Yeh," Maria said. "Yes, now I remember. You said, 'I promise to give you a more meaningful hug next time I see you.'"

"Exactly. I couldn't have remembered it better myself."

And I put my arms around her, pressed her close to me, and put my cheek to hers.

What she did not do during that lovely first embrace is crucial. Seminal. Memorable.

She did not pat my back with the obligatory three pats that signify a polite hug, that triad of *de rigueur* palm taps on the back, signaling time's up, buddy! Time to disengage! But not Maria. Oh no! She hugged me back. We drew each other closer. Her arms were around me and her breasts pressed into my chest. It was a long, long hug. Not a hello or goodbye hug, but the sort of hug you give an old friend whom you love.

"I see you keep your promises," she said with an awkward little smile.

I could have said, I always keep my promises, or some other banal, self-serving words, but I just smiled at her and, with a slow rotation of my head, took in her rectangular living room. Two windows on the left that faced the street. An old dark red sofa against the far wall, the door that led to her bedroom and, by the wall opposite the window, an equally ancient wine-colored easy chair with that little white Bible. To the right of the entry doorway where we stood was a writing desk with a lamp and a birch folding chair. And two steps from the table was the little kitchen and, as I soon found out, the back door that led to the parking lot.

"Nice apartment," I said. "Do you own it or are you renting?"

"I can't buy an apartment because somehow I can't save money. Money seems to slip through my fingers. But renting? No, I'm not renting. Renting?" she sneered. "Are you kidding? I'm leasing," she said proudly.

"Oh," was my muted response. I didn't understand the difference and why she denigrated renting. Maria explained.

"You see, when I wanted an apartment, the management agent asked me if I wanted to lease or rent the one-bedroom apartment. I asked, What's the difference? It's the same apartment, isn't it? Of course, the man said. If you rent, it's $700. But if you lease, it's only $795. I stared at the guy. You see, he said, it's a matter of prestige. It's almost like owning. Like if you lease a car, it has a certain cachet. It's not like renting some used car for a week while yours is laid up in the shop. Like, for instance, he asked me, would you rather marry a divorcee or a pre-used wife? I don't think, I told the guy, either would appeal to me. Sorry, he said, I deal mostly with men. So I asked him, what if I rent and say I lease it? That's a violation of your contract. You would actually be breaking your lease. Look, you're a smart girl, you go with the right crowd, and you'll be better off, prestige has its price, you know, and it'll pay in the long run, believe me. So I leased."

"No wonder you can't save any money. How long have you been here?"

"Ten years."

"How much is the difference over ten years?"

"I'm not good at math," she said.

"That's $95, let's say $100 a month to make the math easier. That's about $1,200 a year, times ten years equals $12,000. That's $12,000 you could have had in your pocket."

"It wouldn't have stayed there long."

"Still, better in your pocket than theirs. And you could have rented but said you're leasing."

"True. But then I'd be lying. And I don't lie. Jesus wouldn't like that. The guy was right. People are impressed when I say I'm leasing.... Do you lie a lot?"

"Never. Except when it's absolutely necessary."

Maria looked at her wrist, which didn't have a watch. With a twinkle in her eye, she exclaimed: "My goodness! You've been here for what seems like hours and I haven't offered you anything yet. What can I get you? Tea, perhaps. A napkin? A dry biscuit?"

"Just a glass of cold water."

"Sure."

I followed her to her tiny kitchen, where one was a crowd. She opened the refrigerator door. I looked in and couldn't believe my eyes. Maria always surprised me. But that wasn't surprising, since she was such an offbeat girl. For instance, how many other modern girls have Jesus embedded into their consciousness?

Her fridge was full of socks. And folders. And a couple of books. And one bottle of cold water. That's it. Not a crumb of food. I didn't say a word. I was too stunned.

But Maria said, "My fridge is a great storage space. And I like cold socks. Not in the winter, but all the other months. Nothing cools you off like a pair of fresh, cold socks."

After I drank the water, I said, "Now I can sign your book."

"Problem is I couldn't find it yet."

"Did you check your fresh fruit bin?"

"Not yet," she said, "but I do have the slides."

Maria pointed to her desk, where she had prepared her projector and a couple of slide trays. She asked me to sit on her chair, then, while standing to my right, began showing slides. She began with her trip to Israel. I thought she would show me Bessarabia, in conjunction with "my" travel book that she loved so much. But perhaps she would show me those slides another time.

The slides were enlarged to about eight by twelve inches, clear and crisp, on the white wall. I praised her photos and asked how many times she'd been to Israel. Just once, she said.

"What still fascinates me," I said, "is hearing those Greek Orthodox priests in Jerusalem, with their big round yarmulkes and long, dark brown hassocks..."

"I think you mean cassocks."

"Maybe. I'm not very good with Christian terminology...hearing those priests speaking impeccable Hebrew."

"You understood them?"

"Not a word."

"Then how do you know it was impeccable?"

"The impeccable parts I understood."

I looked at Maria. I was sitting. She was standing in front of me, slightly to the right. Then I made a move which I didn't mull over at length. Had I thought about it—another time I'll tell you how long I thought of doing something else with her—had I thought about it I wouldn't have done it. But without thinking, without waiting for the stop call endemic in human beings, which binds us, prevents us from doing the things we want to do, I stretched out my right hand, put it around her waist, drew her closer till she stood in front of my right leg, and then I pulled her, guided her back onto my lap. She didn't break off her narration but continued showing slides of Jerusalem and the Galilee and Nazareth and Bethlehem while sitting on my lap, her back to my chest, both my hands now around her waist, my hands clasped tight, she tilted slightly to the right to give me a clear view of the changing slides.

"This is where I walked. Can you imagine, I walked in his footsteps. This where Jesus was born. And here, in Jerusalem, he walked too, poor Jesus. And here he preached."

All this Jesus made me edgy, but since she was on my lap I focused on her tush, which wasn't perfect, but it was okay. A little too long and a little too wide, but from a certain angle, with your eyes slightly closed at twilight, one could say that Maria had a callipygous ass.

•

= Wow! I couldn't help saying. = I haven't come across that word, Katz, since I read *Catch-22*, the funniest book I have ever read. Have you, like me, read *Catch-22* two or three times?

= Never, John. Not even once. In fact, less than once.

= What? Then how can you quote from it? Remember that evocative word?

Katz stared at me. Not answering. Making me feel queasy. Guilty of something. Then it dawned on me. It's not him. He's quoting his brother's work.

= My brother and I may share the same genes, Katz said with exaggerated patience. = But we don't read the same books. I never read fiction that makes me laugh.

•

I liked it. I liked her sitting on my lap. It seemed natural. That's how close to her I felt. I felt I could do anything I wanted with her and I told her that. Not then, of course. But at another time. And Maria liked it too; otherwise, she would have refused my embrace. The fact she didn't say a word—that too was important.

Of course, once on my lap, she could have turned to me with a smile, a warm smile, to show me, to demonstrate that she agreed with my move. Was waiting for it. That's why she stood so close to me and asked me to sit in her chair. Had she turned to me with a smile, I surely would have kissed her. But, as you will see, Maria was not like that. Turning and smiling would have been akin to her saying, I like that. I love what you just did. For her it sufficed to accept my lead without a word. To comply. Yet not to reveal her feelings by word or gesture. She had a mantra that I learned much later, which explained everything. Well, not everything. But a lot.

The slides she showed me went in one eye and out the other, if there's such a phrase. I just reveled having her ass, along with the rest of her, on my lap, my arms around her and, when she leaned forward to change the slide tray, her breast, I couldn't tell if it was just one or both of them, resting on my arm.

"Wanna see more?"

"Sure."

"You're not bored?" Maria asked.

"Nothing about you is boring. Neither you or your slides."

"Nor," she corrected me, then, after a pause, added, "Now for some photos of Romania."

Maria stood to get the slides. Again what she did not do was significant. She didn't resume her earlier standing position. If she had, it would have meant that sitting on my lap was just good manners. But no. Soon as she put in the new slide tray, she again sat down on my lap, unbidden, as though it were the most natural thing in the world.

When the slide show was over, I thanked her, praised her skill as a photographer, and said: "Come, let's talk."

I sat down on her old sofa and expected, fully expected, fully fully expected her to sit next to me, as though it was preordained. In life, one goes from A to B to C. Once you're at C, you don't go back to A. But no. To my dismay and astonishment, she sat down in her old deep easy chair, which, judging by its age and faded deep wine color, could have been a match for the sofa. I didn't like that at all. I wanted her to walk with me to the sofa and sit next to me. Given what had passed between us that would have been natural. Maybe she purposely sat down on the easy chair to wait for me to beckon her, to pat the empty cushion next to me.

But I didn't do any pillow patting. I didn't gesture to her. I didn't bend my index finger and with a few back-and-forth motions signal *come sit next to me*. I didn't utter a word.

I simply got up, walked over to Maria, took her by the hand, and pulled. As I tugged, she rose and, hand in hand, we both walked to the sofa.

I didn't put my hand around her shoulder. Not yet. First we spoke, sitting side by side, she looking at me.

"You're a quick learner," I said.

"Regarding what?"

"Looking at me when you talk to me."

"I am a quick learner, you know. When someone gives me a good suggestion, I pick up on it, you know, rather quickly."

I was about to express my disapproval at the two "you knows"; to tell her she wasn't such a quick learner; that she, a recidivist, was regressing to her old tram mode of speech. Then, bam, it hit me. I realized she had purposely thrown in those phrases. Had she done it once, it would have been a slip. But by saying "you know" twice in one sentence, she signaled her self-satire.

"I'm still looking for your travel book, but I hope to find it before your next visit."

Hearing that, two little sparkles of fireworks lit up in my mind. Again, she invited me to see her again, elegantly and sideways. And also, my brother's book, bless it, dazzled like a firecracker.

That book of my brother's that I passed off as my own, that was one of the reasons Maria and I had hit it off. That brought us together so quickly. Her affection for that travel book was passed over to me. Her familiarity with it made her feel she'd known me for years. So a link was established. I felt at ease with her. It wasn't a feeling I could create on my own. I sort of absorbed it from her vibes. So I too felt as if I'd known her for a long time. Close but not yet intimate, if you know what I mean

•

= Here's my stop, John. I'll elaborate next time.

7

WHAT KATZ NOTICES FOR THE FIRST TIME THE SECOND TIME HE SEES MARIA

THE NEXT TIME I came to her house, I took her hand and walked her to the sofa. I sat down. She stood before me, almost helpless, as if waiting for me to say something or do something. I looked around her living room. She had a small bookcase. She didn't have a TV set; maybe there was one in her bedroom, but I doubted it. With a girl as bright as she, I would have expected some music. None. Instead, the silence created by two people not speaking.

Even though she wasn't mine, I felt she was mine. And I may even have said this the first day I came to her apartment, when she excitedly showed me her travel slides from Israel and Bessarabia. She stood in front of me by the projector while I sat and watched and then I grabbed her waist and plopped her down on my lap and she sat there quite naturally, not twisting away, not eluding me politely, pretending my move had never taken place.

I think I told her right away, when I sensed that electric current flowing between us as if we were two terminals and one wire linked us, I told her I felt I could do anything I wanted with her, that's how close I felt to her. This swift sense of kinship, so out of a movie, had never happened to me before.

Now I gazed into her green eyes. She tried, I could tell she was trying, to maintain a neutral expression. But it seemed to me her entire being was waiting to be told what to do.

"Sit on my lap," I said.

At once she said, "Which way? The slideshow way?"

"No. I want to look at your face when you talk to me."

"Okay."

She bent her knees and slid forward until her knees were almost up against the back of the sofa and her butt sat on my legs. My elbows and arms rested on her thighs, my hands clasped her hips, call it upper buttocks, just below the waist. I was eye level with her boobs. Her crotch was awfully, pleasantly, close to mine. But with my eyes on the same plane as her breasts and her lips about twelve inches above my lips, I had to look up to her when we spoke. Me, who always looked down on everyone, to her, now, I had to look up. Still, I couldn't believe it, having this lovely girl on my lap. You know how I felt? Happy as the first movement of Mendelssohn's "Italian" Symphony.

Then she slid off and sat next to me. I looked down and my heart almost stopped.

•

I didn't notice it that first morning on the Boston-bound T with her. And I missed seeing it first time I came to her house. Not that she hid it, like people who have defects do. I just didn't see it. It wasn't until she was close to me on her sofa, when she began telling me about her poor relationship with her mother and I put my arm friendly-like around her shoulder and clasped her upper arm and she tilted her head so naturally and rested in on my shoulder as if we'd been friends for a long time. She held her hands on her lap, palms down, fingers out, as if wanting me to look, to discover now rather than later, drawing my attention to her fingers, it was then that I looked down and first noticed it.

On her left hand, the ring finger—she didn't have a ring—the top digit was missing. This made her ring finger as small as her pinkie. It sent a shock through me, that finger without a fingernail. I may have made an involuntary motion, as though a spasm went through me. A sudden rill of pain began in my head; I still recall it. I felt so sorry for her. But say a word? Commiserate? Oh, no! And I never asked her about it. Never inquired if it was an accident or from birth. And she never mentioned it either. Not one single word. Until much, much later. Luckily, it did not seem to have altered her life one whit. But then she began telling me about her mother. Maria hadn't seen her mother in months. To Maria's chagrin, her mother was living with another man; she hadn't divorced her father, who was bearing the pain and the humiliation stoically. And as she spoke about her mother, I saw Maria's eyes moisten too.

Then she told me why she never offered me sugar when she made me tea. Which is why she never even kept sugar in the house. "I loved sugar, when I was a little girl," Maria said. "I would stick my finger in the sugar bowl and lick my finger and my mother always reprimanded me. Once, when I was ten and there was a guest for lunch, I had tea and took three tablespoons of sugar and stirred it into the tea. I sipped the tea and enjoyed the half-melted sugary syrup at the bottom of the glass. Since my mother didn't say anything, I thought she didn't mind. But after the guest left, she said, 'I see you like tea with your sugar. So I have a special treat for you.' She took a cup of sugar and poured a little tea into it. 'Now finish this to the last bite.' I started eating and gagged. 'Eat it. Eat it,' she shouted. 'Show me how much you love sugar.' I forced myself, crying, and then vomited all over the floor. My mother made me clean up the mess. Since that day, I haven't touched a drop of sugar. Can't even stand the sight of it."

"I hope you'll forgive me, but that woman is a cruel bitch. A sadist. What she did was child abuse, pure and simple."

Then listen to what Maria did. It was right in keeping with me putting my arm around her shoulder and she leaning her head against my shoulder. And it was only my second time in her house. I saw her hand slowly coming to my face. Then, to my astonishment, she wiped the tears from my face and put her hand on my heart.

I weighed that gesture. I considered that gesture. I was touched by that intimate gesture that could only come from a person you've known and loved for a long, long time. We compressed time, Maria and me; we crumpled it like a plastic cup but without the crunch.

And then you know what I did? For a while I hesitated, then reconsidered. If I let that moment go, I'd regret it forever. A thrill went through me as I took her hands in mine and kissed the tip of each finger, saving the flawed ring finger for last. I didn't look at her as I did this but focused all my attention on her hands. When I looked up at her, I saw tears on her cheeks, two thin rivulets on her sad, happy, now pretty face. But I did not, oh no, I did not kiss her lips.

And you know what? That little missing fingertip, I never noticed it again.

Then, as if sadness dissolved, she looked out the window.

"I wish it would always be ten o'clock in the morning," Maria said cheerily. Maybe she wanted me to forget about her finger. "With a stillness in the house, and everyone in the other apartments gone to work, there's not a sound anywhere, and I can read and there's no traffic noise outside, and it's so quiet and sunny I can see the dust motes on the shelves."

But it's only ten at ten o'clock. In time the shadows lengthen and there's no more sunshine, I didn't say.

"I wish this special aura could last forever."

"And me here with you," I said, feeling a little tightening in my throat with my bold utterance.

"Yes," she said. But no more than Yes. With my heightened mood, I wanted her to say more than Yes. But Yes was all she said. Although it is my habit to put the music of words into a balance and assay their metaphysical weight, once I heard that non-committal, neutral, restrained, polite, conventional, automatic, canny, careful, and circumspect Yes, I no longer lingered on its music nor its metaphysical mass.

And then I thought: nothing lasts forever.

•

I saw Katz a few days later. A look of agitation darkened his face as he slid next to me on the train.

= John, I have to make a correction, an emendation to what I told you the other day. My brother gave me a revised chapter. Katz pointed to a sheaf of papers in his open briefcase. =And he says he changes, has changed, his mind about the finger-kissing episode.

= To what?

= He changed it back to something the protagonist wanted to do but didn't have the nerve to carry out...Does that make sense to you?

= From a fictional or from a realistic point of view?

= Well, both, Katz replied.

= When I first heard it the other day, I thought to myself, as a story it sounded a bit implausible. I don't think a character seeing a girl for the second time in her house would do something so intimate. What drives the hero to do something so dramatic, even drastic, after knowing the girl so briefly?

= My very thoughts, said Katz.

= If they really have affection for each other and both sense this, then after a certain time such a gesture becomes believable in fiction. However, from a real-world perspective, anything is possible. Real life and fiction live in separate worlds and only occasionally intersect...You know how beginning writers excuse a fictionally implausible scene by saying, 'But it really happened!'?

= Right, Katz said. = I asked my brother if it really happened, but he wouldn't tell me.

Good for him, I thought, but I didn't tell Katz that. Why should writers reveal another layer? But I also thought: if Katz is telling me one thing one day and withdrawing it the next, how do I know what is his brother's story and what is Katz's? In other words, how do I separate the truth of his brother's fiction from the fiction of Katz's truth?

But Katz wasn't done.

= And another thing, he continued. = Remember Maria's praise of a quiet, sun-filled morning in her apartment, where she concludes by wishing it could last forever? Then the hero says boldly, And me here with you! And then Maria, in the version I told you last time, Maria gives a neutral Yes. Turns out that's changed too. From Yes, which is at least a kind of affirmative, now my brother has her saying her trademark, neutrally weighted Really?, albeit uttered softly, with an insuck of breath, you might almost say passionately. So I guess if you think about it, that *Really?* is even stronger.

•

After she told me about her mother, Maria said, "You're such a good, sympathetic listener, you could be a psychologist."

"Among other professions, I'm a psychologist too."

"Super. You can listen to more of my problems."

"Gladly. I might even, you know, if I feel it's warranted, create some new ones for you."

"The last psychologist I knew, well, I didn't really know him, but the last one I got to know is a psychologist who is a character in a novel."

"Which one?"

"Oh, a novel I read some years back, I think it was called *Diary of an Adulteress*."

"You mean Charlie?" I said.

"Yes. The psychologist. Did you read that book too?"

"Read it? I *wrote* it."

"Wow! You wrote that book too? Under a pseudonym?"

"No. Under a sun umbrella. In the Bahamas. Well, actually, the author, C. L. Eviant— he doesn't like first names either, based the character, Charlie, on me."

"Amazing! To be in a book. Do you also sleep with all your patients, like Charlie?"

"With as many as I can. Men *and* women."

"Ugh!" Maria grimaced.

"Why the ugh?"

"With women too?" she said.

"Yup."

I don't know who giggled more, she or me.

8

WHERE ARE YOU GOING?

OH, HOW I WANTED to kiss her. Why? What a question, why? Good question, why. I always like good questions. You don't ask, you don't learn. Why? Because it was a natural concomitant to what we were already doing. By now we had everything but that. We had a shared intimacy. It was understood that I could/would come over whenever I wanted. An ease, a relaxation between us. We felt like a couple without the sex.

When she showed me her slides, she sat on my lap, her back toward me, as if I was a chair. Next time she sat on my lap, she faced me, so kissing had to come next. Do I have to spell it out for you? What's the ultimate purpose of a little bud? To become a flower. An inexorable event.

I'll let you draw your own conclusion about the analogy.

This went on for days. I sat close to her every day, and every day I said, today I will kiss her, but I didn't have the nerve. At night I would regret my faintheartedness and rehearse my next visit. Instead of holding her waist as we spoke, I would raise my hands to her face and hold her cheeks and bring her face to mine until our lips touched. How easy, how uncomplicated this was when I planned it at night. And how distant her face seemed when she sat opposite me, her lips no more than ten inches from mine. But the next day would pass like the previous ones. My frustration at myself put knots in my stomach. My desire to kiss her became physical pain.

Then, suddenly, I had a thought. A thought with an umber shadow to it. My God! Maybe she thinks we're having a platonic relationship.

For days I dreamt of kissing her, and at night, before I fell asleep, I thought of it too, seeing it in full color on the screen of my either open or closed eyes. Or maybe I was at the midway point between wakefulness and sleep, bridging the border of that tenuous no man's land, when I tasted her phantom lips. And not a word was spoken in this silent film.

I felt like a high school kid with a crush on the prettiest girl in class. But unlike the high school girl who was out of reach, this one was nearby. On my lap, in fact, facing me, so close and so far away, legs splayed, her knees pressing my hips. A position both real or symbolic, depending on one's taste. I wanted to break the ice of this seemingly buddy-buddy relationship. If I waited any longer, desire would fade. One two more such meetings and something indefinable would slip away and we'd be like two poles set in concrete, unable to touch each other. Perfectly platonic. Achingly platonic. Absurdly platonic.

The next day, I sat her on my lap and we chatted, while in my mind I put my hands behind her back and drew her closer till her lips met mine and my dream of kissing her was realized. Then I saw her little Bible again. Maybe Jesus is the unseen barrier between us.

"Does it bother you that I'm Jewish and you're Christian?"

"No no no," she said quickly. "Not at all."

We talked for a while. Time slid by. I looked at my watch. My goodness. Time to go. I sprang up.

"Tomorrow?" she said.

"Not tomorrow. I can't. Tomorrow I have to go in very early."

"Then Thursday?" she said.

"Sure."

Thursday Maria sat on my lap again, knees spread. There was an erotic charge in the room; you could almost hear the buzzing chemical flow. Her hands were on my shoulders, mine around her waist. She was so close, but her mouth, her lips, were miles away. What prevented me now from doing what I knew was inevitable, erasing those ten or so inches of space between our lips? That first kiss would transport us to a different continent.

I looked at her and said to myself, No more tomorrow. Now! Now is the time. And before I could think some more, postpone some more, I lifted my hands, saw myself doing what I had done in my thoughts the night before and the night before that. I lifted my hands from her waist and I watched my hands moving up up up until they touched her cheeks. I put my hands on her cheeks and pulled her face close to mine and I kissed her. And Maria, totally surprised, but maybe not, maybe not surprised at all, just astonished that it took so long, didn't resist. She didn't twist away. Her lips were not open like mine, but she kissed me back. Her eyes were closed—a good sign, excellent omen—and I kissed her again. Remember, I didn't just suddenly come up to her from across the room, surprise her with my embrace and startle her with a kiss on her lips. I didn't bend over to her as she was showing me slides. I didn't turn her around as she stood in front of me, opening the refrigerator to take out socks, a sweater, or a box of paper clips, and press her close to me. Don't forget she was on my lap. The position was ideal; couldn't be better—legs spread, kneeling, her knees pointing to the back of the sofa, straddling my thighs.

"I've been wanting to do this for a long long time."

Then she uttered a word I gave so many interpretations to:

"Really?" she said, softly, appreciatively, with a tenderness that I hadn't felt with her before.

I ran my finger down her back. A little shudder went through her. I felt that shudder. She tensed; she arched her back. Not many women react that way. But if their backs tense and arch, it's a sign that this will also happen before an orgasm.

Now I wanted to say something. But my lips were sealed, my tongue tied. My tongue cleaved to the roof of my mouth.

Then something phenomenal happened, as if in a dream. Instead of words coming, I saw a grid, a huge square, like an enlarged Bingo card, and from the top, along a horizontal line, letters began falling slowly like thick snowflakes on a calm, windless night. The letters, a mix of consonants and vowels, descended lazily and fell into a smaller grid, but they spelled no words I could understand. Then the grid vanished and I found my tongue again. But Maria was the one who spoke. Either I didn't hear her or the letters of her words, like mine, were jumbled, creating a language I did not understand.

I wanted, I longed for Maria to say how much she loved my kissing her. I knew, I sensed she loved it, but I wanted to hear it from her. In her own words, in a grid of my own construction.

Instead of saying what I wanted her to say, Maria astonished me with:

"Where are you going?"

Oh, what a classic line! It reverberated in my consciousness for ages. And still does. The sudden chill of those words yanked me out of my sunny island and covered me with frost. I could have concocted so many subtexts to that question. But I knew it wasn't what it meant on the surface, for with her on my lap, where *could* I be going?

What it meant was, In which direction are you taking this relationship, which seemed so brotherly up to now? Yeah, like the brother-sister relationship in ancient Egypt which yielded children who had only one set of grandparents. Sure, I thought, that's why you're on my lap, so maidenly modestly with your legs spread, and that's why, sister, you let me pull you onto my lap the first day I came to your apartment to see your slides, and that's why—of course, this happened a few days later—you had that sisterly platonic wet spot when I lay next to you on the sofa with my arms around you and then stroked you with my very best we're-just-good-friends stroke until I put my hand on your crotch and found it soaking wet like a sponge, sister, buddy, pal, part-time platonic partner.

"Where are you going?" was her muted response when I kissed her the second time.

I don't know whether to put quotes around this coming paragraph or not, for I don't recall if I told this to her or just thought it to myself.

On second thought, I did tell her, for in the echo chamber of my mind I keep hearing that delicious, soft "Really?" of hers, her bemusement, her wonder at the metaphysical energy and fervid dreamstuff I expended on her.

"Where am I going?" I repeated and answered my own question, rather hers, before she could open her mouth again.

"Here...and here...and here." And between each "here" I kissed another part of her body. First I lifted up her chin and kissed her throat. "That's where I'm going." And then I pressed a long kiss into her left, let's see, it's like a mirror image, the one on my right side was her *left* breast –yes, that's the one I kissed first. "That one first," I said, "because it's over the heart, is where I'm going," and then I kissed her right breast. "If you want to know my itinerary, it's all printed up. Just send me a self-addressed stamped envelope and I'll mail it to you." And I kissed her lips again. "That's where I'm going, but the trip's not over, for I'm only halfway around the block."

Maria gazed at me, but I couldn't read her eyes. Was she with me or agin me? Yet every time my lips pressed hers, she responded.

"Where am I going, you ask? This is where I'm going. Here and here. And here and there. I am going before, behind, above, between, above, below..."

"That's from John Donne," Maria said.

"How did you know that?" I asked, amazed.

"Knock, knock, knock, three-personed God...It's religious poetry. Very Christian. So I know it."

"Also, very sexy. Erotic."

"Yes," she said.

"You know that religion and the erotic are very closely linked."

"Yes," she said again.

I sensed she didn't want to talk poetry now.

"And I'm also going there...not only here," I said, demonstrating. "I'm going, I'm staying, I'm coming. Like John Donne, I too can play with words and have them mean two things at the same time."

Seeing Maria's pleased look, I added:

"Do you know how long I rehearsed this first kiss, how long I thought about it, dreamt about it? So when I went through with it, it was actually the second time I kissed you."

"Really?"

Ah, I was getting a reaction from her.

"Yes. Really. I've been planning this for a long time."

"How long?"

"For years. Since my Bar Mitzva."

She beamed. She didn't move. On my lap she was, her arms around my shoulders, knees pressing into my thighs.

"Let's backtrack to a few minutes ago," I said. "Here I sit with my arms around your waist, very friendly like, and there was a space of about one foot between our faces. But that space could just as well have been ten miles long, because I couldn't make the leap. For me, for a while, it was forbidden territory, even though I knew as soon as I began talking to you the other day, that wondrous day we met and took that lovely ride on the tram to Boston, that I could do anything I wanted with you."

And I wasn't afraid to say that to her. I thought it absolutely natural to tell her what I felt.

"But by dreaming about kissing you, by wishing I could, by planning that soon-to-be-made move, it made the eventual leap easier."

"Really?" she whispered. Breathless was that second "Really," the vowels tinted, the consonants rounded.

"Did the dream kiss count? You bet it did. Aside from its dream nectar taste, diaphanous, evanescent, good at the moment but great, super, in recall, it laid the rock-solid, steel-reinforced concrete foundation for the real kiss. Go ahead, say it."

"What?" Maria asked.

"Really?"

Her eyes crinkled.

"Where are you going?" I heard her say. Not that she said it again, but I heard it again.

"Paris," I said, "maybe heaven," clicking my seatbelt and flooring the gas pedal, but I meant Miami. With my lips on hers, I was up north and my aim was to go south to Savannah or Jacksonville.

Where are you going? wasn't a geographic question like *Where are you traveling this year, New York, Seattle*? What she meant was, *Where are you heading with me*? *What's your goal*?

But now that I thought of it, I didn't like, sweet as it seemed, I didn't like the tone of her voice. It wasn't said lovingly. Her voice lacked the color, the nuance, the patina, the melody and closeness that I reckoned we'd been building the past three weeks by seeing her almost every weekday and talking on the phone twice a day, she talking so softly that her co-workers or bosses wouldn't hear her, a soft voice that I interpreted as sexy, affectionate, intimate. We weren't just connected because of the phone. We were connected, period. She was sending me that special timbre of her voice, sending it on that wavelength that we, and only we, were on.

But now I heard that neutral, officious, colorless, formal, cool and distant question, those four Icelandic words, albeit softly said, perhaps complaining, surely surprised (but I can't believe she wasn't expecting it), for this was the first overtly sexual move on my part, despite the fact that sex hung in the air, the sex molecules so thick and plentiful they could have been plucked like stars, the air so charged with eros only a self-deluding fool would have averred it wasn't there. And delude herself she did, up to this point, evidently assuming that everything that had been going on between us was friendly, brotherly, platonic. But Platonism, you sexpot, you easily-stirred-up Maria, doesn't cause the crotch of your thick blue jeans to explode with a flood, to salivate in its own fashion, to get soaking wet, does it?

"Hallelujah!" I shouted. Now, for I didn't shout it out before.

"Why are you saying that?"

"Because it shows me you're normal. You're a woman with desires, a girl who can get ignited."

"What are you talking about? Just from that one kiss?"

"Not one...two...three...four...twenty-seven."

And I kissed her again to get the numbers higher. I kissed her long, hard, deep, until she was gasping for breath and banging my back with her fists because she couldn't breathe.

"Where you going?" I recalled.

So it was three Icelandic words after all, not four.

And she didn't mean, like across my waist, up my neckline, down to my panties. Neither Paris, Rome, nor Prague. She asked that question to make herself feel good. Give herself an out. Proclaim to the ether that she could kiss me and still satisfy herself that she hadn't forgotten her self-prescribed boundaries. That Jesus and her little white Bible were still her heart's favorites. Of course, as she kissed me, her slightly compressed lips signaled that those other, real lips, somewhere between Savannah and Jacksonville, would be sealed too. Until the same tongue that broke the seal of the upper kingdom would penetrate the soft barrier of the nether realm.

But first I'd have to scale the walls of Jericho, alas without the help of Rahab or Joshua's trumpets. Seven times around her waist would do me no good. There was no magic I could summon but my own pertinacity. A finger slid diagonally across her back would make her taut, arch with pleasure, with expectant joy. That was the sexiest move on her.

Remember, I said that although she was on my lap, in my mind she seemed light years away. For a few successive days, I had been telling myself, Today I will do it, but I chickened out at the last minute. And then, when the first kiss came, it happened so quickly there was no time to think about it. She was on my lap and I brought her face, I held it with both hands, I decided today's the day, no more delay, and I quickly brought her face, she did not resist, I quickly brought it down to mine and I kissed her lips. She caught her breath and said, Where are you going? But it was too late. That kiss changed everything. Continents drifted. Maps were redrawn.

"Here's where I'm going, I call it Timbuctoo, and I'm taking the train, so get your tickets, choo-choo-choo."

"Where are you going?" she said again.

In a deep voice, I imitated my underling and said: "The Chairman is not taking any questions."

I kissed her again, but her mouth was tight. I had to fight my way in with my tongue, but once I was there she opened up as I knew she would and she drew close and pressed her fingers into my back and kissed my eyes, my cheeks, my neck. Soon her mouth was wrapped around my lips and she let her tongue go like a puppy released from its leash, exploring here and there and everywhere.

After that kiss, she no longer sat on my lap. Next time we stretched out, side by side, on the sofa. A day later I took her hand and led her to her bedroom, but she said an abrupt No and we ended up on the sofa again.

We lay side by side. Now that her face was next to mine, I saw she was a bit older than the mid-thirties. I buried my mouth in her neck. As I kissed her and she responded, I ran my hand over her body, down her back and to her ass, all this across thick blue jeans, no frilly material where I could actually feel flesh, and down to her thighs and quickly up to her crotch, and it was then I noticed, through the thick jeans, that her crotch was wet. I was delighted. So she's actually hot for me. I didn't think of that wet spot, actually it flew by me for it happened so quickly, and I didn't relive it until I asked, yes, I actually asked her about it later and she confirmed it.

After that first kiss, Maria looked at me and said with an admiring tone:

"You have blue eyes."

"Sure took you a long time to notice."

"I'm a slow noticer. But when I notice—I *notice*."

I felt we had become so close, absolutely on the same wavelength, it was as if she were an extension of me. No wonder I liked her so much. Love, like charity, begins at home.

But I wondered how many Jesus hurdles I would have to leap before she devoted herself full-heartedly to me and let go of her white leather-bound Luke.

•

Then Katz stopped and, in a slightly higher pitch, as if he were done with his narrative voice and was now speaking personally, said:

= John, I know you prefer me telling the story, not reading it, but this part I must read to you. My brother has another version of the "Where are you going?" scene. And, anyway, I want you to hear it in my brother's—not my—words.

= Fine with me, I said.

Katz opened his briefcase, flipped through some pages, pulled out a sheaf of papers and read:

•

First let me tell you about a succulent, intimate moment that occurred after that first kiss. No, it's not what you think, but nevertheless it is intimate. Even more than you think. I was saying something she didn't want to hear, I forget now what exactly, probably how sexy she was, so as a way of shushing me, she clapped her hand over my mouth. As soon as I felt the palm of her hand on my lips, I kissed it. She did not remove her hand. I slid my lips over every part of her palm. I licked it. I ticked it with the tip of my tongue. I kissed her fingertips, starting with the pinkie, slowly, intently, intensely. I kissed the tip of every finger and she helped me along by offering, as though she were playing a scale very slowly, one finger at a time, and I heard her giving out a little moan with each note I played on her round little fingertips. It was a duet we were now performing. She hummed, vibrated with "Mmm" and continued that little song for three or four fingers. By the time I got to her thumb, she was already into vowels, 'Ahh" and "Ohh" and "Oo-ooh." Oh, I love those vowel songs; they're sweeter than any kisses. If I had my way, I would do away with consonants and we'd all talk Hawaiian. I lingered on each of her fingertips as if each was a beloved entity, worthy of worship and adulation.

Now back to that seminal question: Where are you going?

But instead of answering where I was going, I answered with another question:

"Do you know how long I've been waiting to do this?"

"What?" she said, as I knew she would.

"This, you silly goose." And I kissed her again as if I owned her, as if she were mine. I spread her lips with my tongue and plunged deep into her mouth and kissed her lips and cheeks, her green eyes, her pressed-shut eyelids, went into one ear with my lips, into the other with my tongue, and then, surprising her with more and more surprises, I pressed my lips into her right breast and into her left and then returned to her lips, taking the top one into my mouth and then the bottom one, my lips moving back and forth until I felt her hands press into my back and she drew me close and her tongue slipped into my mouth and I said, "I've been dreaming of this. Rehearsing this." But she said nothing except that delicious, musical, soft and dreamy, ethereally inviting "Really?"—a word, more an exhalation, that became her signature reply, as if she couldn't believe I had focused my attention on her her her.

But the reality of it, reality always comes out later, the reality of it, there's no avoiding it, reality always shows its ugly mug, the reality of it was that that one word was her exculpation, her little cave of concealment, her hiding place, hiding in, behind, that innocent glowing "Really?" of hers, her way of not having to say anything endearing to me lest it compromise her fidelity to Jesus, lest she betray him by saying an affectionate word to me, for my words to her he could not hear, but he was all ears to anything sweet she might say to me. Talk of having your cake and eating it too, that "Really?" did it for her.

Piece of cake.

I often wonder what my response would have been had she said, "What are you doing?" instead of "Where are you going?" Maybe I would have said something stupid like "I don't know," for my tongue would've been tied by that sudden question, a question a guy who kisses a girl would dread hearing. But "Where are you going?" was a delicious spur to sarcasm. She could have meant, in which direction do you propose to go, up or down? Are you next going to kiss my eyes, my forehead, my ears, my hair? Or are you aiming in a southerly direction?

In short, are you heading for my pussy, Katz?

9

MARIA AS DETECTIVE (VERSION A)

WHEN I FIRST MET Maria, I thought it would be sexier to say I was married. That was my mistake. My grand *faux pas*. I shouldn't have told her that. Even if I were married, she would never have found out. I had my way of keeping my life secret. I said I was married because women sometimes like to have an affair with married men. There is something sweet in betrayal. Screwing your lover and his wife at the same time. An earthly Paradise, as the *Kama Sutra* says. They love the idea of having their smell mingling with that of the other woman's. A kind of long distance *ménage à trois*. But not Maria.

I didn't realize the extent of her piety, a Christian who adhered to all the values Christians nowadays dismiss. She had Jesus perched on her shoulder like a pet parrot. Hearing "married," she wanted to back off. So I confessed I wasn't married. It was just a put-on, I insisted.

"I thought I'd be more attractive to you if I said I was married."

She shook her head. Maria would only go so far with a married man. Up to a certain point but no more. And then her religious guilt rolled in, and like a reformed drunkard swearing not to touch another drop, she put up a barrier, which she wouldn't let herself—and me—cross. That last word is an accident. But for her it was packed with meaning. Her allegiance to Jesus grew greater by the day. Otherwise, she feared she would become another Mary Magdalene.

A couple of days later, when I called her at work and told her I was coming to see her the next morning, she shared some glad tidings with me.

"You're married," she said through motionless lips.

Instead of denying it, I said: "Shh!"

"Why shh?"

"I don't want them to know," I whispered. "Why tell the whole world?"

"Katz is married, Katz is married," she shouted in a teasing singsong, actually whispered it loudly into the phone.

"If I tell you to shout something out loud, will you do it?"

"Depends what."

"Shout: Maria is jealous. Maria is jealous."

"I'm not."

"You're so jealous the white wires on my phone are turning green."

"I'm not jealous."

"Why are you whispering all of a sudden?"

"My whole department doesn't have to know I'm j…." and she stopped.

"Say it. Say it," I encouraged her. "Finish the sentence."

She didn't.

"Are you coming back to your apartment tonight?"

"Yes."

"Good. Leave the back door open for me…I'll see you in the morning."

"But you're married."

Good, I thought. She didn't say no.

"I'll get a divorce."

"Will you be divorced by 7:30?" Maria wanted to know.

"Exactly at 7:30 a.m. the divorce judgment will come through."

"Then come at 7:20."

"Why?"

"I love married men. And I believe in ten-minute affairs with a married man."

"You're delicious," I said. "And capricious. No wonder…." And I was about to say, I'm crazy about you, but I changed it to, "I want to see you. Once in a while."

The following morning everything went well, but the next time I saw her, her welcome was frosty. Turns out that Maria, assuming I was wed, had pulled a nasty trick on me, which you'll hear in a minute. But, nevertheless, I put a positive spin on it. Her sly detective ploy—actually comic, if you take an objective view—showed she liked me.

Soon as I opened the back door to her apartment, which lately she always left open for me, the first ice-capped words out of her mouth were, "You *are* married."

She hadn't even stood to welcome me, but from the comfort of her easy chair came the hissed, "You liar! I saw you coming out of your house with your wife…and getting into your car with her….Why're you laughing? Stop laughing! There you were, the both of you, you and your darling little wife."

"Oh, Jesus!" I exclaimed.

"Don't take God's name in vain," she said.

"It's not my God."

"Still."

"So you followed me," I said, delighted.

I drew near and kissed the tip of her nose. I stood over her, held her shoulders and squeezed affectionately.

"Yes. Yes I did. Yes, I followed you."

"Why?"

"I didn't believe you."

"You'd rather I were not married, right?"

Maria didn't answer, but her silence said yes.

"I told you I wasn't married."

"But you also told me you were."

"That was Version A. Version B is now operative….If it will make you feel better, it was my landlady's daughter, a married woman for your information."

"See? I knew she was married. I could tell. She had that married look."

"…whom I was giving a lift to."

"To where?"

None of your business, I was about to say. Instead, I said:

"What difference does it make? You jealous about that too?"

"No," she said, her voice an ashen shadow.

"I gave her a lift to her house."

"Where you probably screwed her."

Good, I thought. She *is* jealous. Deep green, verdantly jealous. Chic expanse of golf course jealous. Rain forest greenly jealous.

"Only in my mind, so it's no sin. And why didn't you like it when I said Jesus?"

"I don't have to explain it. And because I love Jesus."

That's what they all say, I thought. Then I said it out loud.

"No, really, it's true," Maria said. "I love Jesus. You won't be able to understand it."

"I'll try to. Okay. Listen. Who do you love more, your canary or Jesus?"

She put her finger to the edge of her mouth. "Umm," she said, hesitating. "My canary…just kidding."

"Why do you love Jesus so much?"

"Because he's Jewish, and because all his disciples were Jews."

"Then you'll have to love me too."

"I'm allowed one free pass," was her clever response. But her warm smile told me something else.

"So that wasn't your wife?" she said gently. "Really? Do you promise?"

"I promise. I aver. I affirm. She is not my wife and I have nothing to do with her. And I'm delighted you're jealous, although there is nothing to be jealous about…. Now get up and put your arms around me."

And she did. Then added: "Can you swear?"

"Of course," I said.

"Then go ahead."

Like Eliezer did with Abraham, when he promised him not to bring back a Canaanite girl for Isaac, I put my hand under Maria's thigh and said:

"I'm ready to swear."

"Then go ahead. Swear!"

"Fuck it! My hand's getting numb."

10

WHAT MARIA TELLS KATZ ON THE PHONE (VERSION B)

= JOHN...HERE'S ANOTHER VERSION my brother has of the previous chapter, the one where Maria admits she followed Katz to his house. In this version, Katz hasn't told her early on that he's married. My brother is still deciding which chapter to use. Maybe, like in an earlier chapter, he'll include both.

•

One day I called her at her office to tell her I was coming to see her the next morning.

I expected, I wanted, to hear her happy voice. When a girl likes a guy, her vocal cords are coated with melody, like chocolate on a fine wafer, like grace notes on a Bach sonata. Instead, she stunned me with, "You're married." No chocolate, no grace notes.

I had not told her one way or another. Where she deduced that from, I don't know.

"Hush. Why're you shouting?"

"You're married."

"Will you calm down? Don't shout it out! Why does everyone at your office have to hear fake info about my private life?"

"They don't know who I'm talking to."

"Neither do you, if you think I'm married. And why should your coworkers even think you're talking to a married man? Which, by the way, you're not."

"You're married," Maria said for the third time. Did I hear a sad downspin, a tone of regret in her voice?

"Will you shush? You're killing my chances of making it with Sally and Betty."

"They don't work here anymore."

"You're supposed to say, They don't work here any more than I do."

"You're married." Said a fourth time, a hard edge now replacing the dreamy tone of regret.

"Pure disinformation, initiated by…by…I don't know who's initiating this. Maybe *you*!" Then, *sotto voce*, I added, "I may be going out with one of your office mates. Male or female. Like Goethe said, *Es ist mir egal.* It's all the same to me. Main thing is to go somewhere else."

Maria was silent.

"I'm joking about Sally and Betty. I just made up the names."

"You did? They just fired a Sally and a Betty."

"Why?"

"They were socializing on the phone too much."

"So you may be next…And who, which demon, told you I was married?"

"I know what I know," she said, trying to sound mysterious.

"Tell," I ordered.

"Not now."

"Okay, then. Face to face. I'll see you in the morning. Leave the back door open."

The next morning, she welcomed me with her usual smile and a perfunctory embrace and a kiss on the lips—but on her forehead lurked a frown, whose thin lines only I could see.

This time she sat in her easy chair. Uh-oh, thinks I, this is serious. She's not sitting on my lap.

"You're married," she said.

"One would think you're a wound-up, mechanical doll, who has only one phrase installed in her *pupick*."

"What's that?"

"Sanskrit for belly button."

I held up five fingers to indicate it was the fifth time she said those words.

"You've been married five times?" Maria cried.

"But not consecutively."

"How do you mean?"

"Contemporaneously. I have four wives in five different states. I mean in four different states. Virginia. Carolina. Georgia. Those are not my brides' names, but the names of their states. And let's not forget my favorite, Ippi, who's good backward and forward."

"Who is Ippi?" she wanted to know.

"My fourth wife. Everyone calls her Mrs."

Maria's eyes lit up. "But what about the one in Waltham?"

"Well, I guess that does make it five. But, hold it, I'm not married in Massachusetts."

"But I saw her with my own eyes."

"Your seeing doesn't make her my wife. What did you see? And how? Snooping on my nuptial couch? Peeping Tomishly into my marital bedchamber?"

Maria let out a pent-up breath. "Okay. I'll tell you what I did. The last time, after you left, I sort of, you know, followed you. And just before you got home I parked, you know, within looking distance. I watched you get out of your car in front of that impressive-looking two-story brick house with those two imposing round white columns on either side of the entrance, and your wife, quite good-looking too, just happened to come out of the house as you were going in and you hugged her and you kissed each other. Disgusting, after kissing me just a few minutes earlier—can't she taste me on your lips? Or do you do a quick mouth rinse after you leave me and before you get home? And then she gets into her car and waves to you like a good little wifey and drives off...Why are you laughing? What's so hilarious?"

Maria was shouting now, but there was a little tear in her voice, like an envelope being ripped in half. Her cheeks were flushed, her lips thinner, her nose pinched. "I'm disappointed in you...Well, are you going to talk or will you just keep laughing that supercilious laugh of yours?"

"My God! Little Miss Iceberg is jealous."

"I'm not."

"My hot little tuffet, the sexy Miss Muffet is miffed. My lovely Maria likes me. She's jealous."

"She doesn't. She's not....Well, are you going to explain? To tell me why you're laughing?"

"Sure...Soon as I calm down...Okay, here goes. First of all, I'm impressed that you actually took the trouble to follow me. That's very flattering. Secondly, that alleged wifey in your creative KGB scenario was…is…my landlady's daughter. I hadn't seen her for a period of time. She came to visit her mama and was on her way home when this dysfunctional couple, me and the dotty detective, pulled up, of course in two different cars, as befits a pair of loons. And since I've known her for a number of years, it's natural for me to hug and kiss her on the cheek."

"It was on the lips."

"Wrong. The cheek. But next time it will be the lips. And I will determine which lips, and where those lips are located. And whether they are latitudinal or longitudinal."

"But you kissed her with such…such…"

"Absence makes the heart grow fonder."

"She must have been absent from you for a long while," Maria said. "It was a pretty loving kiss."

"True. Had I met her in the closed entrance hallway away from snoopy eyes, I cannot guarantee what secret places my hands would have been exploring."

"Relish. That's the word I was looking for. You kissed her with such relish."

"I am passing up the opportunity for wordplay. Ah, me, what I could have done with relish."

"She's your wife. I just know it. I know what I know."

"She's not. You know nothing. Will you stop it?"

"Can you swear?"

"Of course."

"Go ahead."

"I can, but I won't. I mean, it's even written all over your Christian theology: do not swear. Jesus would not approve."

"It's okay. I give you dispensation. Go ahead. Start swearing."

"All right…fuck it!"

A stunned silence.

"What's the matter?" I asked her.

"I…I…I'm shocked." Maria's face, yes, it turned red. "You cursed. I've never heard you use foul language before."

"You asked me to swear. I didn't want to. I never swear. It's boorish and low class. But you insisted. So I swore like a trooper. Now you're complaining."

Maria gave a nervous little laugh. Then something came over her. She spread her arms wide and said, "Come here, you big loon. Come and let me hug you...So you're not married."

"You're probably thinking of my brother. Although he was born one year and I the next, some people say he looks like me."

"Then I suppose it's your brother who's been trying to hop into my bed."

"Could be. He likes sex even more than me."

"Than I."

"Probably...no, I take that back. You like it the most. Then him. Then me."

"Then he."

"Who's the fourth guy? For a modest little maiden, you sure keep that bed busy."

"I didn't know you had a brother."

"See? You learn something every day. You also probably didn't know I had a sister, did you?"

"Well, do you?"

"No, I don't. But if I did, she would look like me.... God, would she be a knockout!"

"We're straying from the topic. Let's sum up. So that woman I saw you with you claim she's not your wife."

"That is correct, despite your tainted syntax."

"Excuse me. What is correct? That you *claim* she's not your wife? Or that she is not your wife?"

"What's the difference?"

"I don't know, Katz. I'm all confused. I haven't talked, argued, so much in years."

"Okay, the main thing is she's not my wife."

"Are you sure?"

"Sure about what? This is getting to me, Maria. 'Are you sure?' is one of the dumbest questions in the English language. Want another cup of coffee? No, thanks. You sure? No, I'm not sure. I guess I *will* have another cup. Make that two. No, three. What is there to be sure about? Either she is my wife or she isn't. If she is my wife, I'm sure about that. If she isn't, I'm sure about that too. What you really want to ask is if I'm lying."

"Well, are you?"

"I'm not."

"You sure?"

"Sure about what? That I'm not lying? Or that she's not my wife?"

"That she's not your wife."

"Sure, I'm sure. Who else would I be kissing?"

"Your wife."

"Not while my landlady's daughter is around."

"It's impossible to talk to you. You sure that the so-called landlady's daughter is not your wife?"

"Well, if she were, then her mama would be my mother-in-law, and why should I be paying rent to my own mother-in-law?"

"Why not? If I were your mother-in-law, I'd charge you rent."

There Maria let out a weary sigh and plopped onto the sofa, her head back.

"This is more work than work."

11

MARIA GETS KATZ TO SIGN THE BESSARABIA BOOK

NEXT TIME I CAME to her house, Maria stood in the middle of the living room with her hands behind her back and a naughty smile on her face.

"Guess what I found hidden in a drawer?"

"My alleged wife."

"No."

"Grant's pajamas."

"This." From behind her back she brought out *Travels in Bessarabia*. She held it tenderly in her hand as if it were her book. As if I were the book. I took it and looked anxiously at the dust jacket to see if it had an author photo. But all I saw was a blank space. Seeing that empty spot where a photo could have been, I suddenly remembered—though I hadn't seen my brother's book in years—now I remembered quite clearly that his picture *was* on the dust jacket. And then I began recalling a number of things, as if a blackboard had been put before me with lots of forgotten facts. I remembered the name of the photographer, Abraham Eden. I remembered, as if seeing it now, the small caps EDEN running up the right side of the photo. I remembered that the photo was on top of the inside back flap of the dust jacket and that my brother's unsmiling face was in three-quarters profile.

Where had that photo gone? I looked at the front matter of the book. Same publisher. Could this be a pirated edition, perhaps printed in China? I flipped through the pages.

"What's the matter?" Maria asked. "You're frowning. Is something wrong?"

"My picture is gone!" I said. "There used to be a photo here." And I pointed to the back flap.

She touched the empty space, looked at me, and said: "It's still a pretty good likeness."

Then I noticed another curious change. The page numbers, I remembered, were on the top right and top left of the pages. My brother liked that. Because to find a certain page, you just flip the corners of the pages. But in Maria's edition, the numbers were on the top middle, flanked by little dashes. That too was bizarre. Even spooky.

I shared this with Maria, but it didn't faze her.

"It doesn't surprise me," she said, quite upbeat. "Books do these things. There's nothing spooky about it. Books live and breathe and change too. They're mysterious, with a life of their own. And, anyway, there's another answer regarding the disappeared photo. The best of all."

"Okay, let's hear it."

"Have you read Borges?"

"*Read* her? I wrote most of her stories."

Maria laughed. "But not 'The Lottery in Babylon,' where one sentence explains the missing photo and the changes of position of page numbers. In the middle of that story, Miss Borges writes: 'In Babylon, no book is published without some discrepancy between each of the edition's copies.'"

Then she handed me the travel book. "Now you can sign it."

"With my maiden or married name?"

The Middle

12

AM I PRETTY?

MARIA WAS PLAINLY PRETTY. By that I mean her face was plain and pretty at the same time. Look at her and you see long. Long green eyes. Long brown hair. Longish chin. And thin lips, not full and sensual lips. She didn't have a sexy face or a sexy demeanor. Some girls just have it. Maria didn't. She didn't look at herself in any mirror she passed. It seemed as if she were totally without ego regarding her looks. She didn't wear eye makeup or powder, only a thin, the very tiniest smear of lipstick, and a bit of perfume, not to smell good but to counterbalance the smells of the unwashed masses she passed in Boston. Clothes? Didn't care about them.

Her femaleness didn't overwhelm you. She didn't tilt her head, half close her eyes, lift her shoulder provocatively as she spoke. She had none of the gestures that even teenage girls learn from watching sultry women on TV. She stood there like God had planted her.

Still, once, as we lay together, our arms around each other, she surprised me with—

"Am I pretty?"

It was, on the face of it, a sort of pathetic question that showed she needed boosting, some moral sustenance.

What was I going to say, no? But I liked the question because it was intimate. She wanted my approval. Was leaning on me for support.

Then I was sidetracked by memory. I suddenly remembered what Maria had once told me about life in high school. She had tried to make herself stand out. One of her teachers told her, cryptically, without elaborating, "It's a rough world out there." She assumed he wasn't hinting at her looks; she wanted to believe he was referring to earning a living. Nevertheless, after replaying those words several times, she heard them in a different key signature; she immediately saw herself in a mirror, went into the eyes of her teacher and saw herself the way he saw her. How does a girl who is not stunning make it in this world? She started wearing funky hats, then alternated these with letting her wavy brown hair—where sunlit reddish glints shimmered on the strands along with tiny sprinkles of gold—grow long. She wore baseball caps, cloche hats like women in the 1920's, yellow and blue berets, and, once, a black silk derby. When hats and hair went out of fashion, she moved from dress to speech.

Maria loved words and puns. People would laugh at her wordplays and occasionally too acerbic jokes, which caused her to develop a quirky response—"Just kidding"—if she thought she'd been too harsh or critical.

But that wasn't what attracted me to her. So what kind of magic did this girl have that enchanted me, that made me switch hours in my work just so I could be with her three four times a week?

Maria wasn't sophisticated. Knew nothing about sophistication except perhaps the spelling. High school girls today are more sophisticated than this girl/woman in her late thirties.

Am I pretty? Either her question echoed in my mind or she repeated it.

Of course, I answered right away, knowing that you don't hurt people's vanity, especially the vanity of a woman you're crazy about, especially a woman of a certain age tottering on the brink between pretty and plain, especially if it's a topic she'd never mentioned before and neither had I. I was raised, yes, to speak the truth, except here honesty had to be tempered by the exigency of the moment. I had to do some fine calibrations. And, anyway, how could I possibly fall for an ugly girl? Still, but, nevertheless, let's face it, got to call it as it is, when she walked down the street men didn't turn to look at her. Maria had an appeal and there was, and I told her this, a strong sexuality to that appeal. But it was more internal than external. I broke it down Talmudically by saying:

"You're not pretty..." Her heart, I could see it sinking in the translucent hollow of her chest, her eyes dimming. Suddenly, the shape of her face changed. I could see its bone structure collapsing. I understood, then, the meaning of the word "crestfallen." "Never mind pretty. You're more than that. You're lovely. Just listen to the sound of the two words. Pretty versus lovely. Pretty just has prit in it, but lovely has love. And you're lovely."

"Really?" she said softly, the oxygen slowly returning to her face. I loved that musical, two-note exhalation. And deep down I was touched, honored that she thought enough of me to ask my opinion. Obviously, she wanted to be pretty for me.

"You see," I said, "lovely encompasses a lot more. Your face, your wit, your body, your gestures, your personality. You're not sexy in the glitz media way. I told you that. But you are very sexual. If you can see the difference. You're not cheaply sexy, you're expensively sexual. Do you see?"

"I do...that is, I think I do."

"Then kiss me."

She did. Long, long and slow, with long green eyes closed and a smile, a beatific smile, I hope not an I-love-Jesus beatific in her eyes. Maybe on her lips too, but them I couldn't see.

"Kiss me again," I said, "you who stand at the three-front of my imagination."

"Do you really think I'm pretty?"

"I told you you're lovely, which for me is even more important because it combines your face, your perkiness, your love of words, your intellectual curiosity, your reading, though limited to Bible and Kierkegaard and whatever I recommend, your machine-gun-rapid manner of talking, sometimes out of the side of your mouth like a movie gangster, your subdued flirtiness..."

"Me, flirty?"

I remembered going into a wine shop with her. She was instantly so friendly with the salesman it made me jealous. Like an Arab I felt such a sense of proprietorship.

"Yeah. I watch when you talk to strangers, even though our relationship hardly ever includes a third person, but you, in the two or three times I've seen you talking to someone else, you come on strong by showing off your wit. Your instant palsiness. It's a wonder you don't have fifty boyfriends."

And then she said something that still rings in my ears and somehow encapsulates the entirety of Maria's lonely life.

"Then why do I sit at home on Saturday nights reading?"

"Because you don't like crowds. You don't like people near you. That's why you love Jesus. No chance of him invading your space."

It was only much later that the word I was looking for came to me. What Maria was not: feminine. That's what she was not. Femininity, no—sexuality, plenty. But from within, not without. Yes, she wore her hair long, hair that was brown but when the sun shone on it little tiny dark rivulets of red ran like threads through it. Yes, occasionally, she wore long skirts. Yes, she carried a knitted, shapeless, red and orange striped bag that she had gotten in some godforsaken village in Bessarabia from a gypsy peddler. But feminine she was not. Maybe she took to heart Simone de Beauvoir's view that women can only be free when femininity disappears, that femininity is a form of ideological oppression. But odds are Maria had never even heard of, much less read, Simone de Beauvoir. Maria was female, that's what she was, not feminine. And sexual, yes, sexual to her core, to her essence. Once you put your arms around her and drew her close and felt her lips on yours, the natural, innocent, but wordless generosity of her affection and loving showed her deep-rooted sexuality.

13

TO THE MOVING PICTURE SHOW

One evening, remembering that on Saturday nights (her words) she sits alone at home, I took Maria to the movies in Boston. It was a Monday night. "There's a first," she said. "You taking me out." It was true. We spent so much time together alone, we shut out the real world. Somehow, standing in line for tickets among dozens of people made her more real for me.

When we were about six or seven people from the cashier, a crowd came out of the exit door, signaling the end of the film. Suddenly, Maria grabbed my shoulders, turned me, and pressed her face into my chest.

"What's this all of a sudden?"

"There's a guy coming out of the first show I used to go out with and I don't want to see him. Can you hear me talking into your chest? I don't want to go through the *How are you* routine."

Maria had me turned around so he couldn't see her and of course I couldn't see him. At once a wave of jealousy rolled over me. Had she told me she had gone out with someone, X or Y, it wouldn't have bothered me. But the fact that there was someone alive, hovering near us, a previous boyfriend in back of me whom I could not see, drove a huge nail, an iron wedge of jealousy into me. And all this on the very first time we had gone out into the outside world together.

"Who is, was, that?"

"A guy I once dated," she said flatly.

"And what happened?"

"It didn't work out. He was obstreperous."

"Is that some kind of ailment?"

"Not quite," Maria said.

"Or some off-beat Christian sect, like Anabaptist?"

Maria removed her head from my chest. "He's gone now. Boy, I never thought I'd see him in town. I thought he moved to California long ago."

"How long were you with him?"

"Six months."

"Why didn't you marry him?"

We moved up on the line. I was now before the cashier. I asked for two tickets, and we walked into the dimly lit theater.

Maria's head was down, as if reminiscing.

"I told you. He was obstreperous."

"Spell it."

"No."

"Is that a reason not to marry someone? What are you, against intermarriage?"

"Certainly. And he was Jewish too."

"My God. Obstreperous and Jewish. What a winning combination!"

"I mean, you know. I don't have to explain it to you. Like you wouldn't marry out of the faith, would you?"

We found our seats. The coming attractions were beginning.

I weighed the question, then said, "Depends on how far out."

And then I wondered: So what are we doing pursuing each other? Maybe waiting for a miracle. One morning she'd wake up a Jew. And, my luck, that same morning, I'd wake up uncircumcised—and obstreperous.

The film was about a couple's divorce. The unhappiness on screen made Maria fidgety. She who was not married had to suffer through someone else's metaphysical malaise. Me, I paid no attention to the goings-on, for I had a cloud of discomfort, depression, hovering over me.

14

DIFFERENCES BETWEEN

We talked for hours. For days. But perhaps it only seemed that way because of the intensity of our relationship.

"Remember, the other day we were talking about how sexy you are…not. Do you remember what I said about the difference between sexy and sexual?"

She looked puzzled.

"Okay, I'll explain it again. Sexy is the convention of a girl with just barely parted lips, the over-the-shoulder look, sultry, pouting open mouth. You know the rest. You've seen it on TV, the movies, in ads. It's all around you."

"And I'm not sexy," she declared, but intended an interrogative.

"I didn't say that."

"You did the other day. Change your mind?... Well, am I?" Maria insisted.

"No, you're better. You're authentic. Not phony. You're sexy with the gloss, the dross, the gilding stripped away. For sexy women men turn around on the street."

"And not for me?"

"Wait. They slow their cars down, or like my old friend Guido Veneziano-Tedesco used to do, make a U-turn on a one-way street to catch the last fade of a walk, trailing stars and banners, of a presumably sexy woman."

"And for me no one turns?" Her words more a lament than a question.

"No cars, no planes, not even Superman. Traffic cops love you because you don't stop traffic. In fact, you might even apply for the

Annual Even-Flow Traffic Award. You don't cause no problems. Not on the avenues. Not on the road."

"Because I'm not attractive. Not sexy."

"Wrong on A. Right on B."

"How can I make myself more sexy?"

"Don't even bother. Don't even try. You got the goods. But men have to discover it. It's not visible from the outside."

"Do I look old?"

"Not on your back. It's amazing how a woman, no matter how old she is, looks younger in a horizontal position. A woman flat on her back, the years just roll off her. No matter how old she is, she becomes younger."

"Now I'm old too."

"Nonsense. I just wanted to accent that horizontality becomes a woman. Once you're prone, or is it supine, your true talent shines. Because you're sexual. In fact, it's long been known that sexy women, it's been scientifically proven in all the glossy magazines and gossip columns, sexy women are no good in bed and don't even enjoy sex. But you're special. You got what few others got, deep down, attractive sexuality. That's it. End of story."

For a minute or two, we were silent. Then I added, "One more question."

"Okay."

"Are you formication or against it?"

"With whom?"

"Me."

"I'll think about it."

First time I heard such positive news from her.

"Do you know what formication means?"

"Sure. I wasn't born yesterday."

"What word did I use?"

"Fornication."

"That's what you wanted to hear. But I said formication."

"What's that?"

"A swarming of ants. When ants swarm, they formicate."

"No wonder there are so many of them," said my clever Maria.

15

TO THE BEDROOM

I once tried, I think I told you, I once tried early on, tried leading her, taking her by the hand, and leading her to the bedroom. No go. She refused. Adamantly. I dropped it, courting her instead, patiently patiently, on the sofa, that old, wine-colored, dried-out cotton-covered three-cushioned sofa she must have inherited from her grandma. She could have bought another sofa but didn't. Compared to her long chaise longe chair, which looked like it had grown fur, her sofa was moderniste. I never met a girl who was so uninterested in material possessions. And I told her.

"Disinterested," Maria corrected with a soft, sedulous voice.

"Un-," I shot back, one of the few times I caught her wrong with a polysyllabic word.

She ran to her old unabridged whose white pages had turned beige, a fat and lazy dictionary that never stirred from its place. The sort you find in libraries because no one has the strength to lug that three watermelon-weight home.

"Don't waste your time," I insisted, my confidence slow and sure. "It's an unusual word. Lots of people err with it. Disinterested means neutral, not lack of interest."

Maria grudgingly gave in.

Where was I? Yes, in the bedroom. Rather, outside of it.

But wait!

Astonishments galore! Neverending suprises. I wish English had a dozen synonyms for surprise, like it has for pretty, attractive, lovely, beautiful, gorgeous, stunning, ravishing.

Things change sometimes in Maria's world, that full-of-surprises, that never-to-be-expected world of Maria Christiansen.

One morning, perhaps ten days after my abortive attempted stroll with her to her bedroom, I came to see her. She opened the back door for me. I saw she was wearing an old sweatshirt and a skirt. I saw she moved in two dimensions, her stride forward and her unharnessed breasts swinging sideways like pendulums within her sweatshirt. I put my arms around her, kissed her, then without preamble, without planning, without advance mapping, with no restraints, I lifted up her sweatshirt, gazed at those full breasts, and kissed each, then held the right one up with both my hands and kissed her nipple, did the same for the left, without thinking, because she had done the thinking, the planning for me, otherwise she wouldn't have worn that sweatshirt without a bra, don't tell me girls don't have strategic plans.

Then I took her by the hand, led her to the bedroom, saying, to give her a bit of an out, a little squeeze of salve for her conscience, saying as I crossed the threshold:

"Isn't it more comfortable to lie side by side on a bed?"

We lay down. I kissed her and she responded, her arms tight around me. Seeing how warm was the welcome, unobstructed by landmines of piety, no Jesus peeking over her shoulder, I ran my hands all over her body and heard her singing a lovely song.

I told her to lift up her hips and I pulled her skirt down. I rolled it into a ball and flung it into the air to the other side of the room. It landed, covering her clock. I still hadn't made a move with anything I was wearing. Would she pull my pants down? Never. Rose petals would first fall from the sky. She in panties and sweatshirt; me, fully dressed. I hadn't even taken my gloves off.

•

= Gloves? I said. = Katz, I could swear I heard you say gloves.

= Well, you did, John. I'm joking. Just wanted to see if you're paying attention.

•

So then. I hadn't even thought of taking my shirt off. Now that I had made it to the bedroom, I was proceeding gingerly. But I was under the covers with her, something I couldn't have imagined—well, imagined yes, only imagined—yesterday. Under the covers, wearing my pants. Ridiculous, no? Now I moved. As I pulled my pants off, to distract her I said:

"Ridiculous, wearing these chinos under the blanket."

She could have said, Then take off the blanket.

Then I would have said, I don't want you to catch cold.

I lifted her sweatshirt and returned to her breasts once again, not letting those delicious penduli, those little fawns go. I ran my hands over her tush, down her thighs, up to her crotch.

"How many hands do you got?"

"Five," I said. "No…wait…six."

She said she felt like a dozen hands were stroking her and she was right. Before one sensation ceased in one spot, it started in another.

Maria was on her back, eyes closed. But her closed eyes were not passive. Life sizzled in those closed eyes. I could see the happy, excited vibrations under those closed eyelids.

"Sit up," I said and pulled up her hands and took off her sweatshirt. She looked terrific with her hands up and her full boozies out. I quickly took off my shirt and flung it across the room, then did the same, in another direction, with her sweatshirt. I pulled off my briefs. Hugged her. She pressed her face into my chest.

"Kiss me," I ordered.

She did. Once. Twice.

Quicker her singing breaths as I explored under her panties. Off they came, threw them, it, whatever the correct grammatical form is, to the other side of the room.

A little later, after Maria's song was done, I heard the same notes from somewhere else, a seeming thin echo.

I couldn't place it. "What's that?" I asked her. "Are you a ventriloquist?"

"That's my canary."

"You didn't tell me you have a canary."

"You didn't ask."

"Is it in the room?"

"Yes. It's on the floor right next to the sliding doors of the closet."

"It does a pretty good imitation."

"Yeah," Maria said. "It thinks it's a parrot."

Now we had clothing all over the place, on the floor, in the bed, hanging from knobs, dangling from clock, up and down, here and there, over that and under where. I wanted to cover up the canary cage, but the canary was quiet. Perhaps she, he, it, had gone to sleep.

•

Someone else had gone to sleep too. No, no, don't worry, it wasn't Maria. It was Jesus. The ubiquitous guardian parrot on her shoulder, the omnipresent, intractable watchman of Maria's morality, flew off without a squawk. And perhaps that's why, to Maria's everlasting credit, she didn't inform me that I was married. She kept that good news, that pernicious rumor, to herself. Didn't ask—experienced straphanger that she was—she held onto the vertical of the question mark for dear life, and didn't even give me an opportunity to deny it.

16

MARIA'S SPECIAL KISSING

"A-DOODLE-DOO," I SHOUTED ONCE all our clothes were scattered on the floor and hanging helter-skelter from fixtures, knobs, clock, a Dali-like scene with garments, not melting timepieces, on display.

"What's that?" Maria asked.

"It's short for cock-a-doodle-doo."

"Then why don't you say it?"

"I don't use that word in mixed company...so doodle."

"Now? I don't even have a pen."

"Not that sort of doodling. You heard of Yankee Doodle?"

"Sure."

"Fine. So yank my doodle. Doodle me."

"Oh. Okay. I see. But you speak the queerest English."

"Only when I'm horizontal. It's Vermont street talk."

"Where in Vermont did you grow up?"

"I didn't."

"You're impossible."

"Only when I'm horizontal."

Maria began doodling. For someone who just learned the word, she had a fine grasp of vocabulary, a handy-dandy handle on hands-on horizontal English. After a couple of minutes she said, "I'm doodling, but—"

"But what?"

"Your doodle, or whatever you call it in Middle English, doesn't doo."

"Like in the expression, this won't do?"

"Sort of. I mean it's not doing what it's supposed to do...Don't doodles doo? With two 'o's? Like in the rooster call? Like I want to make a big to-do, one 'o' out of it."

"Because you got the wrong one."

"What is that supposed to mean?"

I reprimanded her with: "You're asking a lot of questions today."

"Well, what does it mean: you got the wrong one?"

"Because I have two of them."

"Two? I only see one. And under the circumstances," she said, "I can't even see that one properly."

"Yes. I have two. One is cock-a-doodle-doo... the other is cock-a-doodle don't, which is the one you have."

"You should have shown me the menu. Never mind. I'll wait until your other rooster crows in the morning."

"Not in the morning. Now."

And because of one of her memorable phrases, I told her what to do. And that's spelled with one 'o' too.

Like Rosina, who chants in *Barber of Seville* that she is docile, obedient, and respectful, Maria too said, "I like to be told what to do." She said it without the slightest tone of self-denigration. And I imagined Maria/Rosina in a house with arches and arabesques, Spanish tiles, balconies decorated with filigreed designs like paper cutouts, and graceful, wrought-iron latticework, and a florabundance of flower pots blooming with roses, carnations, and hyacinths.

Had I told Maria, *You look like the sort of girl who likes to be told what to do*, it might have been taken as an insult, some kind of put-down, a girl who is easily manipulated. But she volunteered, "I like to be told what to do," matter-of-factly, while we were naked. I didn't weigh that telling phrase when I heard it, other than indeed telling her what to do. But, in retrospect, putting it on the balance scale of human speech, it was a rather erotic, inviting set of words that needed an especially sensitive scale, akin to measuring gold dust in avoirdupois.

"I like to be told what to do."

So I told her what to do.

"Kiss me," I said. Again. I didn't elaborate. I just said, "Kiss me." Two words, two syllables, six letters, telling her what to do.

And she did.

As if my body was made of tiny, half-inch checkerboard squares, she began touching her lips to each square. She started with my big toe and gave it three kisses, looking up at me for approval after the third. Then she kissed each of the toes and moved to the arch of my foot, one soft slow kiss sliding up my leg, slowly, unhurried, kissing the bone and the flesh, the seconds, the minutes, slowly spinning by, inching her body up, her breasts now grazing my ankles, and kissed the enormous slow space of my knees, then, surprising me, without telling me what to do, she turned me around and kissed the soft area in back of my knees—where were those lights coming from?—touching one tiny square at a time, not even stopping to breathe, and turned me again as if I were a light Chinese fan, and caressed her loving lips up and down across and back up one thigh and then the other, skipping my urging center, but I didn't say a word for little tingles of electricity danced above my skin; they converged from many directions and gave me light and heat. She kissed above the hairline and went up and down the crossword puzzle of my belly, past the navel, up a square, laterally with soft inexorable force, leaving the imprint of her lips on tiny grids of my flesh that hardly had time to register the pleasure before her mouth moved to the next square, a kiss, then sliding her lips up to my nipple, then taking the caravan of kisses higher, and I tasted nectar of dates and figs in the oasis before she brushed her lips up across my chest to my throat, her big breasts swinging across my chest, her nipples resting on mine as she kissed every centimeter of my brow, nose, but not the lips, no, not the lips, she slipped by my lips, but my lips on her throat now, to my eyes she went, lingered there, did not remove her lips from my closed eyes, I groping like a blind bard, too stunned to sing, but kissing whatever part of her was near my mouth, the blazing meteor keeps shining, no hint of coming darkness, bright and brighter the light, no end in sight. Then she turned me around again and kissed slowly, patiently, with cartographic precision every inch of my back, and down to the curve of my buttocks, kissing without a word the back of my legs and feet until her mouth was on my toes again.

Never before had I been kissed like that. Her previous kisses never gave a hint that she had this in her. As if an angel, or a demon, had just opened a celestial amor book and let Maria take a quick peek. Had some previous guy taught her that caring, driving, determined, unceasing effusion of kisses? Or maybe a gypsy, some Carmen, in Bessarabia. And what inspired her to do this now? Was it just my curt command, kiss me?

A beautiful rhythm, the way she kissed every cell/inch of my body, gliding up and going from left to right, and when she came to the end of her imaginary line, then up a half inch and smoothing her lips slowly to the left, like a printer, methodically crisscrossing. As she moved her hair gradually fell in front of her eyes and with her right hand she threw back the auburn waterfall of her long strands, without ceasing her relentless kissing. I had never experienced anything like it in my life, have you? The hair cascading over her face again, her mouth scudding across my body as if it were a windblown craft, and I heard and saw the trail of kisses on my skin, then she stopped, rather paused, no, she didn't, it just seemed like an eyeblink pause, to take the curtain of her hair and throw it back over her head, with one motion swooshing it back where it belonged and where it would not stay for long because of the wind she created as she sailed over me.

I felt I was in two places at the same time. I felt I was looking at her coming up from my legs to my face, getting closer and closer, her hair over her head like a veil, and then, without missing a beat, a kiss, her hand came forward and she pushed the veil back until gradually that auburn curtain fell over her face again. And at the same time, I was floating up and behind her and had a view of her naked back and my own face, as if I was a camera behind her, seeing her slowly inching up my body, with her slow, methodical, careful kisses, as if I was a map and she, the cartographer, had to record with care every hamlet, village, town, the flood of her kisses not missing a millimeter, every cell of my skin covered by her softly exploring lips.

And, imagine, the sound, the music of the kissing, I'm completely oblivious to it. Only later, as a faint echo, did I hear it.

Maria didn't say a word. But I could hear her thinking: *You said, kiss me*, and I did.

You like to be told what to do, I responded in my thought.

"Um-hmm," she said.

And then I flipped around—my head near her thighs, my knees by her hair—and began kissing her. But not like a mapmaker. I kissed her like a sniper. A sharpshooter. I wasn't all over the map like her. I zeroed in on one township, doing what I was doing in, let's call it Augusta or

Jacksonville, while at the same time I was aware of a slowdown on her part up north, in Albany, shouting at her to continue.

But she protested, "I can't do that."

"What?" I said, coming up for air from the southern side of the bed. "I can't hear you."

"I said I can't do that to you while you're doing this to me."

"I thought you told me you like to be told what to do."

"Except this. I mean that. One at a time. I can't do this and that at the same time."

"So who's doing what to whom first, or 'that' as you so modestly phrase it?"

"Me," she said.

"Me as doer or doee?"

"Me first as doee. Then you."

"Okay," I said, and I wondered if when I finished that she'd still be amenable to this, for once my that was completed maybe she wouldn't want to do that this anymore. But now wasn't the time to teach her the conventions of sexual politesse or give her a lesson in arithmetic that two times 34½ was a concomitant activity, not subject to alternation like an antiphonal chorus nor to a 50% discount.

So I resumed my sharpshooting. I zeroed in on the target, the verdant municipal park south of Jacksonville, and teased her with a momentary pause at which she screamed, "Don't stop, don't stop, don't stop," and I felt her stiffening, her body rigid, the pelvis up, she arched like a bow, and a scream the like of which I'd never heard before tore, yes, I purposely use that clichéd word, tore, ripped out of her mouth, the bow released its arrow, and I, like a cat, twisted and turned, my south become north in a feat of agility and speed, I shifted poles, she held my rigid arms

—then time moved backward and I thought I heard her say, "Wait," in a pleading tone. I honestly don't recall that word, but I distinctly remember saying, "No, I don't want to wait. I waited long enough." So she must have said that word or something like it, which prompted me to say what I said, although here too I only hear an echo of my muttered phrase in and not the words themselves—

she held my rigid arms, her nails digging into my back like a cat, her back up again like a cat, arched again like a cat, and a series of high-pitched, caterwauling yips and yawps tore out of her in tune with mine.

She ravished me, ravaged me, she all-encompassed me, surrounded me with the depth and height, color and intensity, the variety of her wildcat "Ah" and "Oh" cries, cries that ranged from F up to E flat, sometimes sliding up the chromatic scale, sometimes taking a passionate octave leap.

In tremolo sang she and in vowels of ascending rapture ecstatic and adoring notes that inspired my own and that made her repeat in the same way she had breathed before, Don't stopdon'tstopdon'tstop, now she quivered with a luxurious chant, IloveitIloveitIloveit, me wishing the *it* would magically turn to *you,* but it didn't. It stayed *it.* But that delicious cry call affirmation made me delirious. That *I love it I love it I love it* brought ecstasy to me too.

Then Maria heaven a sigh—

•

= My God, John, what a fortuitous typo. Did you notice that? My brother, or his typist, typed "heaven," but it should be a verb, mostly likely "heaved." But the heaven here is a very meaningful error.

•

Then Maria heaved a sigh, a groan, and the next thing I hear, pulling me down from celestia, plucked from heaven with a skyhook, she saying with eyes closed, dreamily, desultorily, not in a plaintive tone, but as if from a distant planet, a remark more to assuage herself than to make me feel bad,

"What if I get pregnant? Please don't get me pregnant."

"Shh," came from somewhere behind my lips.

And those were our last sounds till Maria said later: "No joke, what if you, you know..."

At first I didn't say a word; I was too dazed. Then, through a haze, as I dropped through the clouds, I managed to say:

"Don't worry, you'll take a MAP."

"How will a nap help?"

"I said MAP."

"What's that?"

"Morning after pill."

"Do you realize you can be indicted for spermicide?" Maria said.

"No problem. I have weak, scattered, and scatterbrained sperm. They can't even find an egg with a flashlight. They can't even inseminate a fruit fly."

"Stop it. Tell me. Suppose it doesn't work?"

"Then it will be a blessed love child. My beauty, my brains, and your…your…"

"My what?"

"Your fear of crowds."

"But…but…"

"Fear not. From now on, we'll use a quondam."

16

PUTTING THE DEMON INTO HADES

NEXT TIME I PLAYED a little game with her.

"This is the demon," I told her. Showed her. Demonstrated.

"Last time it was Yankee Doodle."

"That was last time. Now it's this time. Names of objects change. Same item, different monickers. Okay. Here's the demon. So where does the demon belong? Certainly not in Heaven. The demon belongs in Hades. Gotta put the little devil in its proper place. Where it's burning hot. And what's burning hot?"

"The oven at 250 degrees?"

"Shows you don't cook."

"You know I don't. I've never even turned on the oven. Like the fridge, I use it for storage."

"What do you store there?"

"I forget. I put things in there years ago. Maybe dishcloths. I don't remember. Maybe sneakers I don't wear anymore. Probably my iron."

"We're getting off track. What's burning hot?"

"I don't know. What's burning hot?"

"This. Otherwise known as Hades."

"Oh!...Some guys would call it Heaven."

"Yes. The only place in the world that's Heaven and Hades at one. And that's where the demon must go. To Hades. In a game created by Boccaccio called Put the Demon into Hades. Some say, Put the Devil into Hell. Ready to play?"

"What am I, a self-storage unit? Like my fridge? My stove? Oh, all right," she said resignedly. But I knew that seemingly unenthusiastic tone was just a front, a cover for her sinning. Her two-timing her beloved Jesus. So I restrained myself. I didn't sing out enthusiastically: I love your eagerness, your unabashed lust.

Later, in the gyrating gymnastics of bedroaming, after she had accidentally conked my head with her elbow and I unwittingly banged my knee into her shoulder, I said:

"Did you ever wonder how in loveplay people survive all the twisting, turning, climbing, bending, sliding, curling, flipping, moving, stretching, shifting, spinning, without pulling muscles, getting their balls mauled, their knees knocked, their peckers wrecked, their boobs busted, suffering black-and-blue marks, with fingers and hands and toes flying all over the place, coming up suddenly out of nowhere like a missile, without having their tongues tied, their noses bumped, their eyeballs poked, their elbows bruised, without breaking their necks or spraining their backs, without getting contusions, confusions, concussions? I guess some do. And do they make up all kinds of excuses to emergency room docs and nurses? Bumped into a wall. Fell off my seat. I didn't see the hanger in my closet. It's a miracle we emerge unscathed. This danger is even attested to by Shakespeare in *The Merchant of Venice*, where the young virgin, Ophelia, says to Romeo, quoth she: 'If thou givest me a palpable prick, shall I not bleed?' I tell you, sex is a danger to life and limb.... Can I interest you in a sex damage insurance policy?"

"No danger for me," said Maria. "I'm a WASP. I just lie there like lox."

"No. Jewish girls lie there like lox. Goyish girls lie like smoked salmon. Maybe gravlox."

But that wasn't so at all, as you know by now. Maria said that with tongue—my tongue—in cheek.

And then I asked her a question I always wanted to ask her.

Maria didn't like crowds. Barely tolerated the tram. Just the idea of a big terminal in New York like Penn Station or Grand Central or the Port Authority frightened her. She didn't like people swirling about her. Tried to keep her distance. If people came too close, she felt she was suffocating. That's why she arranged her work schedule after both rush hours.

"Okay, you can't stand crowds. You can't stand people crowding in on you. So how do you—I want to say this as discreetly and delicately and politely as possible..."

"I think I know what you're driving at," she said.

"I want to choose my words carefully and be as courteous as I can so as not to offend or breach the standards of propriety or the societal norms and conventions of decent speech that my parents inculcated in me. I want to say it without sounding vulgar or crass. So here goes: How, please, pray tell, with all this phobia about crowding around your personal person, how do you fuck?"

Maria laughed.

"I try to do it from far away," was her quick reply. "Either long distance, or, better yet, by proxy."

"You mean a stand-in?"

"No. A lie-in."

17

MARIA'S SILENCE

=JOHN, THE SCENE WITH Maria kissing Katz all over is another instance of where my brother has another version. I'll share with you now his second version of a similar scene, plus some new material and a bit of astonishment, a surprising twist. Here too I really don't know if the first or the second is going to go into his final draft, or maybe like in earlier chapters he'll include them both. So here it is.

•

She never said it. Not one word. Not a hint. Not even a word of praise. Not a *You're so nice.* Not a *You make me laugh.* Maybe the theological implications on her side, confessing that she liked me, loved me, would have made her sin more obvious to her, I'm looking at it now from her perspective. It would have made it clear to her like a sudden slap in the face. And it seems to make sense. She says out loud she's crazy about me and her guilt stares her straight in the eyes. Displeases Jesus. And another thing she wouldn't do, she was that sort of an old-fashioned girl, besides never ever saying she liked me was that she would never call me. Never. She never even asked for my phone number. Not that she would be able to reach me. Every weekend I was traveling for my business.

Then I decided to tell her straight out:

"You opened me up to say things to you I never said before," I told her. "A stream of continual praise and affection. And I appreciate how you too opened up to me slowly, surely, until every part of your being, literally, opened up. But please, one thing, I want you to—do you know what I want?"

"What?" she said.

I weighed that What. I have a scale in my mind even for one-syllable words. Call it a mental apothecary's balance. I can even weigh a letter as light as 'o'. Add an 'h' and I sense the difference. And so I weighed that What of hers, pondered if it was snippety, like the "What's up?" you hear on the telephone sometimes, that rude "What's up?" as if the guy on the other end wants you to come out with your request fast so he can go back to doing whatever he was doing before you interrupted him. Or if that What of hers was a tender and loving one. Tell me, please, sweetie, what it is you want. I weighed that What, judged it, found it to be neutral.

"I want you to be more verbal," I told her. "Tell me what you feel. Don't just keep saying *Really*? or that noncommittal *That's sweet.* What a clever cop-out those words are. They sound loving but contain nothing personal. Just a cool observation on what I just said. Words without meaning."

And I think to myself, she's bright, sweet, adorable, pretty, a mentch. Witty too. Not outwardly sexy, but inwardly a volcano. That sudden stiffening, the arching of her back during a long slow orgasm. A sexuality one never would have imputed to her by looking at her. Sometimes you can tell by looking at a woman if she sizzles. But not always. It's the "not always" women who surprise you. And that's why women are so much fun. Each one is an astonishing discovery.

But then, to make it less serious, I played a little joke on her. I told her to hug me. When she tried, I slipped away from her. I did this twice, three times, squirming away from her each time, saying, "Hold me." Finally she said, "Come here." Then I said the line I had set her up for, "What's the matter? Can't you hold your licker?"

Then came a roll of hysterical laughter, she banging her heels into the mattress like a tympanist in Stravinsky's *Rites of Spring.*

•

I didn't think it would be polite to stop Katz, but the intimacy of the narrative's sexual details made me uncomfortable. I had a hunch other passengers were listening. I wondered if Katz noticed my discomfort. I made a tone-it-down gesture, whispered: =Shh. I felt my cheeks burning.

And then, as if to add my unease, he said with passion:

=In the throes of love, she scratched. Like a cat. Here. Look. I still have the scars…

Katz rolled up his sleeve, showed me the inside of his forearm below the elbow.

=Yes, he said. =Nails. Nails dug in in passion. Or with malice aforethought.

=Katz, I said. =I thought this was your brother's story.

=We're very close, he said, unfazed. =Like one person. He gets scratched, I bleed.

He looked at me. Not a smile on his face. Then he continued in a softer voice.

•

But, on the other hand, she did show a slight indication of her affection. When the phone rang, she always looked at me and pleaded—way before I even kissed her for the first time—Can I take this call? Do you mind? I'll make it very quick. Of course, I always said yes, but I still think that was very considerate of her. She was always thoughtful of others. Remember that first day we met and how she wished the hefty ticket seller at the tram station a belated happy new year?

Despite her tight-lipped reticence, I know she liked me. A woman gone ga-ga has music in her voice, the strings of her vocal cords tuned a special way. And a special light in her eyes. I just have to recall the way she kissed me; that is, once I started with her and broke the ice, my ice, her ice, our ice, and we began kissing and the rest followed.

One time, when we were in bed and I asked her to kiss me, she began, and I felt the newness of it at once, she began to kiss me. I had never been kissed like that before. She kissed every square millimeter of my body, starting with my instep, on the edge of the bed, on her hands and knees, pushing back her long hair from her face every once in a while, but never stopping the concentrated kissing, her lips moving slowly, methodically, determinedly, as if I were a map and she had to touch every village, moving her head and lips slowly to the left, and then to the right, let's compare it to a typewriter going from the left margin to the right, then going carefully to the next line, her lips touching my skin tenderly, lovingly, but it was actually like a reverse linotype machine, starting at the bottom and systematically working its way up, not missing a line, flicking her long hair back when it curtained her eyes, starting with my toes and going up to my lips, then turning me around and doing the same while I lay on my stomach.

It wasn't quick. It was slow, slow and thrilling. I was watching. Like a wave in slow motion, slowly coming up from my toes, head down, hair over her eyes until she swooshed it back, like a musical interlude, her hand coming up and brushing her hair away from her face, and me, watching her, her lips moving from one knee to another, one thigh to another.

I was so moved, so enthralled, by what she was doing, because I felt it, sensed it, knew it, I called out happily that she was doing this especially for me, only for me, out of love, passion, enthrallment, these things happen in the throes of love, a once-in-a-lifetime event, you do things you've never done before, amazing how love, passion, makes you inventive and creative, it prompts you to do things you've never done before and I was floating, holding onto the handles of a white cloud, floating beneath the bright blue sky to tell her: I know you've created this kissing just for me.

To stop time is what I wanted. I was in a special place, a love-lined glen I'd never been in before. Now she was up to my chest, my nipples, only for me, only for me had she invented this special intimate original kissing only for me, is what this seemingly shy baby/woman had done, never mind that she never said one thing positive about how she felt, what she was now doing was a silent declaration of love, that I cried out, in a high of enthusiasm, "I feel you've never done this before with anyone," I said out of my special place, the one I've called my love-lined glen....

•

= Oops, here we are, John. Gotta go! Katz called out and jumped up.

= But it's not Newark Penn Station.

= I have a meeting in Menlo Park today.

= But where's the astonishment? The surprise twist.

= Next time, Katz said at the door and rushed out into the morning crowd.

18

MARIA'S SPECIAL KISSING, CONTINUED

= WHERE WERE WE last time? Katz asked as he sat next to me in the seat I'd saved for him.

= You were about to say what happened when you blurted out to Maria that you thought her special kissing was invented just for you... The surprise twist...

=Yeah, yeah, now I remember. Let me get the pages straight in my mind. It's as if I'm shuffling my brother's manuscript and coming up with the right page. And don't forget this is his second version of the scene.

Katz looked into his briefcase, nodded as if to say, yes, that's it. Here it is. And he began:

•

Anyway, I'm totally consumed by her kissing and, from my special Garden of Eden love bower, in a nirvana of bliss, joy, childlike happiness, I sing out to Maria, "I know you've never done this before with anyone, I feel it, I know it, you've created this just for me." And she brings me down to earth and pricks the balloon I was sailing on, flattens it, it now looks like a rubber version of a baseball bat, a long, hangy, droopy piece of rubber. It was blue, by the way, that balloon.

So down to earth, whsshht, straight to land plummeted I, holding on for dear life to that punctured, flattened piece of rubber following gravity with a vengeance, as she said:

"You're right. I've never done this before..." And she stopped, then added, what a bitchy thing to say: "...with you."

Cra-a-ck! A baseball bat slamming my skull. I saw stars. And I knew at once who it was. That baseball bat knocked knowledge into my head. That guy coming out of the movies from whom Maria was hiding by pressing her head into my chest. With my back toward him, I couldn't see him; he couldn't see me. And then equivocation set in, muddling my star-flashed, broken-lightning thoughts.

And then I added to my pain by stupidly asking her, "How does a modest, single girl like you have a talent like this?"

"I may be modest and single," Maria answered, "but I'm also enigmatic."

And at once a spurt of evil yellow bile, the same sour taste of jealousy, a jealousy out of hell, a great image from the Song of Songs, swept over me. I imagined a key being inserted into her front door at night and that phantom guy, her ex-boyfriend sliding into her apartment. That hellousy clouded my eyes, constricted my heart, collapsed my conyons. Strong as death is love and jealousy is hell.

Maria knew she would get me with that. And she was absolutely right.

If it wasn't the movie guy, who else could she have done this with? Where did she learn that art, refine it, practice it? But after her nasty crack, the question, *Why couldn't you lie*? runs through my head. Dammit, why couldn't you lie just a little bit, just stretch the truth a bit for this special occasion? And again that scene of unusual loving replays itself in my memory. I can't forget how I still bristle when I recall how she devastated me. After kissing me so lovingly, inch by inch, all over my body, every place I had skin glowed with her kisses. Not just my skin but all of me glowing, I could have sworn I was bioluminescent. And in a high I said to her: "I know you've invented this loving kissing just for me," and she demolished me by saying, "No, I can't say this is the first time, but it's surely the first time with you."

But I still didn't know, who was the other first with?

I looked at her, penetrated her with my glance. But Maria was silent, as she usually was when she had nothing to say, unlike other women who always have something to say even when they have nothing to say.

19

MARIA'S B&BS - HER DIET

WHEN SHE WAS DRESSED you didn't notice her hair, you didn't notice her breasts. But when she was undressed you sure noticed both.

Maria's breasts looked like they were not her own, or at least that she wasn't aware of them. She was totally, as far as I could tell, except for her washed bras hanging from hooks on the door in her messy bedroom, from knobs on her dresser and pegs on her bathroom door, she was totally unaware of her breasts. They weren't pets to be coddled, and the bras she chose didn't do justice to the nice-sized boobs she had. No girlfriend clued her in on what type of bra to buy to bring out the shape, size, and beauty of her breasts. Maybe she didn't want to spend the money or waste time shopping for the perfect bra. Maybe she just didn't care. I suspect the latter. I certainly couldn't help her with that. Anyway, I preferred her bra off, either near the pillow or on the night table. Once, in bed, when she removed it and just flung it up in the air toward the ceiling, in a comic, theatrical gesture, it landed and dangled on the blade of a ceiling fan. When I jumped up to put on the fan, she reached up and grabbed my leg and pulled me back. Too bad, that would have been some fun, seeing that bra in flight.

For Maria, those boozy holders were purely utilitarian, neither decorative, nor enhancing, nor adding to allure. When I asked her if they were 40C, she said:

"How do you know?"

"I have size 40C hands."

I once tried to open her bra with one hand but couldn't do it.

"What is it, on backwards?" I shouted. "Or inside out. I can't open it."

"Because it has three hooks, not the usual two."

"Oh...I used to be able to open a bra with one hand, even less than one."

"How would you do that?"

"I just looked at it and it snapped open...And now I can't even open one with two."

"Open one with two. I like the conundrumness of it. You're having trouble because my big-boobed bras have three hooks."

"In fact, I used to be able to open one with no hands."

"How?"

"I shouted. Open...that...bra!"

Those breasts, they didn't seem to belong to her. She certainly did not shower them with the same affection I did. Had her waist been slimmer, her hips been narrower, her legs less hefty, her good-sized bust would have been more attention-grabbing. But she was what she was and her laissez-faire attitude to her body shaped her shape. She certainly didn't help it along with her spotty, totally unhealthy eating. A cup of coffee in the morning, some pizza for lunch at work, and something or other for supper. I once told her: You need a good Jewish mother to take care of you.

20

KATZ QUOTES THE SONG OF SONGS

I VISITED MARIA ONE Sunday morning after she had come home from church. She didn't attend regularly, she said, and that surprised me, for I thought, what with her religious proclivities, she'd go every Sunday. And that Sunday was good for me too because it was one of the rare weekends that I wasn't away on business doing consulting for my engineering firm.

•

= I thought you were a land surveyor, Katz, I said.

= That's him and this is me, Katz said drily.

At least this time Katz didn't give me his usual lecture on how he is not the hero of the novel, but just the re-teller, copying for convenience his brother's first-person narrative mode. He didn't even make a face, and I was grateful for that.

•

As usual, I came in via the back door. As I stepped into her kitchen, I could have sworn I heard the click of the front door closing. Maria stood in the living room. I hoped it was my imagination, but I sensed a presence in the room, the aftereffect, the aura, of a man who had been there, here. A shadow of a shadow brushed the air, the furniture, the walls and floor, and then it insinuated itself into my heart. A shadowy pain. I didn't say a word, but as I hugged Maria, pressed my face close to hers, I breathed in deeply, carefully, sniffing her face, her hair, for signs of the intruder.

I decided to approach this new feeling—a kind of emptiness soughing through me—obliquely. I had recently reread the Song of

Songs and decided on a different translation of a crucial verse, the one that pertains to jealousy. Now was the right time to share it with Maria.

"You know," I told her, "love is as strong as death and jealousy is hell."

"*Very* original."

"Why the sarcasm?"

"Your translation," Maria said. There was a bright, know-it-all look on her face.

"What translation?"

"Are you playing dumb, Katz, or trying to put one over on me?" Without waiting for my reply, she said: "How you're translating that last phrase with jealousy. Right out of the Song of Songs, chapter eight, verse five."

I don't know if my jaw dropped. But I imagined it dropped. In sheer surprise. She was right: I had wanted to put one over on her.

"I read the Bible every day," she said. "And I love the Song of Songs, which Christian tradition interprets as a love song between Christ and the Church or God's love for Mary."

And I countered with:

"The Christians did this in reaction to the Jewish tradition of reading it as a love song between God and the People of Israel...Neither Orthodox Jews nor Christians can tolerate the overt eroticism of the Song of Songs, so they cloak it, disguise it, emasculate it with sanctimonious commentary."

"Look, Katz, this is one of the most striking images in the entire Bible and one of the greatest metaphors anywhere about love. So, please, be like a good scholar and footnote your sources. One translation reads, 'jealousy is as severe as the grave.' Another substitutes 'cruel' for 'severe.'"

"I'm aware of that," I said, restraining my galloping impatience like a seasoned jockey. "But whereas you know the English translation of the Bible, I know the original Hebrew—and it's verse six, by the way, not five."

Now her jaw dropped. I lifted it gently.

"Wait a minute," she protested. "Remember, when we once talked about the Greek Orthodox priests in Israel, you said they spoke an impeccable Hebrew but you didn't understand a word."

"Right. And I said the impeccable parts I understood. That was a kind of joke. But in any case, all Hebrew is impeccable."

Maria nodded. But I could see she was still confused.

"Just as the poet of the Song of Songs spoke in the contemporary idiom of his day," I continued, "I'm using that phrase, jealousy is hell, in the idiom of our time. The word *she'ol*, although translated as 'grave,' really means the nether world, or hell. And that's what jealousy is—the pits, absolute hell."

"So you know Hebrew?

"Inside out."

"I didn't know that. You never told me."

"I keep my vest close to my cards."

"Why didn't you become a rabbi? With your knowledge, you should have been one."

"Knowledge is not enough. I actually did study for the rabbinate, but my secular knowledge and education were held against me. The authorities didn't want anyone too bright to lead a congregation. And then there was a prob—"

"Why did you stop? What was the prob? Probability? Probe? There was a probe into your political activities. Proboscis? Your nose was too long? Tell..."

"Problem. The problem was that although I could rein in my head, I couldn't rein in my hands. It was too tempting."

"Naturally," Maria said. "I could have predicted that at your first interview. You couldn't keep your hands to yourself. Touch. Grope. Fondle. Feel. Any girl thirteen to seventy. That's always a problem with clergy. With the Catholics, it's boys; with rabbis, it's women."

"Wrong! I couldn't keep my hands off the books. I abused them. In the library. The rabbinic authorities don't like a rabbi more well read than the congregants. So I decided the rabbinate is not for me."

With a glint in her eyes, Maria said: "Shall I call you Rabbi Katz?"

"Please do. For with me you've now hit the clergy jackpot. You're the only woman in America who has unclothed all men of the cloth: ministers, priests, rabbis, even an imam or two."

What could she say in rebuttal? The only thing she could say was:

"Are you jealous?" she cooed. "Song of Songsly jealous?"

This was the first time I heard a coy femininity in her voice. For one brief moment she dropped her mask.

"Of what? And of whom?" I said, offended. "Well, actually, there's a vague presence of someone here." I sniffed. "It's in the air...Who was visiting you?" I asked, my heart palpitating.

"No one," she said.

"I could swear I heard the front door clicking shut as I came in. It's like out of a farce. Just as one chap leaves, another comes in." It was that guy from the movie theater. I just knew it.

Maria was silent. She stared over my shoulders.

Then she sang, "Katz is jealous. Katz is jealous. Katz is jealous," stretching the "is" to two notes, i-is, like children do when they tease each other.

Besides the phantom guy, I was also jealous of her silence, jealous I couldn't make her say sweet things to me. Can you understand that? Not jealous of another lover, well, yes, that too, of course, that above all, but jealous of the gap between what is and what could be. Can you imagine that? Jealous of a gap. In addition to the other jealousy, which ate into me like a ravenous beast, I was also jealous of nothing I could put my finger on or point a finger at.

"Nah! Are you kidding?" I told her. "For jealousy, you have to be jealous of someone."

"Not necessarily," Maria said. But this time there was no tone of coy flirtatiousness in her voice. "Sometimes people are jealous of a phantom. Suspicious."

My God! She read my mind.

"Okay," Maria with a slow, shy smile. "I'll confess. Your instinct is right. There was a guy here from church who came in for a few minutes to borrow a book."

"That means he'll come back to return it."

"He can always return it to me in church, when he sees me. But if you don't want him to come back, I'll tell him and he'll mail it. In fact, I'll tell him he can keep the book."

That made me feel better. I sensed the phantom starting to drift away.

This wasn't the first time Maria made me jealous. I think I told you that once at a café, we were both sitting opposite each other in a booth and for some reason a guy sitting behind her reading a book made a comment out loud. At which she turned and began talking to him. Not only that, after a minute or so, she even exchanged first names with him, it enraged me, I'm fuming, and then she even introduced me as K, me who never likes to talk to strangers or to be introduced to people I don't know, she suddenly becomes buddy-buddy on a first-name basis with that creep behind her, and later she said, trying to exculpate herself, boy how she would love that word, *But I didn't tell him my last name or yours, for you I just said K,* she pleads. *That's café politesse. No last names. You don't want the guy to look you up in the phone book.* It drove me wild, she was purposely doing that to infuriate me, to make me jealous, well, at least, I calmed myself, mollified, at least she likes me, because if you don't like a guy, you don't drive him jealous, but still it annoyed me, I never thought she would display a trait like that.

But first let me back up. What was I, who never sets foot in a café, doing in a café? Not my choice. Here's the story. The day before, we'd decided that I would come to see her. To my shock, dismay, and disbelief, when I arrive, I go to the back door and, instead of finding it open, I see a taped note stating that she had walked over to the Brandeis Café. At once I see that she did this to annoy me, to vex me. To show me I can't perpetually set the agenda. Come to her and slide into her bed anytime I want.

I don't know if she started talking to that guy to make me jealous. What do I mean I don't know? What am I, an idiot or something? Sure I know. Of course I know. She did it purposely. Calculating. To make me jealous. Yes, in her piquant phrase, Song of Songsly jealous. A jealousy as cruel, severe, unfeeling, unrelenting, tormenting, as hell. The pits. The worst. No rotten feeling can compare to it. When your insides are inside out and there's a hole in your heart bigger than your heart. I didn't like that purposeful calculatingness. I thought she was out of the orbit of being calculating. She always struck me as an innocent. Until I discovered otherwise, later. So I resented that entire calculating scenario, wherein she purposely planned not to be at home, in bed, waiting for me with the back door open so I could come in without being seen by prying neighbors.

Instead, the door was locked. And I had before me the product of a calculating mind—a note left for me. To wit: If you want to see me, I'm at the Brandeis Café. *If!* Why the If? Why that nasty little If? Obviously I wanted to see her. Otherwise, I wouldn't have come. I knew she was doing that just to tick me off.

And in the café, where she gives me a smile wherein lurks both shyness and shrewdness, she purposely—in five words: cal-cu-la-ting-ly—tries to pick up another guy and subtly meld, weave, interlace me into the conversation. I can't stand calculating behavior. Especially if others do it.

Whether she chatted with him to make me jealous, that's not the issue. I *was* jealous. But more than jealous, I was furious that she wasn't at the apartment and made me come to that stupid café, me who hasn't foot in a café since I was in Paris years ago, sitting there with those pretentious morons pretending to read but looking up each time a girl came in, ready to pounce for a pickup. But I politely cloaked my rage with smiles.

That's the first time she pulled a trick like that with me. I just couldn't believe she had that in her. Between the two of us, one calculator was enough. Usually she was so compliant, cooperative. Remember, I told you, when the phone rang, she'd ask me, Do you mind if I take this call? If you don't want me to, I won't.

On our way back to her house, I asked if she purposely went to the café and left me that note just to annoy me. Although she had a sly little smile on her face as she admitted doing just that, the tone of her voice, not the words, mind you, but the tone of her voice had the ring of apology. That tone made me forget the whole thing. But had the reverse happened and I started to speak to some young chick in her presence, I don't think, well, I can't say one hundred percent, but I'm pretty sure she wouldn't have been jealous. And that I didn't like either.

I never would have dreamt she had such slyness in her, until much later, months later, she revealed an incident in her past that showed me that when it suited her needs, wants, desires, she could summon those traits with a snap of the finger. It also revealed to me, it sort of closed the circle on her never-ending battle with guilt and her faithlessness to Jesus. This sin and repentance cycle reminded me of an incident I had heard about years earlier, when I was working one summer in New Hampshire.

There was a small resort in a pretty little town where a good-looking bookkeeper would do a striptease late at night at the hotel bar.

The owner would invite her to the bar, treat her to a few drinks, dance with her on the small dance floor to the music of a three-piece band, and then ask her to do a solo dance on the bar. I never witnessed this, but I heard she would start dancing, then the lights would dim and a soft spotlight would shine on her and then, as if in a trance, she would slowly lift her sweater and take it off and dance a while and the men at the bar would shout their encouragement while she just hugged her breasts and danced solo so slowly, We're all family, we're all friends here, go go go, and the guys in the band would shout go go go and blare some go go go sounds with their instruments, and then she would put her hands behind her back and unhook her bra and reveal those two perfect gorgeous pendulous boobs of hers and not one minute would pass and she put her hands to her face, began bawling, and said, I'm never doing this again, pick up her bra and say, Help me down, and run to the bathroom and rush out of the bar to her room. The next two nights she'd say no to this addiction, but on the third night she was lured into her act again. But of course on the night I sneaked into the bar she didn't show.

You see what I'm driving at? This cycle of joy and guilt and rage. Every third or fourth night, the bookkeeper would go into her trance and do the naked dance and then tears would stream down her face and she would stop and run away.

But despite that little blip in our relationship, the sense of rapport I felt with Maria was unique. Unusual. From the very beginning I felt it. As if someone had slipped me a ticket that said: With her, you're going to feel something special. And quickly. Presto.

No matter how many ways I try to express it, I think I still get it wrong. It's as though we came out of the same cell. Cellmates? I think Maria would appreciate that pun. If we were talking now, I'd say wordplay. She'd say foreplay. I'd say foreskin. She'd say two play at foreplay—but which comes first? I'd say, fourhanded foreplay comes before foreskin.

We were on the same wavelength. I sensed, I felt, she was mine, and that accounts for my jealousy when she spoke to another man. Soon after we met, I felt I could do anything I wanted with her. How did I know this? By the way we chatted with such ease. By the way we laughed with such familiarity. By the way we loved words. By the way we liked the same author: Katz. By the way she remembered *Travels in Bessarabia.* By the way she invited me to her house by saying simply, *When we get home.* By the way I put her on my lap the first day I came to her apartment. By the way, did I tell you I liked her? So when I first kissed her, I felt I was claiming what actually was mine from the very beginning.

21

TOGETHER WITH MARIA

During a pause, catching our breaths, Maria mock scolded me:

"You rascal! You woke up the beast in me with the real thing. Till now I've been singing solo. But now I realize that a duet is preferable."

Until Jesus comes along, I thought, and gives you a solo in the church choir.

"How about a trio?"

"No thanks. Now with the awakened beast, now I'll want you to come every day."

"Your feline, felid, felix beast never went to sleep. Your beast is on perpetual no-doze."

To that she did not respond, but later, in the midst of our embrace, out of the blue, she asked:

"What did you do today?"

"This."

"This?"

"Yup. This. This morning. I was practicing."

Her eyes darkened, but since I smiled, she began laughing.

•

= I didn't know about this other one, I told Katz. = Did you really have another girl on the side?

= First of all, the protagonist is joking. Second of all, John, once again you're mixing up me, the mouthpiece, with the I of my brother's story.

Katz then went into his briefcase and pulled out a sheet of paper.

I have mentioned that on occasion Katz read from a typescript. And sometimes, even with the pages in front of him, he narrated as if he had memorized the text, and, like a good actor, was truly the person he was so successfully imitating. Katz had taken on the "I" of his brother's story so well, I often thought of the two as Siamese twins, indelibly attached.

•

She was a wild one, she was. She made me laugh. When I was flying high, somewhere above and around Saturn, hanging on to one of its bright moons, wearing sunglasses, I giggled, giggling higgledy-piggledy, gaggling a high-pitched *gelekhter*, the Yiddish word for laughter. It just sang out of me, those jiggling giggles of joy. At that moment a scene from the Bible became clearer to me. Remember, in Genesis, when some little kinglet peeks out a window and sees Isaac sporting—the Bible says 'making his wife laugh'—with his gorgeous Rebecca? That's the laughter of passion, joy, release.

On the edge of the bed lay I, my feet hanging, draped on the floor, my hands, palms up, stretched out horizontally. Had I been standing, I would have been in a surrender position.

The naked Maria crawled between my legs and bent over me. Contemplating my crucifixion position, she asked, "Do you feel like Jesus?"

Which surprised, actually astonished me. Under these circumstances I never would have expected her to invoke her idol's name.

"What?"

"I said, do you feel like Jesus?"

"I feel like fucking. Again."

She made her mildly disapproving "Pshh," which was also used to express incredulity.

Then I added, "I hope Jesus didn't feel as bad then as I do now."

Perhaps she thought, because of the ambiguity of the words, that I was insulting her. What I should have said was, I feel great with you above me, about to make love to me. Come to think of it, I don't even know what I meant by that.

But then Maria began cogitating, and I could tell, see, every word flying through her febrile mind. Then they appeared, letter by letter, on the flashing screen: on the face of it, thinks she, what he just said is funny. When isn't he funny? Everything he says is funny, or at least every other, even though he claims he doesn't like to laugh. But when he says, "I hope Jesus didn't feel as bad then as I do now," there may be a theological import to what he's saying or feeling. Maybe he means he feels guilty at what he's doing at this moment, and then of course it's not funny but a touch of the spiritual during this very physical moment. Or maybe he's putting me down, as he usually does, declaring that even though he's about to make love to me, he really doesn't enjoy it that much, maybe because I'm not that pretty, or maybe because he thinks I'm not that good at this, my God, I've been celibate for years. I should have taken that fucking internship I was offered last year.

Then I began pulling Maria's leg, teasing her, toying with her. I shouldn't have. It wasn't right. She didn't deserve it. Even though I was still annoyed at that guy who came to borrow a book—maybe that guy from the movie theater, maybe not; his shadowy presence constricted my heart with jealousy. Still, she didn't deserve it. Maybe later she deserved it. But not now. But I couldn't help it. Sometimes a mean streak comes out unannounced and we seem to watch it from a distance. A boulder barreling down a slope. Impossible to stop.

"So you want to get laid, huh?"

"Yes."

"Say it."

"I want to get laid."

"Screwed?"

"Yes. Screwed."

"Poked?"

"Poked."

"Say it."

"I want to get poked."

"You wanna be fucked?"

I looked at her. I didn't say, say it. But she knew what I meant.

"I wanna be fucked."

I watched her as she said this. She spoke the words matter-of-factly, compliantly, without a shred of irony that would have indicated she was obeying against her will, realizing that I was playing with her, attempting to demean her, to put her down by progressively more vulgar statements. After all, remember, she once declared, I like to be told what to do. So I told her.

Then Maria surprised me, as she usually did, she surprised me with, threw me off balance with, threw me for a loop with, now took the upper hand with:

"And I don't care by whom."

She watched my sudden change of mood, with utter detachment, gazed at me with her big green eyes, then said, "Just kidding. You know, you're talking too much…get to it, or do you like talking about it better than action?"

Later she came out with one of her rare phrases of praise. "You know, I want to say that you have such a magic touch. You give me so much pleasure."

"To who do you want to say this?"

"To whom," she corrected.

"Wait a minute! We're upside down in a position one integer less than three score and ten and you correct my grammar?"

"If one is…devoted…to…the…Englaaaaaaaooooohh," and she couldn't continue but was able only to mutter, "Don't stop don't stop don'tstopdon'tstop…pleeeeeeease don't stop."

But I stopped to declare:

"People devoted to the English language do not use pro- or contractions. They say: Do not stop…"

And I did not, neither with contractions nor without.

You see, despite her religiosity, Maria had an erotic turn of mind—and body. No doubt about it, the two go hand in hand. I've previously observed that in mysticism the imagery for the spiritual is very sex-oriented.

Here's how I once assessed her frame of mind.

Once, we passed an outdoor vegetable market. I saw her looking at thick white asparagus with the suggestive tips. I knew her. I entered her mind with the ease of a car entering a tunnel. Knew what she would say.

"Did you ever notice asparagus is the only vegetable sold standing up?" Maria said.

See? I told myself. Do I know her erotic mind or do I know it?

"But not by itself," I said.

"What not by itself?"

"A solitary asparagus," I said, "does not, cannot, stand up by itself."

"Right," Maria said. "It's always tied up with others, rubber-banded so it shouldn't run away." And she broke into a merry laugh.

•

We now lay side by side. I turned and noticed the sliding door of her closet was open half an inch. I jumped up and shut it.

"You're more meticulous than me."

"I told you first day we met I don't like open closet doors," I said. "I don't like my ties staring at me. There's lots of things I don't like."

"And mostly?" Maria asked.

Again the demon of nastiness overtook me. But once I said what I said there was no taking it back. At once I regretted what I said. But, like most hurtful words blathered in haste, it was too late. I liked her so much, but yet a perverse imp—the wise-guy demon, the comic insult devil—made me say:

"Mostly you."

Maria paled. My words thrust her back, as though I had shoved her, as if a stormwind had blown her, as if I'd just slapped her face. A slap in the face hurts momentarily, but words wound the heart and never go away.

"That's not nice," was all she could say, this Maria who usually had a sharp reply for everything. My cruel, thoughtless phrase must have knocked any comeback out of her. Was it her stinginess with words of affection that had prompted me to say those two dumb words? Or was it the shadow of my two rivals, the movie guy and the book borrower, that forced those words out of me?

I felt awful, terrible, as if she'd said those words to me. Suddenly, my head pounded. What prompted that stupid crack, one she'd never forget, one I'd never forget? Would she turn away from me? Or say: In that case, you can leave now.

I bowed my head. "You're right. I'm sorry. I apologize." I fell to my knees in contrition. I felt like weeping. Then, saintly, lovely girl that Maria is, she pulled me up.

"But I couldn't resist," I added, "when the truth is, among other things I like, you're at the top of my list."

"That's all right," she said softly. "Don't worry about it. You're near the top, no, actually on the top of my list too."

Was I hearing right? My God! Maria finally said something loving to me, and after that nasty jibe too. Like her hero she was turning the other cheek.

Maria paused and added, "If you turn the list upside down."

Then, without even stopping for a breath, Maria thought she would surprise me with, catch me off-balance with:

"What does your wife do?"

"This is becoming annoying. I told you a number of times...Lay off!"

"I know. I know. Of course I know you're not married." Oh, the muted bite in her voice. "But if you *were* married, what would she do?"

"Divorce me."

"And I can see why. I can never get a straight answer out of you. But come on, really, what does your better half do?"

"I can tell you what my lower half does that my upper half doesn't do. But when I look at both my halves, I see them both as better and not worse. Both are ungainfully employed."

"And both of you, to my chagrin, all of you, are impossible. Can't you answer?"

"Okay. I will. First of all, I told you about my marital status...And second of all, if I *were* married, he's a traveling salesman."

"Really?"

"Is that really a really the way I love to hear it, or is that really a matter-of-fact really, the synonym of a flat *Is that so*?"

"The latter. Is your better half really a 'he'?"

She said it so hesitantly, gingerly, as if treading on broken glass. She wanted so badly to be politically correct. But I could see a dark cloud settling on her brow and slowly making its excruciating way, pore by pore, molecule by molecule, down to her cheeks.

Carefully, she asked, "You're not gay, are you?"

"Only when I'm happy."

Maria looked confused. She was teetering on a tightrope.

"You look, sound, so disappointed, Maria. Didn't you know I'm a bi-..." and I lifted my fingers and began counting, "no...tri-sexual?"

I saw her mouth opening, her jaw moving lower and lower.

"Yes, I was gay. And little by little you've helped me come out of, or go back into, the closet. You don't know what a great mitzva you've done for me."

"Bi-...tri-...how's that possible? You don't look...."

"Listen. I'll explain. My spousal partner is male. For extra-material, sorry for the metathesis, for extra-marital affairs, I go for women who remind me of him...in other words, a girl like...you."

"Okay, that's bi-...But where's the tri-...?"

"I try to meet as many sexy women as possible who remind me of—and at the same time can make me forget—my husband."

Maria did not laugh. I wanted to make her laugh. I loved her laugh. But she didn't laugh. She looked overwhelmed, not knowing where to draw the line between incredulity and belief. Now that I think of it, I should have taken that as a positive sign. She was jealous. As some sweet words of hers a few days later showed me. She didn't want me to love anyone, neither man nor woman.

"Let me correct that. The tri- actually refers to plants. I would screw a chicken, but since I'm a vegetarian, for snacks I go for plants. There you have it. In a nutshell. Which I also go for, especially pecans. Now you have a list of all my sexual preferences. What do you think?

"I think you're a pervert."

"Only on meatless, fleshless Fridays," I assured her.

Only then did Maria offer a tentative smile.

22

WHERE LOVING JESUS AND LOVING GOD COMES FROM

THEN CAME THE TIPPING point. Began little by little the trouble. She slowly filling with guilt.

"I still feel bad doing what I'm doing." At first the words seemed to come from somewhere else. She hardly moved her lips. Then I realized it was Maria speaking. "Just because I enjoy it, it doesn't mean there's no payback."

"Convert," I told her. "Become Reform. Then you can do anything you like."

"I can't. I love Jesus too much."

"In a liberal Reform synagogue, you might be able to get away with it."

"I can't," she said again. "I really can't. My love for him knows no bounds."

I didn't like that line and I told her so. "In the course of history, too much love of Jesus always led to disaster, misery, murder of Jews. The Crusades. Easter fanaticism. Pogroms. The line of Jew hatred that led to the Germans. God- or Jesus-intoxication has always made Jews jittery. Cautious. Anxious. Nervous. Jews could, can, never understand this combination of love of Jesus and murder of Jews. I'm sure you're sensitive enough to understand that."

"I didn't, I don't, want to offend you. I'm sorry."

"You're not offending me. I'm stating a historical truth. Your feelings do not offend me. But I would advise you to tone down your love of Jesus. Too much loving. Put a little Christian hatred into your heart."

Maria's eyes twinkled. She was a good sport, was Maria. She scattered her kindness, niceness, affection, and love like a peasant woman sowing seeds.

"You know what the difference between us and you is? I'll tell you. In 1933, before they started killing and burning Jews, the Germans burned books. My mother always taught respect for books. How you treat books, she said, is how you treat people. It began with the pernicious burning of secular books, which Goebbels, the noted PhD in literature, led at a bonfire where the books of Freud and Thomas Mann, Mann wasn't Jewish, and other German writers were publicly burned. Then, on the very first day the Germans invaded Poland, September 1, 1939, they took the entire library of the great Yeshiva of Lublin, the greatest Talmudic library in Poland, thousands and thousands of books, to the market square, and there they set fire to the sacred texts. The blaze lasted twenty hours. All the Jews of Lublin assembled and wept bitterly. The weeping was so loud it almost silenced the roar of the flames. Then the Germans summoned their military band and with their joyful noise they tried to drown out the cries of the mourning Jews. You see, that's the difference. Jews weep over destroyed books. You don't."

"Jews like to cry," Maria said. "We love to laugh."

I was stunned at her callousness. "There's a difference between loving to do something and having to do it because of circumstances."

Nevertheless, despite her flip comment, I saw tears in her eyes. I could have hugged her for her tears and smacked her for her words. Then I shouted louder than I had ever shouted before.

"Jews invented laughter, for God's sake! They also invented the question mark, by the way. It's the Christians who made us weep throughout the centuries."

"I was just kidding," she said. "That story touched me."

"I know," I said, "but you still have a nasty tongue."

"Well, I'm a Christian, after all. Can a leopard change its spots?" she quoted Jeremiah. "But I try every day, do everything in my power, try as hard as I can every day to become a better person…so I beg forgiveness for my tartness. What those poor weeping Jews did not know was that in a year or so, your mother was so right, they would be consigned to the same flames with the same military band cheering."

Bless her, she understood, was sympathetic. Still, I wasn't through with her.

"Do you know where this love of Jesus comes from?"

Maria thought a minute. She pressed her cheek with an index finger. "Actually not."

"From the Torah, where it says, and Jews recite it twice a day as part of the *Sh'ma Yisrael*: 'You shall love the Lord your God with all your heart, with all your soul and with all your might.'"

"See?" she said. "There's your love of God."

I held my peace, then tried to continue calmly. Nevertheless, I noticed a nervous tremor in my voice.

"But you will never, never, never ever hear a normative Jew say, 'Oh, do I love God! I just lo-oo-oove Him.' In all my years I've never heard a man, woman, child, rabbi, layman, teacher, or any other Jew ever say 'I love God,' rolling their eyes heavenward in prayerful ecstasy. Never. Like some women purr, 'I just lo-oo-ove my canary'...Or, 'I love my cats,' with a capital K, of course. Never will you hear a Jew ecstasize his love for God. You will hear a Jew say, 'I love the Torah, the mitzvot, the traditions, the Sabbath, the holidays, the literature.' You will hear, 'I love the Mishna, I love Maimonides, I love Rashi's commentary. The Midrash.' But God? Never. Ever. Because for a Jew the love of God expresses itself in doing good, obeying the commandments, caring for the sick, helping the poor, being a decent human being. Judaism is all about doing, while Christianity is all about belief and faith. God. Good. One little 'o'. One little circle. One little orb. One round little 'o' is the difference. The dividing line. That's the difference between Judaism and Christianity. Loving good and loving God. Loving God doesn't do anyone any good. The Christians have loved Jesus for two thousand years and look how much havoc and bloodshed this love has wrought. But loving good means doing good; it brings the subliminal God down to earth."

But dear Maria wasn't fazed by my speech. She wasn't taken aback. She just nodded slowly, seemingly accepting what I was saying.

"And as part of that divide, don't you think of me, the Jew, as a foolish sinner, a member of a stiff-necked tribe that still doesn't have the good sense to accept Jesus as a son of God, the redeemer of the world, and hence be saved unto all eternity, amen?"

"No," said Maria, "and I'll disregard that none-too-muted tinge of ridicule. No no." I sensed the kindness in her voice. "But one day I'd like to talk to you about Jesus and why he can be important for Jews too."

"It won't happen. Please, Maria. No proselytizing. No attempts at conversion. We like each other too much for that."

"Of course. No proselytizing. It's not for you. It's for me."

"You got the wrong guy. It will make no impression on me."

"Can you just listen to me one day? It will clarify belief for me."

"We'll see. But the whole premise is so absurd, an absurd which is the bedrock of your faith. It just doesn't make any sense for me and you to delve into this subject."

"And you, on the other hand, I assume you have a certain view of the stupidity of Christians, who..."

"...who believe, as I hinted above, that the one and only God would anthropomorphize himself and then deign to screw a poor Israelite woman without the benefit of a wedding canopy, and who worship said son of that illicit and impossible union and his mother as deities. Indeed, you're absolutely right. But I have nothing against you personally. Some of my best friends are Christians."

Maria took a deep breath and let out a sigh. I saw her open her mouth. She was about to say something.

"Look, I didn't want to tell you this because I didn't want to brag. But since you think I'm a kind of a callous, you know, anti-Semite..."

"No no no," I interrupted her. "On the contrary..."

"Let me finish. I want to tell you that affection for Jews and hatred of anti-Semites and fascists and Nazis, etc., has been part of my heritage for generations. My grandfather, Loritz Christiansen, who emigrated to the United States after World War II, had a small fishing fleet in Copenhagen. He was instrumental in saving the Jews of Denmark, in that daring and historic operation where, during one night, almost all the gentiles in Denmark cooperated to bring all the Jews into ships and boats of all kinds and spirited them over to safety in Sweden. On the night before the day the Germans were going to round up and take away all the Jews. My father's father was one of the leaders, the organizers, of this fantastic mission....And when the Danish Jews came back home to Copenhagen and other cities, unlike in Poland, where the villagers immediately looted the Jews' houses once they were taken away and hounded the few survivors when they returned in 1945, in Denmark everything was left intact; in fact, when the Jews returned they found welcoming flowers in their apartments and houses."

"I'm touched, I'm proud," I said.

And I gave Maria a warm embrace.

"They all did it because it was the right, the humane, the godly thing to do." She stopped. Did not say it was the Christian thing to do. Maria watched her words carefully.

Then she asked an unusual question.

"I've often wondered how a simple person of flesh and blood like me, like us, can conceive of God. I've given it some thought. I conceive of God as a vast space with infinite power. How about you?"

"I'm a left-wing agnostic. But if pressed, I'd say that I think of God as a circle whose center is everywhere and whose circumference is nowhere."

"Wow! That's superb!"

"I wish I could take credit for that wonderful thought, but it's a definition of God by a twelfth-century Spanish philosopher, probably an Arab mathematician."

"How do you know so much?"

"I don't," I said. "But if you talk loud and quick and don't stop for breath, people assume you know everything."

"All this theology talk distracts me —but it can't wipe away the bad feeling in my heart, the guilt that is stirring there. In fact, the more I talk about God and Jesus, the stronger is my feeling of guilt. Please. Please understand...Too bad you've never experienced Jesus."

"But I have."

"You have? Really?"

"Yes. I was once at scientific retreat in Italy sponsored by some international organization. In the middle of dinner, a tall, beefy African, dressed in his voodoo robes, clinked a spoon on a glass and, unbidden, rose and said: 'Ladies and gentlemen, let us thank our Lord Jesus Christ for this meal.'

"I jumped up. Infuriated. Outraged. Seething. 'What chutzpah!' I hissed. 'This is not a Christian institution, and not all of us are Christians, and there probably are a few atheists here too who resent this unwelcome intrusion. How dare you invoke Jesus into a meal and turn this into a Christian sectarian ceremony where people like me sit who are Jewish? What nerve! Who gave you the authority to do this?' I clinked a spoon on a glass too. 'We will not thank Jesus for this meal. We will thank the Institute that sponsored this conference and gave this meal to us and to you too. And we will thank no one else.' The guy was so shocked, I could have sworn he turned white."

I wondered what Maria would say to this.

"Good for you, Katz," she said. "The Inquisition has been over for years."

23

CONVERTING FOR MARIA

ONCE, SO CRAZY WAS I for her, and only a crazed man would do this, I even had the wild idea of converting for her. First I told her to convert to Reform, an offer she declined, and then I figured if I converted, accepted Jesus, even pro forma, like Felix Mendelssohn or Gustav Mahler, then everything would be smooth sailing for me. But I didn't realize how many glass shards she'd strewn on the roadway. The more religious I became, the more religious she. Converting wouldn't be enough. She wouldn't even screw with a Christian. She had to marry first. I could imagine her saying after I converted:

"What?! Me?! Marry a goy? Never!"

Because she loved the Jew in Jesus even more than she loved the goy in me.

Then I told her:

"I dreamt I'm wrestling with an angel made of fire and water but don't know why."

"I know why," says the nascent therapist in her. After all, she'd been listening to one for nearly eighteen years—she had recently told me that in passing—so something must have rubbed off. "You feel guilty about going with a *shikse*. That is why the angel has come to you in a dream. He is struggling to find mastery over you and send you on the right moral path. I wish I could get a clear message like that. 'Maria! Renew your links to Jesus. Stop sinning.'"

Poor thing. Always torn between sex and Jesus. If only we could combine the two. But although she always threatened to stop sinning, she couldn't. She loved sinning too much.

"So you believe in dreams?" I asked her.

"Yes. I do."

"I will remember that," I said.

"And what's more," Maria added, "with your dream, now it's easier for me to separate from you. I won't use the argument that you're married. I'll use the intermarriage prohibition."

Me and my big mouth. Every time I tell her something, she uses it to my detriment.

"I told you, God knows how many times, I wasn't married," I fumed. "You probably saw my brother, who resembles me, and his wife."

"Is your brother really married?"

"I don't know. I don't see him that often. And anyway," I said, "I have this wild idea of converting. Since you won't convert for me, I'll convert for you."

"What?" she screeched. I had never heard her raise her voice before. She was truly shocked. My pronouncement had set her off kilter. She lay in bed, but metaphysically she had fallen off the bed.

"Yes. Convert in a sort of semi-conversion. I mean, I wouldn't bow down to Jesus, but maybe, just maybe, I would become part of the most liberal of the Christian denominations, the one closest to Judaism, maybe a far-out, far-left Unitarian, let's say, almost a Reform Jew. So for you I'd be a Christian."

To which the clever logician retorted, "You might be a Christian for yourself, but for me you'd still be married."

"If my brother divorced his wife, would that help?"

"Maybe him and her. But not me, not you."

"You just said you won't accent the marriage issue but focus on the intermarriage aspect."

"It still bothers me."

My knowing that Maria would only marry a fellow Christian prompted my idea of asking her, just for curiosity's sake, if she'd marry me if I became a goy. But I refrained from asking her for fear she might assume I was proposing. It would only have been a theoretical question, for I would not cross-marry either.

Then I thought, why waste time with theory when we live in a world where practicality is king. So instead I said:

"Why don't we celebrate my religious conversion with a passionate fuck? In Jewish tradition, when there is a spiritual celebration, some kind of food or drink is served, but what better physical pleasure can there be above food or drink than sex? After all, we read in the Bible—the same Bible you and I, or as you put it so colloquially, me and you, read—that religious pagan rites were always connected to sex. Jews and Christians alike separated God from sex, but the Jewish medieval mystics, at least theoretically, restored it. No wonder it's a mitzva to screw your wife on Friday night."

"Right you are. On the mark. Your wife. Not someone else's."

"You're not someone else's wife. Wanna celebrate my conversion?"

"How about if we just celibate it?"Maria countered."I made up my mind. No more sex for me until I'm married."

I looked at her. Stony-faced. I drilled my stern glance into her.

Did my sneer, my hard, down-putting, impatient, cold, unrelenting look persuade her? Or was it my flawless celebratory logic? I can't tell. But *I* almost fell off the bed when Maria said:

"Well... Since we're both in bed, why waste proximity? All right. One more. One last time. I can't help it. I'm addicted to you."

"That's the nicest, warmest thing you've said to me."

"Really?"

"Except for that."

"Okay, one more. One last time. But…that's…it."

An hour later she called me, "Faaahlshe kahhhtz."

Where she got that Yiddish expression I'll never know. When I asked her, she shrugged her shoulder.

"Why am I a *falshe katz*?"

"Because of your false conversion ploy."

•

= Do you know what that expression means? I asked Katz.

= Yes, I do, John. It means a false cat.

= So what's so bad about that?

= First of all, it's a clever pun on my name. Katz in Yiddish means cat. And in Yiddish culture, a cat is considered false, duplicitous, fickle, disloyal, undependable. So *falshe katz* really means two-faced rascal or scamp.

•

"That's what you are," Maria said, "a false cat. You and your faux conversion."

Again I asked her where she learned that phrase.

"Never mind. I learned it. And I used it well, didn't I, *falshe* Katz?"

And again the evil flower of jealousy bloomed in me. Why did I have to take her to the movies? We should have done what we had always done. Stay at home. The guy she had seen coming out of the theater. That Jewish fellow she had dated that I was not able to see because Maria had turned me and hidden her face in my chest so he would not see her. And it was *me* she was calling *falshe katz.*

A cat was always considered deceitful and conniving, I told Maria. Unlike a dog, a cat won't lift a paw if you're in trouble. A cat couldn't care less. A dog is loyal. My good-humored mother always called me a *falshe katz*, especially when I hugged her just before asking for something. It was a lifelong, loving monicker she gave me. But her way of calling me *falshe katz* was not as catty as Maria's.

24

JUST TWO LETTERS - MARIA'S RIDDLE

"JUST TWO LETTERS," SHE said as we lay in each other's arms in semi-celibacy.

"What two letters?"

"T and r."

I didn't understand. What was that supposed to mean?

"Think."

"Teddy Roosevelt?" I guessed. "He too was in your apartment, along with Ulysses S. Grant, on the night Lincoln was shot?"

"It's not initials. Those two letters are in the middle of a word."

"Betray."

"No, but that's appropriate too."

"Troublemaker."

"Absolutely. But still no."

"Untrustworthy."

"On the button, *falshe katz*. All applicable, but the word I'm thinking of pertains to *me*."

"Strumpet?"

"What's strumpet?"

"A baroque instrument that you blow with tongue and lips."

"Still no," Maria said. "Give up?"

"Yes."

"T and r are the two letters that separate misses from mistress."

I got it but didn't say a word. Had she read my mind? After the failed conversion on both sides, she wasn't hinting that I marry her, was she? I had never heard Maria express a thought so indirectly direct. For, remember, she had never once articulated affection for me. Or was she just making an observation about her ambiguous role? I didn't have the faintest idea. As I said, I wouldn't have married her and she wouldn't have married me. There was, remember, a religious divide.

But I did ask her, surprised her with:

"Did you ever thank God for me?"

Maria looked at me in silence.

Cornered, forced to reply, she had no choice but to answer:

"Well…"

"That's all you can come up with? A noncommittal monosyllable?"

"Well, I do thank him." And then her voice dropped, shifted to a different, maybe minor, key. "For sending me, my luck, a married man who lured me into sin."

"That's it. Finished."

I got up.

Maria's face fell. "Are you leaving?" she asked in a thin, a thinning, voice.

"After seven hundred and seventy-seven denials," I shouted in a huff, "you're still at it? First of all, the marriage issue is closed. Maybe it makes you happy to peak, to tweak, your guilt, to satisfy that incipient Catholic guilt you glory in. And secondly, I didn't lure. Your penchant for disinformation matches that of a dictatorial Sixth World regime. It was you, you, you who, the first day we met on the tram, did the loud, lewd luring by shamelessly declaring, 'When we get home' when I hadn't even the slightest intention of seeing you again. Ever!"

"Still…" was her lame reply.

"If I met a guy like me, I would fall on my knees, if that's permissible for a non-Catholic, and thank Jesus for sending me such a great guy."

Maria smiled; she laughed; she beamed. "They broke the mold when they made you."

"And I broke the mold when I made you. You hadn't been laid for so long your pudendum was covered with an almost impenetrable coating of mold."

"But I do pray for you. I pray to God and ask Jesus to bless you."

"Hold it! Please rein in the zealous horses of excessive piety. The first part I accept, but in reference to me, leave Jesus out. Or shall I repeat that anti-Jesus speech I addressed to the African who turned white with shock, Caucasian white, within a minute?"

"Okay," she said, shamefacedly. "And I do fall on my knees when I pray for you."

"Just don't pray that I convert. That's over and done with."

"That I don't do. I'm not that sort of Christian."

25

THINKING ABOUT MARIA'S LIFE - HER EASY CHAIR

Sometimes I thought to myself, What was her life? An armchair. Yes, an oversized, comfortable, nondescript, aged, lumpy-looking, wine-colored, has-been, velveteen and elephantine easy chair, on whose armrest lay a little New Testament open to Luke or Matthew. I remember reading one of Sholom Aleichem's absurd and hilarious comparisons: "A man's life may be compared to that of a carpenter. A carpenter lives and lives until he dies. And so a man." Maria's life couldn't be compared to a carpenter. Rather, to a chair.

This was her livelihood. With her minor in labor arbitration and a couple of psychology courses, she passed herself off as an expert in employee relations and worked as a kind of floating ombudsman. Companies called her to arbitrate certain employer/employee problems. She sometimes worked from 11 a.m. to 10 p.m. for two weeks in a row, including occasional weekends. Then she took a couple of days off and waited for another call. I asked if her minor was useful. "No," she said, "all you need is common sense. Even a moron could do my job," and she looked at me intently, giggled, and kissed me on the nose.

When she came home, that armchair was her companion, friend, co-renter, into which she plopped herself and read for hours, sometimes till the morning. I can imagine her snuggling into that chair, encapsulated into her little world. This, basically, was her social life. I couple this with her sitting home alone on Saturday nights, reading comfortably—sad but comfortable. Comfortable but sad. A sadness she would not admit until it popped out once—not in person but over the phone—as she bethought her life and uttered that pathetic line: "It's been a sad week, a sad life."

When I asked her about it later—I had been too stunned to react—she claimed I had misunderstood her. That's not what she meant at all. But it reminded me of State Department or White House "clarifications" of offhand but gut-honest comments. True feelings come out first, explanations afterward. Explanations afterward attempt to flatten, cloud, distort, undo, sterilize, emasculate the original honesty.

I knew nothing about Maria. Except what she told me. Could compare her to no one. Had I known one of her coworkers, someone in town who knew her, I might have been able to glean some rumors, some background, some backbiting, some stories. But the fact is, she was a loner, a solitary figure in my ken and in my imagination. When people's lives intersect, you get a three-dimensional picture. With her it was one dimension, maximum two. No one could round out her personality for me, or provide shadowing for my portrait of her.

•

Katz turned to me.

= The protagonist's relationship to Maria was perhaps like you and me. The only thing we know about each other is what we have revealed during our meetings. There are no outsiders, no one to fill in and make an in-depth portrait. No one to add juicy or boring details.

Katz looked down. I thought he would resume his narration, but instead he looked out the window.

= See those pathetic cars parked beside those pathetic cookie-cutter bungalow houses whose outer shape reflects the tiresome and monotonous existence of their inhabitants? Now come the characteristic warehouses. Listen to the mournful moaning of the train's whistle. Not a stretch of happy greenery in this somber Jersey space. I'll have to suggest to my brother to include a scene like this. Where geography parallels a person. It's apropos. Somehow all this recalls for me Maria's sad easy chair, with not an ounce of ease.

= And I remember reading, I interrupted Katz, = an apt phrase in a novella by the Italian writer Natalia Ginzburg. She wrote about a single woman, unloved, and she uses the same words you just used, a woman who led a 'tiresome and monotonous existence, with worn gloves.'

That little detail marked that line in my memory.

= Wow! exclaimed Katz. = What a wild coincidence. And I never even heard of Natalia Ginzburg.

= Yes. 'With worn gloves.' That extra touch gives splendor to that whole line.

= I imagine her sitting there, in her sad, big armchair reading, and daydreaming about God knows what. Pehaps God. And Jesus, of course, who was more important for her than God.

Then Katz resumed his narration.

I wanted to ask Katz if, as he read his brother's novel, if he thought there was some meaning to Maria's life. It seemed so empty. I hesitated. The question was so banal, so Chekhovian. Instead, I said:

= I can imagine Ivanov, Oblomov, Onanov, Korsakov, Gorbachov and Taykitov, and other characters in *The Seagull* wandering about the living room, wearing pince-nez and exclaiming tragically—even though Chekhov marked all his plays comedies and wanted us to laugh at all these chaps. I hear these characters declaiming, *Is there any meaning to our drear lives here in the country? We must move. All six of us. We three brothers and three sisters, we must leave our beloved cherry orchard. We must go to the capital. To Dnepropetrovsk. To Dnepropetrovsk. To Dnepropetrovsk.* By the time the character says it three times he's halfway there already. And most of the first act is over.

Katz seemed delighted at my parody.

Then I asked my question about Maria anyway. Katz said he didn't know.

Then—he must have thought it over—he said:

= Remember what I said earlier re Sholom Aleichem and the life of a carpenter? I would say Maria's life, as I judge it from my brother's pages, her life was like that of a carpenter ant, slowly devouring the wood of her chair. Until she finally became her chair.

•

Her easy chair and living room were her safe haven. Ensconced in her old easy chair with a light whose wattage was just below comfort, she felt like a baby swaddled and pressed to her mama's bosom, or a baby bird in the nest with a warm wing spread over her.

Maria had absolutely no interest in money, in improving her financial state. She still had college loans debts from seventeen years ago. Other students had their loans forgiven, but she continued paying through the nose, year after year. She owned no stocks, just had a small checking account that paid no interest where she kept four thousand dollars.

She also had little interest in buying things. On rare occasions she would splurge, buy an expensive toy like a Cuisinart, and then the unopened package would just sit there in her living room until she hid it in her closet. She had no desire to buy clothes or items to make herself feel good or look good. She didn't want to impress anyone. I think I've already said that a touch of lipstick was her only makeup.

"I can't stand odors, smells, fragrances. Even facial cream is foul. A jogger's sweaty sweatshirt. The warm air from a hair dryer makes me gag. Steamed broccoli and burnt toast—yek! And...let's see...perfumes give me a headache too."

"Me too. But you, you yourself put on perfume. I've smelled it. Didn't like it either. Asked you not to put it on when I see you."

"I know. I put on just a tiny dab. Reluctantly. To drive away other smells elsewhere. I'd rather smell me and get a headache than smell them and gag."

In her living room, I felt I was walking through an apartment store display. Temporariness incarnate. She had unopened packages, impulse purchases she would never use, like a vacuum cleaner that she said ate up dirt. It never had to be emptied. It also did handstands. Or a multitask Kitchen Aid juicer with a reverse gear. You put in orange juice and out came an orange. Bake? Not on your life! She didn't even boil an egg. Tea was the only thing she prepared in that sad little kitchen with its lone silent yellow canary. She thought of that living room as her return to the womb, although she didn't much care for her mother. With all those unopened packages, I expected the movers to barge in any moment.

•

= Sorry for interrupting, Katz, but I think you once told me that you, or rather the narrator, liked Maria's apartment.

= Yes, correct. According to my brother, when she was there and when it was sunny. Listen.

•

Then I looked at her, not the walls. At her face, not the floor. Her eyes, not the furniture. Her face was the sunshine that camouflaged the drab, even when the sun wasn't shining. Even when the sun wasn't shining and she was there the place had a different feel. But when Maria was not in the room, a curtain fell over it.

Exit sunshine, enter drab.

•

One day I called Maria; she answered on the first ring and said, "Hello."

"Maria?"

Why did I say Maria? Who else could it have been? But the Hello was a little off. Not her usual voice. Perhaps she had a cold or a sore throat.

"Yup."

Her voice did sound funny, deeper, guttural, as if she had swallowed a mouthful of lemon juice. And what's this Yup? I had never heard her use that word before.

"You okay?"

"Yup."

"I wanna come over, Maria. Leave the back door open."

"Okay. Yup. Come over. Back door open."

"Sure you're okay, Maria?"

"Yup."

Suddenly, I heard a shriek. "Give me that phone, you bastard."

And then came the guttural, lemony voice: "You bastard."

Again my heart fell. That book-borrowing guy from her church came to borrow another book. Or to watch slides of Christian sites in Jerusalem and *kvell* over Jesus together. Or maybe she made up with her ex-boyfriend, the moviegoer, who has the temerity, the nerve, the gall to make a fool of me, trying to imitate Maria's voice. The bastard.

"Who is this?" Maria asked.

"Who was that?" I countered, an ill feeling souring in my gut. Who was in the house whom she knew well enough to call bastard?

"It's you."

"Of course it's me. And who, what, was that? That bastard that answered the phone."

"My parrot."

"Your what? Did I hear parrot?"

"Yes."

"Where's your canary?"

"He or she or it up and died. This is my loaner bird till I take delivery on a new canary."

Well, at least that news made me feel better. Better a bird bastard than a male bastard.

"Next time I come, I'll tell you a great story about a talking parrot. Leave the door open for me for tomorrow morning."

"Yup."

"Is that you or the bastard?"

"Me."

First words she said the next morning were: "Lemme hear that parrot story. I love talking parrot stories."

I put my arms around her and said:

"A language died in a remote mountainous area south of Naples, but an old parrot remembered quite a lot of words. This language had a tense system—verbs existed only in the future—so complicated you needed a slide rule or an abacus to figure out the pluperfect. It was like trying to explain color to a man blind from birth. Since the language had only a future tense, you needed certain head gestures, a lift of chin, a raised eyebrow and a slight wink of the right eye to indicate the past tense."

"You're making this up, Katz."

"No, I ain't. I read it in the *Science Times*. Only in the nineteenth century did a philologist suggest saying 've' before each verb to indicate the past and thereby eliminate all facial gestures. You see, they had no present tense because their philosophy of time was that all present becomes past and only the future counts. For the imperative they sharpened their glance, furrowed their brows, and jabbed the other person in the chest with an index finger.

"The parrot's vocabulary was quite extensive, but he never accepted the 've.' Rather, he continued with head, eye, and facial gestures when he wanted to use the past tense. But he was able to teach an almost full range of vocabulary of this dead language to philologists and Italian linguists before he died, exhausted by facial expressions."

"Get out of here," Maria said with a laugh, pushing at my chest with both her hands. "I've never heard anything so absurd."

26

NO REFLECTION IN MIRROR

In her bathroom, Maria stood before the mirror, patted her hair. That was unusual, for I had never seen her looking at a mirror. And I wondered, what did I look like when I wasn't looking in the mirror observing myself? At a mirror I adjusted my face to look nice, welcoming, beneficent—and not morose or arrogant or disappointed with the way the world treated me. But it was tricky. I only caught part of my unaware self before noticing my true self and adjusting to what I thought I should look like.

As Maria patted her hair, I saw—how odd!—only one hand, not two. Then she stepped aside. Curious, I too looked in the mirror—but I couldn't see a reflection. Uh-oh, I thought. In folklore, if you can't see yourself in a mirror, you're dead.

I sensed a quaver in my voice as I asked Maria, "Do you see your reflection?"

Suddenly, as if a stopper in me had become unplugged, I sank into fright. My knees shook. My hands trembled. I held, rather, something, some vise beyond me, held my breath.

"No," she said.

I pinched her cheek.

"Ow! Why'd you do that?"

I exhaled. If Maria wasn't dead, there was hope for me too.

"I wanted to check if you're dead too."

"What's got into you?"

"According to Fourth World folk belief, if you can't see your reflection, you're dead."

"Don't worry," she said cheerily. "It's a special dark mirror. My non-mirror mirror. It doesn't reflect."

"Then why were you looking into it?"

"Where else should I look?"

"So what use does…?"

"It helps reduce egotism, vanity. I bought it to practice reduction, elimination, of pride."

Catholic, Catholic, Catholic, I say to myself, and then out loud:

"I look at myself and don't see myself and I think I'm dead."

"Not yet," she says.

"Where'd you get this dark glass?"

"At the beauty salon I go to, Figaro's. I could have bought one that would reflect anyone else's face but mine, but it was too expensive, so I got this one. And anyway, who else uses my bathroom?"

"Figaro…I like the name. Does he do men too?"

"Yes. Figaro is bisexual."

"I just can't imagine you at a beauty parlor."

"I don't go every week, like other women. I just go once at the end of every fiscal quarter. I'll take you, if you're free, next time, but it's about an hour north of here. It's a fun place and you can meet Figaro."

"He's actually a person?"

"Yes. He's the owner and his motto is: We don't do hair: we do happiness. It's a perpetual party there. A place with offbeat things to buy."

"Do you know where Figaro got his name?" I asked her, but she didn't know.

Maria had once used the word "saltational," which drove me to the dictionary. It glided off her tongue as though it was one of the seven words she was born with—but she had no clue if Figaro was a pet, a food, or an Italian belt.

"The Mozart opera, *The Marriage of*…Also, Rossini's *The Barber of Seville*."

"I've never been to an opera," she said, "but once at his salon, I heard him sing a song they said was from an opera. He stood on a little stage in the back, mic in hand, and began a catchy little ditty. He had a good voice, but in the middle of his song he repeated words, as if a needle got stuck in a record. Then he ran off, collapsed in a chair, and began crying. Later I realized that he had been lip-syncing to a CD and something went wrong with the record."

When I asked Maria if she knew what Figaro had been singing, she didn't know. She was there and she didn't know. I wasn't and I did. I told her about that famous aria and later made her a present of the CD.

For a girl who loved words, books, intellection, her taste in music was primitive. She had never heard of Vivaldi. She liked mild rock and was especially fond of a Jesus-loving female singer—she played a CD for me—who had eros, tease, directed at Jesus, packed into her suggestive voice. The eros part Maria did not recognize. It went past her, through her, above her, around her. Maria only heard Jesus in the vocalist's melodies. But I, an objective outsider, I heard sex in those stretched vowels, the moans and teasing sounds, the sudden drop to low-pitched sultry notes. The singer was working in the centuries-old, universally practiced tradition of combining religion and sex, especially in music. But Maria's mind censored that part, more likely was oblivious to it, and reveled only in the spirituality of the song, her lord transubstantiated into melody.

27

MARIA'S WATERS OF BITTERNESS TEST AT FIGARO'S

I GOT TO SEE Figaro's sooner than I thought. Here's how it happened. It was all connected to Maria's dream one hot late August day.

"I had this weird dream last night."

"Tell. Tell," I said. "You never told me about dreams before. I love dreams. Let's hear it."

"In my dream, I have this feeling that, you know, I'm an adulteress and I must undergo the Biblical Waters of Bitterness Test. And then I suddenly woke up. Now I feel I have to go to Figaro's."

"And get your hair done? But it isn't the end of the fiscal quarter yet. And what's one thing got to do with the other?"

"I told you last time that his is a unique place. He'll administer the test. I'm going and I want you to come with me."

"I'm not drinking that stuff. No way."

"It's only for a woman, silly. Men can do what they want. I hope you don't mind, we'll park a couple of blocks away and go in separately. I don't want anyone to, you know, think that..."

"Fine with me," I said. "I understand. Perfectly."

Turns out, in light of subsequent events, that that was a good idea.

At Figaro's, I saw the full name of the salon: Figaro's Femme Fatale Fricasee. Maria entered first and I came in about five, six minutes later.

She must have slipped me a mickey or flipped me a hickey, for as I entered I felt I was in a different world. Dance music overwhelmed me, a soft, insidious Latin beat. Four Latina girls were cutting the hair of four women with elaborate, ballet-like movements. I looked closer. There were two more girls in the back I hadn't seen before. Six girls at six chairs next to six sinks were cutting hair in perfect synchronization. They opened the hot water faucets with their left hands with rounded gestures as they closed the cold water with their right, bending now this way, bowing now that. All at the same time, in a set choreography worthy of a 1940s Hollywood musical.

Did Maria give me some potion, some drug? Had I inhaled something in Maria's messy apartment? For at Figaro's I was in a psychedelic world. It was unreal. Figaro himself was a character out of a Thomas Mann short story, some kind of Mario the Magician, casting a spell over us. First of all, his uncanny ability with numbers. I had once read about people like that, a quirk of the brain, inexplicable, they didn't have to be smart or geniuses, but they could, like a calculator, multiply two three-digit numbers in their heads at once, but couldn't tell you who was America's second president.

At once, I was so excited by what I had seen I wrote it down, but when I reread it later, it was not what I had written, what I wanted to say. For example, I jotted down that Figaro had been asked to multiply 342 by 243 and came up with the answer, but when I read what I had written the words spoke of a special hair-dyeing formula Figaro had invented.

I felt I went into a time warp. For an hour or two, time was compressed, like one of those huge vises that crushes wrecked cars into a pancake. What happened in over an hour felt like minutes.

But let me backtrack. Soon as I came in, a man in his late thirties, tall, with slicked-back black hair and an open, friendly face and crinkly-eyed smile, came up to me.

"How can we help you?"

"Just a haircut, please."

"Shave? Facial? Massage?"

"Uh-uh."

I looked for Maria, saw her talking to a young woman.

"Short, medium, or long."

"Make it short."

"You're not supposed to answer. It's a rhetorical question. We decide these things."

"And who are you?"

"My name is Figaro." He danced around me as he trimmed my hair. "By the way, I'm an expert at geomancy. You know what that is?"

I said no to make him feel good, even though I knew it was divination by means of figures or signs.

"Neither do I," said Figaro, "but I'm good at it. Here we want to make you happy...See those shelves full of lotions, notions, and oceans of potions, and all kinds of specialty items you will find nowhere else? If you need anything, let me know. Any of these girls interest you, I'll introduce you. Want to meet that girl with the long brown hair who's getting her nails done now? She's an old customer. We're gonna have an interesting ceremony here with her in a few minutes."

"No, thanks, I have a girlfriend."

"Another one or two won't hurt."

"Won't help either," I said. "Betraying one's wife is okay, but betraying one's girlfriend is unconscionable."

Figaro stopped cutting; he leaned in close to me.

"Why, you married?"

"Who said so?"

"You did."

"I did not."

"Well, I gathered that from your inferences."

"Inference is not fact," I said.

"Well, I'm a married man and I have a girlfriend or two, but I'm not prying into your personal affairs. I'm not one of those hairdressers who, while clipping, snipping, trimming, cutting, slyly slips in questions about his client's private life."

Soon as he said that, I felt as if stardust had been sprinkled on me, or as though he had poured some truth syrup into my ear, like the character does in Hamlet's play that mimes the murder of his father, the king. I felt as if someone had hit the proper numbers on a combination lock. And I began reciting to him all kinds of personal details.

"I'm a travel writer," I said, "and I have one older sister who lives either in Austria or Australia, I don't know which, for I can't read the postmark on the letter she sends me once a year, and my big toe..."

"Whoa! Whoa there! Hold it!" Figaro said. "I didn't want your entire biography or details about your foot problems."

I couldn't stop. "And I have a Siamese twin, a sister who after reading *The Castle* became a land surveyor."

Figaro looked at me. He shook his head in bewilderment.

"I thought a Siamese twin is supposed to be, you know, attached."

I began to laugh. "We were attached at the shoulder but we separated years ago. I got the house and she got the children."

"Mister, I still don't know your name but you're nuttier than me."

I chanted, "My name is Sam, that's who I am. I'm half a twin, a semi-Siam."

•

= I see your brother disguised you pretty well.

= But he still gave Figaro my profession.

Suddenly, Katz began rubbing his left shoulder; his face was twisted, seemingly in pain.

= What's the matter?

= It's the point of separation, John. It still hurts.

•

The mention of Siam, now Thailand, and twins reminded me of another twin incident. Once, Maria and I sat in a Thai restaurant—one of the few times I took her out—and there she came up with one of her great lines. When she looked around and saw we were the only white people there, she said, "You know, we're the only goyim here." During the meal she went down a broad set of stairs to the ladies room. When she came back up slowly a few minutes later, I thought I was having a vision. She had descended as a single, was returning as a twin. There were two of her, as if she quite by accident had met her sister down there and now both were coming up together, or as if some kind of parthenogenesis had taken place down there and she duplicated herself. Then she stopped. Both girls looked at me. Where, when, how had she planned this surprise for me?

What a gift! Two Marias. She had told me she had a sister, but never mentioned she was a twin. Twinship has always fascinated me, in real life and in literature. But then she rose up one more step to the floor and her twin vanished. As if a stage mist had been blown in and made one disappear. But which one remained, Maria or her twin?

At the table, I asked her about her missing twin.

"You silly creature," she said. "Didn't you see the mirror on the wall?"

"No. But then, how come it's the mirror image that's here now, eating voraciously, while your twin I could swear went down the stairs again?"

"She had to pee too," Maria was quick to reply.

•

"Okay, okay, okay," Figaro said. "Thanks for the details. Can I interest you in one of our specialty mirrors while you watch the ceremony? We have one where only you can see yourself but no one else. Or vice versa, everyone can see their reflection except you."

I didn't answer.

"Come. Everyone," Figaro called out. "We're going to see a marionette show that's going to be like an overture to an opera. It's the overture for the special ceremony that follows.... Come, all of you, come back here where the platform is."

The lights dimmed. The girls stopped working and they and the customers gathered in the back.

"Soon you'll see. You'll see soon. You'll soon see," said Figaro.

By the rear wall, a little black curtain parted and a small stage appeared. I couldn't tell if it was a slideshow or a TV screen or if there were real marionettes up there.

Judging by the names, Giuseppe and Gina and Giovanni, the marionettes acted out a Napolitan story about a young married woman whose husband had lost interest in her. Meanwhile, she's studying art at an institute and meets a young artist to whom she's attracted. She invites herself over to his house. They embrace each other passionately and the curtain falls.

I was watching Maria watching the show. As the action proceeded, she leaned back in her chair and stiffened. Stretched out like a board. It reminded me of the way she stiffened just at buildup before letting go and, like the mystics of old, summoning Oh God, Oh God, Oh God at the height of her religio-physical ecstasy. It confirmed for me that the bed, not the foxhole, is atheism's greatest enemy, verifying Goethe's pithy bon mot: "No woman is an atheist when she's horizontal."

That was the end of the show. Figaro then summoned Maria over to one of the chairs. None of the girls resumed work. I stood at a distance.

As if rehearsed, one of the girls asked, "How do you do it, Figaro?"

"It's because I'm a barber, a surgeon, snoop, mind-reader, backbiter, double-dealer, prestidigitator, legerdermainiac, matchmaker, magician, and dispenser of magical lotions, notions, and oceans of potions."

Everyone gathered near Maria's chair, where she sat covered with a white protective cloth. Figaro, following Biblical procedure, began to dishevel her long hair, throwing it here and there, this way and that. Then he gave Maria a glass full of some transparent liquid.

"Drink it."

I thought Maria would refuse, would back out. But she sniffed it, raised it hesitantly to her mouth. Figaro didn't say what was in the glass and Maria didn't ask. To me it seemed I was watching a film from a distance.

Maria took a sip and said, "I don't taste anything. What's going to happen next?"

Figaro did not reply.

I saw Maria looking at herself in the mirror.

"My face looks the same," she said. "My eyes are not bulging. My belly isn't swelling. My thighs are not falling away. So maybe, maybe I'm innocent after all."

And I whispered to myself, "You're innocent. Of course you're innocent. In my book, you're not guilty of anything."

Figaro must have heard me—not the words, just the mumble—and he shouted, "Shh! No talking during the ceremony." And then he began his quick, soft chant.

He spoke in a language I, we, didn't understand. It sounded like English, had its rhythms, sounds, and intonations, but I couldn't understand a word. The words seemed to be tilted at a forty-five-degree angle. I saw Maria tilt her head down to the left. I too in sympathy, standing in the back, did the same.

And Figaro, seeing Maria doing this, also tilted his head, assuming she'd absorb the words better that way. This seemed to help, for when he spoke now, the words, the sentences, although jagged and maimed, at least were recognizable English.

"One spreads the lie, one spreads the lie, one and one and one and two and one and three, one after the other. Another spreads the lie, sows the lie, until the lies get darker and mix and mingle, ming and springle, sprink and mixel with other lies and poison, and you drink the potion and more lies come out and more deception, which leads to accusation and self-incrimination and excoriation, on and on until all of this seeps into your hair, all of it..." and Figaro came close to her, his face changed, looking like a demon, about to swallow her, and he shouted, "which now must come off…"

And from behind his back he pulled out a pair of scissors so huge they looked like hedge-clipping shears.

I had to restrain myself not to jump up and shout, *Don't let him do it*, but I sent Maria a silent message. *Don't let him*, I prayed.

Those big shears unnerved Maria. Just as Figaro's face almost touched hers, Maria leaped up, threw off the white cloth, which floated like a cloud and landed elsewhere, and screamed:

"Stop! Stop! Don't touch me. Give me those shears and I'll clip *your* hair."

And then Figaro, his personality changed, said calmly:

"You're innocent. You passed the test."

"How do you know?" Maria asked.

"Because you jumped up. If you were guilty, you'd have let me cut your hair. Only the guilty women let me guillotine their hair. Congratulations. You passed the test."

We both left separately and met at the car.

In the car Maria began pummeling me lightly, beating me gently with her fists.

"What are you doing? Stop it!"

"You rat. You did this purposely."

"What? What are you talking about?"

"The marionette show. You set it up."

"I don't know what you're talking about. I didn't even know there was going to be a show."

"You knew. About a girl who's promiscuous. Like me."

"Stop it. You passed the test."

"I didn't. Figaro just wanted me to feel good."

"I didn't see your belly swelling up."

"It was just plain seltzer water he gave me."

"Plenny women swell up from that."

"You arranged it."

"Will you stop? You're not making any sense. I didn't even know who Figaro was before you told me."

"Do you swear? No, cancel that. I still remember the invective that followed."

"I swear I won't swear no more. Come, let's go. It's been a long day. By the way, what made you jump up from the chair when he was about to clip you? I was sending you a silent message, *Don't let him do it.*"

"You know what rattled me? It wasn't the disheveled hair that frightened me. And not the drink, the supposedly bitter brew, the waters of bitterness, which was just plain old soda water. It wasn't even the shears. What got me was his wild jabbering, his nonsensical patter, the wild look in his eyes, as if *he* had been affected by the drink."

"Well, I'm glad you jumped up. It would have been a pity to lose that gorgeous hair."

Driving home, Maria said, "I always wondered if there are any post-Biblical stories about the adultery test that shed some light on the ceremony. In other words, if it was ever actually done."

"I know of one. In Jewish folklore, I think it's in the Midrash, there's this story about a woman who took the test about two thousand years ago. It's about twin sisters who try to outwit the test. One twin who was accused of adultery admitted to her sister that she was guilty and afraid of drinking the bitter waters. Her twin sister offered to substitute for her. She drinks the water and obviously passes the test. Nothing happens to her. Then when she comes home, her adulterous sister is so pleased and grateful, she embraces her sister and kisses her on the lips and at once falls to the floor dead."

Maria was silent. She didn't like to hear about such punishment.

"When we get back home," I said, "you'll make me a cup of tea, okay?"

"It's not tea you want, but it's only tea you're going to get. My mind is made up. I'm through with adultery."

28

MARIA TO KOL NIDREI (VERSION A)

A FEW DAYS PASSED before I saw Maria again.

"You won't believe this," Maria said, beaming, "but guess where I went last Friday night."

"What was last Friday night?" I said cagily. I think I knew what she was getting at.

"Oh, you must know."

"From my point of view or yours?" I asked her.

"Yours."

"Kol Nidrei night." I looked at her. Felt my mouth opening in surprise. "No!"

"Yes," Maria said. "Yes yes yes. I went to a shul in Brookline on Yom Kippur night."

"What? You? To shul? To a synagogue?"

"Yes. To a synagogue."

"Why? Whatever for? Were you agog with sin?"

"I wanted to. I wanted to experience what Jews experience. After my mony cerephony at Figaro's, I wanted the real thing. True atonement...didn't you go?"

"No. Not this time."

"Don't you ever pray?"

"Yes. Sometimes."

"For what?"

"For laughter. Since I rarely laugh, I ask Him for the ability to laugh and make others laugh...and since it's an unusual request, it gets His attention."

"Has it helped?"

"Not a bit."

"Why didn't you go to shul on Yom Kippur night?"

"I don't like confessing. And anyway, I have nothing to confess."

"I thought all Jews go to shul on Kol Nidrei night."

"Plenny stay home...Did you go to an Orthodox or Conservative shul?"

"I'm not sure. Maybe Conservative."

"And how did you handle it? You can't read Hebrew. Didn't you have problems following the text?"

"Nope. I had a Siddur with an English translation, and the gabbai or caretaker announced the pages."

"Did you like it?"

"I loved it. I was very moved being with all these Jews on the holiest night of the year. And all those different beautiful melodies. Especially that haunting Kol Nidrei. And the entire congregation knowing all of them. I could have floated up to Heaven listening to all those moving melodies. And it was impressive, thrilling, seeing the entire congregation beating their breasts as they confessed their sins. And I joined them, confessing my sins, and it was almost an epiphany for me. I felt purified, praying with a people whom my God thought of as His people....And everybody in shul so religious. If I were a Jew, I would be an observant Jew."

"Come on a Tuesday morning."

"Why?"

"Then you'll see what the shul attendance is really like. Probably fifteen men, not two hundred and fifty."

"You mean these people don't show up every day ?"

"No, these are the twice-a-year Jews. At least most of them. Rosh Hashana and Yom Kippur. And that's it."

"But you know, that doesn't make any difference to me. What I experienced, I experienced. And it was very moving. Only thing I missed is hearing the shofar."

"Not on Yom Kippur...The shofar is blown on Rosh Hashana, during services. And at the end of the Yom Kippur prayers at night, to signal the conclusion of the holy day."

"Oh my. I would have loved to have heard the shofar. As a clarion call to repentance. To reform."

"Okay, enough talking. Come here."

"I am here. What do you think, I'm there?"

"I mean *here* here. On my lap."

"I'll sit on your lap. But we're staying in the living room."

"I want to stretch out with you. On the bed."

"No. I can't. No more."

"You've become Orthodox. Ultra. Soon you'll wear a wig."

"No. I realize now that what I have done is wrong." And she began quoting from the Yom Kippur service. "'For the sins we have committed by being promiscuous. For the sins we have committed by being lascivious. For the sins we have committed by illicit sexual relationships.'"

"So you go to shul on Yom Kippur night and actually reform your ways. What are you, crazy Jewish?"

"No. Sane Christian. Very Christian. And those Hebrew words. Listening to those Hebrew words, I felt closer to the Hebrew-speaking Jesus."

"He didn't speak Hebrew. He spoke Aramaic. Before he was crucified he said, it's right there in your New Testament you read twenty-five hours a day, he said, '*Eli, Eli, lama sabatani*?' That's Aramaic. 'My God, my God, why have you forsaken me?' Had he spoken Hebrew he would have said, '*Lama azavtani*.'"

"How do you know this?"

"I was there."

"What were you doing?"

"Holding the nails."

"You're terrible," Maria said, kind of admiringly. "Anyway, those Hebrew words of the Yom Kippur prayers drove my errant Christianity, my forgotten-by-the-wayside morals, home to me…Why're you laughing? Cackling? That's not nice."

"Only a goy would take Kol Nidrei night seriously. No Jew actually reforms after Yom Kippur. Reforming after Yom Kippur! You gotta have a *goyishe kop* to do that. Relax. Don't take those words so seriously."

"But I have. I do. They struck home. I feel His eyes are on me."

"His eye is on the sparrow. So how can he be looking at you? He's not cross-eyed."

"I'm telling you, I feel His eyes on me."

"Looking doesn't count. Where are his hands?"

For a moment she was quiet. As I had expected her to be. She suffered my slings and arrows without contumely. Then she surprised me with:

"Sarcasm isn't an expression of intellection. Neither is contemptuous or arrogant language. Or scornful insolence. Or insult. All of which is contumeliousness of the first order. Number one. Number two: you sound like you're an inside-out anti-Semite…i.e., an anti-Christite. If I would say nasty things about your belief and faith and practices the way you do about mine, you'd call me an anti-Semite."

"I'm not anti-Christian. I'm just being gently contumelious with my favorite *goya*. Even though she doesn't paint or make canned beans."

I held my chin, thinking how to phrase what I wanted to tell her.

"Look, this is what I want to say. You know, human beings love resolution. You know what a scale is?"

"Yes. Fish have it."

"Not that scale."

"On which you get weighed?"

"Not that either. Think music," I said.

"I should have known. Up and down the scale."

"Exactly. When you play seven notes, C to B, and stop, that's how I feel with you. There's no resolution. The scale is not complete until you play the eighth note, the C again. It's like climbing up the ladder to the next-to-last rung and then, instead of going up to the last rung, you turn around and go back down."

"So you want resolution?"

"Yes, Maria, I do."

"Okay. My resolution is: no more sex."

What a turn of events, I thought. I go to shul only briefly on Yom Kippur night, but she, a Christian, goes for the entire Kol Nidrei service, on the holiest night of the year for Jews, and in an instant learns moral behavior and actually repents, paying attention to words that for most Jews go in one ear and out the other. What a fix! Instead of being screwed in a normal fashion, I'm screwed by Yom Kippur prayers.

"Okay. Then just sit next to me and let me put, like this, my arm around you."

"You mean you're accepting what I'm saying?"

"I too am moved by your Jewishness, your Christianness, your Christian Jewishness, your Jewish Christianness. Put your head on my shoulder. Good, like this."

"You don't know how much I appreciate your acceptance of my feelings."

I didn't want to scare Maria off. Especially after Yom Kippur. But I was biding my time. Walking softly. Like a Katz. For I knew her neo-virginity would not last long. So I made a pretense of complying with her wishes. Just stroking her hair and arms and holding her close to me. Could it be, I wondered, could it be that she was what she was because of her name? That one's name is one's fate? Could a certain name draw you in a certain direction like a magnet? That her personality would have been different had she been named Carol or Gwendolyn? If you're a Maria or a Kristin, it's going to have some kind of effect, because maybe a name sets you on a certain destined course in life. Especially with a family name like Christiansen. If you're called Maria or Christopher, the walls in the corridors become narrower, and you're guided—you can't help it, you cannot resist—along a certain path.

And maybe because she lived such an insular life, she was able to focus all her attention on Jesus. She might as well have lived on an island. In all the days I was with her, no sister, no parent, no relative ever called. Not even a friend. Only agencies to discuss a possible job.

I didn't press her for two weeks. As if I forgot about sex. But gradually, day by day, each day very gradually, a little more and more, we stretched out on the sofa, as in days of old, and she began to return my kisses. Still I did not press her. We stayed in the living room, on the sofa. She did not hear the word "bedroom" pass my lips. But again, moving slowly, stealthily as a Katz, I forcefully restrained myself, for I knew if I pushed too hard I might lose her.

One morning—after two weeks of modest romancing, as if a plank were between us, as you read in old medieval fabliaux, or as though we were kissing through a veil—when I passed my hand down, sort of innocently, as though I were out for a little stroll, toward her knee as I stopped for a rest on her crotch, as I once did in days of old, through the thick jeans I once again received a silent, beneficent message. My little Yom Kippur nun was no longer the cold chaste moon; my nun was now, again, yes, hurray, hosanna and hallelujah, my little nun was once again a sizzling sun.

I couldn't wait for the Kol Nidrei syndrome to wear off. Down with drome, up with syn. Out with gogue, in with syn.

Nevertheless, I knew she could turn on a dime, reverse herself in an instant. So I decided it was time to use extraterrestrial help.

No no, not prayer. A different type of help.

29

THE REFORM
(VERSION B)

= John, here's a different version of my brother's Maria/Kol Nidrei chapter. With a fascinating twist....Guess where the protagonist and Maria are.

•

Yes, we were in the bedroom. Again. Patience rewarded. In the bed.

She bit her lips, crossed herself and then her legs, and panted, "Stop!" her face ecstatic, like St. Theresa pierced, in the Bernini sculpture. "No...I can't...I won't do it...no more!"

I saw black. I saw red. I saw a gray wall of swirling emptiness. I saw ice out of Dante's Hell. Ice so cold its edges flamed. I don't know what surfaced first and most. Disbelief. Anger. Shock. Feelings turned inside out and upside down.

"Now? *Now* you shout Stop? At this point? What's wrong with you? Are you out of your mind?" I raged.

She drew a deep, slow breath. Her temperate tone surprised me. "I have to withstand temptation. To reform. And I thank God I succeeded."

My head was spinning. Seeing fire and ice. But I managed to say:

"But you failed."

"I did?" And you should have heard the innocence in her suddenly girlish voice and in her big—what color did I say her eyes were? "How?" she wanted to know.

"By failing me."

Maria thought about my words. As if we were having a friendly debate. Some debate, the two debators, me and her, lying next to each other naked. The frustrater and the frustratee.

"I had to reform," was her considered reply.

"To lure me? Tease me? Then deny me? What in heaven's name has gotten into you?"

"I went to shul."

"What? You? To shul?"

"Yes."

"What does *that* have to do with *this*?"

"You'll see," Maria said.

"When did you go?" I muttered. But even before she began to reply, I knew. I knew deep in my gut, even though it wasn't yet articulated, I sensed the entire scenario as if some painter had lightly brushed the information over my skin.

And she began singing a familiar Jewish melody which, like magic, like a lullaby, like a draught of a potion, calmed me. I had never before heard her singing, and right on tune, with a fine soprano.

"Where did you get that?"

"I learned it."

"You know what that melody is?"

"Of course. The Kol Nidrei."

"Where did you learn it?" I asked. As if I didn't know.

"On Yom Kippur night. A few days ago. The chazzan chanted it three times, with the congregation humming along, so it was easy. Did you go to Kol Nidrei? I shouldn't even ask. Of course you went. What Jew doesn't go?"

"Yes. I went. But plenty Jews don't." But I didn't tell her I came only to hear that haunting five-hundred-year-old melody. Then I left before the breast-beating communal confession. But I didn't tell her that either.

Still, I held her. Despite what she did to me, I held her. I should have gotten up and left, but I didn't. I held her. Held her next to me. She didn't slip away and get demurely dressed, turning away from me, or ask me to look the other way, which I certainly would not have done. We were touching, knee to knee, chest to breast, almost nose to nose. What a crazy reform! A reform like this has never been seen before.

One would have thought that, after absolutely and resolutely resisting temptation, she'd get up and put her clothes on. And of course turn around, on her modest high horse, with malice aforethought, as she hooks on her bra. But no. She remained. I minded it and I didn't mind. I understood but didn't understand. But I realized one thing. I realized that Maria was totally, absolutely and resolutely, off the wall.

I don't know why but my fury abated. Maybe because she did not demonstratively run away from me but kept holding me. In retrospect, viewing the scene objectively, as though it did not happen to me, seeing what she had done—we were about to enter each other—anyone else would have pushed her away, gotten up, dressed and walked out, reveling in his dignity. But instead I lay there. I too was off the wall—who needs dignity when you're holding a naked Maria?—and asked her why she went to the synagogue on Yom Kippur.

"Because I wanted to. I wanted to experience what Jews experience on that holy night. And I wanted a true atonement after that phony Figaro scenario."

Maria began to speak quickly, hyper, one thought tailing the next.

"I was very moved being with all these Jews on this night. You know, the rabbi in white. The chazzan in white. It was impressive, moving, thrilling, seeing the entire congregation beating their breasts as they confessed their sins in unison. And I joined them, confessing my sins. Beating my breast for my lustful behavior. It struck home."

"Like this?" And I beat her breast lightly with my fist.

"Stop making fun," she said. "It was almost an epiphany for me. A cathartic experience. I felt purified, praying with all the Jews."

My luck! This Christian gets religion in a shul. By now her nasty religious trick had killed all desire. I might as well have been a eunuch, singing my lament castratoically.

I regarded this unnatural situation I was in. First she turns on the fire in both of us, then she crosses herself. And double-crosses me. All this was a religious exercise for her. She used me, methodically. A kind of ass-backward seduction. A rape in reverse.

But Maria, Maria was as full of explanations as a pomegranate is of seeds.

"You see, I'm afraid if I don't control myself totally, I'm going to go the other way."

"You mean become promiscuous?"

"Yes."

"Spell it."

"No."

"In other words, you're going to fuck every man in sight."

"Yes. That's what I'm afraid of."

"And who says every man in sight will want to fuck you?"

"That's their problem."

"You think you have that propensity?"

"I might. And I'm not spelling that, either."

"And then maybe even lose your amateur status and turn pro? Become a whore?"

"Who knows? But I want to be on the safe side. I'm like the sixteen-year-old girl who says I'm afraid if I start I'll never be able to stop. One never knows the dark shadows that lurk within oneself."

"Have a little faith. Get thee to a nunnery."

"That's exactly what I'm afraid of," Maria said, looking me in the eye.

"What do you mean?"

"Don't you know what Hamlet meant when he said those words to Ophelia?"

"No."

"It means go to a whorehouse," Maria explained.

My silence was an angry, rock-heavy, seething silence.

Then Maria spoke and put her hand on my face.

"I had to stop," was her feeble excuse, using her own brand of logic double threaded through an invisible needle, "even though you may not be married, even though I suspect you are."

"And what if I am married?"

"Then I'm committing adultery," she said.

"But it's not adultery if *you're* not married."

"Then what is it?"

"Delicious," I said. "And I've told you seven hundred seventy-seven times I'm not married." And I pressed her tight to me. "So let's to it."

"Not so fast. Even if you're not, *I'm* not married, and certainly not to you. So it's fornication. The promiscuity, the illicit passion, I vowed to stop."

"So I'm screwed if I am married, screwed if I'm not."

"In a manner of speaking. And even if you're not married, there's something married about you."

"Like I have horns, right?"

"Right. Like I'm screwing your wife and putting horns on you." Then she became serious. "I learned something that Yom Kippur night and it hit home. A sin unconfessed and unrepented is a sin constantly committed."

"That's good," I said. "Very profound. I didn't know you were a profundist."

"Did you know I was good?"

"Yes. Up and down."

"I don't get it."

"You're good in two ways. Standing up, you're good ethically. Except today. And lying down, you're good sexually. Except now."

"It's not me that's profound," Maria admitted. "That line was the rabbi's. It was in his Kol Nidrei sermon, which affected me deeply. If you don't repent, it's like you're sinning constantly. Repeating the same sin again and again. It makes a lot of sense."

"At which Jesuit seminary did this purveyor of relentless guilt get his rabbinical degree?"

"Don't mock. Sermons sometimes do touch the heart and make people change their ways. The rabbi also said something else that was very powerful that I took to heart. He said that true atonement and reform, as stated in the Talmud, occurs, you know, when one is placed in the very same situation of temptation and then resists the temptation to sin. Like a cashier who regrets taking money from the till and requests a different position in the shop. He shouldn't do that. He's supposed to continue working as a cashier but totally resist temptation to help himself to money in the drawer. Same thing, I concluded, with sex. You're supposed to place yourself, you know, in the same situation you were in before, but now you have to be strong and say, *No, I won't do this again.*"

You jerk, I thought. You dunderhead. "With the cash register," I said, "there's the cashier and there's the cash. Inanimate. Without feelings. But with sex, with sex it takes two. There's a human being, a partner involved. So where's my role in all this?"

"You don't have any role in this. It's totally my call."

That selfish attitude blew my mind.

"Uh-huh," I say. "Okay. You're the fuck*er*. So it's your call. But me, I'm the fuck*ee*, and he's got a word to say too. But no, he's suddenly out. Like an old dishrag."

And then it hit me what she'd done. Using my body for her own nefarious, sanctimonious agenda.

"In order to expiate, to cleanse yourself, to atone, to reform, you violated a whole laundry list of "For the sin we have committed…" I shouted. "Some religious epiphany. Some catharsis. You used me. Teased and seduced me to the point of entry. You showed no regard for my feelings, you who worry about a tiny canary."

And then I jumped off the bed and headed for her tight little kitchen where she had lately hung the cage so that the bird wouldn't witness her lascivity.

But Maria sprung up too and began yelling, no, screaming. I'd never heard her shout before. Never even heard her raise her voice. "Help! Someone! Stop him! He's going to kill my canary."

She ran around me and blocked my path. She spread her hands like Jesus on the cross.

"Don't you dare touch it! What did it do to you? What I did is my fault, not his—hers. What do you want from that poor little creature?"

I pushed her aside. "I'm not going to touch it. Even if I wanted to, I don't how to kill a canary. I'm not a canary *shokhet.* Relax. Do you think I'm going to hurt it?"

"I don't know. I've never seen you so angry."

"Have patience. Calm down. I'm not angry yet. I'm just getting there."

I took the cage—the tiny bird, scared out of its wits, began dropping its droppings all over the place and started singing, off tune—and carefully carried it back to the bedroom. I stood on the bed. First Maria sat on the bed, watching me warily, then she stretched out. She didn't cover herself with the sheet. I held the cage in one hand and waved the other.

"You have more sympathy, more concern for this little thing than you have for me."

I pointed. I gesticulated. I mimed. Then I put the cage on the floor, jumped back onto the bed, and stood up straight, calling down to her.

"You dumped me. I was dumped. Dumped at the height of loving. Dumped like a bag of trash."

"I didn't dump you," she said softly. And she rose and kissed the soft part of my neck next to my collarbone. "I had to do it for my spiritual health."

"And what about *my* spiritual health? My sexual health. My mental health. My psychological health. My metaphysical health. My emotional health...But your lust..." And I stopped. Oh, yes, I stopped for dramatic effect. It was a calculated pause. "...your lascivious, untrammeled lust for sinlessness, for purity, made you commit six other sins."

And I raised six fingers—unfortunately, I had to use two hands for this—I raised one finger after another, listing one sin after another, each time with a sharp forward movement of my hand, as if I were snapping a whip.

"You wanted to be free from, pure from, promiscuity, from unauthorized, forbidden carnality..." I stood straight on the bed, me as naked as she, as Adam and Eve in Eden, can you imagine how provocative, how desecratory it would have been had I been wearing a tallis, that's a prayer shawl, I can just hear the cries, *For shame! Scandalist! Scandalous! Shame on you*! As I pointed down at her I thumped my breast, listing the six sins, yea, the seven, no, eleven, she had been guilty of.

I felt like Isaiah or Jeremiah, righteously indignant, cataloguing a list of misdeeds, hurt, sore, upset. Used.

"'For the sin we have committed in dealing treacherously.' You have dealt treacherously. With me. 'For the sin we have committed in dealing duplicitously.' You have dealt duplicitously with me, leading me on just to prove to yourself your sanctimonious, your holier-than-thou ability to resist temptation. So you used me. Just like guys use girls you used me. 'For the sin we have committed with evil intent.' Your deed today was one of evil intent. Against me." My tone grew sharper, higher pitched. "'For the sin we have committed in acting callously. For casting off responsibility. For the sin we have committed by plotting against men.' Me! 'For the sin of sordid selfishness. For the sin we have committed with a confused heart.'"

I think my voice cracked. She must have thought I was about to break into tears. Her face darkened. I swear, I saw an umber shadow filling her cheeks, the skin of her face. Drops of perspiration stood out on her forehead. I was getting to her.

"You fooled. You seduced. You conspired. 'For the sin we have committed with lying words, in malice, with unclean lips, with secret planning.' Want more?"

As I preached to her, her face darkened even more. Her lips trembled while I dramatically pounded my chest with stronger and more forceful and more passionate blows until the room sounded as if a bass drum were being banged. Then, suddenly, the tears. I had never seen Maria cry.

"Stop it. You're hurting yourself. I'm sorry, Katz. I truly am."

And then she too began banging her chest and pleaded, "Come back. Come back. Come back next to me. Hold me."

At that moment, the beginning of this entire scene flashed before me. I came into her bedroom and lay naked next to her. Usually, I initiated everything. This time, she began. She began slowly, methodically, to unbutton my shirt, going about that seductio ad absurdum until her goal of ecstatic refusal was accomplished.

•

= Katz! I interrupted. = This is indeed a dramatic point. But the hero is naked already. What's with the shirt? There's a scribal error here.

= Oh, my God! You're right. My brother must have gotten so deep into righteous indignation, and me too, in retelling it, that he... me...I...we forgot important details. It's hard to unbutton a shirt on a naked body. Unless it's a zipper.

•

I obeyed. I came down from my preacher's pedestal and lay next to her. She put her arms around me and held me close. My hands were stiff at my sides. Asleep. Dead. How come, I thought, one day can be so good and another so awful? But at Maria's questioning look that said, *Well, where are your hands?*, I moved my arms and placed them around her waist and now both of us were locked in an affectionate embrace.

Maria was touched by my plosive words. She wasn't stupid. She saw my side. At least I imagined she did. And I began to warm to her again. And, against my inner wishes, I felt myself stirring. She pulled back an inch or two.

"Don't get any ideas. I mean it. Please consider me too. I want to be whole. I beat my breast with all the Jews and on that Yom Kippur night I felt myself Jewish, just like my lord is, and I recited 'For the sin we have committed with promiscuous behavior.' And I said 'we' for both of us, for me and you, for we both have done this. It was a very moving experience. At that moment, during that night, I felt like a Jew and regretted that I didn't have that marvelous four-thousand-year-old heritage. You're lucky, you."

You can always convert, I didn't tell her. I heard that "lucky" echoing in my ears until it sounded ridiculous, like the noises someone makes licking a lollipop.

"Very. Very lucky. My arch-Christian sweetie goes to a Kol Nidrei service on Yom Kippur that I didn't even go to..." It slipped out.

"You said you went."

"But I didn't stay till the end. She goes, I don't, and I end up screwed."

"Screwed one way; unscrewed another. Consider it a blessing." And Maria kissed me on the cheek as I held her, naked and chaste, next to me, drained of all desire.

I sat up. "Okay, since you're quoting the rabbi, I'll quote the rabbis. Plural. Of the Talmud. The formulators of the Jewish tradition. They taught that God favors the true penitent over one who is blameless, who never sinned at all. I.e., the truly penitent comes even closer to God than those who have never sinned."

"Then there's hope for me," Maria said. She hung onto every word I said. Every word I said was another lifeline drawing her closer to safety.

"Much. Much hope. And I have an idea of how we both can come even closer to God."

"Uh-oh. Let's hear what's coming."

"No joke. Why don't we both find grace with God by sinning lustfully together again? Then both of us will repent, and you and me, me and you, you and I, all six of us will find even greater favor in the eyes of God. I'm willing to do this for you, knowing how close you want to be to Him."

"That's so sweet of you. But I think this time I'll go it alone."

Then Maria, that big, overgrown baby, a nearly forty-year-old like a little girl, abruptly changed the subject and said enthusiastically:

"Look at my canary. You scared the poor little thing. Look at her shivering. Isn't she gorgeous? So cute and tiny, a tiny little living creature. I just love her. Tell me you don't love her."

"Okay. I don't."

"Why?"

"You just told me to tell you I don't love her. I'm just following orders."

"But you do love her, don't you?"

"Actually, I don't."

"Why? Just look at her."

Instead I looked at Maria enthusing over a little yellow bird with a big appetite—her only friend in this sad little apartment.

"It's nothing personal, Maria. I'm afraid she'll start loving me back. And I don't want to be screwed by a canary. Oh, the shame of it!"

The emotions that zigged through me were like a ride on a merry-go-round, on a painted plaster horse that bucks up and down, and then goes wild and slaloms in and out between the other fixed-in-place horses, dashing clockwise to the counter-clockwise canter of the carousel. First rage and disappointment surged through me; then I was whiplashed by her softness. I realized that what she did was not done out of malice. She didn't jump up and ask me to leave. Instead of getting up and dressing, she remained by my side, holding me, and tried to explain the reason for her wild behavior, calmly, quietly, even affectionately. And then, imagine, she even began to express her gratitude.

"Thank you, thank you. Thank you and, above all, Jesus for helping me. Saving me."

"What does Jesus got to do with it? It was the rabbi quoting the Talmud that did it. Thank him."

"But it was Jesus who inspired me to resist. I prayed to hHm and He answered me."

"In the synagogue? To Him?"

"No no no. Not in the synagogue. But I did, and I do, pray to Him. He answered me and gave me strength."

"Hallelujah! Son of a g...g...god! A new rival. And who gave me the strength not to explode?"

Maria was silent. She wanted to, I just know it; she wanted to say, Jesus, but held back. She had given me enough religion for one day.

With her still holding me, it was hard to jump up in a huff, put on my clothes, and run away. When Maria, and other girls, would tell me that God broke the mold when He made me, I didn't believe them. What's so unusual about me? But I can honestly say that He broke the mold when He created Maria.

"I didn't want to, I wasn't able, to correct you when you said before, I'm not doing this no more."

"Great!" Maria clapped her hands in joy. "So the Kol Nidrei mood has inspired you too. What a quick reform! Now we both see eye to eye."

"No no no. I'm correcting your grammar, Maria. I won't do this no more is wrong."

"It may be wrong grammar. But it's correct morality. In any case, it was a new thought. I'm not doing this...pause...then a short, interjectory phrase—No more! So now my grammar is as clean and pure as me."

"As I..."

"I'm glad you agree."

And then I decided to use my trump card. "What about your addiction to me? Remember?"

"I got a prescription to counter it. Double strength Niagara."

"Never heard of it. What kind of medication is that?"

"It makes your libido plummet," she said.

And I thought to myself, why is it my misfortune to meet a girl who at precisely the wrong moment cries out: "I hate sin! From now I'm going to do my best not to sin anymore." Why can't I meet a normally amoral girl who proudly declares:

"I love to sin. I'm crazy about sinning. I go to sleep thinking of sin. I dream, and in blazing color too, about sinning. First thing that pops into my head when I wake up is: I can't wait to start. Maybe even before ten. Today I'll begin to sin without even brushing my teeth. Sex and sin keeps me nice and thin."

That's the sort of girl I want. Normal. Without hangups. Who doesn't think of sex as sin. But thinks of them as twin. Who is not coated with pious Christianity like chocolate on a graham cracker. Who can honestly assert: "As a girl I enjoyed my girlhood. As a maiden I couldn't wait to lose my maidenhead. And now, as an adult, I'm nuts about my adultery."

•

It was then that I thought, now's the time to use some extraterrestrial help. No no, not prayer. A different kind of help.

I decided to go to Figaro's Femme Fatale Fricassee.

30

PREPARING THE DREAM POTION

THERE WAS SOMETHING EXTRAORDINARY about Figaro's beauty salon—I wonder if it still exists. Happiness and good cheer all over the place. The employees, on a perpetual high. Living in a Rossini or an Offenbach overture. Figaro himself, besides cutting hair with ballet-like gestures and floating with dance steps around his client, also sold, mixed them himself, he said, herbs and, to quote him, oceans of potions.

One Saturday, when I knew Maria wasn't due for another visit to the salon any time soon, I drove out to see Figaro. His eyes opened wide and his Italianate eyebrows went up to his forehead.

"With no appointment?" he said.

"I'm not here for a cut," I said, and I motioned him over to a quiet corner. "I need an herb. A potion."

"For what?"

"For a dream."

"To interpret a dream?"

"No. To make a girl dream the sort of dream I want her to dream."

He didn't ask me who the girl was and I wouldn't have told him.

"What kind of dream?"

"You mean you have potions sub-categorized into type of dreams?"

But Figaro either missed my joke or disregarded it.

"She can dream of success for you in business. She can dream of gaining self-confidence. She can dream that she loves you."

I knew Maria loved me, but that I did not tell him. Why should I share my intimate thoughts and feelings with a stranger?

"Or you can have her dream an erotic dream."

I didn't respond.

Figaro laughed. "Oho! So that's it. *L'elisir d'amore*. The elixir of love. Well, I don't hear you saying no, so I assume yes."

"It has to be soluble."

"Soluble."

"What I mean is, it shouldn't be visible."

"Be visible," Figaro said.

"No, on the contrary," I said, feeling a bit edgy. "Not be visible. The potion shouldn't be leafy, grassy, or have any particles that float or sink to the bottom of the cup like tea leaves. It has to melt, like instant coffee."

I half expected Figaro to say, *Instant coffee*. But he did not. While we were speaking he was opening and closing small wooden drawers, the sort you see in a carpenter's workroom, where each little drawer contains different-sized nuts, bolts, screws, or nails. He took some powder from one and sprinkled it on an apothecary's scale, muttering, "Eros and sex, sex and eros," either as a spell or as a prickly or snide comment directed at me, like a woman saying indignantly, *Men, you're all alike*, while struggling to quickly take off her pants.

He mixed the powders and placed them in a tiny envelope.

"Shall I label it?"

"No," I said. "I'll sniff it here."

We both laughed.

"Sprinkle it into her tea and she'll dream what you want her to dream."

I wanted to ask him a question, but I knew what his answer would be.

"It's safe, right?"

"Absolutely. It's only a mixture of extracts from various plants and herbs. Part of it is ground-up mandrakes, like, you know, love apples from the Song of Songs. Like the ones," Figaro continued, "that Reuben finds in the fields and brings to his mother."

What could be better? A biblical potion for someone who loves the Bible.

"And, anyway, would I keep, store, sell, even give away something that might hurt my friends?"

"Okay. Fine. I thought so. How much will it be?"

"Nonsense. It's yours. Take it."

"No no no. This is your business."

"It's just a teaspoon or so."

"I insist. You don't give haircuts for free."

"Listen to me. I know you. I'm giving the potion to you."

I inclined my head. "Please," I said. "Your generosity is making me uncomfortable. Tell me the price of the potion, and I will take it and go."

And Figaro answered me, saying, "Hear me out, this potion worth," and here he mentioned a reasonable sum, "what is that between you and me?"

I paid him. He hugged me and wished me luck.

"Wait. Before you go. Would you like to look at the new *Universal Dictionary of Neologisms*?"

"Actually, I got to run now. But what is it?"

"It's a dictionary that not only has newly coined words but also words not yet coined, in every single language in the world. Three thousand pages."

"Next time," I said. I marveled at the absurdity of it. A book that has neologisms in every language, even words not yet invented. I shook my head. Figaro was either pulling my leg or living in a dream world. Drinking his own potions.

31

GIVING IT - THE METRO POSTER SCENE

THAT NIGHT, AROUND 10 p.m., I came to Maria's apartment for a brief visit. Through the back door, via her little kitchen. She had just come back from work, looked exhausted. I didn't even hug her.

"Working till ten? Unconscionable. A violation of child labor laws. Take two aspirins and see your lawyer in the morning. You look bushed. Sit down. I'll make *you* tea. You always make it for me. This time, now, I'll make it."

I wondered if she could sense the tremor in my voice.

"That's so sweet," she said. Then she narrowed her eyes. "What's wrong? You look so funny."

Which made me even more nervous. But instead of replying, I made a face, crossed my eyes, stood on my tiptoes, and began crowing like a rooster, which made her laugh hysterically, and me relax.

In the dim kitchen, I did not turn on the light. I boiled water and prepared tea in one of her big mugs. A quick peek into the living room. She sat with her feet curled under her on the sofa, reading a book (I never saw a newspaper or magazine in her apartment). I took Figaro's little envelope from my shirt pocket and sprinkled the dream potion into the mug. So as not to make noise with a spoon, I used the top of my ballpoint pen to carefully stir the powder in the tea.

"Here. Sweet dreams."

"Aren't you having any?"

"No. Not thirsty."

"Want first sip?"

God, no! I almost shouted, afraid she would subject me to the tradition of king's taster.

"Uh-uh. No, thanks," I said, pleased nevertheless that she wanted to share her drink with me, a kiss by proxy.

Maria took the mug. Touched the side. "Ouch! Too hot. What did you put into it, fire?" Then she gave out a big yawn. "Set it on the side table. I'll drink it before I go to sleep."

Darn it! On this I hadn't planned. Maybe she would forget and go to sleep without it. Maybe she would decide not to drink it later. If the tea cooled down too much, she might just pour the brew down the drain. And I couldn't be too insistent and say, *Why don't you have it now? It will relax you*. For then she might say, *Okay, if you'll share it with me*.

We chatted a while. Half the time I looked at Maria, half at the untouched, unmoved, cup of tea, and half, surreptitiously, at my watch.

Then it was time to go.

"Gotta go. I'll see you in the morning?"

"What time? I leave for work at ten."

"Is 7:15 okay?"

"Fine," she said.

"Leave the back door open."

I liked, I loved the fact that she left the door open for me; I thought it a physical extension of that tender "Really?" of hers. It was an intimate, romantic gesture, even a shade illicit. She didn't appreciate the idea of neighbors on both sides of the street seeing she had a male visitor early in the morning. Neither did I. The parking lot in the rear of the complex offered more privacy. By using the back door, people would assume I was returning to my apartment from the refuse bin.

Before I left, I kissed her hair, held her forearm, slid my hand slowly, sensuously, down to her hand, clasped her fingers—I told you, I no longer feared, or paid attention to, her flawed ring finger—and said, "Good night."

•

At seven the next morning, I let myself into Maria's apartment and locked the door. Through the dark, little-used kitchen I walked into the living room. Didn't see the mug on the side of the table where she kept a few books. Good, I thought.

Maria liked her apartment. "It's nice, isn't it? Comfortable, cozy, right?" she would say. I agreed with her. What could I do? Comment on its dull, shabby look? The scruffed, colorless carpet, furnished by the landlord, was bare in spots. Her dull sofa and sad wine red easy chair were forty years old, about the same age as Maria. The walls needed painting. With the money she earned, she could have freshened the place up. But Maria claimed she didn't know where her money went. She hadn't balanced her checkbook in years.

The door to her bedroom was open. Maria was asleep, hadn't even heard me coming in. With her several pillows and folded and unfolded blankets scattered on her rumpled bed—poor, nay, pathetic stand-in for a man—it was hard to discern where she began and her bedding ended. I closed the door. In front of my nose swung three bras hanging on a hook on the verso side of the door. Wooden cubbies with sweat-shirts and slacks filled half a wall. It amazed me that she who could not stand closet or sliding doors open even half a centimeter tolerated all these open cubbies. The closet door was tightly shut. Maybe that's where she kept her skirts and dresses.

I slipped off my loafers and slid under the blanket. I put my arm around her head and brought her close to me.

"Hi," she said sleepily, in a contralto lower than her usual mezzo timbre. Cascaded an intimate melody from that soft and sexy "Hi," followed by "Good morning." Two words sweetly chanted in three notes. Now, eyes still closed, she turned to me and threw her right hand around my neck.

"Sleep well?" I asked, reveling in that warm, melodic welcome.

"Mmm," she hummed. "I had this fantastic dream...and I rarely dream."

Bless you, Figaro, I thought. Maestro Figaro. Bravo, Figaro. Figaro, la. Figaro, qua.

"Actually, a sexy dream." Still closed her eyes; on her lips an enticing, sleepy smile.

Seeing this, hearing this, sensing this, I decided to risk it and say:

"I'm hungry for you."

Still that dreamy, satisfied smile on her face.

"Well, say something. Say, I'm hungry for you too. I'm thirsting for you. I'm starving for you. I'm fasting for you. I'm slowing for you.

I'm longing for you. I'm shorting for you. Try I'm rooting for you, or even I'm neutral for you, but say something!"

But Maria kept her peace, held her silence. She just smiled, stroked my hair and my face, and pressed close to me. Then she said: "Do you want to hear the dream?"

"Sure. A wet dream, right?"

"Yeh, right," she said and laughed. Not her little off-center laugh, but a full and rounded laugh, a well-balanced laugh.

"Tell."

She opened her eyes but wouldn't say a word, the tease. My heart sank. I feared she wouldn't tell me her dream, and then what good was the potion? Meanwhile, as my left hand clasped her waist—it wasn't lost on me that I was holding her close and yet all I wanted was yester-night's dream—my right index finger traced a straight line along her spine. That gave her a special charge, I remembered. I had never seen anything like it. That touch made her tense up erotically. Ready for pleasure. Her rigid body became shaped like a bow. Maybe Maria did dream the dream I wanted her to dream, but still I could enhance the unpalpable with some palpating here and now. As we spoke I drew her heavy flannel Brandeis University nightshirt above her waist and held her naked back.

"Tell," I said softly. "I'm excited about your dream."

"Well, I guess it *was* the female equivalent of a wet dream."

"Was I in it? Was it me, Maria?"

Wait till you hear her reply. I often complained about how stingy Maria was with words of affection. But this one did the trick. She could have waited a moment to increase the tension. But she didn't. To my question, "Was it me?" she came right back with—

"Of course," Maria sang out. In mezzo. In soprano. In melodic delicioso.

I couldn't believe it. Was the potion working its magic already?

"Of course," was the aria that Maria aired.

Can I replicate that "Of course"?

Soon as I heard that "Of course," time was suspended, upend-ed, downended, plain ended. Time ascended, descended, as I compre-hended those two words said as one and sailed heavenward on a clock with no hands.

I can try and try but I'll never be able to imitate the glow of her inimitable, silken "Of course" that in just two syllables was otherspeaking for "Naturally! What did you expect?" And more. Those two syllables turned into three notes as the second word was chanted as "caw-orse". Play F, A, F in that order on the piano and you'll get the melody of her two words.

I can try and try but never in a million years will I be able to recreate that soft and warm and cozy electric current I had never sensed before. Up went my heart and I followed, holding the string to my balloon heart, smiling at the people below getting smaller and smaller. Up so high did I sail I looked down, yes, down at the stars that glittered and sparkled like the Eiffel Tower when it sprays light every hour on the hour after sunset.

Now I felt as if I had two Marias in my grasp, the Maria of now and the dream Maria, like the phantom twin Marias I had once seen in a Thai restaurant. Does holding both the physical and the metaphysical at once defy some natural law? Of course, I would never tell her how happy she had made me with those two words uttered as one. Those two words played as three delectable notes. Maria wasn't very sentimental, you know. Maybe that "Of course" was inadvertent, a kind of sleepy mutter. Maybe she didn't mean it to be so loving. It just popped out of her. But if it was the potion speaking, it sure packed a wallop.

Her almost breathless "Really?", whispered on a musical scale somewhere between an upbeat major key and the Jewish sadness of minor, when I said something in praise of her, that "Really?" uttered without even moving her lips, was a perfect match to her "Of course."

•

=John, here in the margin, my brother writes: "Perhaps use the paragraph below, which has a slight change of nuance." So here goes:

•

That from-the-heart "Of course" was one of the sweetest things I ever heard that reticent girl say. Yes, I keep dwelling on it because it meant a lot to me. Along with her breathless "Really?" chanted, sung, exhaled, with the faintest patina of incredulity, when I said something in praise of her, like how bright and witty she was, how adorable.

When I thought about it, analyzed it objectively, I suppose that velvet "Really?" of hers was another way of saying, "I love you," a kind of negative, solo, selfish, egotistical way of saying it. Expressing it, yes, but not saying the words. Left-handed, ass backwards mirror image. Upside down and inside out too. How limited is language when articulating the nuances of love.

•

And added to that short list of noncommittal sweet words was another confessive line of hers. You see, I rarely ever called Maria by her name. Change that to hardly ever. Maybe on a subliminal level the sound "Maria" was so chillingly Christian to me. For a long time I couldn't say it. Somehow, the name's theological implications, you know, the alleged mama of god, got stuck in my throat. Can you imagine if her name had been Kristin, Christa, or Christina? Months and months had passed before I used her name for the first time, for when I once called her Maria, said softly as I embraced her, she noticed and said blissfully, "Do you realize it's the first time you called me Maria? You never say my name."

"I know, Charlotte," I said at that time. "And this is also the first time I've called you Charlotte."

"I love it when you say my name," she whispered, uttered it so tenderly and slowly, it sounded to me like a declaration of love. "I never hear you say my name."

How hard it must have been for her to come out with that nice line, but say those words she did, unhesitatingly, even though she may have regretted them when and if she ever replayed that warm, revelatory line later in her mind, which started with "I love" but lacked that cosmic third word—which never slipped forth from her lips. That was the closest she ever got to saying she liked me, when she said, "I love it when you say my name."

Analyzing it, that's me, the analyzer of words, the splicer of phrases, thinking about that line later, I realized it reflected her me-oriented attitude. *She* loved it. *Her* name. True, the word "you" (meaning me, Katz) was there too. But perhaps only for syntactical ease, for grammatical felicity. It's awkward to say, *I love it when my name is said.* Awkward and insulting.

But, basically, it was I, me, myself centered. She didn't say, *I love to say your name, Katz.* Or, *I love it when you hold me.* But in the tender music of her soft-spoken words, like rose petals floating, she cleverly gave the impression of tenderness and love without actually saying the words I wanted to hear.

Then I reflected on it and thought, You know what? I'm not being fair to her. Too harsh. I'm analyzing too deeply, applying tendentious speculation to make my point. In retrospect, her whispered, "I love it when you say my name," was honestly and deeply felt.

So let's go back to that melodious "Of course," which she said so merrily, so graciously, so quickly and naturally, without hesitation, without planning or guile, as if to say, *What a question*! I think the word "alacrity"—she'd love that word—fits in here perfectly. She said that tender "Of course" with such alacrity, so spontaneously, I could have sworn we were man and wife, exchanging dreams on a morning when neither of us has to go to work and we can enjoy another relaxed hour in bed.

It may not be proper to mix theology with amour, even though cults have been doing that for centuries, including Jews with kabbala and mysticism, but when Maria uttered that "Of course" of hers, an ecstasy, an almost numinous ecstasy swept over and through me. A thrill of joy. Just like on Yom Kippur night, when I hear that soul-stirring melody of Kol Nidrei. And thinking of Yom Kippur, I remind myself that's why I am here, now, to attempt to reap the benefits of the magic dream potion, to reverse Maria's Yom Kippur reform that elevated religion and deleted me.

Given how warmly she received me, I wondered if that potion was already working. Dear Figaro, maestro, master, wizard! How did you do it? I seem to be getting what I wanted even though I used underhanded tactics.

"Of course", she said with multi-toned intimacy, when I asked her if I was in her dream. I was tempted to say "polyphonic" before and still want to say it to describe the many layers of loving music in her two words, as if we'd been lovers for years. I know that more than one voice is needed for polyphony, but maybe I too was singing in, at, of, above, between, below—there's that echo of that John Donne poem again—with her voice, singing along with the invisible trope of that efficacious dream potion I had given her the night before in that tea I hadn't seen her drink.

No no. I'm not going to declare she loved me, but, then again, how can I not say it? Even though she didn't say it. I can't imagine her saying anything bordering on those three golden words that all girls love to hear. But she said. She said it. She said it in two words. Maybe one.

After that Edenic "Of course" I buried my mouth—it was an automatic, almost instinctual gesture—in her neck, the soft part just below her ear and above her shoulder. A long, arduous kiss.

"Tell it, Maria," I said. "Tell the dream."

"Okay," was her whispered response. I loved that whisper too. Perhaps it was I who had drunk the potion. Perhaps I too, like Chaucer's Cressida should also say, half dizzy with love, stumbling, smitten, staggering, when she sees Troilus for the first time: "Who hath given me drinke?"

Now Maria pressed up to me, knee to knee, hip to hip, waist to waist, breast to chest.

And my pants still on.

Speaking her dream—my dream; yes, Figarissimo, my dream—speaking it into my ear.

"Listen to this," Maria says.

"How can I not listen with your lips whispering 's'-laden sibilant syllables into my ear? I can shut my eyes to not see, but unlike a moose, I don't have flaps to close my ears."

"Do mooses really…?"

"It's not mooses," I said. "It's meese. Goose, geese. Moose, meese."

"Do meese really have ear flaps?"

I put, I pressed, my index digit on her lips.

"On with the dream!"

"Okay." She took a breath. "Remember that travel book of yours?"

"Sure. Katz's one and only. Published years ago. The one you remembered with your perfect pitch for title and authors. The one with which you guilefully and shamelessly lured, seduced me into your abode, ostensibly for me to sign it…and I've been your unwilling sex slave ever since."

"Shh. Listen. Here's the dream."

32

MARIA'S DREAM

"IN MY DREAM," MARIA said, "you've written a novel and it's been published."

"Oh, may it be a reality, not a dream. From your mouth to God's—the Jewish one, of course, who doesn't gad about seducing voluptuous married virgins who are named after you—to God's ears."

"Not only that, but your book is a sexy love story that's been translated into French and it's being advertised all over the place because it's such a big hit. And on the cover is a stunning naked woman with full-size boobs."

"Wow! As big as yours?"

"Bigger. No, let me think."

"No thinking! Look!" And I lifted her nightshirt and let her look.

Maria looked bemused. "Well, maybe the same size. But mine are nicer."

"That's what I like. Self-confidence. Yes, yours *are* much nicer… Okay, let me have a go at those twenty-five-year-old tits."

"What?" she screamed. "They're thirty-nine. Almost forty."

"No. You got them at fourteen, and so they're twenty-five. Now watch. Look. See the demonstration."

And I demonstrated. Step by step. First, I ated. I rated. I trated. Then I strated, monstrated, and emonstrated. Then, finally, I demonstrated by diving under the cover and kissing her nipples, holding the right breast with one hand and kissing the left, then holding her left breast while nuzzling the right, and then holding both heavy boobs with two hands while she sings "Mmmm…" and then ascends the scale, jumping from consonants to the vowel cries I approve of and adore, "Ah" and "Ohh." She knows my line, "Now we're getting somewhere. Sailing from consonants to vowels."

The taste of those luscious breasts, one of my supreme gustatory experiences, is like a dream taste, a taste sweetened by the potion that prompted her dream, which in turn enchanted her to respond to me freely, following her instincts, inclination, desire, following her heart, her affection, unshackled now from Jesus and her New Testament morality which had cast an iron spell over her. She knew she had to, was destined to, come to me but she couldn't find her way. Until now, infused with magic, with potion, with compass that set her on the right path.

Now we were in a different world. Floating in a magic dreamland, a ride you can get only in dreams, where there is no gravity and when you speak you speak in color. And the taste of her soft skin, the suppleness of her full breasts, and her unrestrained ecstatic cries as I kissed the unexplored territory between her breasts, those cries could only have come from a fairytale land or from a wishful dream dreamt during a happy twilight sleep.

And I'm listening to her singing Ahs and Ohs, absorbing the vowels we all know, and then hearing vowels, non-consonantal notes that haven't been heard before, for from her lips flowed in delectable contralto notes and sounds and words that linguists, philologists, and the editors of the *Universal Dictionary of Neologisms* haven't even dreamed of.

"After an objective comparison test," I told her, "I must regretfully conclude that yours are nicer. I don't care what the dream cover of my book is like. Yours are much nicer and far more delicious. I'd call it a memorable culinary adventure. Sorry, I interrupted you."

"It's all right," Maria said pleasantly. "I forgot to tell you, did I tell you where we are in my dream?"

"No. Where?"

"We're in Paris. At a Metro station."

"Super! Which one? I love the Paris Metro. When I go to Paris, I don't even check into a hotel. I just spend all my time in the Metro. Is it Pigalle? Or my favorite station, La Motte-Piquet-Grenelle?"

"How should I know? I've never been to Paris."

"But it's your dream."

"Will you listen? You want to hear the dream but you keep interrupting. We're at this Metro station and we see this big poster, and I mean it's huge, about six feet high…"

"You mean taller than me?"

"Yeah. Six feet high and about three feet wide. It's the cover of your book and your name is on the bottom and the title is on the top."

"What's the title? What's the title?"

"I didn't pay attention. It's your book, for goodness's sake, you wrote it, you should know the title."

"But it's your dream. Think."

Maria closed her eyes as if re-entering the dream. "Oh, now I remember. It was called *Journal of an Unfaithful Wife.*"

"Not sexy enough," I said. "Too lumpy. In French they'll probably call it *Journal d'une femme adultere*. But I'm going to call it *Katz*. This way my name will be on top and on bottom."

"Fine. Now listen. The poster, this huge ad of your book in this Metro station features a very handsome, elegant, and attractive woman with glossy black hair. Her hand is upraised as if holding onto a post that is not visible, so that's why her amazing full breasts are uplifted. And the poster is causing quite a stir. People are stopping to look."

"The pigs. Perverts. They probably jumped the turnstile too. Why don't they go out and buy a copy of the book instead?"

"Passengers crowd around," Maria continued, "to stare at this unusual poster. And I see a mother walking by with her gaping, pop-eyed little boy, about six or seven, and she covers his eyes and tells him not to look. And then I have an idea. The Metro comes. People board. Now no one is around. The poster is at the end of a series of poster ads for cars, hair lotions, films, clothing, soda, liquor, and I see a little niche, a door, that leads evidently to an area behind the posters. We go into a narrow dark space and pull the door shut. I take a pencil from my bag and poke two little holes…"

"Ouch! I hope not where the breasts are."

"No, silly. On two sides. So we can watch the people looking at the poster unobserved and gauge their reaction to that huge ad. But you stand behind me in that narrow alcove and I feel you rubbing up against me. You run your hands all over me and it seems you have six, eight, ten hands and then you touch and press and rub my you-know…"

"Like this?"

"Oh, yes. Something like...God, does that feel good! Where did you learn to touch like that?"

"Hebrew school. I majored in touch and tell."

Maria reacted with a disparaging wave of her hand. "Back to dreamland...And you press up hard against me and I start moaning and—listen, you'll laugh— through the hole I made in the poster I see one man staring at the nude and he says, 'Disgusting! What will those desperate booksellers think of next? Not enough they plastered an ad of a naked woman in a public space, but they also have her moaning...' And then the man walks away."

"That's hilarious. What a dream! What an imagination you have." And I run my hands all over her body and I tell her: "Say, pet my pussy, Katz."

Maria giggled. "Wait. That's not all. Then you pull my pants down and I feel you, you know, into me from behind..."

Figaro, I underpaid you. Figaro, you wonder worker and potion provider from a lively beauty salon miles from Waltham, you who weaves the medieval magic of *The Decameron* and *Thousand and One Nights* into today's real world. Your potion worked and opened up the Bible-driven, prissy Miss Maria and made her dream the dream I wanted her to dream. Your potion made her mine.

"Like this?" I said as I pulled her panties down. Not only didn't she resist, she raised her hips to speed the process. Wait! Maybe she wasn't wearing panties. Maybe it was only a long flannel nightshirt so easy to pull up. But I distinctly remember her lifting her hips. Well, maybe that was another time. This all happened so long ago, it's easy to mix up facts. Anyway, I almost regretted giving her the dream potion. Imagine me using a crutch instead of my own male manly masculine skill. But I went at her with enthusiasm. I worked with many hands, the many hands she thought I had in her dream. Then I sat her up.

"Hands up," I said suddenly.

Maria raised her hands, amused, astonished, compliant. I pulled the gray nightshirt over her head. She remained with her hands up.

"This was the girl's position on the cover of your dream book," she said. "And you got me so hot in that little cubicle."

I began to kiss her. I started with her forehead, looped back to her left ear, then down to the back of her neck.

She turned and looked at me. "Wouldn't it be polite to, you know, take your pants off?"

"Your command is my wish," I said, complying with the aid of four hands.

I could and couldn't believe what was happening. If it was the power of the potion, I could believe it. If it wasn't, I couldn't. How she had turned 180 degrees. Or is it 360? But I wasn't going to quarrel with her evanescent nature. Nor ask why she had changed her mind again. What was I, crazy? I just thanked my good fortune, my good Figaro, and put the puzzlement, the confusion, the contradiction, the unpredictability, the abrupt switch of moral and religious behavior in a file in the Siberian exile recesses of my mind.

"Wait," she said. "I was making so much noise behind the poster of your book in the Metro station I didn't even pay attention that someone had drilled two more tiny holes in the poster and, instead of us—or is it we?—looking out watching them, some guy was spying in on us. 'Who needs a naked photo?' I heard a guy saying. 'Wow! The real thing is much better,' until I stuck my finger in the hole and poked it into his snooping eye and he ran off screaming."

But I hardly heard those last words of hers, for I was busy recreating the dream, her dream, my dream, making her dream mine and my dream ours.

Part of that dream is Maria's singing. To get a flame, you have to strike a match. My fingers were the match, her voice the flame. I ran my index finger vertically from the rear of her thigh up her ass to the back of her waist, then shifted, slowly shifted direction and moved my finger with slow turtle sloth h-o-r-i-z-o-n-t-a-l-l-y from her spine to the edge of her waist.

A melody came from somewhere far away. It took me a while to discern how close it really was. I felt her stiffen.

"That...is...so...goo-oo-d," she said slowly. "Did you learn that in Hebrew school too?" was the song she sang with a flirtatious lilt in her voice.

"No. In sex school. Want more?"

"Uh-huh."

As I kissed her tanned knee, going in little clockwise circles, her happy noises began. Smack in the middle of the alphabet commenced her sounds of joy, with a lower case "m" that gradually grew to a capital "M." And then, as I slid my lips up her lubricious thigh, she moved up to "N," which had more vibrato and was on a slightly higher pitch. After which, like a slingshot in reverse, she sailed down the sliding pond of consonants back to *aleph*, the primary vowel, and sang "ah" and "oh"—the vocal signs under the *aleph*—in no particular order, but switched the melody of the vowels in direct proportion to the kisses.

At first, I didn't hear her singing vowels.

"How come you're still with the consonants?"

"Consonants are no good?"

"Vowels are on a higher plane."

"You haven't gotten to the vowel spot yet," she teased.

So I explored some more. I sought. I found. The magic dot. Then heard the cascade, the refreshing gush of vowels. She even invented a letter that wasn't in the alphabet, a consonant that bridged "m" and "n"; it had the force of the former and the vibrato of the latter. It quivered like a dozen overhead tension wires, like a loose electron caught in a rush-hour crowd. And she came up with a new sexy vowel sound too, "uh" with the "h" aspirated. And I discovered another nuance, perhaps the difference between hearing a Bach Chaconne on a Strad or on a Guarneri. I commended her on her subtle musicality.

"I guess you really do believe in dreams," I said.

"What are you trying to say?"

"Remember, you once told me you believe in dreams and I said, I'll remember that."

And then came that surprise—in a morning full of surprises, and a bigger one yet to come. As she got out of bed, still glowing, a happy smile on her face, like a cat that has licked the butter pan clean, she took one half of a giant step into her little bathroom.

"I'm going to shower up," said she.

"Me too," said I, as I leaped up and ran to her.

"No," she said, each letter cast in steel, its timbre a trap springing shut.

And that surprising steel-trap "No" sucked the music out of the air.

"Why?"

"Because."

Had the potion worn off once my dream was fulfilled? After the glory of that "Of course" and the ecstasy of that other course, that "No" stabbed me in two places, both of which now ached.

The surprise, the suddenness, of that "No" rattled me, although I understood it. She felt guilty enough. Screwing was okay. But a shower with me, a perfect stranger, violated her tenuous, penetrable balance line between right and wrong. Jesus would not approve.

Her mood change confounded me. Surprised me. Given the Paradise she'd just visited, the celestiality she had just experienced, that "No" should have been tinged with warmth and grace. But I suppose you can't argue with a potion. Its efficacy went just so far.

Later, I understood her "No." She ventriloquized that "No." It wasn't Maria speaking. It was her guilt, her Christianity. She couldn't resist the guy who stood in front of her. She hadn't had loving for so long and I made her sizzle.

But then came her "No" to a shower together. She put the brakes on. Fucking fine; shower, shame.

All smiles was she, when she came back from the shower, wearing a robe.

"Okay, now I'm all cleaned up. Now we can get dressed." She looked at me, noticed my face. "What's the matter?"

"You're absolutely nuts," I cried. "The way you switch. On and off. Loving one minute. Fury the next. You blow hot and cold."

Usually, she would react to the possibility of a double entendre. A lusty laugh. Or just roll her eyes. Or say "Pshh!" But this time the possible paragram passed her by.

"I feel guilty," she explained. "And the guilt gradually builds up like water slowly filling a bottle. And when it gets to the top, it overflows."

"Then..." I jumped up, dashed to the bathroom, grabbed a bottle from her shelf, and opened it. "Then pour guilt out before it gets to the top. Like this." And I poured the contents into the sink.

"Stop!" she shrieked. "You crazy? What're you doing? You idiot! That's my expensive perfume...Why? Why?" Her voice broke.

"I'll get you another one..." I passed the bottle under my nose a couple of times, sniffing it carefully, "...this cheap Woolworth eau de cologne. And, anyway, I told you I don't like perfume."

Then she was crying, suddenly deep in tears. I couldn't believe she was so upset. No, I realized, it wasn't the bottle that distressed her. It had to be something else. She was probably sorry for suddenly yelling at me. Or maybe it was the sin.

I sniffed the sink. "Expensive perfume, my pelvis! It's just a pale imitation of perfume. And it's already giving me a headache. The more awful the cologne, the mightier my malaise. I think I'm going to faint. Where'd you get this so-called perfume?"

"A friend gave it to me."

In English one can't tell the gender of "friend." In other languages—a cinch. Probably the book borrower. Or maybe the movie chap. Trying to blindside her with cheap, cloying cologne.

I dried her eyes with my sleeve.

"Choose your friends more carefully."

"I'm trying," she said pointedly.

"Tell me. Where am I now in the bottle?" I held the empty cologne bottle before her, as far away from my nose as possible. "I want to be there at the bottom before it fills up."

"I can't tell you how quickly the guilt fills up. It might go slowly or quickly. I'm not in control..."

To distract her I picked up another little bottle filled with a thick golden liquid.

"What's this?"

"Why didn't you pour *that* out? It's baby shampoo."

"My my. Expecting a little one? Is your tummy filling up like the proverbial bottle, slowly, growing with a love child?...Is it mine?"

She rolled her eyes. "It's baby shampoo, for my eyes. My eye doctor told me to use it to clean my eyelids. But I don't use it anymore. It makes my eyes smart."

"But not the rest of you."

She suddenly straightened up. "That's it. I can't. I won't. I won't do this any more."

I felt my stomach tightening, dropping away from me. "Just because of that dumb phrase?"

"No. It's because the bottle is full. Overflowing. My cup runneth over."

"Then let's seal your decision with a kiss."

Again Maria stunned me. "All right."

She put her hands on my face and brought her lips to mine. Now her hands were around my back. I opened her robe. She pressed close to me. She hugged me tight and kissed me with all her fervor. I don't think she ever kissed me like that before, her tongue moving, lost in my mouth.

My God! I thought. She's crazy about me. But I didn't move my hands from around her back.

She moved her head back.

"I mean it," she said crisply. "Jesus is looking over my shoulder. Unhappy with me."

That "No" to the shower was for her a salvation. It made her feel better.

And me—worse.

But that feeling didn't linger. And I'll tell you why.

Leaving her apartment, I walked through the kitchen as usual to the back door. I was happy. But around that halo of happiness was a second halo, heavy as lead, frayed at the edges, symbol of my gloom. Why? Because human beings are never satisfied. She had opened herself up to me, in every way. Yes, I had revved up her feelings toward me, but with the help of a magic potion. I recalled how I had warmed her months ago on her sofa without outside help. And now, to my shame and ignominy, I had to rely on extra-terrestrial power. And that sudden switch. That adamant No to a shower with me, and a renewed threat to cease and desist from all loving. Nunnish again. In the ying and yang battle between sex and piety, piety and Jesu had taken the upper hand once more.

While still in her kitchen, full of the above thoughts, I looked to my left and looked again. Couldn't believe it and looked again. I stare and—guess what?—I see her mug on top of the refrigerator. I looked into it. Full as the night before. She hadn't drunk a drop of it. You hear? Not a drop of it did she drink.

Who gave her drinke? No one. She did not drinke the drinke.

Had Figaro warned her? Impossible.

She hadn't drunk the potion.

The leaden halo vanished. It just floated up like mist into the ether.

I could have jumped for joy. Gone up to the stars following the path I had sailed a couple of hours ago when I heard that sweet "Of course" of hers.

Maria loved me for me and not through magic.

I took the mug, poured out its contents, washed it and put it away.

Now that she had washed herself without me, I washed away the magic potion without her.

But I wouldn't ask her why. Wouldn't dare. Didn't want to ruin the mood my own magic love potion had created. Didn't want to jinx it. Had her Kol Nidrei night reform worn off? Her self-alleged promiscuity returning? Unable to resist temptation?

A while later, I told her: "Remember how you once asked me, "Will you sleep over with me one night?"

"Really? Did I say that?"

"And do you remember my answer?"

"If I don't remember my question, how can I remember your answer?"

"Easy. Selective memory."

"Well, what did you say?"

"I said I will. And I'm prepared to any day."

"What will your wife say?"

I rolled my eyes. "She won't miss me because she's sleeping with her husband."

Maria gave me her noncommittal "Pssh."

I wanted to ask her—again, again, again—why she started becoming intimate with me again. But I didn't want to jinx the current situation.

It was Maria who initiated the conversation by saying:

"You broke me. Subtly. Gradually. Inch by inch. One patient day after another. I wasn't even aware how by degrees you were ducing me."

"Ducing? What kind of verb is that? Is it short-speak for something else?"

"Ducing," Maria said. "The ABC thereof. A-ducing. B-ducing. C-ducing. Re-ducing my ability to resist."

"Yes. It was me. I. You had nothing to do with it. Except maybe donating the lubricating fluid."

She paid no attention to the satire of my words.

"I let myself go. I let the wild side of my nature surface. You brought it out. I couldn't resist. I love it. I was crazy about it. It frightened me because I had this in me some years ago, when I was married."

"WHAT? Y...y...you," I sputtered, rather stuttered, because there is no 'p' in You. "You? Married? You never told me that. I'm shocked. Speechless."

"It slipped out. I didn't want to tell you. You see how you make me do things I don't want to do. But that's from long ago. Not important now. I had it in me and I thought I had gotten rid of it. But I didn't. You brought out the slut in me again."

"Stop it!" If there was ever a time when I felt like smacking her, it was now. Not to hurt her, but to bring her back down to earth. To reality. "You like me. Otherwise, you wouldn't be doing this." And I marveled at this forty-year-old neo-virgin agonizing about her sex life. "You're not a slut whom anyone, everyone, can grab. And you don't drop your pants, I hope, for everyone." And then I saw those two guys, my nemeses, the book borrower and the film lover, screwing her. Both of them. "I don't want to hear denigrating talk like that. You're insulting the girl I'm crazy about."

Maria put her hand on my arm. "Cancel that marriage business," she said softly. "I threw it in to tease you."

"I knew it," I said. "Who would want to marry a girl who refused a co-ed shower?"

33

HER ONE-PAGE DIARY

I REMOVED MY BRIEFCASE from the seat I had saved for Katz. He began speaking even before he sat down next to me.

= Another wrinkle to our story, Katz said as he peeked into his briefcase. = Once, when Katz was in Maria's bedroom…

I think this was the first time he used the name of the protagonist but soon switched back to his normal mode of narrative.

=…remember, I told you that I never heard the words "I like you" or "I'm crazy about you" from her, unlike me who told her that a number of times. Another time…and here Katz dropped his voice, not quite to a whisper but a notch above it, = she coaxed it out of Katz again by cooing, "Do you really like me?" And that led to, that was the prelude to another shock that hit me square between the eyes.

•

"Why do you ask?" I said to Maria.

"Because," she said, "I once read a novel whose exact title I forget, something like *Diary of a Lady Adulteress*, similar to the book you wrote in my dream, *Journal of an Unfaithful Wife.* In any case, it's about a guy who loves women. He goes from one to another. A real hedonist. Are you a type like that? A hedonist?"

"Me? Not at all. And you have the word wrong. A girl who likes guys is a hedonist. A guy who likes girls is a *she*donist. I used to be a hedonist until I came out of the closet. Now I'm a confirmed shedonist."

"Come on. Really. Do you really really like me, or are you like that guy in the novel?"

"You mean sex crazy? Are you kidding? Nah!"

"Tell me. Tell me. Tell me straight out."

I couldn't delay any more. And then, fool that I am, naïve to the world, knowing nothing about verbal games, sexual upsmanship, I immediately asserted, "Like you? I told you a long time ago I'm crazy about you. For me, you are Maria, mia aria operia."

Then came that wry, crooked, endearing little smile of hers, happy and satisfied.

I didn't say to her, *Well, now let me hear it from you, Do you like me?* I just sort of lowered my chin and peered over glasses that were not there and glared at her, seeing if I could mesmerize her, enchant her, jinx her, spellbind her into saying something I'd like to hear. But no. Dead silence.

•

Katz looked out the window at the desolate Jersey marshland, perhaps imagining his brother in that situation—or perhaps reliving those moments, if they happened to him.

•

I was in her bedroom and Maria got up, excused herself. She had to go to the bathroom. Instead of just lying there in bed, I got up. This is where the drama begins. I noticed the top drawer of her chest of drawers was open. And this is a girl who shuts every single door, every single drawer. Remember that first day I met her? That's one way we got chummy. She gets up and closes the slightly ajar door of the tram and I tell her, Me too. Exactly what I do. Anyway, her drawer was slightly open. God, was I tempted to peek into it. I don't usually do this. I respect people's privacy. Would never read someone else's letter. It's an old mitzva among Jews. A rabbinic edict about a thousand years old. Tried hard to resist. Put my hands behind my back. Clenched my fists. But I couldn't fight it. I opened the drawer and saw a typewritten page.

I read that page. Swallowed the words. She was writing about the unmatched thrills some guy gave her. Read quickly just before she opened the bathroom door. That night I jotted down what I remembered.

•

= My brother has this on a separate page, Katz said, = as if it's Maria's own document. He won't say if it's a real letter or if it's just another fictive device. As you can see, it's on a blue sheet of paper and the type font is different. If it's Maria's own page, she must have typed it in the place where she works, for according to my brother's novel, in her apartment there was no typewriter.

Katz began to read.

•

"I had never experienced anything like it before. He made every part of my body tingle. He made love to every pore, starting with my fingertips, kissing every one of them. Then he closed his lips around each one as if my fingertips were lollipops and gave each one of them a sucking kiss. He massaged my toes, my instep, my heels, forming a cup of his hand and rotating it around my heels. I loved that. I loved each of his touches, and I began to moan. He kissed my legs up to my knees and then moved to my inner thigh, and a thrill I had never felt before thrilled through me, tingled through me, shivered through me, vibrated through me. I arched my back not because I wanted to but because I couldn't help it, it was like a reflex and I was like a taut bow, and the arrow instead of leaving me would enter me."

I stopped reading because pangs, fangs, and wangs went through me. I wish there were more synonyms for jealousy. And in color too. The dark heart downspin combined with blood-red rage, impotent purple fury, blue depression, weed green jealousy, that poison toad yellow feeling when the pit of your stomach probes the top of your heart. What a palette for a dejected painter. That movie guy, Maria's faceless ex-boyfriend, now assumed a huge golem-like presence in my gut. Why did I have to take Maria to the movie theater that night? That black night that cracked my nerves and twisted my stomach into knots. But I can't keep repeating that dumb and useless question. Once you do something, it cannot be undone. Only in daydreams can we reverse time.

I continued reading Maria's handwritten words that seared my hands:

"My head on the pillow, the heels of my feet pressed into the sheet, and my midsection raised. Was I in heaven? In Paradise? I don't know. But I certainly felt I was in a place where I had never been before. I couldn't think. I was all sensation, a fire, a burning in me. A gorgeous, delicious flow. I wanted more. I wanted this to continue forever. "Don't stop. Please. Please. Please don't stop," I shouted in ecstasy, as if from another world. Where I had the strength to say those words, I don't know. They burst out of me in the fire of my absolute desire, which joined my other desire to make time stand still. And then I began to remember things that hadn't happened yet. A mingling of so much desire and happiness. Hours later my insides are still tingling, trembling, tremoring, vibrating. I feel it from the bottom of my feet to the top of my head. I don't see how men can enjoy it. They spritz it in and leave. And I, I have a phantom pecker in me for hours. I only wished I could make him…"

•

= There's something crossed out here, Katz said and stopped. = There's a word, probably a name, written before "him" and it's carefully blotted out. Impossible to read. And then she continues, "make him feel as good as he made me feel."

= Is the name long or short? I asked.

= I tried to figure that out too, John. But it's hard to say. Certainly more than two letters. So what do you make of this one-page diary of hers?

= Sounds like she adores you, likes you, appreciates you. That is, Katz, the protagonist…Don't you agree with me? Why're you making a face?

= Because maybe she didn't mean the novel's hero, Katz.

= Can you explain?

= Well, John, according to my brother's manuscript, that drawer was partially open. Maria went to the bathroom. Maybe it was a setup.

I looked at Katz: = You mean, as if she purposely lured Katz to look at it?

= Yeah. She sort of knew Katz would look, and prepared that page on which she had written about someone else. You know, those two guys the narrator keeps mentioning.

= Maybe there was no someone else, I said.

= Maybe, John. Maybe she wrote it to make Katz jealous.

= If Maria wants to make him jealous, it's okay. It's a sign she likes him.

= Or maybe she just did it to make Katz angry, Katz said. = *And* jealous. And she sure succeeded on both counts.

= Or maybe, I said, = since we're slicing reality into so many possibilities, maybe it's just simply about Katz.

= Do you really think so? Wow! If it were about Katz, I would be happy for my brother. Or at least for the fictional Katz.

= Would you mind reading that part again, where Maria describes the thrill?

= Sure.

Katz opened his briefcase and pulled out the page.

= Here it is: "A thrill I had never felt before thrilled through me, tingled through me, shivered through, vibrated through me. I arched my back not because I wanted to..."

= Okay. That's enough, I said.

I didn't have the nerve to ask Katz if Maria's description accurately reflected what his brother, or the character Katz, had done to her. Katz admitted that his brother didn't share personal details with him. And even if it had been Katz himself who had experienced this, there was a protocol of silence and distance that I had to observe.

= Well? Katz asked, hanging on my reaction like a litigant awaiting the judge's decision.

= Let me think. Meanwhile, let me ask you this. Within context of the novel, does the heroine realize that Katz looked into her open drawer and read that page?

= Katz made one mistake, but it was too late to correct it.

I sort of upticked my head to signal him to continue.

= When Katz heard her flushing, he replaced the page and closed the drawer. Only after she returned did he remember that the drawer had been slightly open.

= Does your brother indicate if Maria noticed this?

= He doesn't say. But given her character, as developed in the story, she must have. She's very sharp. But she didn't say a thing.

= What would have happened had she caught Katz?

= It would have been very embarrassing.

= Suppose she came out as the narrator's back was to her and he was reading that page.

= I can't speak for a character in a book. But had this happened to me, I would have done what I once saw Harpo do in a Marx Brothers film, or maybe it was a Chaplin movie. I would have eaten the page, chewed, and swallowed it.

= Could it possibly be Maria's wishful thinking?

= No! Katz shouted. Then, as people turned to look at him, his face flushed. He gazed down at his loafers. = No, he whispered. Given what we know about Maria, I assure you it wasn't wishful thinking.

I was on the threshold of invasion of privacy. But Katz had already answered my question. I gathered that he—or, if going by his continual remarks, his brother—had had such an experience with Maria.

But one puzzle remained. If Katz or his brother didn't make the whole monologue up, how could he have remembered the nuances of her feelings in such precise detail?

The answer, the explanation, came somewhat later.

34

THE PHONE TRICK

AFTER THAT DIARY DISCOVERY, I wanted to test Maria. After all, she once tried to check out if I was married and followed me to my house. I recalled that she had once told me about her visit to a girl friend named Amy, where she met Amy's boyfriend, a guy with the offbeat name of Stajko. He had southern European dark good looks, curly black hair, long lips, very masculine.

Another guy to be jealous of, I thought. Another guy to give me twangs and drangs.

"When Amy left the room to make tea, I sensed Stajko looking me over," Maria said with perfect innocence, not trying at all to brag, or upset me. "It made me uncomfortable, especially since he's supposed to be her boyfriend. Among other questions, he asked me about my schedule, if I have any free time during the day."

"Did he speak English well?"

"Pretty well."

"With an accent?"

"Of course."

With that at once I had an idea. I waited a few days and called her. I told her, "Hi, I'm Stajko. I'm in Boston for couple days and would like to see you." First Maria hesitated. She didn't ask how I got her number. But when I told her how impressed I was with her and with her sexy good looks, she agreed. We arranged to meet at a designated place and then I hung up. Devastated. Jealous. Furious. Two days after the "date," I asked her how was her encounter with Stajko.

Without thinking she immediately said, "He didn't show up." Then, a moment later, "Hey, how did you know about it?"

"Stajko told me. Very nice. Accepting a date with your girlfriend's roving-eyed roue boyfriend. What's the matter? I'm not good enough for you? Trekking all the way to Boston just so's he can grab you?"

Fickleness, I thought, thy name is woman. Two-timer, deceptive Maria.

Can a jealous heart be larger than the body that contains it?

35

DIARY, CONTINUED

A COUPLE OF WEEKS later, Katz clarified for me the mystery of Maria's one-page diary that the protagonist found in the open drawer in her bedroom.

= There's yet another wrinkle in the Maria diary page that I have to iron out, a story that is getting to be as wrinkled as a linen suit. You may have wondered how Katz could remember that monologue of Maria's word for word.

= Indeed, I did, I said, and added, = I read something by Maxim Gorki the other day and I jotted it down. It might shed some light on Maria's diary page. Gorki wrote: "A woman's body is more sincere than a man's, but her thoughts are false. When she lies, she knows she's lying, but when a man lies, he believes he's telling the truth."

= You know, John, on the face of it, it sounds impressive. But when you look closely at the words, every phrase contradicts the one before and after it. It almost sounds like Gorki is thinking, I'm going to say something seemingly profound that people will quote later, but I myself don't know what the devil I'm talking about. Now I'll narrate what happened, as my brother tells it. He revised and expanded that marvelous scene. Yes, Maria went to the bathroom. But stayed longer.

•

She said, "I'm going to take a shower and do my semi-annual hair wash."

"I'll join you," I said. Her No was so adamant it could have cut a diamond. Here we had been as intimate as a married couple and suddenly No to a shower. This was the second time she banned me from her bathroom. She said she'd be finished in half an hour. I lay on the bed, heard the shower, then, bored, got up and saw the open drawer.

•

= You know what happened next, John. No need to retell it. But here's my brother's expansion of that scene.

•

I wanted the text of that piece of paper. Reading it, trying to recall it, having those words flutter in my mind like butterflies, was not enough. There was no way I could remember it. She said thirty minutes. With a woman, a shower, hair wash, drying, it's forty-five minutes at least. Since I thought I had plenty of time, I took a chance, grabbed Maria's page, and ran out the door. Did I tell you I dressed first? A couple of blocks away was a convenience store that had a Xerox machine. My luck. A woman ahead of me was Xeroxing five thick documents. "Would you mind if I went ahead you?" I asked. "I just have one page and I'm double parked." She looked and said, "But there's no car out there." "Oh, my God," I said, "they towed it already." "Okay," she said. And then they ran out of paper. The owner had to open the machine and reload it. Time ticks; my heart racing. But no quicker than my legs back to the house. Softly in. Hear her hair dryer, noisy as a lawn mower. Fold the copy into my wallet. Return her page. Close, stupidly close, her drawer. Take off my pants and slide back into the bed just as she opens the door and says, "There! There's a task I won't have to repeat till next December."

•

= What a story! I said. = Another complication could have been if the narrator put the original in his pocket by mistake and left the Xerox copy in her drawer.

= Yeah, but that would be fiction and this is real.

= But I thought your brother's story is fiction.

And, cryptically as usual, as though speaking Sanskrit, Katz retorted: = Yeah, that's what I mean.

The "I" and "me" in Katz's narration kept bugging me. I wondered how he felt about this switching, which by now came so naturally to him. He spoke of Maria with such enthusiasm, I could swear he had fallen in love with her, although he had never met her, if indeed she was a real girl. I had to shake my head at the concentric levels of reality or imagination that had been created here. Could all of this be Katz's own creation, and not his brother's? Based on a girl he had known fifteen, twenty years ago? Or was she his brother's fictional creation? Being immersed so deeply in all the details of the young woman, wouldn't I, as reteller, have fallen for Maria myself?

I decided to break train protocol and ask him:

= Tell me, Katz, with all this retelling of the story with Maria, don't you feel drawn to her, wish you could have known her?

= Absolutely. I won't deny it. And when I tell it in the first person, I imagine that I'm the hero, crazy about Maria, and it gives me a thrill.

= Okay, then I have another question. I think I detect a contradiction which, as is your penchant, you'll no doubt explain. You told me early on that your brother said you have total recall. So how come you had to run out and Xerox that page?

= John, now it's you who is confusing writer and teller again. I didn't run out to Xerox the page. The protagonist did. It's my *brother's* story, and he's not the one with total recall. Moreover, from the novel's point of view, with a document as important as Maria's one-page diary, one doesn't, one shouldn't, rely on memory.

= Katz. You still owe me the ending of that faux date story, which you dropped abruptly. What was Maria's reaction when Katz confronted her?

= I have it right here, John. Katz went into his briefcase. He quickly retrieved a page and read:

•

"I didn't even go," Maria said.

"You didn't?"

"No."

"But you said Stajko didn't show up. How do you know he didn't?"

"Because..." Maria came right up to me, face to face. "Because, you rascal, you sting operative, because I recognized your voice. You rat!"

And all I could say was, "I knew you'd recognize my voice. How could I possibly imitate a south European Croatian accent? And you know what? I didn't show up either. Who wants to go out with my girlfriend's girlfriend anyway?"

•

I looked about.

= Katz, your station has arrived.

At the door, Katz said, = Actually, it's the train that arrives, not the station. That's one of the anomalies of English. See you next time, John.

36

WHY'D YOU DO THAT? - TWO WIVES?

THAT NO TO THE shower of a few weeks earlier put her in a tougher mood. She said, "No more. I mean it." She was edging to celibacy again. But I was biding my time, for I knew her neo-virginity would not last long. So I made a pretense of complying with her wishes. In her apartment, Maria and I were playing the chaste patient game again. She, chaste; I, patient. For two or three visits, I didn't even kiss her. We just lay on the sofa, as beforetimes.

Then I had to go on a business trip for two weeks. When I returned and saw her, the warmth within me for Maria overwhelmed me and I drew her close and kissed her. She did not resist. But she spoiled my joy by saying:

"Why did you do that?"

It wasn't the first time she asked me a question after a kiss. Remember that four-word "Where are you going?" first time I kissed her?

"It wasn't me," I said.

She looked around. Perhaps looking for my twin. "Then who was it?"

"My willpower."

"That's a new one," Maria said.

"Look." I went into my pocket and pulled out a prepared note. "I swear to God," I read, "I didn't want to do this. Why should I want to kiss you, anyway? But my willpower overwhelmed me."

"But if you wrote the note in advance, you could have controlled yourself."

"Shows you how weak is my will. Not like yours. Made of iron. Fortified by your Yom Kippur visit to that No More Shall I Synagogue."

"Why did you do this?" she said sadly. She didn't whine; to her credit she did not whine. Still, even without the whine, regret quivered in her voice. "Why? You know my attitude. You seemed to be accepting it so nicely. Why?"

As an answer, I gave her an entire sermon.

"Do you think you can ride that saintly train forever, smug, blameless, and pure? With an unlimited ticket that gives you my presence, my hugs, my affection, without it costing you guilt? Uh-uh. Never. Enough! I had to show you that that newly invented caboose riding the rails between Platonism and Eros, like a nation half-slave, half-free, does not, cannot, will not endure. It is a unicorn, an angel, a phoenix, a legendary, mythic creature found neither in heaven nor on earth."

And later I thought: Was she testing herself with me again? Seeing how long she could resist temptation? And, in a macabre way, did I fiddle with her to see how long it would take her to betray her love for Jesus? Like trying to seduce a nun?

For Jesus-loving Christians like Maria, it was far easier to say I was the devil who compromised her, broke her, damaged her, defiled her, made her tainted goods, made her keel over from her pure sanctity into disgrace, into the sullied pit.

But how delicious the disgrace, how celestial the sullied pit!

I stunned her with my words. She opened her mouth but only air came out.

"Anyway, I didn't go it alone. You kissed me back. Was it good?"

"I'm not saying."

"You're not saying. Typical Christiansen attitude."

"This is the first time you called me by my family name, Katz."

And I thought to myself: If your family name were Katz, you'd be related to me. Maybe even my wife. And then you could honestly claim that I was married and that you were having an affair with a married man.

"Typical Maria. 'I'm not saying.' But that's not an acceptable answer. For that answer I'll give you a B, no, a B minus. If it wasn't good, you'd have said no."

"It wasn't good."

"Now you get an A for lying."

She laughed. Her old laugh. Then erased it as if shutting a light.

"Come back to me, sweetheart," I said.

"This is the first time you've called me that."

"It slipped out. A typographical error. Come back to me and I'll say your name all day long. Maria. Maria. Maria. Your name is like an aria operia."

I looked at her. Her eyes were closed. She was whispering something. I thought it was Katz, Katz, Katz, and it made me feel good. Then I realized she was muttering the next best thing: Jesus, Jesus, Jesus.

And I countered that by thinking of the Yiddish expression: *ess vet dir gornisht helfn*. Nothing will help you. Not incantation, nor anything else.

"You don't understand, Katz."

"I love it when you say my name, Maria. You know, you hardly ever say my name."

A beatific look glowed in her eyes. She got the echo of her words of a few months back.

"You don't understand. Something can be good, terrific, sensational, the best. But not acceptable. Good. Great. Delicious. But morally wrong. Don't you understand? I want to be true to Jesus."

"This above all, to thine own self be true. In kissing me, you were true to yourself. Now close your eyes."

"No."

"Close them. I want to see if I can resist. You proved you could. Now give me a chance. I've been practicing at home."

"With your wife, no doubt."

"Back to that again?

"Yes. Again. And again. It bothers me."

•

= Katz, let me interrupt with my own take on the story.

= Sure, John. Go ahead.

= With Maria's constant banging away re Katz having a wife, the reader, listener, me, has to get the feeling she may be right.

= John, you know how some readers who start a book turn to the last few pages to know what will happen. Don't be like them.

= In other words, you want me to be patient, like Katz.

•

"Jealous?" I asked Maria.

Of course she wouldn't say.

"At home I myself have been practicing to resist the temptation to kiss. Now for the crucial test. You told me, once, when we were naked. Remember that glorious time? That you like to be told what to do."

"Yes. That's right. I like to be told what to do."

"Well? I'm telling you."

"Only when I'm naked," was Maria's quick, teasing, response. And again she laughed that raucous, naughty laugh of hers.

"Then take your clothes off."

"No."

"I see you have a very limited vocabulary today. Okay. Compromise. Everything below the waist."

"No."

"Who said I can't compromise further? Or negotiate. Okay, Maria, just shut your eyes."

"All right."

That surprised me, it did. Like I've said before. She always managed to surprise me.

"Are your eyes closed?" I asked.

"Can't you see?"

"No. My eyes are closed too. Tell me if yours are shut."

"Wait. I have to check," she said. "Yes, now they are... What now?"

"I'm bringing my lips closer. Do you sense them?"

"Yes."

"My lips are getting even closer. Ladies and gentlemen, will Katz be able to resist temptation?... Do you feel my lips quivering at kissing distance from yours?"

"Yes."

Softly said. Very. Almost missed that pianissimo Yes.

"Now my lips are drawing so close one has to have the power of Goliath, the will of a Leviathan, the self-control of a saint—not a Catholic one, of course—not to press forward like this and put your lower lip between my two lips like this and take them into my mouth and envelopmmmm..."

Maria pressed closer. I felt her fingers clawing into my back.

And through both our closed eyes and open lips, she snapped:

"Fuck your temptation and kiss me more, you dope. And stop talking so much. You haven't kissed me in what feels like years. That's it, you failed."

"I know," I said with mock sadness.

"But what a delicious failure."

"Maria Maria Maria. Sweetheart, Maria."

She opened my lips with her tongue. I opened my eyes and saw her eyes passionately shut, a dreamy look on her face. Not a hint of Jesus on her lips. And I kissed again each of her fingertips, including the missing one on her ring finger. Then I kissed her eyes, each one three times, her ears, her throat. I slid my lips up from her throat to her cheeks and then went back to her lips again.

"Here's your epiphany," I said, then added, as I held her breasts: "I want to keep kissing you like this."

"For how long?"

"For…"

"Not five?"

"Forever," I said.

I knew what she would say next. Either "Really?" or "That's sweet." And she did say, "That's so sweet," but surprised me by adding: "That's how Marquez ends one of his novels, with that one word: forever."

And then she ruined it by returning to her old bugaboo.

"Wouldn't your wife be jealous if she knew I was kissing you?"

"You can't resist, can you? You sense how good, how delicious, how glorious we're both feeling, so you have to kill it by articulating your guilt. Feeling guilty makes you feel good, right? It's the counterbalance to the kisses. There's something off-kilter in that Christian piety of yours. We were flying so high. Do you know how rare it is to achieve such a balloon flight for two, and then you stupidly prick the balloon and send us plummeting."

Maria opened her mouth, but I didn't wait for her to respond.

"My wives aren't jealous. They don't mind."

"Your what?" she screamed. If she was sitting, she jumped up. If lying down, she sat up. I don't recall. But she shrieked out in surprise, in astonishment, in shock. "Your what?"

"You heard me."

"Maybe I didn't. I thought I heard you say wives. Plural. With an 's'."

"All correct...Wives...Plural...With an 's'."

"Now I understand. When you once said I'm not married to a single woman, you were telling the truth and lying through your teeth as usual...You have two wives?"

"I do. Which is the exact phrase I said twice at the ceremony."

"How do you do it?"

"You mean, when, where and how often."

"Yes. When? Where? How often?"

"Long distance—and by proxy. Just like you. By proxy."

"This is unbelievable. How did you meet?"

"It was easy. They're twin sisters."

"But how can you marry two...?"

"It's quite legal. You see, I'm practically a Yemenite, on my grandfather's side. He was a half-brother. So by law I'm permitted two wives. It's an old Yemenite custom."

"Are they identical?"

"In their love for me? Absolutely. To the max. They're so alike even their parents can't tell them apart. I can't either. Sometimes when I call one, the other comes."

"That's queer."

"Because they can't tell each other apart either."

"You're making all this up."

"Yes."

Maria rolled her eyes, as if saying: *I should have expected this from him.* Still, she was pleased, entertained.

"In short," I said, "there's nothing to be jealous of. Or about. I told you my situation long ago."

"If you introduced me to your wife, I could come over to see you without pangs of guilt."

"Maria, sweetie. Your idea of me introducing you to my wife, if I had one, or my husband, if I had two, is absolutely brilliant. In fact, this might even induce me to get married so I could introduce you."

"Okay, but if you had one, how would you introduce me?"

"Ve...ry...care...ful...ly."

"Come on. Seriously."

"I would say, Mrs. K—for I always call her Mrs. K, because I keep forgetting her first name—this is Maria. Remember, I told you about her? How she likes Jesus more than me. And her canary more than Jesus. How she would leave the rear door open for me and how I would creep into her bed almost every morning before she went to work, how she loved all the sweet things I told her but would only say 'Really?' instead of saying she was crazy about me, and how in the middle of sex play, when I asked her if she liked this position or that, she would answer, 'You choose, I like to be told what to do,' and when I finally uttered her name for the first time after knowing her for several years, she said at once, 'I love it when you say my name,' and how when I began to—"

Now Maria clapped her hand over my mouth and muzzled my lips.

"…she sang out, I love it, I love it, I love, don't stop, don't stop, don't stop, don'tstopdon'tstop, is how I'd introduce you."

At this point, for some obscure reason I can't fathom, the roles reversed. Maria took me by the hand and led me to her bedroom. Lots of thoughts flew through my head. A: She really wanted me. B: Maybe she'll do again what she had done before. To show herself she really could withstand temptation. No, she wouldn't have the gall to do that post-Yom Kippur trick again. C: Her desires have peaked and everything will be fine. D: I'll play along with her piety and say no. To make her feel good. Grateful. And to bide my time.

In the bedroom, I hugged her and said:

"No. After Yom Kippur, when we were in bed, you said no at the height of our passion. I'll say no now before we even begin. To help you remain pure."

"Thank you. Thank you, Katz. What you've just done is helping me enormously in my quest for purity, my path to purity and wholeness."

"Fine," I said. "Can I just puss your kiss-kiss once more before it goes into permanent permafrost exile?"

"No. But you can kiss my top lips. But just once. Once hello and once goodbye."

I kissed her but I said, "Au revoir."

"Thank you for understanding. You don't know how much this means to me. It's as if Jesus himself is standing before me."

I took the halo from above my head and folded it—it was as light as light—into my back pocket.

That night, I don't know why—could it have been somehow related to the day's events?—I had an amazing dream, whose meaning would delight interpreters of dreams. A dream which Maria, alas, read to my detriment.

37

KATZ'S FLYING DREAM - MARIA SAYS: I'M OFF...

It's not the first time I had a flying dream. I can't remember any of my previous flights. Not a single one. But I knew as soon as I had that dream, while I was in it, dreaming it, flying it, I knew that I had flown in my dreams before.

I don't remember if the previous dreams were monochrome or in color, but this one was in shining, blazing color.

As I flew about fifty feet above the ground, in a walking position, my legs did not move. I stood upright, propelled through the air by willpower alone.

In the distance I saw a huge blue lake amid mountains. I felt as if I was in a balloon sailing between the snow-covered peaks. I looked down on forests, rivers, and lakes, and sometimes even skirted close to magnificent waterfalls.

Then, in midair, I recalled that my family was flying to a local airport and I had to meet them. I forgot the name of the airport but vaguely remembered it was somewhere to the left. And then I looked down, saw a group of people, descended, floated down, and landed in a little square.

"Do you know which way is the airport?" I asked a woman.

"For which town?"

I knew the name of the town, but I couldn't pronounce it. Do you know what I mean? I sounded it out in my head but in typical dream fashion couldn't articulate it. The bridge between my thoughts and my tongue was broken. Put another way, a tight, silken, banner stood between my knowing and my ability to express my knowing.

Finally, I babbled, "Biarritz," even though I knew that Biarritz was in southwest France by the sea and I was flying in a land of lakes surrounded by mountains many miles away, in mid-country, far removed from the sea.

The woman pointed to the left, in the very direction I thought I had to fly. Then I leaped up, rather, levitated, gradually rose and began flying, enjoying the ecstasy of it, flying over a narrow lane on a hill where people were walking in my direction.

Down below, another woman walking raised her head and looked up at me, totally surprised. She made a large O with her mouth. Her hands moved quickly to her bag; she took out a camera and aimed it at me. I should have told her, What's so amazing? It's only a dream.

"No pictures. No pictures. The use of cameras or recording devices is strictly prohibited. Put that camera away!" I shouted down at her.

But she pressed the shutter anyway. Suddenly—it had nothing to do with me—suddenly there was a flash of light that extended in a huge bright hoop in front of her that hid her completely. The light receded. Her camera had disintegrated. I flew away.

"What do you make of it?" I asked Maria after I told her the dream.

"I think your subconscious is telling you that one of us—me!—should take a trip. For weeks I've been thinking of going to Europe. Now this dream clinches it. My mind is made up. I'm going."

"What? Now that we've become so close, you're leaving me?"

"Only for a month. I've been thinking about this off and on, and now your dream comes as a clear message. Maria: go! And I am. I'm flying to Europe."

"With a plane?" I asked.

"Of course. You think I have your magical powers?"

"But how could my dream be a message to you? It's only a dream."

"I told you I believe in dreams," Maria said.

Me and my big mouth. Dammit! Why did I have to share my dream with her?

I became jealous. Again. But this time not of anyone in particular. Rather, of everyone in general. A supremely friendly innocent unattached lonely girl who loves loving traveling in Europe for a month, and all those European guys ready to pounce. So all I could say to protect my interests was: "Remember Jesus."

And all she could say was: "Don't worry. I shall."

Another stupid Katz suggestion that bounced back at me like a sudden slap in the face.

But I wanted to show her that even though she had flown away from me, she hadn't flown away completely. When she made her arrangements a few days later, I had asked her the name of her hotel in Athens and I remembered it. A day after her flight, when it was late at night in Greece, I called the hotel, praying she would be in and not galivanting around with some Greek god. She answered. I said this was her bastard parrot calling to check on her health. God, was she surprised. She even thanked me for the call.

And then all those postcards came.

Which banished jealousy.

In its stead came something worse.

Gloom.

38

MARIA'S RETURN

Okay, she's back. Thank God. Mine, not hers. All smiles. I welcome her back. She brings me a beautiful souvenir from Venice. I say nothing about the postcards she sent me.

•

= Wait a minute, Katz. There's something wrong here from a psychological and also from an artistic/aesthetic point of view.

= What?

= The gap. One minute Maria's gone. Next chapter she's back. What about Katz's reaction to her going away? What he felt during that month? Didn't your brother say anything about that?

Katz slapped his head.

= My God! You're right. Of course he did. In my anxiety to get Maria back, I've skipped over an entire chapter. And I just reread it a couple of nights ago. This has never happened before…me missing, skipping over, an entire chapter of my brother's book. But I don't have it here in my briefcase. I'll tell it to you next time.

And then we did not say another word. Katz smiled at me once, with his pleasant, open, friendly face. When he smiled, his entire face lit up, his eyes almost shut, and two little dimples appeared in his cheeks. Then he opened his mouth as if a vowel was about to form, perhaps the pronoun "I" with which he began most of his thoughts. But then, inexplicably, he closed his mouth, as if censoring himself. What made him suppress his words? Or was it just my imagination, since we had never before ridden in silence? All of our trips were suffused with words

words words. What had made him stop even before he began? A simple answer is: perhaps he had nothing more to say. We looked at each other once. I too did not speak.

It was a strange ride to New York. For almost one hour, we communicated in absolute silence. We did not even take out a book or a paper. And I think it no exaggeration to say that the silence we experienced had a certain fervor. Which was why when Katz had to leave we both rose spontaneously, shook hands in formal fashion, and, as if we had both rehearsed it, said, "Thank you" at the same time.

39

CENTER OF GRAVITY

= Here's the missing chapter, John, Katz said next time I saw him. = The chapter that fills in the gap between Maria's departure and her return from Europe.

And Katz began to read:

•

As soon as Maria left for Europe, I felt ill at ease. As the days passed, I realized how much I missed her. I felt off balance, like a man groping in the dark. Not that I couldn't stand or walk. But something within me felt that way. My center of gravity was off. Where had that thin little critter run off to?

•

Katz gazed out the window as if looking for it there. Cheap bungalows swooshed by. The poverty of the houses seemed to affect nature too. In this poor zone on the wrong side of the tracks, even the sky was gray, and the trees, instead of being brightly colored on this sunny fall day, were skimpily clad with sad, moth-eaten brittle yellow leaves.

= How different is the scenery down here from up around Boston, Katz said. = My brother told me about elegant houses, mansions even, and in the fall, seeing blazing colors, yellow, ochre, screaming orange, a shiny fire engine red leaning toward wine, that bright red nearing purple you see only in New England, a backlit, translucent red, occasionally some leaves tipped with gold, the sort of polychrome that if an artist were to imitate it the result would be pure kitsch, and the bright blue shrubs…"

= Blue? I said. = There is no blue in nature, except for flowers.

= I know, John. I just threw that out to check if you're paying attention. I wonder where Maria is now?

Was that in the manuscript or an interjection? Katz looked lost. He lost, and I, confused. Again the old question. Was he telling me his story or narrating his brother's? Or had Katz so perfectly assimilated his brother's tale that he was relating to it as if it were his own? The way Katz told the story and created the portrait of Maria, it sounded so personal. Or was he just conveying, like a good photographer or painter, his brother's portrait? But, then again, wasn't it he, Katz, who was now wondering where Maria was?

Katz did look as if his own center of gravity had been misplaced. He seemed dazed. Memories of Boston and the ride through shabby, hardscrabble New Jersey towns with their neo-welfare ambience were more than he could handle.

= Where was I? Katz said.

= Your, or your brother's thin, fragile, reed-like center of gravity... Katz, I want you to know that you throw *my* center of gravity off...I can't separate you two. You're like Siamese twins because the way you keep saying "I" makes one think it happened to you..."

= I told you, John, I'm just the medium. When Laurence Olivier declaims "To be or not to be," is he the author of that soliloquy or is it Shakespeare? When I first began this narration, I said I'll probably mix up the "he" and the "I." But I decided the "I" would be more comfortable, especially since my brother is writing the novel in the first person. Would you rather I switch to the third person?

= No, Katz. Continue the way you've been doing it. I've gotten used to it already...Let's get back to the story.

•

Okay. So I wondered, did I leave it in her house just before she left? Perhaps in her bedroom mirror, as I glanced at my rumpled hair and pillow-creased face. Where did my center of gravity run off to? It certainly was not with me.

•

I wondered if Katz losing his center of gravity was a kind of depression, his spirit longing for something more that Maria wasn't giving him.

= Does it come back? I asked carefully, realizing too late that I was addressing my seatmate Katz in the present tense about a malaise that a fictional character of the same name written by a writer of the same name had suffered some years ago.

With Katz narrating about Katz, people and time zones were both fluid and fused. He had indeed made Siamese twins not only of himself and his writer brother, but of time and space as well. Einstein would have been proud.

= Oh, yes, Katz was saying over my thoughts. = Eventually…it slides back into me and I don't even notice it, like when you're feeling ill and wonder if you'll ever feel well again, and then, when you're well again, you don't even remember what troubled you. Same thing with her. That off-center feeling vanishes. Unannounced.

Now I decided to be less circumspect.

= Your brother's creation has affected you, hasn't it? You're taking the separation very personally.

= Yes. As if a girlfriend of mine had left me. Just like I told you the other day. I sometimes imagine it's me who is the hero of the book. But you have to remember that in human relationships, there are always surprises. What you expect to happen does not.

Katz looked into his briefcase at some pages. He took a deep breath as if to clear his head. This time he read from a page in his hand.

•

When Maria left, my center of gravity was tilted, misplaced, lost somewhere, although I suspected, I had a hunch where it was.

Mine was metaphysical, if you will, but hers—hers was quite physical, touchable, actually, and if you paid attention you could actually see it, it was quite manifest. Her center was really off. And that's why there was disorder in her life. I told her about various approaches, suggested how she could put some order into her life and she said, I know, I'll look into it, I'll work on it.

I'll give you a couple of examples. Some I don't want to talk about lest I betray her privacy. But this I'll share. For instance, I told her, *You know what you need? You need a good Jewish mother.* To watch her diet. Guide her to have three healthy meals daily. Here's her breakfast: a cup of coffee sipped on the tram on her way to work. That Jewish mama would also noodge Maria about her careless way of dressing. Pressure her to pay more attention to jeans than to Jesus.

What exactly she did to earn a living I forgot. Some sort of consulting or arbitration. Perhaps financial planning? No. Not that, because she couldn't keep her own finances straight. Was still paying off her college loans eighteen years after graduation. But, on the other hand, who says you can't be a good financial analyst or advisor while your own finances are screwy? It reminds me of the famous Yiddish folk expression: a shoemaker always goes barefoot.

I had a terrific idea for her. I told her to keep a running account of her expenses in a booklet. That means I have to buy a booklet, she quipped. I accented that a running record for a month would show her where her money went. Of course she didn't do it. Wouldn't do it. A creature of habit, she never changed.

She never shopped for food. Only thing she cooked was water for tea on the one burner she used. The other three had dried up from underuse, atrophied. She showed me her pantry. That's with an 'r'. Empty of food, but filled with old books. Opened her fridge. Not an edible thing in it. She kept everything in it but the kitchen sink.

I still don't understand where her money went. And *she* certainly didn't know. I told her to force herself to save. She had no pension. No health care. I can't afford to get ill, she said. And I don't have the time. She had hourly wages but no vacations. A queer way to work, an even queerer way to run a life. No wonder my center of gravity was off kilter. It rubbed off from hers. If you look at her life objectively, you had to conclude it was pathetic.

Thinking of her thus while she was in Europe, probably getting picked up left and right, me pondering her off-center of gravity threw mine off even more. If you're lonely, some magnetic pole sucks away your center of gravity.

I said pathetic. Yes. Despite the fifty g's she pulled in during good years, which was a lot of money in those days, it was still a pathetic life. A much more honest word would be miserable.

Of course, she would never admit it. Like the Yiddish folk expression has it, a worm in the horseradish thinks it's in Paradise. Let's face it, hers was a miserable life. Lonely. Not married. No kids. No lovers. Okay, except me. No money. No father. A distant mother who'd run off somewhere with an alleged boyfriend. And one sister she hardly saw. Out of touch. Not even considered family. And slowly the biological clock ticking. Approaching forty or forty-one. And a missing fingertip on her ring finger to boot.

So what did she have? My rival for affection: Jesus. And me, sometimes. Can religion fulfill one's life? Perhaps if she deluded herself.

But, still, despite all this, most of the time she was in good humor. Aside from one bolt of anger directed at me that surprised me—about that I'll soon tell you—I never actually sensed she was unhappy. Except once, when I wanted to get together with her, she said: *No, this hasn't been a good week.* And then, without a trace of drama, she let slip matter-of-factly, *It hasn't been a good life.* In fact the two sentences were one thought: *It hasn't been a good week, it hasn't been a good life.* And she said the second sentence without even stopping for a breath.

So you can see how all this, me missing her, me re-creating her to help assuage my missing her, can tilt my center of gravity.

I can't say I dropped the phone in surprise when she said it hasn't been a good life, but truth is I had never heard her utter such a shattering thought before. As if she was negating her entire existence. To which I said:

"First time I've ever heard you say something like that."

To which Maria said something even curiouser:

"I don't feel it or believe it."

What a lot of hooey, goes through my head. I've never heard anything more absurd.

"I don't believe a word of those two sentences," she added.

Those words were totally illogical. At once, her true feelings came out. The cat was out of the bag and couldn't be put back in. Or is that applicable only to a genie? Those words of hers, their order, their syntax, the pathos of those heartbreaking lines—and its denial so illogical, so patently false. It was as if her autobiography were compressed into those two sentences.

"So if you don't feel it or believe it, why did you say it?"

And then she comes up with that dumb follow-up, and I can imagine the pain she's going through trying to explain away those sad words.

"I'm saying it just to you."

"What in heaven's name is that supposed to mean? I still don't understand why you said those words."

To a degree I was proud that she trusted me with such an intimate revelation, her soul's confession, her spirit's lament.

Still, if she didn't feel or believe those words, why did she say them, even if just to me? She probably *did* believe them, otherwise they wouldn't have slipped out. She said them and then tried, awkwardly, to cover them up. She said, *I'm saying it just to you*, as if me she could trust, she could trust me with her innermost feelings, a girl who never once expressed verbally her feelings for me. And, as I once or twice told you, I felt so at home with her from the very beginning, even during our first tram ride together into Boston, that's when I told her, Look at me when you speak to me.

And those were the sad thoughts about Maria that went through my mind during the month she was away, completely ravishing my center of gravity. I checked my calendar every day, urging the days on, despite the postcards she sent me. If she only chose to, she could have had a happy, a good life with me. And deep down she knew it, she felt it. But her guilt about sinning with a married man...

•

I couldn't control my impulse.

= Are you married, Katz?

= First of all, John, my brother writes, "her guilt about sinning with a married man." That doesn't mean that the protagonist is married. It just refers to what she, Maria, the character, perceives and feels guilty about. And second of all, replay my first-of-all. And third of all, John, you're obviously addressing this question to my brother, who shies away from all personal questions. Moreover, I have to repeat again and again, we're dealing with a work of fiction, so you're asking a question of a character. The main thing is that in the novel Maria considers Katz a married man.

And then Katz, like clever Maria, changed the subject.

= Remember, John, in the novel, the hero actually considers conversion just to make it easier for her. A pro forma conversion, not a theological one. For how can a Jew believe that God consorted with a woman? Forgive me for offending you, John, but in the absurd matrix of human belief that takes the cake, or wafer, for absurdity.

= No offense, Katz, I allowed. = I too consider it absurd.

40

MARIA'S RETURN, CONTINUED

Okay, Maria's back. In her apartment I welcomed her. I said nothing about the postcards she sent me, informing me that things between us would have to change.

Her new attitude expressed itself at once in the seating arrangement. She sat herself down in her old, deep easy chair, which left me no choice but to sit on the sofa. This time I didn't stretch out my hand to take hers.

"Look, I hope you'll understand. Our relationship, as beautiful and special as it is, has been troubling me. You know that. And in Europe I had an epiphany."

Yeah, I thought. Because of me and my dream.

Then, with closed eyes, Maria told me she had gone into a church in Slovenia, no one was around, it was the middle of the afternoon, very quiet, eerily silent, the place was ice cold, and she suddenly broke into tears in an act of repentance or contrition, or whatever the correct Christian term is for this feeling, crying her eyes out, remembering Jesus, praying to Jesus, and she vowed, she promised Jesus she would no longer be intimate with me, because it was a sin and she was trying, she would try, to lead a life free of sin.

"But I'm not married," I cried out. "I told you that a million times. So what's the sin?"

"Because I'm not," she said. "Sex without marriage is fornication. And that's the sin. And that's why I can't no more." She looked at me and gave me a half smile. "Remember, just before I left, you told me to remember Jesus? And I did. Even though you were probably being facetious when you said it. But you told me and I like to be told what to do."

That last line of hers annoyed the hell out of me. Using the same line now for Jesus and Christian piety that she had used for sex. I could swear there was a faint sparkle in her eyes and a tease in her voice when she said those words, the witch!

Indirectly, maybe even directly, it was I, me, Katz, who was responsible for her European epiphany, her uptick in piety. My telling her often enough about the beauty of Slovenia, Greece, Ferrara, Padua, Venice perked her interest in traveling again. When I spilled my flying dream to her, she decided on the spur, I'm going. And by leaving, by leaving me, by not seeing me almost daily, I gave her the respite and time to reflect and genuflect, to cogitate and meditate, to reassess her religious state, to feel guilty, to see how far she had strayed from, and betrayed her other beloved, Jesus.

My luck, there were churches all over the place with long fingers beckoning. Of course, if not for my big mouth, she would have tamped her sky in the piety, nurtured her carnality.

"You're a reincarnation of Mother Ann Lee," I told her.

"Who's that?"

"The eighteenth-century founder of the American Shakers. Like you, she believed in confession and celibacy, of course after being knocked up seven or eight times...So you can be a Shaker too."

After a moment's thought she said, "I'd rather be a mover."

"Me too," I said. "That's part of my six-part sexual motto. Waker. Taker. Mover. Shaker. Quaker. Then maker."

"Faker," said she.

And then, her face beaming, she went into a little bag lying on her dictionary stand and withdrew a small box, which she gave to me.

"Open it."

Inside, on a bed of absorbent cotton, lay a beautiful, handblown Venetian glass gondola about four inches long, so delicate and fine it looked like it was fashioned out of blue water and sky blue air.

"It's stunning...Thanks for thinking of me."

I hugged her. She hugged me back.

"I always think about you," Maria said. "But my decision, it's irrevocable. What's that bag on the floor?"

"Something for you. A welcome home present. Open it."

She held out two leather bags. One a pocketbook; another, of matching design, a bigger bag in which she could carry all the things she lugged in the gypsy sack she'd been using for years.

"Oh my God, it's so beautiful. Thank you. That's going to be my new travel-to-Boston bag."

She came and kissed me on the cheek, thought a moment, then kissed the other one too.

"But please respect my wishes, okay?"

I made no such promise.

What a turn of events! Under normal circumstances when a guy is let go, there's another chap in the picture. But here my competitor was not another man, but Jesus himself, who had insinuated himself into her, inveigled his way in. She got religion. Became his disciple. He got in—I got out. That son of a god ruined it for me. He screwed me good, which is precisely what I wanted to do to her.

Enter morals, exeunt sex.

It distressed me, her new attitude, but I wasn't despondent. I had been on that path before. Maria's life with me was a zigzag between sin and sainthood, between open and shut doors. *My beloved is a locked garden*, says the Song of Songs, but I had a key. She had reformed before and I had deformed that reform. She would put up a valiant struggle but, in the end, she couldn't resist me. My rival, Jesus, could stay on top of the seesaw only for so long—and then I would bring him down again.

Had we agreed that she would leave the back door open for me again, so that I could come in very early when she was still asleep? I don't recall. But the next morning I decided to go anyway and, to my delight, found the rear door open. And you have to understand there were two doors. The back door, which gave entry into the hallway shared by two apartments, the upstairs and the downstairs tenants, and the back door to Maria's apartment. So it couldn't have been an accident. It takes will and motion to open up both back doors.

Into her bedroom I went. She was fast asleep. Previously, before her trip, I would let myself in, she's a heavy sleeper, nothing wakes her. I would take off my clothes and slip in under the covers with her. But this time I did not do this. Under the blankets, fully dressed, how undignified. Okay, my shoes were off.

Half asleep now, she welcomed me and snuggled into my embrace. Maria was on her back, wearing her long loose gray flannel nightshirt with the deep V-neck. I had my right arm around her neck and shoulders, my left hand holding her right breast, and I was kissing the outer edges of her lips and she was responding, albeit hesitantly, restrainedly, holding-back-edly. If you want to put it into percentages, me giving 85% to her 20%. I know the numbers don't add up. In love, percentages are fluid, illogical, like everything else. And I whispered into her ear, "I'm so glad you're back, safe and sound. You must have missed me something awful."

And a moment after her lips were on mine, and while my hand was still clasping her right breast, she started complaining, softly, calmly, that I had wormed my way back into her bed and was trying to get her to break her bond. And as she spoke she slid her glance down my right arm to the hand, wrist and fingers resting on her bared breast as if to say: "*See what I mean*?" What in heaven's name is *that* doing *there*?" A look like a mother would give her five-year-old son for picking French fries from the common bowl with his fingers. But Maria didn't tell me to remove my hand. Of course I didn't move it. I liked it where it was. Instead, I kissed her cheek, her eyes, her hair. She did not turn away from me.

That's why her later reaction was so incredible, astonishing and disappointing. I mean, it wasn't as if she woke up to find an intruder in her bed. And anyway, remember, my clothes were on.

Religious fanatics are touched with madness.

In fact, I may not have mentioned it, but before she left for Europe, Maria asked me if I wanted the key to her apartment. This way I could come and go as I pleased.

It was a moving, lovely, intimate gesture, but I declined. Her offer was more touching in a way than the words she could never bring herself to utter. If you ask me now why I said, no thanks, or maybe I didn't say that and just didn't take the proffered key, I don't know the answer. This happened more than twenty years ago. Maybe I didn't even know then. Maybe because a key was like an exchange of rings. Maybe because she never articulated that she was crazy about me. I just don't know.

This came about in typical Maria loop-de-loop fashion. Like her indirect invitation for me to come to her house first day we met. Not in a blaze of passion or love which prompts one to say: *Come whenever you like, day or night; I want to see you.*

This had never happened to me before, the offer of a key. Sometimes I had a girlfriend with no apartment. Sometimes I had an apartment with no girl. Sometimes I had a key without either an apartment or a girl. Isn't that every guy's dream? The offer of a key? It's not just the key, it's a symbol of the girl's trust. And most of all, her commitment. I mean, a girl doesn't give out multiple keys. Unless she's a locksmith or in business. With that key I wouldn't be surprised by finding someone else in the apartment with her. Leaving through the front door as I entered through the back. By giving you her key, she's saying: *You're the only one who can put his key into my lock.*

A couple of days before her trip to Europe, I asked, "Who's going to feed your replacement canary?"

At which she repeated her earlier offer: "Let me give you a key and you can come in whenever you want and feed it."

She pointed to one hanging on a nail near the rear door. "Revel in my absence. And feed my new canary."

"Is this for keeps, or for just when you're away?"

"Hold on to the key," she said astutely. She didn't even say, Keep the key, for by using that word she would have affirmed my question. And so she avoided, as she usually did, a direct response to a sensitive question. But I didn't take it. I didn't take the key. Still don't know why.

A few weeks passed. I mulled over my crippled center of gravity. Now Maria had returned from Europe. I let myself in via the back door which she had left open and I slipped into her bed fully clothed. Then, after that lukewarm welcome, I left her house and said I'd be back in an hour to take her to the tram.

What happened in her head during that house I am only imagining. I wasn't there. Wish I could have been. But during that hour while I floated in joy that I was slowly getting back to her despite her vow to Jesus, during that hour the demon surfaced in her.

Could she too, like most of us, possibly be two people, one evil twin lurking hiding within the other benign, outwardly beneficent good twin, to be revealed only when an imaginary border is crossed, a line of stress violated, then the inner demon surfacing, when she feels her honor has been compromised? How otherwise to explain Maria's behavior only one hour after I lay next to her?

•

= Katz, it's interesting that your brother accents Maria and her evil twin. Especially after that anecdote from the Midrash or Talmud about the twin sisters and the adultery test.

= I'm glad you noticed that. Yes, the notion of twins and twinning fascinates him. As it does me.

Katz stopped, narrowed his eyes as if trying to remember something, then said:

= Faulkner once wrote: "A book is the writer's secret life, the dark twin of man. You can't reconcile them." Like my brother, I too have a fondness for literary twins. Thomas Mann loved them too. The dwarf twins in his *Joseph in Egypt.* Also in his *The Holy Sinner* and in his long story, "Blood of the Walsungs."

= But the last two also deal with incest, I reminded Katz.

= That I don't recall, John. Last incest I know is *Oedipus.*

= But, Katz, I said, = that's mother and son. The Mann fictions I refer to are brother and sister incest.

= Like the brother-sister relationships in ancient Egypt that the narrator refers to after Maria asks him, "Where are you going?" When he kisses her for the first time.

•

I don't think anything untoward happened to her during that hour we were apart. No lightning strike of moral relevation. I know it's a misprint, but that's the way my brother wrote it. Maybe purposely. No otherworldly vision. She got up, washed, brushed her teeth, didn't eat of course, didn't put on and then tear off three or four outfits, didn't carefully choose which bag she'd take today, purposely rejecting the new one I had given her just yesterday, she took the one that had become part of her skin, a colorful, loosely knit multihued sack made by native women in some misbegotten Fifth World country. When she looked in the mirror—I mean she *had* to look in the mirror once or twice, didn't she?—Maria didn't see a face distorted with rage. But it was brewing. Building up. A coiled spring about to be released. And it was only when she saw me that the spring sprung, the cork popped, and out spewed fury. Venom. Religion. It was her reading of the Testaments that did it. The Old Testament—the way the Christians see it: wrath.

Maria sat in the car and faced me, but her eyes, her glance, were set beyond. The little space of my car could not contain her indignation. It needed a larger forum. So she stared out as if to a broad distant vista.

Her flare-up, disjointed, ungrammatical, illogical, unlike anything I'd heard from her, was directed, as much as I could make of it, to me. Because of the sloppy grammar, I knew it wasn't Maria speaking but her evil twin. All the more surprising was her volcanic eruption because it came at the cusp of my euphoria.

Things were going so swimmingly now, I thought as I left her house that morning. Despite her vow in her postcards to me from Athens, or maybe it was Venice, despite her epiphany in a Catholic church, she who detested Catholics and Catholicism for its pagan qualities, for its impure Christianity, for its un-Christian theology, she found solace in an empty ice-cold Catholic church in Slovenia, the locus of her penitent tears, the place where she sobbed out her guilt and made her I-won't-sin-anymore decision. I suppose when your own religious shrine isn't around, you grit your teeth and go over to the competition.

Of course, it was all my fault. None hers. She was just a passive bystander, or, better, by-lier, an innocent page in a book, and I was the demon who defiled the page. From in between the lines of her jagged chatter, I gathered that it was I who had led her into temptation, me, the snake, and she, weak Eve creature that she was, slave to her sinful desire, bit into the juicy proffered apple, good Christian symbol nowhere to be found in the Bible or other Jewish sources, the fig is probably the correct fruit, given the fig leaves with which Adam and Eve covered their nakedness, although personally, if you consider what might be the most tempting and delicious fruit in the world that opened their eyes, I'd vote for the ripe permission—another salient, meaningful, Freudian slipcover, penetrative typo—ripe permission to continue nefarious loving, although the mind wanted to write *ripe persimmon*, the cagey, lust-driven fingers fingered *permissio*n.

So despite all that I was back in her bed, holding her, and she was, albeit s-l-o-w-l-y, even grudgingly, semi-responding to my kisses. Lying next to her, I figured if I didn't rush her we'd be back to the same intimacy we had before she left for Europe.

It was only months later, late one night, coming back from a trip we had taken together to Connecticut, that she told me details, and what exciting details they were—God, I kept replaying them in my mind like a racy video one hides from one's family and views repeatedly when no one is around—of an earlier incident in her life. It was then that I came to appreciate her scrambled egg mix of rage and reform, of desire and delight in Jesus.

Now, in my car, about 9 a.m., taking her to the T, Maria's face changed. It was almost magical, not magical in the heavenly sense, rather sorcerical, in the demonic sense, the evil twin surfacing within her. The sort you read about in a fairy tale or see in a dark brooding film by Ingmar Bergman. It was no longer the warm, smiling, friendly, open Maria, radiating innocence and light.

Now her face was tight. Her voice became thin, high-pitched, compressed. She spoke in staccato bursts. I use the word "burst" because it's as if something broke in her. You should have seen her face. I had to watch the road. There was lots of traffic. Didn't want an accident. Her face became distorted. Contorted. Her throat pulsed, her cheeks dark red. Whoa! I wanted to say. Rein in the horses. What's the matter with you? Too bad she couldn't see her face. Once, with my right hand, I twisted the rearview mirror in her direction so she could look at her face. She twisted it back, screaming, ranting, speaking in a language invented on the spot.

I no longer recall precisely what she said, but her new tongue had lots of *ex* and *on* sounds, like ablixeron, hexerex, ontexeris, entlonxin. Maybe a pharmacist would have helped me decipher those words. I should have written them down when I got home. I just remember the tone, the rage, the vehemence—how she had twisted the rearview mirror back as if she were twisting my neck off—a side of her, a face of her, that I had never seen before.

In her tirade, Maria railed against every single one of my limbs except the one she loved most. My hands should be tied. My legs bound. My tongue cleaved. In her fury she babbled, *Your lox lipped*, but she didn't catch that and I wasn't in the mood for humor. I wish I could have recorded her poliloquy. It would have made fun reading.

Maria berated me for corrupting her, for taking her along a path of sin, for forcing her to break her vow to Jesus.

You've become a Catholic, I said to myself. *Get thee to a nunnery. You're done with funnery.*

"I promised Jesus to give up sinning when I was in Europe."

About which she had written to me. Yes, those accursed postcards.

"I'm not going to do that anymore." Her missive from Venice. "We will have to have a different type of relationship."

And now she was giving me the glad tidings in person.

"We can meet in cafés, restaurants, wherever. But not in my house. If that suits you, fine. If not, I don't care if I never see you again."

What an insult. Banished from her house.

"What am I, some kind of disease, a pariah?" I said. "Become a nun," I told her. "So now it's all my fault, huh? I went at it solo, right?"

"I'm not blaming you."

"No. Of course not. You're blaming my car. My belt. The ceiling fan," I shouted.

Her harangue continued, but in a different language. I had always wondered about the expression "speaking in tongues." I never knew what it meant until I heard Maria doing it. In her emotive harangue, delivered in an obfuscative doubletalk that made the language strain at the edges, it was obvious who the culprit was. Whodunnit? Hedon it. Hedonist. I'm a hedonist. But she, she wasn't a shedonist, God forbid. God, how she hated sex, screaming out her hatred of it while going at it full speed. With her the me-you changed places. The you-me exchanged personalities. The you-me fused. The *y*M*o*E*u* slid down, loudly down a slippery slope. And it was I who provided, generously, energetically, with sneaky, irresistible eros, the ice, the wax, the rollerblades, the sleds, the skis, the bobsleds. I even provided the slippery in one beautiful gift box and the slope in another.

"You left the door open for me, for crying out loud!" I yelled. But I stared straight ahead, didn't want to look at her because in my state of agitation, while driving, turning to her would have been a mistake. "Just an hour ago, you snuggled up to me in your bed. How did I get in? Through the window? Down the chimney? What am I, some friggin Santa Claus with holy claws? You left the door open for me. I was kissing you. Holding your bared breast. You didn't ask me to leave the bed. When you're having fun, you tuck away your morals into that freezer you never open."

"I wasn't kissing you."

"You sure were. If you kiss me now, you will taste your lips on mine, you who are a number-one seeded World Class taster."

"I didn't kiss you."

"You kissed me, you did. Any DNA test will confirm it. Only later, when the fun is done, when done is the fun, when you've had your pleasure, then, and only then, do you start with your moralistic philosophying. Then your Jesus comes knocking at the door. The hour we spent in bed you were getting warmer by the minute. Just an hour ago."

"You broke me. You seduced me. You're a demon, a devil," she screamed.

"And with what enthusiasm you put that demon into hell!"

I heard her taking deep breaths. Seethe came out of her in foreign-sounding polysyllables.

"Where does this rage come from? I don't recognize you. I bet you don't even recognize yourself. What's happened to you during the past sixty minutes? Have you taken one of Figaro's mood-altering potions? Answer me why you left the door, both doors, open for me? Because you wanted, you desired me to come. Wanted. Wanted. Just an hour ago. You're being 'illogical, oppressive, and absurd.' Not my words. They're from Mann's intro to Kafka's *The Castle.*"

I wished I could do something dramatic. Like jump on the bed holding her canary cage. Or, to make a point, pour down the drain her cheap eau de cologne which she thought was expensive perfume. But what could I do in the close confines of a car? Ram into a tram?

I reached for the rearview mirror again and tilted it toward her face.

"Look at yourself. Just look at yourself. Do you recognize your evil twin? It's you, you who's the demon, not me. This isn't the Maria I know."

"Slopery slip. Me. You. Down. Pushed," she frothed, foamed, wrathed in inside-out English. Now at least she was talking in one of the known Indo-European languages.

Slippery slope. My goodness! Now that I think of it, that's the madeleine in Proust's milk tea. I remember when she first told me she was afraid of going down a slippery slope. She'd have to hold back with me because if she started, there's no guarantee she would or could stop.

It's the old fear of the young virgin. *Once I start I'll love it so much I'll never be able to stop.*

"Do you think you have the potential to become a whore, a sleep-around?" I once asked her.

"Yes," Maria had said, surprising me. Constantly surprising me. She said if she didn't watch herself she had the propensity—she loved that word—to become a slut. And I thinks to myself: she has a Maria Magdalena complex. Wants to be crucified next to her lord, after being nailed by a horde.

It was only later, a while after this tirade against me, that Maria explained that yes, and it kind of made sense.

When I heard that surprising Yes, I said, "You're off your rocker. You should see a psychologist."

"I have been," she said.

"Oh, yeah. Now I remember. For how long?"

"Seventeen years."

"Drop the crook," I said. "He's been milking you. That thief has no shame. He should be brought up to the shrink-proof ethics committee, if they have one, for grand larceny. I'll fix, I'll analyze your problem in one second, in one sentence, and I won't charge you a dime...well, maybe a quarter."

"Go ahead." Said through tight lips. "What's your analysis?"

"Not so fast," I said. And I remembered the first question a doctor's secretary invariably asks you after you spell your name and before you're allowed to tell her you've just had a heart attack and haven't breathed for ten minutes.

"What kind of insurance do you have?"

She didn't laugh.

"Here's my analysis, in one second. No charge this time. It's a split in your personality between your religious purity and your overwhelming love of fucking. Between your desire for sex, for loving, and your desire for and love of Jesus, which is as powerful a pull on the spiritual side as is the other one on the physical side. That's why the mystics always saw God in physical, even sexual terms. They sublimated their sexuality to the spirit but often couldn't control it, so they founded cults that had lots of God and lots of sex. Those are the most successful religions. Without any tensions."

She didn't say a word; stared straight ahead.

Then, from the silence, another barrage of vituperation. And among the loose pages of her maledictionary came the word "loser" or "looser." Then it became clear. I was a "ducer." She meant "seducer."

I dropped her off at the station. Looked at her face. Gone the wit. Gone the courtesy, the decency, the *mentchlikhkeyt* of my first meeting with her, when she was so gracious to the hefty ticket booth clerk in wishing him a belated Merry Christmas and Happy New Year. Now she was transformed, transfigured, transmogrified. Her evil twin had germinated.

She walked out of the car without even a goodbye. Just slammed the door. Not even *thanks for the lift*. Her I gave a lift; me she gave a down. I felt aggrieved. All she had to do was say, *I'm sorry*. I'm a sucker for apologies. When I hear someone say, I'm sorry, tears come into my eyes and I feel as if I'm at fault. But that's not Maria's style.

Before I drove away, I shouted at her:

"You left the two goddamn doors open for me purposely, didn't you?"

I said that to her back. As those words hit her, I saw her back tightening, as if a missile had struck her between the shoulder blades.

•

For a long while I didn't call her. Except for one brief call that same week just to get something off my chest.

Months later I spoke to her about her transformation that day. I said I couldn't believe the rapid change in her personality. She didn't want to hear. I had planned an entire speech, but somehow, because by now she was back to her old self, calmed, changed, in better humor, my complaining words were no longer relevant. But, as you can see, I did not forget that awful day. It made a lasting impression on me, those ten, twelve minutes of her mania.

After Maria left, I stepped out of the car stunned, dizzy, shaken, hearing her rant again word for word, as though she had magically, Figaristically, programmed it into my skull while she was riding off to work in Boston. My head pounding as if the flu, or some other illness, had suddenly sent me into a spin of delirium, my center of gravity off again. I stepped out of the car. Needed air. Her rage had sucked the oxygen out of me. Stepped out of the car to contemplate my fate. I had never contemplated my fate before. Felt like a character in a Chekhov story or play. Obviously, we were now parted. She, there; I, here.

I imagined her on the tram, putting her big colorful bag, not the new one I had gotten her as a welcome home present, on the seat next to her, opening her Bible, and joyously immersing herself in Jesus. Was she thinking of me as I was now thinking of her? Or had J.C. effectively expunged me completely from her consciousness? Perhaps I would appear in her thoughts but only as a black-and-white image on a negative—she would only see my negative aspects so as to mollify herself, exculpate herself, forgive herself.

But unlike a Russian literary character, I would not exult in self-pity in monologue or burden another with my complaints. Perhaps now was the time to start jotting down my experiences with Maria. I would take Maria, change her, subtract her, expand her, write about and around her. Yes. That's what I will do, I decided as I stood outside of the driver's side of my car.

I went back into the car and, less dizzy now, drove home.

•

Katz stopped narrating. There was a satisfied look on his face. =Well, what do you say to that turn of events?

= Fascinating, Katz. I wish your brother well with the book. He seems to be following the rules.

= What rules?"

= I'm thinking of one of Somerset Maugham's lines. "There are three rules for writing a good book."....Katz, here's your station.

41

KATZ'S DREAM AFTER BREAKUP

THAT NIGHT I DREAMT about Maria, replaying the last few things we said to each other. And I realized, when I woke up, that I had never before dreamt about her. A few days later I called her and, after a polite, meaningless exchange, I asked her:

"Did I hear correctly the other day that you would maintain a friendship with me but never again see me in your house?"

"Yes."

"What's the matter?" I said, insulted, aggrieved. "Afraid you'll plop into bed with me again and tell me, 'I like to be told what to do'?"

"No," she said. But she was lying. That's exactly what she was afraid of. "I'll see you in the Brandeis café but not at my apartment. A lot of time will have to pass before I invite you in again."

"Do you know, do you realize what an insult that is? Every jerk can come in to see you, borrow books, everyone but me. Me, I'm a persona non gratis."

"Grata."

"I like gratis better. It helps pay the bills."

"You know why I said what I said?" she said.

"Why?" I said, falling oh so neatly into Maria's sweetly baited trap.

"Because you're not your every day run-of-the-mill jerk. You're special."

"A special jerk, huh?"

"Yes," she said, and I could sense the smile in that Yes. "A very special jerk."

"Okay," I said slowly. I didn't know what else to say. "Stay well, Maria."

"You too."

The following night my sleep was so dense, so deep, that when I woke I thought I had been in a different era, a different time and space zone. I felt myself groaning, three times, I remember, and I woke suddenly. I felt demeaned. I heard again what Maria said and her words hurt me again. But the curious thing was that while sleeping I didn't feel ill at ease; it was only when I woke that I felt I had been released, and here the old phrase, *bonds of sleep*, is right on the mark, absolutely applicable: released from some kind of deep, ominous experience.

Of course, all this was connected to her, to Maria. Her nasty attitude, it affected my sleep. My sense of time. I knew I'd seen her recently. But time was so squeezed it seemed it was just a moment ago. I needed the crutch of a calendar to orient myself.

•

= John, I'm leaving for about three weeks on a surveying assignment I have to supervise in Chicago. Would you mind if I left you two chapters to read and I'll pick them up next time I see you?

= Absolutely, I said.

= Absolutely yes, or absolutely no?

We both laughed.

42

MEETING MARIA AFTER LONG ABSENCE

I HADN'T SEEN MARIA for months. This didn't mean I didn't think of her. I did. She was on my mind every day during the long winter. Every once in a while I thought of calling her. I imagined my rather long conversation with her, and this seemed to satisfy my need to talk to her. I would go to the phone, then back away, as if from some sacred shrine. I still thought of her as mine.

Then one day, as March was ending, I said, *Enough postponement,* and, with the metaphysical equivalent of fifty chin-ups, I willed myself to call her. It was a Sunday. I told her I had had long, imaginary conversations with her every day. I thought I heard the plosive "M..." coming out of her mouth, then a sudden hesitation, a brake, as if once again she was holding back from saying, "Me too!" And I added, "Conversations in which, to my acute astonishment, you're actually funny."

Then, without saying, *By the way*, or *To change the subject*, or *Listen to this*, or any other pedestrian pleasantry as a segue, after I said, "you're actually funny," without letting her say a word, without a pause, and without even asking her how she was, I immediately said, "I have a business meeting in Dalton, Connecticut, on Wednesday..."

"Where's that?"

"West of East Dalton. Actually, just outside of Norwich."

"What kind of meeting?"

It was a mundane consulting engineers meeting, but I told her:

"Travel Writers Guild. I'm still a member, even though I haven't written any more travel books."

"Yeah," she said. "*Travels with Bessie in Arabia*."

"Which brought me to you. Wanna come along for the ride? The meeting lasts about two hours, during which time you could sit in a bookstore or see a film. It would be so nice."

I thought for sure she'd say no, offer some polite excuse. But Maria immediately, happily, gave an upbeat, delightful, "Sure. So nice to hear from you again."

•

The next day, on March 30, I called to wish her a happy birthday.

Given her unconventional attitudes, I never thought Maria would pay attention to such a mundane topic, but during the time I knew her she had repeated, like an enthusiastic child, that whenever she looked at a digital clock and saw 3:30 she was reminded of her birthday. It got to the point that 3:30 also always reminded me of Maria's birthday.

But to my "happy birthday" came her wry comment:

"Remember your mistake of last year, when you called me on March 10 and thought it was my birthday and I told you it was 3:20 and not 3:10? And so we established that my official un-birthday was March 10. And today is March 30."

And then Maria came up with one of her most memorable lines:

"You can't even get my wrong birthday right."

"Impossible. It was always thirty minutes after three; hence, 3:30."

"Don't you think," she argued, "I should know when I was born? It's my birthday."

"It may be yours," was my rebuttal, "but since it's others who wish you happy birthday, it's others who do the remembering."

"Well, you remembered wrong. Twice. My birth certificate says March 20 and so does my driver's license."

"You see how one scribal error at the beginning of one's life can cause a domino effect of unstoppable catastrophic consequences?"

"You remembered wrong."

"I remembered right. I checked with your mother. She should know better than you."

"You don't even know her."

"I do."

"How?"

"I'm not getting into that now…and, anyway, why should the person who is born be wished happy birthday? It's the mama who gave birth, so *she* should be wished a happy birth day. On that special day, all the attention should be directed and focused on the mother and not on her squealing, squalling, bawling, red-skinned seven-and-a-half pounder…You may have popped your head out on March 20, but you didn't emerge until March 30."

"Anyway, thanks for the good wishes. Even…though…they…are…WRONG…as…you…usually…are. See you Wednesday. What time should I be ready?"

"I'll pick you up at five. And by the way, if you want to sleep over, I booked a room with three beds."

"Who's the third for?"

"My receptionist," I said. "She'll guard you from going to me. I'll guard her from going to you. You'll guard me from going to her."

Maria barked a laugh. "I'd rather be coming than going."

•

Soon as she got into the car she began talking quickly, hyper—did I tell you I gave her a hug and she hugged me back?—nervous, as if wound up, just like she did the first day I met her in the tram waiting room in Newton.

"Slow down," I said, patting her knee. (Had she lost weight? It seemed less fleshy.) I didn't pat her knee out of affection or desire. I patted her knee to show her—and me—that I wasn't bound by any of her don't-touch-me rules. I stroked her knee to demonstrate that I still, to a degree, called the shots.

"Slow down, okay?"

And she did slow down. For a sentence or two, then she sped up again, hyper^2, hardly moving her lips, she couldn't control it, it was beyond her, joining her words like a typist tapping twin-fingeredly sans space bar. Noroombetweenwords. Between words she left no room. The oxygen was drained out of her long run-on sentences. But at least she was talking English now, not condensed Sanskrit.

You know what it felt like, listening to Maria? As if she were programmed, destined, to say a certain number of words during one evening before the bell tolled midnight and she had to say all of them at once, quick as possible, without punctuation marks, the consonants compressed—just look at her lips—the vowels deflated like a limp balloon, her O's like parentheses coupling, so she could say what she had to say before midnight when she'd turn into a pumpkin.

This speech babble, her lips barely moving, reminded me of those radio announcers who at the end of a commercial, when by law the caveats, restrictions and exceptions have to be stated, are spurred into an abnormal gallop of words, most of which are unintelligible. Maybe—what do I mean maybe, delete maybe, cancel maybe—I'm absolutely sure she was nervous seeing me, because a minute later, mightily aware of her speed talking, she did slow down and admitted, "Do you notice I've slowed down? Now you don't have to tell me to slow down anymore."

I didn't respond.

"Well, why don't you say something?" she said. "You do notice… how…slowly…I…am…speak…ing."

Yes, she had put the brakes on her speed speech. But stubbornly, stubbornly, I did not answer. For. A. While. I. Did. Not. Answer. I stubbornly, ob-sti-nate-ly, did not reply. It came over me suddenly, that mood. I didn't plan it. I was probably getting back at her. Stubbornly. There was a subliminal anger in me. It lurked. Ready to pounce. I hadn't seen her in months. I was angry at her for writing to me from Europe, just days after that ecstatic encounter in her bedroom for most of the day. On the eve of her flight (and flight it was: her flight from me) to Europe from Boston's Logan airport—to which I had driven her. Furious at her for writing to me, a week later, I think it was from Venice, that she could not continue in the same way. And all this on a picture postcard, the dummy, emasculating me in front of my female mailman (a strange combo of words, no?) who no doubt read every piece of mail that wasn't sealed and shared it with her colleagues during their overly long lunch breaks. Compromising my privacy, despite the miniscule script, and spreading news about Maria's decision all over the block.

In Slovenia, Maria had another of her religious epiphanies. Tears and prayers in a Catholic church no less. The closest one that happened by when Jesus's halo landed on her head. And then, when she came back home, I inveigled myself into her bed one morning, fully clothed, except for my shoes.

I don't recall precisely the sequence of events. It happened so many years ago. I visited her the day after she came back from Europe. She told me that she can't, won't, do "that" anymore. When I left, I told her I'd see her early the next morning and to leave the back doors open. The next morning both back doors were open. I was relieved, happy like a kid in a folktale lost in the forest who follows a trail of bread crumbs along the way.

Finding the door open, I was ecstatic. Things will go back to the way they were. I loved slipping into bed with her and surprise her with my embrace. I saw everything was rumpled. Clothing scattered on the floor. All the drawers were pulled open, the sliding closet door too. Gone her mania for closed doors.

Maria was asleep, hugging a pillow that could have been a dream of me. Three other pillows next to her. I took off my shoes and slipped into bed next to her. She turned sleepily and through half-closed eyes noticed me and made a sleepy little mutter that sounded like, *You're here.* I embraced her and she smiled happily, dreamily, and chanted pleasant little notes that made me feel good and I slid my hand around her neck and down into her flannel nightshirt and held her beautiful ample breast. I kissed her ear and cheek and lips and we began to talk. As I held her, I asked her to tell me about each city she had visited, and in between cities I kissed her and at first she responded feebly, her teeth pressed like a teenager on a first date, but finally when she got to the fourth city, Rome, she kissed me hard and good as if she meant it. And then, Oh Lord, I still see that look on her face, the way she slowly moved, turned her head away from me, tilted down her chin to get a better view, and slid, yes, slid, I can still that glance sliding, she slid her icy glance down to my hand and did not say a word, but that cold look of disdain in her eye, on her face, seemed to say: What's *that* doing *there*? No, not seemed. It flashed those words in bright orange red neon letters. Of course, I didn't remove my hand. Why should I give her the satisfaction? She had a mouth, didn't she? Her look said that that foreign object on her naked breast was a kind of alien invader, an unwelcome interloper, a plastic or wooden extra hand that seemed to come from somewhere but really should go somewhere else. And, notice, not once during this entire comic scenario did she look at me.

But the truth was she didn't *want* me to remove my hand. That look with those big long green eyes of hers, like a camera dollying, the chin slowly tilting, was just a salve to assuage her guilt.

Her Christianness weighed heavily on her, like a prisoner with a ball and chain. There were good reasons why she didn't have a boyfriend. I don't know if I counted or not. Why she was not married—or maybe she was, like nuns, to Jesus. Why she spent Saturday nights alone in her apartment reading. Why she herself admitted that it had not been a good life.

And don't think that while my hand was on her breast that I wasn't kissing her lips, her face, and she responding, which is why her vehement spew of opaque, Greek-sounding words in the car whacked the wind out of me, and I didn't see her again for months until I extended this invitation to her to ride with me to my meeting.

So, you see, I had reason to be angry. Had cause for a bit of revenge. A longer than normal silence. Harmless, it's true. For a long couple of minutes, sensing the tension building, I let her hang there with her question. Stubbornly getting back at her for banning me from her apartment, for flaring up at me after she had returned from Europe, after I had spent a delicious hour or so early that morning lying next to her, her pre-Europe warmth rekindled, for she had left the back doors open for me and was kissing me with the old fervor. Did you ever hear of a guy having Jesus as a rival in a love affair? In fact, I was toying with the idea of calling the book *How Jesus Was My Rival in a Love Affair.*

"Why don't you say something? Have you become mute?" Maria asked.

Now I opened up.

"Why did you leave the door open for me?" I hissed at her, making each word a screw that I sent into the palms of her hands. "You wanted me to come. That's why you left the back doors open. Both of them. You were hoping I would come despite what you said. Otherwise, you would have locked the door, just as you lock your front door every night. I'm not a Freudian, only his curious and dead wrong work *Moses* interests me, but you don't have to be a Freudian to know what that unlocked door stands for. Some women put a lock on their portals. Some leave them unlocked. Some men lock their wives' portals when they travel abroad. And one doesn't have to be a psychologist to understand that it's always easier to lash out at someone else than at oneself."

Then I fell silent again. She may have spoken, but I paid no attention.

•

"Don't you hear me?" she said while I was driving. "Hey, there! What world are you in?" Said at a quicker pace than before.

"Oh," I said, pretending to return from whatever planet I had supposedly been distracted to. "What did you say?"

Maria drew a deep breath. "I'm speaking slowly," she said, not so pleasantly this time. I can't say it was a contentious tone, but it was three degrees down from pleasant. Stripped now from her words was the patina of laughter.

Now *her* center of gravity was off kilter. I could see it on her tight face. But what good did it do me? You can't win when a nunnish, popish, anti-Catholic Protestant has vowed to love Jesus above all other men. I still longed to touch her, hold her close, kiss her lips, nuzzle into her great full breasts, lie next to her, fuck her brains out. Tell her I was crazy about her. But I couldn't even kiss her lips.

Now she was in a different sexual zone. We were both the same, she and I. Look in the mirror—I mean a normal mirror, not her dark, antipodal, anti-pride, non-mirror mirror—and we look the same, but some evil witch had come to cast a haze over her. I wished we could work out some compromise. I'd even be willing to forget the screwing, if we could still have the holding, the loving, yes, even without the sex that was against her newly evolved religious principles, but have her hands around me and her lips, her eyes ecstatically closed, her lips on mine, a beatific little smile on her lips as she lovingly said, "Really?" in that soft, intimate cadence, that "Really?"—her code word for "I love you."

"You couldn't bring yourself to say you liked me, could you?" I said to her suddenly in the cozy, protective dark.

It took her by surprise, that sudden question.

She didn't say. Now her lips were clamped shut.

"It would deprive you of some of your holiness, right? To say you were, and still are, crazy about me, just like I said those words to you. In fact, once, when we were stretched out on that old sofa of yours, you asked me straight out, 'Do you like me?' And I answered, do you remember what I said?"

"No. I don't remember."

"Do you remember asking me?"

"No."

"Sure you remember, but you're tight-lipped. Every single one of your paired lips, all of them, are now tight. You remember every word I said. Every letter. And where and when I said it. And what time it was. And what the weather was like. And whether the shade was up or down. And what music was playing. And even what color socks I wasn't wearing. 'You asked me, 'Do you like me?' I didn't beat about the bush but shouted, 'Like you? I'm crazy about you!' And it was around that time too that you asked me, and we hadn't even moved from the sofa into your bedroom yet, you asked me if I'd ever spend the night with you. And do you remember what I said? I bet you don't remember."

"You won the bet. I don't remember. I don't even remember asking you that."

"You do. I said, 'Sure I will.' And you probably don't remember telling me that I can have, that I should have a key to your apartment."

"That I *really* don't remember."

"And when you suddenly announced you're going to Europe for three or four weeks, I said, 'I'll miss you, but even more I'll miss your apartment.' I was joking, of course, for what's your apartment without you in it, but you took it seriously and said, 'I'll give you a key and you can come in whenever you like and you can feed my replacement canary. You should have a key to my apartment anyway,' is what you said."

To that too she was tight-lipped. Trying to play my game.

It was on the tip of my tongue to tell her, tell her, mind you, not ask her, because it wasn't a question. It was something I knew; something I didn't have to inquire about.

It slipped out, out of my control, as a partial interrogative.

"You really loved being with me, didn't you?"

She did, but didn't want to admit it, lest it affect her conscience even more. For if a woman offers you the key to her lock, and you assume you're the only guy on the block who has the key to that lock, isn't that like saying I love you in a different way?

I tried a different phrase.

"You were crazy about me too, weren't you?"

"Let's drop it, okay? I don't want to revisit that time."

"But I do. I must. I am oppressed by the dense melancholy of memories."

"That's very beautifully said."

"But it's not my line. You see, I'm footnoting it. It's from the opening line of 'Gedali,' that great short story by the Russian Jewish writer Isaac Babel....This is what I wanted to say. We liked each other. Me, you. You, me. Would it kill you to say, to admit, to articulate that you liked me? Would some piece of your heart be compromised, sacrificed, tainted?"

Maria looked down. Probably thinking of her sin against Jesus.

"Why is it so important for you?" she added.

"Because I'm a woman at heart and women like to hear these things."

I turned to her. She had pulled the sun visor down and was looking at herself in the mirror.

"Will you pull that back up and stop looking at yourself when I talk to you? Why don't you look at me? "

"But I like the way both of us can focus on what you're saying, me and my evil lying twin."

So she had remembered my epithet.

Out of the corner of my eye, I caught her sly but by no means nasty smile; in fact, there was a touch of good humor in that smile.

"There's a first for you, looking at yourself in the mirror."

"I don't have a real mirror at home, so I'm looking here."

"Please look at me."

"Okay," she said, and pushed the sun visor back up.

"You're actually listening."

"Sure. I like to be told what to do."

Oh, the echo of that phrase, now cleverly said in a different context.

But I didn't let go. I didn't relent. One never relents when one has the upper hand. The minute she had looked down, I knew I had the upper hand.

"The way you kissed me, slowly, on every part of my body, after I asked you to kiss me, you obviously were as crazy about me as I was about you."

Should I say, *And still am*? I wondered, then quickly added, "And still am. That was some surprise, the way you kissed every cubic millimeter of my body. It felt so good. It was heavenly. Special. I had never before felt anything like that. In. My. Life."

"Really?" she said, that word like velvet, that word like down, that word like the nap of a fine Persian carpet, an all-silk Ghoum with the sheen of sunrise, made by the little hands of eleven-year-old girls.

"Something you invented on the spur of the moment for me. I said, 'Wow! I feel, I just sense that you've been inspired to do this just for me, that you've never done this before. It's so new, so loving.' And you," *you bitch*, I didn't say, "you couldn't lie, could you? You said, 'No, but it's the first time I'm doing this to you.' You said those words with an edge, reveling in the nastiness."

"I didn't say it with an edge. I didn't mean it to be nasty or cruel."

"But you had to be honest, right? For my sake, at that special moment, you couldn't lie just a little bit, could you? Remember how you once asked me, rather told me, 'Please don't break my heart?' Well, with that remark you broke *my* heart."

"I'm sorry, Katz."

"I was—you put me—on such a high. I was floating above the stars, and you brought me crashing straight down to earth."

"Don't! Please!" she said, actually commanded, in a very tender tone. That surprised me, that tone, for I half expected her to explode in that rage I had experienced with her last time, months ago, when I gave her a lift to the tram station.

For a moment we were still. Then she said:

"If it will make you feel better, you, I have something to tell you about kissing."

"Okay. Go ahead."

"Do you remember," Maria said, "what special thing I did when I was kissing your back?"

"No."

"I was kissing you in one spot and making little bird-like sounds. And you said, 'Did you bring your canary too?' That you don't remember."

"I don't. I guess I was off in another world."

"And you even asked if I took an ornithology course to learn to imitate all these bird chirps."

"Well, what's the point?"

"The point is that I invented *that*, those little bird songs, for you. Especially for you."

Still, I did not relent.

"But your Jesus-bewitched tongue doesn't, didn't, still doesn't, let you say what your heart felt, what your body so obviously expressed toward me. You never said a word. Closest you got was that sweet, soft 'Really?' when I said something nice to you, a 'Really?' that had as much beautiful, tender music as those three un-uttered little monosyllabic words that every woman and every man with a woman's heart longs to hear."

Now her "Please" was pleading, and then she surprised me, she always surprised me, by saying:

"And, by the way, you never once, never once offered those three little monosyllabic words, as you so eloquently phrase it, to me."

"You heard it in a thousand different ways, including, 'I'm crazy about you.' And, anyway, would it have made a difference? Would it have been the magic elixir that oils the rusty closed gate and opens it?"

"Probably not," Maria sadly. As though sadness was destined for her and no deeds, no words, could change that ineluctable fate.

"And I said other things besides I was crazy about you."

"Please..." Maria said softly.

Legato. Rubato. Pianissimo. Tenderissimo.

I pulled over to the side of the road. I couldn't resist. I bent toward her and kissed her softly on the cheek, just to let her know I still cared. And also, calculatingly—do we ever act or speak without a tinge of calculation?—to show her that I totally disregarded her wish: *I don't want to revisit that time.*

"Please..." she said again. The fourth or fifth time.

At that moment I felt that had I thrown my arms around and drawn her close, she would have kissed me with the old abandon.

"...I don't..."

"...want to revisit that scene," I mocked her.

Then I was purposely tight-lipped, as though complying with her wishes. But I liked, I loved, to recall, to talk about the past with Maria. Recalling, reliving, reveling in those delicious moments I knew her, that delectable time space, or "revisiting" as she so formally, distantly, neutrally, put it, as unsentimental as an accountant with his numbers, was important for me. For her, I suppose, it may have been a kind of psychological torment.

Maybe Maria thought I was purposely reminiscing to hurt her, to enhance her guilt. What with her wish not to recall it, it very likely did bring back guilt, a guilt she wanted to suppress, block, wipe away altogether.

But guilt is not like chalk marks on a blackboard. You can't swoosh it away with an eraser. You can't press a button and make guilt disappear. The therapists union would howl Unfair.

Maria had been chewing the cud of various guilts for years and still couldn't—maybe deep down didn't want to—extirpate them. A nice old guilt gets to feel cuddly after a while, like a favorite teddy bear you hug to your chest when you go to sleep. As I would soon learn, she carried deep within her an old guilt—a guilt that would explain, perhaps in part, some of her current obdurate, unyielding, flat-out flinty attitude toward me. And if not toward me totally, then at least toward my exploring, movable parts.

Despite her anathema against Catholicism, she behaved like a Catholic, and I told her so, what with her nunnish behavior, her strict moral sexual code. And now—my luck!—I was her religious dart board. And, above all, haloing goldenly above all, let's not forget her love for Jesus, which grew day by day, and of which she never tired speaking.

"Convert," I told her once, "and find salvation and grace and a snuggly eiderdown goose quilt guilt."

Now, in the intimate darkness, in the dark that cloaked the two of us in a cocoon, in that darkness I looked at her and said softly:

"That was a special time, wasn't it, those few months. I think I told you, didn't I, that I felt such a close link between us, and it was established at once, the minute I told you my name was Katz, which you liked right away, and you recalled the title of that little book of travel essays I'd written about my trip to Bessarabia and other backward southeastern countries. And I felt I could do anything I wanted to you, with you. Remember, on the tram to Boston that delicious first morning, I was bold enough to correct your habit of saying, 'You know,' with a squeeze of the hand? And remember the first time I came to your house, you showed me slides of your trip that was inspired by my book? I was sitting on the birch bridge chair by your desk and you stood next to me and I plopped you down on my lap and put my hands around your waist and you sat there and continued your narration. You didn't stand up. You didn't say stop it. And you didn't say no. In fact, when you got up to change slide trays you sat right back down on my lap quite naturally, as if that's where you belonged. I tell you that feeling of having known you began in those first few minutes. We seemed to be on the same wavelength."

Then Maria surprised me once more by saying, by continuing my song in the same key signature:

"Remember how afterwards you sat on the sofa and I sat myself down in my comfortable easy chair and you…"

"…I patted the pillow next to me on the sofa, indicating that you come next to me and you did."

"Yes," she said. And I liked the tone of that Yes.

"I still can't forget how I pulled you onto my lap and you sat there as if it were the most natural thing in the world."

"Yes," Maria said dreamily.

Again that magical moment occurred. I sensed it flowing between us. In the dark, love was floating in the air. Again I could have put my arms around her and kissed her and she would have responded—but I did not. But in my dream I touched her face and brought it close to mine and I kissed her lips.

"Will it hurt you to say, just once, that you liked me?"

"Is this why you invited me?"

"No. And I must say you've been very patient with me. I thought you'd say, *Stop the car, I want to go home*. But you've been listening to me and for that I thank you. I just want to hear from you that you liked me."

"Remember what I said before?"

"Yes. About revisiting."

"Then please. Stop."

"I can't. I invested lots of moral and soul energy in you, and you hardly said a word."

"But you sensed it."

"Yes. That's true. I sensed it. That's why I felt so comfortable with you. As if you were mine. But something in you held you back. As if by saying something nice you would be confirming aloud what you were feeling, and confirming it aloud would have made it true, and making it true would have compromised your religiosity, and compromising your religiosity would have meant you're sinning, and sinning would have meant you're betraying Jesus—and so you would rather fool yourself and hurt me."

"Hurt you? Never! How would I hurt you?"

"By not reciprocating."

"You put in an extra 'r.'"

"See how you mix me up? And there wasn't one 'r' in that previous sentence."

"You're very perspicacious."

"Spell it."

"No. And smart. How do you know so much?"

"Like Delilah, you asked me that once. Now I'll reveal it. Broccoli. The brain food. Eat of that tree of knowledge and you'll be as smart as me."

"As I," she corrected.

"So you *were* crazy about I."

I saw a happy look on Maria's face. But she didn't say. Didn't admit. Didn't confess. She just smiled her enigmatic, secretive smile. I'll bet at that moment she thought she was Mona Lisa, a smile that obviously answered my semi-interrogative.

Then I asked her, "What do you think is the most tender thing you said to me?"

"When I said 'Really?'"

But that wasn't revelatory at all. No big news. She was just repeating what I had told her long ago: "You couldn't come up with a sweet word of your own? You could only utter 'Really?' as though you couldn't believe or didn't deserve, all the nice things I was telling you."

Was that a play, a calculated gesture, her silence, her reticence to say a loving word to me? By remaining silent she was able to be in both worlds: receive my affection and yet remain moral and religious because she didn't verbalize her love. And so, in her skewered piety, she wasn't sinning by fornicating without marriage. For fornicatus = "I love you." Without the said out loud, *I love you*, no sin, no transgression, no wrong. Nothing peccable.

I paused. "Wasn't it, isn't it, good with me?"

But her countermove on the verbal chessboard was:

"I promised Jesus not to get physical with you..."

"Where did you promise this?" I asked Maria.

"In an ice-cold Catholic church in Slovenia. And I was bawling like a baby."

"Doesn't count! A Protestant vow in a Catholic church isn't kosher. You can't stand Catholicism anyway. You are hereby relieved, freed, exonerated, absolved from your invalid vow...And what's more, in all my forty years as a sexagenarian, you're the first girl I met who used Jesus as a chastity belt."

Maria giggled.

"Now you slow down."

"But I'm not even talking," I said.

"I'm not talking about your talking. I'm talking about your driving. You're driving like a cowboy. Please slow down. It's making me uncomfortable. Why're you driving so fast?"

"It says 95."

"That's the route number, not the speed limit."

"I go by the numbers. On Route 55 I do 55. On Route 66, 66. On 80, 80."

"What do you do on Route 1?"

"Take a bus."

"Please. Slow down."

"Okay. I like to be told what to do."

I didn't look, but I sensed the crinkle in her eyes.

But despite her vow, her promise, she didn't mind, didn't protest, didn't tell me to stop when I touched her face, her shoulder, her knee, when I stroked her hair, when I took her hand as I drove. When I stopped for gas, I bent forward on an impulse and kissed her neck. In other words, receiving affection was okay, as long as you're not caught giving affection. And when I asked her at the start of our trip to kiss me on the cheek, she refused. Why? Listen to this absurd answer.

"Because you asked me to."

Why can't we live in a world of musical comedy, where with an upbeat orchestra reprising the happy overture and the audience feeling the love and optimism of the show, Maria, hearing that music, would realize it was the third act and time for the ingénue to confess her love, and she would throw her arms around me and, if not explicitly cry out, "Screw religion and then me," at least she would give that impression. For love is more potent, more powerful than religion. Love is a kiss; religion, a dream thirsting for lips. Love is life, body and soul; and religion, religion is just an echo, a mirror, a dark shadow that compels you to aver you've just seen the sun.

43

ON THE WAY BACK FROM CT

It was already late when we drove back to Waltham. It was a special time, me and her in the dark. Friendly. Alone. Close, yes, but not that close. For instance, unlike months earlier, before our breakup, when I was in the car with her I would slide my finger, while keeping my eye on the road, from her knee along her thigh. You get the picture. Now I couldn't do that. Still, there was a warmth in the car. I told her it was sweet of her to join me on my trip to Norwich. And how patiently she waited for me in the lobby of the hotel while I was at that meeting. And she, who never expressed one word of affection to me in the months I had known her, she even made me feel good by saying she was glad she took the trip with me.

And then I gave her some advice. I didn't really want to. Why make it easier for a rival? But I did it anyway. I suggested to her if she wants to meet a fellow goy, she should tamp down the Jesus stuff. Keep it private, I said. Don't wear it on your sleeve.

"You'll never find someone as nuts as you are about Jesus. So tone it down. Don't sprinkle Jesus into your conversation with every other word. Consider the apothegm that's given as advice to budding writers: less is more."

"I don't tone it down with you. But even when I mentioned Jesus it didn't seem to overwhelm you."

"Me it didn't bother because it went in one ear and out the other. But you probably go at it even stronger when you meet a goy guy."

"Maybe."

"I'm giving you good advice. Don't flaunt it. Maybe you scare off potential goy boys. You sit on the T with that underscored, notes-in-the-margin Bible and a guy goy who sits next to you goes goodbye. You look like a nun."

"I'm not a nun. I can't stand nuns. I told you, I abhor Catholicism."

"I've heard that from you many times. Have you ever seen a nun on a tram?"

"No. Have you?"

"Yes," I said.

"Where?"

"Sitting next to me. A Bible is open on her demure, virginal, granny glasses lap…You're a nun without the habit."

"I could pun on nun, but I won't," she said. "I'll think about what you said, and I do thank you for the suggestion. Yes, I will seriously consider it."

And she bent over and gave me a schwesterly kiss on the cheek.

Then we chatted about nothing memorable. For instance, she said:

"You know, I never asked you if you liked your name. I remember when we first met I told you I loved the name."

"I'll answer this way. When I was a kid, I loved the name Phil and I wanted to live in Philadelphia and become either a philanthropist, a philatelist, or a philanderer—but I didn't know which is which."

"You knew, you knew," Maria said. "Deep down, you knew."

Again some more inanities until we both fell silent.

I felt there was a subtext to our idle chatter. It was a nervous prelude to something else. She was a high tension wire. Ready to give off, radiating, energy. And maybe that's the reason she consented so readily to ride with me. Then she spoke some words which I can remember, word for word, to this day. Maria filled the small night space of the car with a couple of unforgettable adventures. I still don't know how that car riding through the chill early spring night was able to absorb the drama.

Then, through the silence, came her words:

"I have a few things to tell you. Three things, actually, that will help explain," and she stopped for a breath, "who I am and what I am." Then she gave a little laugh. "I was about to say, 'a few things about me,' but then I thought, I just used the word 'things' twice. Katz won't like it if I use it a third time. Sloppy thinking."

I couldn't imagine what she planned to tell me. Still, I was very excited, pleased to be reconnected with her.

"First I want to tell you why I am so fearful of promiscuity. When you hear the story, you will understand why." She took a deep breath and continued.

"When I was twelve or thirteen, I came home early from school one day. I wasn't feeling well. Maybe I was, you know, getting my period. But that not feeling well was nothing compared to the sick-to-my-stomach feeling and heartache and heartbreak I felt later. I let myself in quietly with my key. I didn't shout, 'Ma, it's me, I'm home,' because I knew she was at work. I went to get something from my parents' bathroom, I forget what. But given what I discovered, I can, you know, be forgiven for forgetting. I go into the bedroom, the door is wide open, and there I have the shock of my life. The sort of scene that pastes itself on your eyelids and never goes away. In the big closet with sliding doors, I see my mother totally absolutely stark naked, giggling her head off, and a man, not my father, a man I couldn't see well for he's hidden between clothes, his face I can't see but he has hair and my father is bald, and I do see he's a slim guy, my father's sort of chubby, it's not my father, for sure, that much I can tell, and the other man, he's naked too. I see his waist, his hip, his naked leg. I don't know what kind of, you know, fantasy game they were playing in there. But I know some force within me stopped me from crying out, from screaming.

"Seeing my mother in the closet, I felt a rage I never felt before, rage and shock and embarrassment and shame and disappointment and disbelief. The floor caved in under me, as if my whole little nest-like world had collapsed. I closed my eyes. This must be a nightmare and I must wake. I opened my eyes and still saw what I saw. I ran to my room and fell on my bed, weeping and sobbing into my pillow, shouting, me, who as a thirteen-year-old never used curse words, I kept repeating, 'Why couldn't you at least shut the fucking sliding door, you whore? Why don't you shut the door at least, for Chrissake?' And then I realized I had never before taken my lord's name in vain and I never have since."

"Oh my God," I said, sympathizing. As my heartbeat accelerated, I slowed the car down. I couldn't drive fast and digest this story at the same time. "Your mother screwing around with another man. And you discover it. You must have been...." I couldn't finish the sentence.

"If you're thinking traumatized—trauma isn't the word for it. It broke me. It marked me. That night I fell on my knees and prayed to Jesus for guidance."

"Wait a minute," I shouted. I was so excited I pulled over to the side of the road and stopped the car. "That explains it. It just clicked."

"Explains what? What just clicked?"

"Do you realize what you said before, when you were sobbing into your pillow?"

"That I took God's name in vain."

"No. Not that. The words before that."

"Yes. I said, 'Why couldn't you at least shut the door, the fucking sliding door?'"

"And so?" I said.

"And so?" Maria repeated.

"How many years of analysis have you had?"

"I told you. Seventeen. Going on eighteen."

"Seventeen years of shrinksmanship and that fool of a shrink, he—"

"She."

"Okay. She. Even worse. Someone who shares a chromosomic makeup like yours and can't, didn't have enough *seykhl* to see the light? Seventeen years and she couldn't come up with an answer?"

"For what?"

"Tell you in a minute...How many thousands of dollars has that shrinkage cost you so far?"

"Oh, tens of thousands."

"You could have put a down payment for an apartment or house of your own...purchased it outright. Saved years of rent. Sorry, lease. Tell you what I'm going to do. I'll charge you seventy-five cents and give you an answer."

"Last time it was a quarter."

"My rates have gone up. And I don't accept Medicare anymore. Okay?"

"Okay. Go ahead."

"Lemme see cash."

She proferred a dollar bill.

I took it.

"Lemme see change," Maria said.

I gave her a quarter.

I said, "There's your penchant, your fixation, for shutting doors and sliding doors and dressers and drawers and everything else. You want to erase that scene from your mind, consciously or unconsciously. This traumatic event with the open doors that should have been closed—especially the bedroom door and the sliding door of the walk-in closet—don't you see?"

Maria looked blankly at me, then closed her eyes, and leaned her head back on a pillow that wasn't there. A bulb lit up in Maria's face. I saw it in the dark.

"Oh...my...God!" She leaned her head back again. Clapped both hands on her cheeks. "You're a genius. I never thought of it before. You're right. That's why I shut doors. I want all open doors closed. Now I realize why I do this...Here..."

She gave me the quarter.

"You deserve it. How come I didn't think of this?"

"Because you probably didn't act it out for that goniff like you did with me, thereby recreating the scene in its full intensity. To your shrink, that leech, that bloodsucker who's been milking you for years, you probably told the story matter-of-factly."

Maria looked out into the distance. Nodded. "I probably did. But wait a minute...what about you?...How do you explain your *meshugass*"—and here she used the Yiddish word for mania, madness—"for shutting doors, sliding doors, closet doors?"

"Simple," I said. And I stopped. Was purposely silent for a long moment.

"Is this going to cost me another seventy-five cents?"

"No. This one's on the house."

"And so, why do you shut doors?"

"Because I too was traumatized. By an open sliding door."

"How so?"

"It was me in the closet with her."

Maria looked at me skeptically and gave a disparaging wave of her hand.

"I'm going to disregard that absurdity." She gave me a half smile. "Now I'm going to tell you something about my mother—this is still part of story number one—that reveals her personality. I think I told you I had an older sister, Laura, but I don't think I mentioned she's ten years older than me. My mother had her when she was nineteen, so that makes my mom sixty-nine. You know my links with my mother are, to be polite, tenuous. But what is annoying is that she still has no shame. My sister went to see her on one of her annual visits, when she spends a weekend at her house in Clittfield. Its ironic pun value isn't lost on me and won't be lost on you, either, when you hear this story.

"Clittfield is a little town west of Harrisburg, Pennsylvania, where my mother and her boyfriend, who's three years younger, he's a vigorous sixty-six, live together. Gregor, some immigrant, probably illegal, from Bosnia, is her latest beau. God knows where she picked him up, probably at some construction site. Anyway, Laura is sleeping downstairs, they're upstairs, and early in the morning, before the birds start to sing and before the traffic picks up, the noises begin upstairs. Shameless. They're at it early in the morning, my mother and her stud, and my sister tells me she tries to close her ears, puts a pillow over her head, after all, it's her mother, and Laura is ashamed, embarrassed, out of her skin. Some sort of restrained familial code of propriety operates in her. She tries not to listen, but at the same time she's human, she uses the phrase, 'I'm only human,' kind of apologetically, 'and I can't help listening,' Laura says.

"First there's the laughter, then giggling. Okay, they could be telling jokes up there, but then the rhythmic thump, thump, thumping begins and Laura says, she admits, it's exciting. She wants not to listen but can't help it, listening as her mother is crying out, I love it, I love it, I love it, oh God, I love it, don't stop, don't stop, don't stop, and then the shrieks of ecstasy. My mother has no shame fucking, excuse me for using that ugly, low-class word, but that's what it is, animal fucking, within earshot of her daughter and making those obscene sounds with her daughter downstairs, can't she at least control herself?

"She's an old woman. Into her seventieth year. She has white hair, for goodness's sake, and I bet her hair down there is white too, if she doesn't dye it, the slut. And her boyfriend, Gregor, Laura tells me, she calls him Rasputin, built like a bull, he has no hair. And my mother chooses, purposely, the one time in the year that my sister visits for a weekend, to put on her sex act. To show off. To show how appealing she is, despite her seventy years and her white hair, in contrast to her unappealing, fifty-year-old daughter. Now isn't that absolutely disgusting?

"What is she, a nymphomaniac who can't control herself? She could go at it three four times a day, like a human bonobo, you know, those apes that have sex all the time. The one weekend a year Laura comes to visit and my mother has to show her, I'm sure she did it to show off, as if to say, 'See? I may be seventy years old, but I'm still desirable, not like you at fifty, whom no one wants.' What a bitch!"

What could I say? I had no desire to argue with Maria about her mother. I looked at her quickly as I drove. Maria was seething. And her long-standing antagonism to her mother was bolstered by that story. Hatred blazed from her eyes.

I didn't want to tell her that a woman's sexuality doesn't end at forty or fifty or sixty. But if someone is blessed with a strong sex drive, like her white-haired mama, that person is very fortunate and should make the most of it. Age-shmage, the minute a woman is flat on her back the years just melt away. But a seventy-year-old woman crying out, I love it, I love it, don't stop—I think that will give any man pause. It's rather sexy in itself. Had I heard those cries of ecstasy, I would not have put a pillow over my ears. I would have taken out my ear trumpet and then my tape recorder. Maybe even my video camera.

"And anyway," Maria continued, "what's so good about sex?"

"That's an odd question, coming from a sexpot like you. It's like Einstein saying, 'What's so good about physics?'"

"Still, what's so good about it?"

"Here, I'll show you."

"Please don't. It isn't that good anyway."

"Right. With others. Only with me. Come here."

When Maria imitated her mother singing, *I love it, I love it, please don't stop. Oh God, don't stop*, I didn't remind, I didn't want to remind Maria that the very words she criticized her concupiscent mama for using when she was screwing Gregor, showing off her desirability at seventy to her unattractive single, boyfriend-less daughter, Laura, Maria herself sang out those very same lyrics with me in the same key signature and to the same melody. That unbearably delicious sensation made both mother and daughter sing the same tune. Don't stop, don't stop, oh God, don't stop. If I were mean I could have snapped, *Like mother, like daughter*. But then, just like Laura couldn't help herself, couldn't resist, but removed the pillow from her head, she *had* to listen to that Siren song, so I too could not resist and said:

"Remember? You once used those two words on me. Don't. Stop. Don't…stop. Don't stop…oh…please…don'tstopdon'tstopdon'tstop—and then joined them into one ecstatic cry?"

"That was then and this is now," Maria said with twilight calm. You would have thought that my comparison would plus her. But Maria was completely and totally nonplussed. "I won't. I told you. I made a promise. Sex is not that important."

"That wrongly puts sex on a scale relative to other things. But you cannot do that. Sex is *sui generis*. Sex stands apart and alone. By using the word 'important,' you infer that some things are more important, some less. But sex is there, like sky and water. It's the elemental force that propels the world. Plants, animals, fish, humans all love it. Cells too. Even your God, as you should best know."

Maria gave a little smile, a weak little smile, as writers sometimes put it, not knowing what to say. That last line took her, caught her, by surprise.

But that story taught me something. I realized that when Maria said she had to restrain herself because she feared she might have a penchant for becoming a slut, she was afraid of becoming like her mother.

"Okay. We're done with my mother. Now I have something more important to tell you. Drive! And don't pull over to the side again."

"I'll call it as I sees it…"

"All these things are interconnected," Maria said, "and they help explain my feelings to Jesus and my attitude to you."

"I'm glad we're in the same sentence, but I resent the order of placement."

"Please don't joke around, Katz. I'm sharing my broken heart with you."

Without looking at her, I stretched out my right hand and stroked her face, slowly, tenderly, once, twice, three times. The third time I slid the palm of my hand over her lips. And again, once more, yet again, once again the surprising Maria surprised me. She gave a light kiss to my fingers as they touched her lips. I made no comment on that; neither did she. I think it was wise on both our parts to revel in that moment of affection without calling attention to it or analyzing it.

"I have to tell you I was once married."

Two astonishments within one minute?

"What?" I yelled. "You told me that a while back and then withdrew it."

"Yes. Then it slipped out and I didn't want to tell you. So I said, It's not true. But now I do. It is true. I was married. Really. I was. Don't slow down. Keep your foot on the accelerator."

"You? Married?"

"You didn't think anyone would want me, right?"

"What nonsense! I just thought with your independent spirit, your particular tastes, your low standards…" I couldn't help throwing that in, but in her state of excitement, she either missed it or disregarded it, "your piety, that you wouldn't marry anyone."

"I got married young, at twenty-one, and I was married for about five years, to a guy I met at school. And I was divorced about thirteen years ago."

"You stun me. What madman would want to divorce you? He should have his head examined."

"He should indeed. By the way, it was him coming out of the movies that evening whom I didn't want to see. I told you I had gone out with him. But that part was made up. Yes, that guy was my ex-husband. He's supposed to be in Texas. I didn't want to talk to him."

"Me neither." At once a brick of jealousy fell off my heart. The movie guy. One less chap to worry about. "People should marry you, not divorce you."

"That's very sweetly put. But it had to happen, and I'll tell you why. After two or so years my husband began, you know, to lose interest in me."

"Jerk! Asshole! Shmuck!"

"I never told this to anyone before," Maria said softly, "not even to my sister, and I doubt I'll ever tell it to anyone else. It's not the sort of thing one is proud of sharing. But during our marriage, when I would come into bed—he usually went to bed before me—his back was toward me, as if to say 'I'm not interested.' Before I went to bed, even though I knew nothing would happen, still I was hopeful, maybe this time. Anyway, in the bathroom I would wash up. I'm sure he could hear me, even though he made believe he was asleep. He could hear the water flow stopping every once in a while as I put the washcloth under the faucet. I would wash up, hopeful, and went to bed, wanting him to turn to me. But in vain."

"Unbelievable!" I said. "Me, first of all, for me you don't have to wash up. For me, you're not like the guys say about dried peaches, a godawful smell, but delicious. For me, you're sweet as is. Me, if I heard you washing up, I'd jump out of bed and dash to the bathroom. I'd take you then and there."

At once I thought of Maria's special kissing, inch by inch, grid by grid, left to right, up up up. Could she have done it first to her husband, her sexless, feckless—substitute, those of you in the letter substitution game, you code breakers, a "u" for the "e" in feckless, yes, that's right, feckluss, that's exactly what I mean, you got it right—her feckluss husband? To try to interest him? Nah, I thought. Never. Then to whom? Those two guys, now minus ex-, who drove me up the tree of jealousy, with scrapes on knees and wounds in heart?

"Boy, you have the patience of Job," I said.

"And the horniness of Tamar."

"Was he perhaps gay?"

"Even for that you have to have some interest in sex, don't you think, no matter where it's directed? But he was completely neuter. As if some creature had come in during the night and snip-snip, cut it off. After a while, in frustration, although I wanted to be loyal to him, I got keyed up. I'm not made of flesh and blood, you know."

"Do you know what you just said? You just said a mouthful. It describes you to a T."

"I said, I'm made of flesh and blood."

"No, you didn't. You said, 'I'm not made of flesh and blood, you know.'"

"I did not. And, anyway, that's what I meant. I'm not made of stone. Then I went back to school and audited evening courses at Brandeis. In one class, Labor Relations, I ended up studying with a guy my age. Barry was his name. And at first he resisted me too. I thought there was something wrong with me."

"Believe me, there's nothing wrong with you. At. All."

"He was Jewish too. I guess you're all bright, attractive, and magnetic, except you of course."

"Goy girls go for that extra piece of excised skin."

"Shh!... And, can you imagine, me, who is shy, anything but forward."

"Picking me up at the tram terminal in Newton during Have Relations With the Author Week."

"Shy goy girl asks him if he'd like to take me to dinner. But Barry knew I was married and he just wouldn't pick up on my signals. We continued to study together before and sometimes after class. Once, I gave him a lift home when his car was being repaired. It was a cold day and I said I could use a cup of hot tea."

"I never heard that as a code word for lust before."

She didn't respond.

So I tried with forked tongue, "Were you that thirsty?"

"No. Not thirsty. Hungry, as subsequent events proved."

"Tell me more."

44

THE PHONE BOOTH PLOY

THE NEXT TIME I saw Katz, I almost didn't recognize him, but I knew it was he because who else would slide next to me in so familiar a fashion? We exchanged greetings like old friends. Katz looked older. It took me a couple of seconds to realize why. In the three or so weeks I hadn't seen him, he had grown a beard. Moreover, it was all white, which was surprising since his hair was black and gray. The contrast was stark. When I first met him, I thought he was in his mid-fifties, but it's hard to determine, so I won't even guess. I know that Jews in mourning don't shave for a month. But I didn't know how observant he was. Had he lost a mother or father? I didn't, wouldn't, ask him. If he made no comment, neither would I. After thinking about it, I concluded that the beard was a personal choice and not a sign of mourning. For if the latter, human nature would have prompted him to share the news with me, to welcome some words of condolence and explain the sudden change in his appearance.

I opened my briefcase and returned the chapters he had given me.

= What a fascinating turn of events, Katz. Constant surprises.

= Glad you liked it, John. Even more surprises are coming. Now you'll see something new in the narrative, for at this point, my brother purposely breaks into the return from Connecticut chapter to present this one. For the next few chapters my brother uses the medieval storytelling technique known as *interlacement*, where one chapter breaks off and another is introduced, and then both are continued in alternation. In my brother's manuscript, the next chapter is typed on yellow, not white, paper.

Katz opened his briefcase, took out a folder, and showed me the pages.

= This way, he creates, at least for himself, the illusion that it is written by the heroine herself. In fact, in this chapter the first-person narrator declares that Maria recorded the adventure for him, which he then transcribed. Or, maybe, like a lot in my brother's novel, this is just another one of his authorial devices, and the whole thing is made up.

•

The following chapter was recorded for me by Maria, who wanted to recount this adventure firsthand. But she wanted to record it privately, saying she didn't want to look me in the eye when she narrated her story. After she made the recording, I transcribed it. Here it is, in Maria's own words:

There was one time when I wanted a call from my friend, whom I'll call Sam. He had to go down South temporarily, and I couldn't receive his call at home for, you know, obvious reasons, for my husband's schedule as a social worker was unpredictable. So I arranged with Sam that I would be at a women's shop in the Waltham mall at 11 a.m. on such and such a date. That shop still had a couple of those old-fashioned phone booths with a sliding, folding-in-half wooden door, a little rounded triangular seat, and a sour, close smell. The little fan that was activated as soon as the door closed didn't bring in fresh air; it only fanned that awful stale air around the booth quicker. I gave Sam the number. He said he'd call me from Virginia or D.C. I couldn't call him because although local calls, you know, didn't appear on our bill, long-distance ones did. Before he left, we repeated the date and time of the call.

Actually, I gave Sam two numbers, in case one of the two booths was taken. On the appointed day, I went to the back of the store, to a quiet little dead-end hallway, to the two phone booths by the left wall. Bingo! The first booth was occupied. Boy, was I glad I had scouted the place and given him both numbers! My heart began racing. What if the other booth had someone in it too? What would I do? That was one contingency Sam and I had not discussed. Maybe he'd think that I, you know, purposely took the phone off the hook on both phones because I had changed my mind about our relationship and didn't want to speak to him. But that's illogical, right? Downright silly. If I didn't want to speak to him, I could just stay home and let that phone ring and ring.

It seemed I was rushing to the next booth and yet it also seemed to take forever. In that dark first booth sat someone I couldn't see, cloaked in navy blue. My entire being was one gigantic hope that the second booth would be free. It was empty, thank God! I opened the door, sat down and closed the door. And I waited.

I look at the phone, wishing, hexing it, ordering it to ring. Look at my watch. It's almost two minutes after eleven. He's late. Is Sam stuck in traffic somewhere? Forgot he was supposed to call at eleven? Maybe he lost the second number. Maybe he's frustrated he can't get to the phone and worried that if I don't hear the phone soon I might leave.

With my heart frozen by the silence of the phone, I'm suddenly jolted out of my reverie by the loud ring. I'm so excited, so confused. I don't pick up till after the third ring, a split second before the fourth.

I say, "Hello."

"Hi," he says. Of course it's Sammy. Who else would be calling me here? "Sorry, I'm a couple of minutes late."

"It's okay," I say. And suddenly, I don't know what to say. I'm at a loss for words. I realize I've never spoken to him on the phone before.

"I was waiting here for you," I say lamely.

"Yes," he says flatly, "me too."

"Where are you?"

"Outside D.C."

"My God, you sound, you know, so close."

"You too. As if you're right next door. I feel I can just reach out and touch you."

"Please do," I say. "Where it pleases most."

"Your voice is so enticing," he says. "So close. It's vibrating right into me…Is it warm in that booth?"

"Very," I say. "And getting warmer."

"I wish I could see your lovely face," he says.

"Me too."

And we continue talking about this and that, nothing memorable, for another few minutes. But the end of the conversation, that's something I won't ever forget.

"Close your eyes," he says, "and think of me. Are your eyes closed?"

"Yes."

"Imagine I'm knocking on the phone booth door."

"Okay."

"With your eyes closed, imagine I'm kissing you. Take a deep breath and with eyes closed tight, imagine I'm sliding next to you."

Now it's really become warm in the booth. Maybe it's warmer because my eyes are closed. Maybe because I'm taking deep breaths. With the receiver pressed close to my left ear, I imagine Sam kissing me. Then I don't hear his voice. A wave of panic, hot and acidic sweeps over me. In a fright I shout, "Hello, hello? Are you there, Sammy?"

"Yes, I'm here. If I'm not there," I hear him saying, "then I must be here."

And before I know it, someone opens the booth door and grabs me. I shriek and pound the intruder with fists and scream—

•

Katz stopped. Closed his briefcase.

= This is where my brother breaks off and continues with the rest of the Return from Connecticut chapter. We'll do that one next time I see you.

45

BACK FROM CT, CONTINUED

"NOT NOW," MARIA REPLIED, when I asked her to tell me more. I didn't pursue it. For I knew she would talk; she was dying to talk. I had a hunch that's why she came with me on this long ride. So she could open up. As we drove in silence, the buzzing of our thoughts was louder than the engine.

"Once I was up there in Barry's apartment, alone with him, he couldn't resist me," Maria said suddenly. "I had forgotten what it felt like to have a man's affection and love."

"Give me fifteen minutes and I'll show you."

"Don't interrupt."

"Your husband was so neutral to you?"

"That's a polite way to phrase it."

Poor Maria, I thought, and put my right arm around her shoulder and tried to draw her close. *You're committing adultery with Barry, you pious Christian*, went through my head. *Did Jesus close an eye*? And I began to stroke her hair.

"Did you continue to see him?"

"I saw him three or four times a week."

"And your husband didn't know?"

"He was asleep."

"You mean you did this at night?"

"Yes. In the middle of the night. That was the only safe time."

"Wow! What drama. Out of Flaubert. Tolstoy. Glenn Miller."

"You mean Henry."

"Sorry. You did this when he was asleep?"

"Fast. I would slip out of bed at 2 a.m. when he was sleeping, drive to Barry's apartment, spend a couple of hours with him, and then sneak back by 5 a.m."

"And your hubby never knew."

"Never."

"He never heard you leaving or coming."

"Apparently not," Maria said.

"Never woke. Never made a comment."

"Never."

"Impossible. This is too absurd. There's something wrong with this story."

"But that's the story," she said.

Listening to her, hanging on to every word, I was, I became, an avid participant. I didn't know if I was Maria, her husband, the lover, or all three. It excited me, that story. I kept asking questions. How would she wake on the nights she went to see her lover? Obviously, she couldn't use an alarm clock. Did she go to sleep at all on those nights? Did she lie awake in excited, exalted anticipation? How long did the trip take? What a name, Barry. As romantic as a dented, gray tin cup. Did she ever skip a night, thinking her husband was restless and might wake? How long did this relationship last? Is it really possible her husband didn't know? Did he really never hear the creak of the bed, the click of the closed door, the ticking of the forlorn clock? Maybe the poor guy got some queer thrill out of it, since he obviously—I think, I presume—didn't like sex at all, at least not with her. What did she enjoy more, the game or the sex? Did she want to be caught? Did she ever imagine the poor simp was in on it, making believe he was sleeping but aware of her every move? Or imagine coming to the bed, her bed, his bed, their bed, and he gone? Did she ever think, in the middle of her adulterous, deceptive drive, of turning back?

Then I realized—turning back? From where? Once she left her boyfriend's house, turning back and staying with him? Or turning back on her way *to* the affair, and returning to her house? Did she ever feel guilty? Didn't her fucking Christianity, her sin-oriented, Jesus-loving religion ever overwhelm her? I had more and more questions. An infinity of questions.

"You were just aching for him to catch you," I told Maria.

"I don't know."

"Any psychologist, even Charlie Perlmutter, will tell you that. Even those phony therapists, with an Ed.D. that permits them to call themselves Doctor, will tell you, despite those idiotic education courses they took instead of real courses. Maybe insipid hubby even knew, sensed you leaving but kept it to himself. For how could a husband not sense his wife slipping away at 2 a.m. and returning at five? If my husband would do that to me, slip out of bed, while I was asleep I would know. I'd catch him, the rat! And I would cut off everything on him that protruded. Fingers and toes. Pecker and nose."

"So you *are* married, you rascal," Maria said with a smile.

"He knew. He knew. How could he not know?"

"He was a sleep deeper. I mean, a deep sleeper. And he slept way on the other side of the bed."

"Absolute, total, and unmitigated nonsense. He knew. Not only did he know, but with his feckluss sex drive he even got a mild charge out of it."

"Maybe you're right."

"When I'm right, there's no maybe...Now tell me, did you feel more guilty then, with him, when you were actually married..." Now I came out with it; now I didn't pussyfoot any longer—"a married woman, an adulteress like Hester Prynne, more sinning then than you are with me now, unmarried yourself and me as well?"

"Now," came Maria's bold and brave response, "now I am more religious. I have no excuses. All I can do is quote Jeremiah 17:9, where he says: 'The heart is deceitful above all things and is exceedingly weak—who can know it?' Now I understand the gravity of my sin. Then, then I just thought of my body. Now I think of my soul."

I could have poked fun, but I didn't. But to myself I think, I hear in that echo chamber we call total recall, I hear Maria's ecstatic, soulful command, her joyous cry: "Don't stop don'tstopdon'tstop...I love it...I love it...Oh God, oh God,IloveitIloveitIloveit."

And I was angry at myself for being so considerate of her duplicitous, hypocritical, phony, new-found holiness—that fool's gold, clinquant, tinsel saint who screwed other guys while she was married but suddenly zipped up her zipper after meeting me.

"Maybe you just enjoyed it more then? Maybe the very act of slipping out of your husband's bed and going to a middle-of-the-night assignation was more exciting, more romantic, than the actual sex itself? I tell you, this story is like out of a film, a great novel."

Maria nodded slowly, pensive, as if thinking of a title for the book.

"Could there be the slightest likelihood that the lover contacted your husband?" I narrowed my eyes as if I was a detective grilling her. She came right back with:

"Again, you're very astute...In fact, he wanted to call my husband. Wanted to meet him."

"Did he?"

"He never told me. Maybe it was just a threat."

"He was probably tired of the game. He wanted you off his back. And I want myself back on yours."

I may have asked most of the above questions. In retrospect, I may be thinking now of more questions than I actually asked.

But, I tell you, those were two exciting hours, when she sat in the car with me and revealed a side of her, a story, an adventure, I never would have dreamed she was capable of.

•

And then I interjected.

= Katz, could it be, could it possibly be, that Maria was, for whatever reasons, making this story up?

= Never, John, Katz said. He said it loud. He may even have shouted, for I distinctly remember looking around in embarrassment. = But it's a very perceptive editorial question for, as you'll hear in a minute, my brother deals with it too. And my view too is: impossible. Never, I conlcuded.

I looked at Katz when he said that word.

= It's an aural typo, I know. But I like the sound of it.

•

Is it possible that Maria was making all this up? To provide a background for her current abstinence? I thought about it and decided: absolutely not. Not at all. She could be a bit manipulative, like the time she left me a note on her back door that she was in the Brandeis Café and purposely stretched out her coffee drinking at the table to tease me, displease me, vex me, unsex me, and then she began talking with that guy in the booth behind her and even exchanged names with him, which also bothered me ("I never told him my last name," she said, to justify herself).

Then, on her way back to the apartment with me, she confessed she did that as a little game, that note on the door. I guess she didn't want me to feel that I always had the upper hand and could do whatever I wanted with her.

But lying? Concocting a story, an adventure, like that? Impossible. Never! No. No. No. A hundred twenty times no. She might conceal, as she had done until she admitted, revealed, confessed her adultery story—that's why I told her she'd make a great Catholic, a wonderful nun, turning the screw into her, for I knew she detested Catholicism. Conceal, yes. But lie, fabricate outright? Never! How forthright, adamant, rock hard on this can I be? Sooner would the tide go backward, sooner would the sun rise and then retreat, sooner would a summer rain turn into purple snowflakes than Maria lie, create, concoct that story of her adultery.

Loads of questions bubbled in me, but I didn't ask all of them. I kept mulling over this exciting story which sprang straight from a novel. It was something totally out of character for her.

"Now you know," Maria said suddenly, "why I began pummeling you in the car after Figaro's adultery test."

"No. Why?"

"Remember, I thought you had planned that marionette show of his, with Giuseppe, Gina, and Giovanni. Gina is married, her husband has lost interest in her, and she meets Giovanni at an art exhibit and they begin an affair."

"Wow! That *is* your story. But I didn't know it then. How could I have known it? You just revealed it to me now. But the real question is, how could Figaro have known about it?"

"He's a wizard. He knows everything."

"Nonsense. It's just sheer coincidence. That sort of story is typical of the commedia dell'arte in Italy."

"Still, it made its point. To me."

As I drove into her parking lot, Maria held up her left hand. She spread her fingers. To catch my attention. I had to look. There was no way I couldn't look. Could not avoid the ring finger with the missing tip. Which is exactly what she wanted me to do: look, gaze, stare, take in that missing part of that digit. Focus on it to the exclusion of everything else. She had never before drawn my attention to her flawed finger. And I, I had always pretended that it wasn't there. But her doing this at the end of her confession, attracting my gaze to her ring finger—what did this mean?

Did she want me to make a connection between her adultery and her flawed ring finger? Some kind of symbolic link? Perhaps to show that just as her ring finger was flawed, so had been her marriage? I looked at that missing fingertip as if I was a camera and drew closer and closer with my lens until I saw only the empty space that once had a living fingertip. As I once told you, I didn't know if it was an accident or a birth defect. Never asked. But why did she make this gesture now?

Suddenly, a shudder of horror ran through me. I felt like a character in a story, perhaps by Edgar Allan Poe, who realizes something awful, otherworldly, is happening to him. Every hair on my body bristled. I thought that after what I was thinking, my hair would turn white.

With an electric jolt that seared me, I imagined that her husband, in retribution, to punish her for breaking her marriage vow, had chopped off a piece of her finger. So he had known all along, suspected, and had it confirmed by Maria's boyfriend.

And while this morbid thought made my skin feel creepy, as if bugs were running over it, Maria leaned toward, threw her arms around me, and began bawling like a baby, the tears running down her cheeks and mine.

"Tell, tell," I consoled her softly.

"Can't. I told you enough. Too much."

Second time I saw her cry. First time it was for that idiotic perfume, that cheap cologne that gave me a horrendous headache. But you can't compare this crying now to that crying then. That, then, was for nonsense. For some stupid eau de cologne that I had dumped into her bathroom sink. But now the crying was for real. Looking at her ring finger and seeing her crying, I saw the entire immolation scene at once, and my head began to spin.

What cruelty! Sadism. Her husband discovers, how could he not when she left his bed in the middle of the night, something had to go wrong, and either she was caught and confessed, or the lover delivered the glad tidings by mail, phone, or in person, infuriating the husband.

But what a punishment! Something out of the Dark Ages. How come she didn't resist? Could it be, no, it couldn't be, that she cooperated?

I tried to imagine if a wife of mine, if I ever had, have, or will have one (or two), did something like that. Chopping off a piece of finger as punishment for adultery. My God! It was straight out of a Saudi Arabian court, where they still chopped off arms and hands and legs and feet and other offending appendages. Never in a million years would I have dreamt of such cruelty, of such a bestial act. Medieval punishment? Me? Never. I just would have killed her.

Now I understood why Maria wanted to undergo that adultery test at Figaro's. She wanted to purify herself, strip from herself once and for all the shame, the sin of her adultery. And that's why she was so careful, so insistent, when the guilt bubbled up up up, on not involving herself with me, lest adultery, albeit a mirror image adultery, haunt her all over again. And then it hit me. Of a sudden. In a flash. I understood something else. I recalled the first time I was in Maria's apartment, in her tiny kitchen. As she was making me a cup of tea, I saw her drawer with only two teaspoons in it. Suddenly I realized, now it dawned on me, why she kept no knives at home. Maybe that's why she didn't even eat at home. She excised from her house, banished from her kitchen—read: her consciousness—all knives. And forks and soup spoons too. And then that elaborate charade of having no need for utensils.

Then I took her left hand again and brought it to my lips and I kissed that orphaned ring finger gently, made love to it as if that poor, orphaned, humiliated finger were Maria, as if all of Maria's essence were in that maimed digit. She placed the palm of her right hand on my left cheek and stroked it and my other cheek slowly, lovingly, for which I thanked her in my heart.

For a while we sat in silence. I felt I was hurtling through space with her to an unknown destination. Then, to distract her, I said:

"You know, we never danced."

"We didn't do a lot of things," she said. No complaint in her tone.

"But what we did was primary, essential, and good—good like the first days of Creation."

But Maria did not say yes. Still the same Maria. Unable to come out and say what we had was good.

•

That night I thought about what she had told me. Not about the finger. I couldn't bear thinking about that. But I tried to imagine Maria sneaking out in the middle of the night, an adventure filled with danger.

Her husband catches her at the door. *Where are you going*? Trapped, she quickly says, *My father isn't well.* In the dark, every night, every moment, she stands on the cusp of being discovered: when she dresses, when she moves to the door, the long minutes she is away, when she returns, a careless move, a door closing too loudly. Her car breaking down. Someone smacking into her car. What a risky caper! And I didn't explore this with her. We could have spent hours discussing every wrinkle in this fabulous scenario. She must have been in love, crazy in love, or so hot in the pants, that she took this tremendous risk every night.

That night I fell asleep but only for an hour or so. Suddenly I was wide awake. Looked out the window. Thought I saw snow on the ground. I opened the door to see if indeed it was snowing. It wasn't. I clicked the door shut. At once Maria came to mind. Again I thought of her leaving her house on her way to see her lover. I couldn't stop thinking of how many things could have gone wrong. A shoe falling in the dark. Bumping into a door. Being taken for an intruder by a half-asleep husband. The sudden roar of the car engine.

Now I understood her. Maria was really, truly, afraid of herself, of her, in her estimation, uncontrolled desires. She feared her own lust. Transmuted into her by blood from her mother. Was afraid that her promiscuity would bring on a tragic end. And the only way she could stop herself was by taking on religion, with as much fervor, devotion, and single-mindedness as her love for fucking. Jesus was her Alcoholics Anonymous.

•

When we got to her house, I shut the engine and did not say a word. Was she waiting for me to ask her, *Would you like me to come in and you can make me a cup of tea?* No. I would not do that. I didn't want a refusal. Didn't want to give her that pleasure, especially after this beautiful evening.

I stepped out of the car. She came toward me. I gave her a big hug and kissed her cheek. She threw her arms around me, hugged me, and kissed my cheek.

"I'll call you," I said as I held her.

"Yes," she said. "Yes."

46

PHONE BOOTH PLOY, CONTINUED

= JOHN, NOW I have the continuation of Maria's tape about the phone booth incident.

Katz opened his briefcase, took out a few sheets of yellow paper and began reading:

•

And before I know it, before I have a chance to shriek, someone grabs me and my lips are pressed shut, clamped by other lips. I pound the intruder with my fists and the thought runs through my head, *I'm going to be raped in a phone booth.* I'm overwhelmed by the man's big slouch hat and bear-like coat, by this attacker in this tiny space. But still, I know the taste of those lips. It's his kiss. I taste it even in the dark of that enclosed space. I think my eyes were shut. But how could it be Sam if he was hundreds of miles away? In that tiny space, even when I opened my eyes I could, you know, hardly see him.

A bunch of question words streamed out of me at once, as if I were in some new dimension where one can utter many different words at the same time.

"What? When? How did you do this? I thought you were in D.C. Wait a minute! So it was you all along in that other booth."

There was a mischievous look in Sammy's eyes.

"You planned this out, you rascal. You checked out this place before you left. If you left at all. But what if that other booth had been occupied?"

Sam shrugged.

"You cut your trip short?"

"Of course. I wanted to see you so badly."

"Me too," I said. "This is the most delicious surprise I've ever had. The most original, creative, delicious surprise of my life."

•

= Wait a minute, I interrupted Katz. = If I remember those booths, there is a bulb in them that lights up when you close the door. So you can see who's inside.

= Right you are, John. Although it's not in her tape, my brother did mention that he imagined Sam either partially unscrewed the bulb or kept the door slightly ajar with his foot so the light wouldn't go on, I forget which.

•

So since Sammy sits in the first booth, he sees me passing by and in a minute he can start dialing. Of course, he delays a moment, the rascal, to make me sweat, to give me palpitations. And that explains why he speaks so softly. Had he spoken any louder I probably would have heard him....I tell you, this phone subterfuge was as exciting as sex.

•

Katz stopped. Saying, reading, the words "exciting as sex," his voice caught in mid-breath.

The consonants cracked. The vowels, their pitch changed, pincers on the 'a's, pliers on the 'e's. As though a skyhook, sharp and unfeeling, had caught his throat.

I think it was the first time, or maybe the second, I had seen him affected by the manuscript he was narrating.

= What's the matter, Katz? I asked. For up till now, his reading had been objective and unemotional. I saw his face was flushed.

= Do you see the way she loved that Sam? Do you see it?

I half expected him to grab hold of me and shake me until I saw it.

= Why couldn't she express her feelings to me that way? With him, with that Sam, she didn't hold back. With him, not shy. That kiss of his she recognized, the taste of his lips with her eyes closed. That whole phone incident, to quote her, as exciting as sex. With him she had vocabulary all over the place. But for me, nothing. Not a tender word. Why couldn't she give me just a little more than that soft, ambiguous "Really"? And at that time, remember, Maria was married, that duplicitous pious Puritan Protestant qua semi-quasi-Catholic, while with me she was long divorced. So why did she have to hold back with me? Get religion on my watch? I know she had those feelings in her. There's not the slightest doubt in my mind she loved me. There, now you've heard me say it. She loved me. As much as she loved Sam, or whatever his name was. If not more. Certainly more. Absolutely more.

= If you know it and are so sure, Katz, I asked him, = then why do you need words? Shouldn't the feeling suffice?

= Now you sound like Maria, Katz said. = I need to be told.

Katz's tone wasn't petulant, but one look at his face and you could see petulance blooming in every pore.

Again I was holding back, but I couldn't hold back any longer.

= Katz, I said. = Again I'm confused. You keep confusing me. You're showing me how thin, and how impenetrable, is the line between fiction and fact. Like a membrane that resists penetration and yet certain molecules float through with ease.

= A hymen is impenetrable too. Until it gets penetrated.

= You're relating, you're retelling your brother's novel. Or is it, and I looked him in the eye, = yours? Whose book is it?

= His, Katz said drily.

= So how can you be so affected, so mournful about Maria's attitude to the protagonist vis-à-vis her attitude to Sam? So personally involved with a character your brother created?

= Or didn't create.

Was Katz suggesting it was a true story? Or one not written by his brother at all?

= I keep asking you, Katz, ab—

= And I keep telling you, John, I read this novel and I retell this story and I get involved. I bet if you would spend as much time with this novel as I do, you'd fall in love with Maria too. You wouldn't be able to help yourself. You'd be addicted. Like me.

= But still. It's your brother's story.

= I'm sensitive. I'm a good reader, John. I take it personally. Great theater, great books, great films always move us. I cry at movies about strangers' lives. Don't you? Don't you get emotionally involved when you see a film? Don't you relate to characters in a book who are just black print on white pages? Why should I be any different? Just shows you what a good writer my brother is. And, anyway, we're blood. Whatever affects him, affects me. We're very close. He's hurt, I cry.

I remembered Katz's wisecrack, Prick my brother, I bleed. As if they were Siamese twins.

= Okay, enough of this, Katz said. = Let's get back to the phone booth ploy. Only in a novel, a movie, or a play can a surprise scene like that happen. In real life, it would be too incredible...Just like Maria's midnight escapade. And whether this Sam is Barry or not the reader does not know, including this reader, me! The author keeps us guessing.

Katz looked out the window. It was his stop.

= Next time, we'll continue *interlacement* with the chapter where Katz and Maria return home from Connecticut.

47

FROM CT, STILL CONTINUED - IN THE CLOSET

MARIA LEFT OUR EMBRACE, I would like to think reluctantly, and began walking back to her apartment. I still felt my arms around her, hers around me. I went back into my car and watched her. Then she suddenly stopped—what made her stop suddenly and turn?—and walked back toward me. Now that our moods had changed, would she invite me into her house? Should I say, like Maria said to Barry*: It's a cold day and I could use a cup of tea, either with or without an elixir?* Nah, that was too much to hope for.

"Katz," she said as she sat in the car again, "before you asked me some questions. Now I have one for you. The other day on the phone, regarding my real or faux birthday, you mentioned in passing that you knew my mother. When I asked you how, you said, 'I'm not getting into that now.' And during our trip, you said you were in the closet with her that awful day. What's going on? Tell me. It bothers me. Please tell me. How do you know her?"

I imagined a trade-off. You invite me in for tea and I'll give you all the details. But I did not say that. Why give her an opportunity to rebuff me? To keep her in suspense, I counted to sixty, to make her think I wasn't going to answer. Then I said:

"Okay, I'll tell you. Yes, it *was* me in the closet with her. I wasn't joking. That's when I learned about your real birthday."

"You told me that twice, but I paid no attention to your obvious joke."

"But it's no joke."

First Maria said nothing. Just looked at me, blinked once, and exclaimed, "No,"—a no that sounded like a downsloping sigh.

"Oh, yes!"

"That's what you discussed when you were allegedly in the closet with her?"

"Uh-huh! You think I was after sex? I'm not like you. It was purely an informational visit."

"Nonsense."

"What else would you do with a woman in a closet full of itchy clothes?"

"Why itchy?"

"Wool clothes," I said, "on naked skin is itchy."

"Now you're naked in the closet."

"Well, why else would I be in the closet? I'm not a coat, you know."

"You were naked in the closet with my mother? Why?"

"Because my clothes were off."

"That's circular reasoning. Why were your clothes off?"

"Why not? If you're hiding in a closet with a woman in heat, it's not polite to keep your clothes on."

"That means you were completely naked."

"Well, you saw me, didn't you? Yes. Totally. Completely."

"Then it *was* you I saw that awful day."

"We're talking in circles. I already told you that."

"And that shameless hussy was naked too."

"I don't really know. It was dark in there. But I suspect yes since she too is very polite."

"Which town is she in?" Maria said quickly, trying to catch me.

"Clittfield."

"Son of a gun. So you *were* there."

Maria was silent, considering all the angles, the ramifications, the morality.

"I wouldn't put it past her, the slut...That's some achievement, screwing a mother and her daughter."

"But not at the same time," I said.

"Wait. Let me backtrack....You said, 'informational.' I know you're going to lie your way out of this as you usually do. But what kind of information were you seeking?"

"If she had a daughter, what her birthday was, what her phone number is, and if that daughter was as sexy and sex-starved as her mother."

"I don't believe a single word you're saying. If you were really in the closet with her, what's her name?"

"I don't take the name of the person I worship in vain."

"Then how did you call her?"

"By snapping my fingers. And sometimes, Honey."

"You have some wild imagination."

"Not that wild. You weren't really there, were you?" Maria said, staring at me. With a smile she tried to straddle two nuances: words declarative in tone but interrogatory in intent. She put on good front, did Maria. Trying to sound jocular, as if playing a let's pretend game with me. But she couldn't disguise the tremolo in her words, the trepidation in her voice.

I met her gaze, unflinching. "I was. Indeed."

"But wasn't she older than you?"

"Then, but not now. Anyway, neither of us minded. Do I mind that you're older than me?"

"Prove it was you."

Oh, she desperately did not want it to be me.

"Okay. First off, it was dark in that closet with the doors closed. Second, she was mad as hell that you came in without knocking."

"Some proof. She didn't even know I was there. What color eyes does my mother have?"

"I couldn't see. It was dark in there. But, as proof..." and I pointed to my eyes, "she told me I have beautiful shiny blue eyes."

"If you couldn't see her eyes," was Maria's feeble attempt at rebuttal, "how could she see yours?"

"Because mine shone. In the dark. Hers didn't. Sorry. No reflection on your haunting, gorgeous green eyes. You can ask her if she remembers."

"I hardly talk to her. You know that."

"All right. Then when you have your annual phone spat with your mother, ask her if she remembers the guy in her closet who mistook her fur coat for her. It took me twelve minutes to discover my error."

"She never had a fur coat."

"How do you know? She had one then. An old beaver or mouton coat. I couldn't tell in the dark. But when you touched it, it was as smooth as your mother's skin. And it even cooed 'Oh' and 'Ah' once in a while, which your mother couldn't do."

"You're lying, as usual." Then, after a pause, she said, "Still, it's something, isn't it, mother and daughter."

"Yes."

"But not at the same time," Maria teased.

"'Tis a consummation devoutly to be wished."

Then I added:

"Don't you remember? It was in the news. All over the place. I still recall the headline in the *Harrisburg Herald*: 'Travel Writer Katz Komes out of the Kloset... Again!' Now isn't that a headline one will never forget?"

"With an imagination like yours, Katz, you should be writing novels, not travel books. I know you're joking. You know you're joking. And I know that you know that I know you're joking."

Then we said goodbye again. She threw her arms around me. I hugged her and kissed her cheek and neck. She kissed my cheek.

"I'll call you," I said again.

And once more she said, "Yes," twice.

Then, from her bag, she pulled out a piece of paper. "Here's my work number for the next couple of months. It's a long-term temp job."

I sat in the parking lot for a few minutes, thinking about her affair with Barry, and I realized it was he, Barry, to whom she gave that special kissing, millimeter by millimeter, grid by grid, covering every room, house, street, town on the topographic map; she invented that kissing for him, practiced it with him so she could years later have it perfected and offer it to me. No way was it given to her husband who, thankfully remained without a name. I would have hated to think of him with a name. To do that special kissing with that other guy, with the ridiculous name, Barry, that was okay. It wasn't against her Thou Shalt Not Commit Adultery guidelines to betray her husband, become an adulteress for a period of half a year or more, taking risks like out of a movie or suspense novel—but not with me.

In her shifting landscape of definitions, with me it was adultery, or fornication. For it wasn't kosher for her to screw a guy who for a very brief time pretended to be married. But for her, as a married woman, to screw a single guy, what was that? That wasn't adultery, right? That wasn't being unfaithful to her husband, right? That wasn't betraying her faith in Jesus, right? Then what was it? How to label that?

Easy.

That was fun. Pleasure. Adventure. Fulfillment. Passion. Lust.

And then I imagined a scenario where Maria is bubbling over, she just has to tell someone about her affair, her sin, and so she confides in her sister, Laura, and swears her to secrecy. Laura lifts her left hand up as though she's in court and places her right hand on her heart and swears she won't tell a soul. What goes into her ears is locked in there. Period. End of story. A day later Maria hears from her mother, who over the phone says tartly: *Welcome to the club.*

•

Katz looked at me, as if to say: Isn't that amazing? Then he said:

= Remember, John, you once mentioned Somerset Maugham's line, "There are three rules for writing a good book." And then it was my station and you said you'd tell me next time. I'd like to pass them on to my brother.

I laughed. = Maugham's maxim was the equivalent of a trick. He paused teasingly after those first few words and then the famous writer continued: "But, unfortunately, no one knows what they are."

48

MARIA'S ATONEMENT

= You remember, John, I told you about Maria and her midnight escapades.

= Yes. Does your brother have another version? I wouldn't mind hearing it again. As long as it's not gossip.

= No, it's in the manuscript. Not another version, but the hero's analysis of it.

= Then it's okay. For if it's gossip, I won't listen. I can't stand gossip. In fact, I make it a rule never to listen to gossip, except if it's interesting.

•

Maria had withdrawn physically from me. She would see me, but no kissing, no touching. Was it just religion with her? Her love affair with my nemesis, my rival, J.C.? Not really. For she had been religious all along and still there was a time—before she went to Europe—that she wound herself around me. And then the electricity was cut. Why? Why?

I moaned and bemoaned.

Then one day it hit me. Bam! Like in the comic books, all the typographic signs for surprise, astonishment, knock-me-over-with-a-feather—!X#&*$! It hit me. Why she was so hard-nosed about sex.

The answer dawned on me of a sudden. Why she wouldn't touch me. Of course, she didn't mind and, I assume, carefully eyeing her reactions, she was rather pleased, when in the car I stroked her hair or patted her face. Even when I bent toward her and kissed her neck. To that she did not say no.

The whole picture suddenly unfolded before me, as if someone had slipped me a secret code that was applicable to her mystery. Why she wouldn't enjoy sex anymore until she stood under the canopy, i.e., no bedding sans wedding. Why?

Here's the answer:

It was atonement. It took her a while, but now, without even realizing it, she was now, finally, atoning for that caper when, while married to that dodo, she was screwing that guy she met at school, that romantically named Barry, when nightly she would slip out of her passive, ball-less husband's nuptial couch in the middle of the night and drive an hour or so to her lover, then, before dawn, drive back and slip silently back into her hopeless husband's bed, her body still warm and pulsing from her lover's embrace.

But I tell you, even by proxy, that story excited me, that wild caper of hers. It's like out of a romantic novel. Maybe she was even subliminally courting discovery. To put an end to that hapless and hopeless, that feckless and fuckless marriage. But it didn't happen, at least in Maria's version, and I'm only repeating what I heard, word for word.

How long did this continue? I asked Maria. *Oh, about a few months.* Then I asked, *Every night*? I forget what she said to that but it was certainly a few times a week. *And the guy at the other end, he didn't initiate this*? I wanted to know. I was dying to know without letting her know how much I wanted to know it. *Oh no*, Maria said. *He didn't.* She didn't say she this proudly or with a touch of triumph, but it was she who began it. At first the guy was, can you imagine, dilly-dallying on such a luscious proposal, at first he was reluctant, knew she was married, didn't want to do anything with an affair. And only when she surprised him one afternoon—

•

= Wait a minute, Katz. Last time in your narrative, you said Maria drove him home because his car was being fixed and then she invited herself up to his apartment for hot tea.

= I know, John. But what can I do? My brother has changed the narrative to make her more aggressive.

•

And only when she surprised Barry one afternoon, after class, and dropped in on him at his apartment, unannounced, did the affair begin. With that delicious girl in his apartment, it was mightily hard for him to say no. And it was he who ended it. And, believe it or not, he even requested a meeting with Maria's husband. Maria was vague on that too. In her estimation, this whole meeting business was just a device, perhaps a threat, on Barry's part to put an end to the affair. But what was known was that she divorced soon after.

And you know what? Maria's husband knew. And I think Maria too knew that he knew. And what's more, I think that she wanted him to know.

•

= John, if you don't mind, I've been called back to Chicago. Probably be gone a couple of weeks. Can I impose upon you again and give you two more chapters? I think we're coming near the end of my brother's narrative. Would you mind?

= Not at all.

= And you'll see that I made a couple of comments in pencil in the margin in two or three places.

I hesitated, then went ahead with my question.

= Katz, I'm curious. In this long narrative you've been telling, have you—I know it's always tempting—have you changed anything?"

= Are you kidding? Katz said indignantly. = Does a scribe who copies a Torah scroll change a word or name or phrase he doesn't like? Never! It's an almost sacred obligation to be faithful to the text.

49

ON THE TRAM

I PURPOSELY BEGAN TAKING a later tram so as not to meet Maria. I wanted to put some time/space between us. Still, so many questions reverberated after that marriage and adultery confession.

One day, just as we're approaching Boston, I heard a woman's voice behind me, one I really couldn't recognize. It sounded like it had an Irish brogue.

"Excuse me, sir," she said softly, "but aren't ye the author of *Travels in Bessarabia*?"

I turned and saw her smiling face.

"When did you get on?"

"In Newton. Just caught the tram."

"Why didn't you come up to me right away?" I looked out the window. "In another minute or so, we'll be at the terminal."

"I was trepidating."

"Great word. Also great way to meet guys."

"And then I finally succumbed. So I guess you won out."

"No. You won out. Too bad you didn't come up to me sooner. I have so many things to tell you, ask you. Almost as many as on our first ride to Boston."

"Do you have time to sit in a café?"

"Absolutely."

In the coffee shop we took a small sofa.

"What did you want to tell me?" she said, an expectant smile on her face.

I waited a moment, took her hand, and said, "I'm thinking of converting."

She removed her hand from mine and clapped her hands once. "No!... But you said that once before."

"But that was different," I said.

A bridal roseate suffused her happy face. She looked beatified, like a Mother Superior in prayerful ecstasy. A loving light shone in her eyes.

"You're doing this for me?" She sang the words softly, like a lullaby, rocking a make-believe me in her make-believe arms. In a crèche, I must add.

"I've thought about it seriously, and I want to consult you. You're the one to speak to."

"Really?"

And she said that "Really?" in the same soft loving tone as the "Really? she used to whisper to me in response to all the sweet things I said to her.

"Yes. But first I want to spend a couple of days with you in a cottage I have in Pennsylvania."

I thought she would say, no way. But she said:

"Well..."

And hearing that *Well*, I thought I had won.

"Is there a church in that town?" Maria asked.

"I think so. It's not the first thing I check when I buy real estate."

She let that snippety line fly by her.

"Then let's go to services when we're up there."

"What?"

"I want you to join me for a Sunday prayer service."

Now it was my turn to say:

"No way."

"How can you convert without going to church?"

I began to laugh.

"What's one thing got to do with another?"

"Simple," Maria said. "It's like a goy"—and she purposely used the Yiddish word to unite with me, to show me that we're one, on the same side; that she, like me, knows the code word, the right vocabulary—"who wants to convert to Judaism but refuses to go to shul or to be circumcised."

"But I am circumcised. As you well know."

"I know you're being funny. Purposely obtuse in your usual comic way. But either you don't get the point or are making believe you're not getting the point. How can you possibly *not* want to go to church when you're thinking of converting to Christianity?"

"Christianity?" I exploded. Everyone in the café froze. As though a film had been paused. The waiters stopped serving. Patrons stopped sipping. A priest holding a croissant dropped it and crossed himself.

I exploded in all sorts of ways. I exploded with laughter. I exploded with astonishment. I exploded with disbelief. I also imploded with dismay. I pointed to her. I pointed to me. I turned my index fingers around each other, making little endless circles.

"You? I? You think? Me? That is…" And again I let my hands be the spokesman for my mouth. Like those villagers near Naples who used eye motions and hand gestures to indicate the past tense in their now extinct language. I moved my hand as if leaping over a barrier, a long horizontal parenthesis.

"You crazy?" I whispered harshly. "Or do you think I'm crazy? Me converting to Christianity?" And I actually gave out a fake, melodramatic laugh: "Ha! Ha! Ha!"

"Then what kind of conversion where you thinking of? Surely not Islam?" said a taken-aback, unsettled Maria.

"Of course Islam."

"Islam? Really?" she said. "You know I abhor Islam even more than Catholicism."

And I began laughing again.

"You really think that after all this time you know me," and I tried to express my consternation with some hand motions. I'm sure she didn't understand. I hardly understood them myself.

"You thought I was about to come over to your side?"

"Yes. Converting."

This time I didn't laugh. But I did shake my head.

"I wanted to consult you on a financial matter. After all, you specialize in labor relations and deal with economic issues as well, even though you can't keep track of your own expenses. From a business point of view. The economics of it."

She still didn't understand. Or didn't want to. But the roseate glow on her cheeks had faded. Blush had turned to ash.

"You mean, you might earn more money if you became a goy?"

"No no."

"You mean, like, if the church will give you a stipend, or pay you, or pay me a finder's fee for you to convert to Christianity?"

Now I felt bad for her. I put my hands on her cheeks and held them affectionately.

"No, you silly girl. I was thinking of converting materially, not spiritually. Of converting my cottage from oil heat to gas heat. They just installed natural gas lines up there. And I wanted to know if in the long run there would be cost savings if I converted."

"You're pulling my leg."

"I'm not."

"You know, Katz, on second thought it might not be such a good idea even if you thought seriously about it. You're too much of a wag. To you everything is one big joke."

"I know. I would even have had Jesus laughing on the cross."

"Anyone who says, 'I was holding the nails' when asked what he was doing at the crucifixion is not a serious candidate for conversion."

"So I was right. You do remember everything I say."

"There's nothing funny about Christianity. It's a serious business."

"If you remove the word 'serious,' you're absolutely right." Then I added:

"How can Christianity be a serious business if its First Premise, its basic tenet, is one big joke?"

She digested that without comment and then said:

"Then why did you ask me to spend a couple of days with you in your cottage—which, by the way, you've never ever mentioned before?"

"Why not? And by the way, I just bought it a month ago."

"Do you always answer a question with a question?"

"Do I? Did you know that Jews invented the question mark?"

"I heard that good news from you before." Maria looked about. "Can we have a drink somewhere? After talking to you I need one."

"Do you still have time?"

"They can wait for me."

I paid, took Maria by the hand, and walked into the pub next door. Here was something new. Maria drinking. In the back was a dimly lit little booth, where we sat next to each other. We had never before had an alcoholic beverage together; she did not even have wine in her house.

"What will you have?" I asked her.

"Whatever you have. I like..."

"...to be told what to drink," I finished for her.

There was a warm look in Maria's eyes. I ordered two glasses of Johnny Walker Black Label.

"Drinking Scotch at eleven a.m.," I clucked. "Very nice. Coming to work shikker. Reeking of liquor."

Maria clinked glasses with me, said, "L'chayim!" and sipped the Scotch.

"It's nice to sit in the dark with you." I leaned toward her and spoke softly. "I have one more question for you. Regarding what you told me in the car. About your husband's lack of interest. I'd like to know, what does a woman do when her husband loses interest in her? In other words, what do you do when love is dead, and before a new love is found?"

She spoke quickly, around and around the topic, as if trying to avoid zeroing in on the answer, beating around the bush with a feather-light Chinese fan, the sort she used when she turned me around during that memorable kissing months ago when we were together, really together, so together you couldn't slide a joker or a credit card between us. At times it sounded as if she were speaking Danish again. I told her, "Slow down your speedspeak." At first she listened but soon backslid again.

Finally, when the roundabout carousel ride wound down, she answered my to-the-point question with a sad little smile. She put her cheek almost next to mine and confessed:

"I play with myself."

This annoyed me, depressed me. I finished the tumbler of Scotch and began my moralizing reprimand with:

"You can get so used to masturbating..."

Then we both began speaking at the same time and, seeing she wanted to say something, I said quickly, "Let me finish...For once you get used to going it alone, you can easily forget that the self-abuse is just a third-rate substitute for the real thing. What were you going to interrupt me with?"

Maria brightened. At once she placed her hand over my mouth (I felt like holding it there and kissing her palm) and said, "Shh, that's precious...'You were going to interrupt me.' You have to write that down. It's like out of a book, you know."

"I'll remember it, like."

Maria made a face and said, "Soon as I said 'you know,' I tried to catch myself. I know it's a vapid interjection, but it was, like, too late."

"Okay, okay," I said impatiently. "Let's hear what you were going to interrupt me with."

"I was going to say, I don't do that any more."

"Hmm," I muttered. "So what do you do instead?"

"I pray."

"For what?"

"An orgasm." And she gave out a bold, assertive, teasing laugh I hadn't heard before, which made me want to put my hands around her again and bring her close to me, like I had done before our split. I felt a wave of desire rising in me, from my knees up to my loins and to my heart. Seeing her now made me realize how much I missed her.

The waiter suddenly loomed over us. Maria quickly finished her drink. I told him we didn't want any more of anything. "And, please, we'd like to have a bit of privacy for a few minutes." Abashed, the man slunk away.

"Just kidding," Maria said. "I said that only to amuse you, to say what you expected me to say...But I do pray, and that's the truth."

Maybe her good humor was a mask, a grand personality deception to cover up a basic malaise. There was a split in her personality, I concluded, that demanded attention, that needed healing. No wonder she had been in therapy most of her life, if one part of her was subservient to Jesus and the other to Eros.

"I'm going to save you seventeen more years of therapy," I told her. "And thousands and thousands of dollars. And I'll charge you only five dollars and forty-seven cents."

"How come your rates keep going up? Last time it was seventy-five cents."

"My malpractice insurance has skyrocketed."

Now her "Really?" was not in the same league, not in the same musical language as usual. This "Really?" was more incredulity than affection. Although I am sure the reverberations of that other "Really?" sang and tingled through her.

I looked at my watch and stood. "Let's continue this later. How about if we meet here at seven thirty?"

"Fine," Maria said. "But make it eight fifteen. I'll be working till eight."

On the sidewalk, before we parted I drew her close, brought her face to mine, and kissed a whisper into her ear.

"Just one more quick question."

"Okay."

"When you began with me again after stopping, what was your motivation? Tell me. Tell me. What was going on inside your head, your heart?"

"I don't know."

"You know. Think. You thought I was married. You know I'm Jewish. You had Jesus to contend with. Your perpetual brake. Why did you keep going, when, when...?"

Maria looked down, then looked up at me, right into my eyes.

"I couldn't resist you. I was lonely. You made me feel so good. So loved. So special. And..."

How good I felt hearing those words.

She stopped..

"And...?"

"And I guess I'm my mother's daughter."

Which wiped away at once the good feeling.

Although that's what I had thought all along, hearing her say it made me change my mind, and so I shouted. No. What am I talking about? We were standing in the street, people passing all around us. But I said it forcefully, passionately, in a loud whisper.

First I put my hands on her shoulders, then I brought her close. We were pressed up against each other, and my loud whisper was only an inch away from her lips, maybe closer.

"Stop it! Stop berating yourself. You're not a victim of genetics. You're not a character in an Ibsen play. You know what you have to do? This!"

I bent down and pressed my ear to her left breast, right into her heart.

I think she got the point.

50

IN THE PUB BOOTH

At eight-fifteen we sat in the same little booth. Maria's eyes, there was a happiness in them. As in days of old. Expecting to hear some truth from me. In the pub the sounds of the superb Handel harpsichord and violin sonatas filled the air. Another first for us, going out together right after work. But this time it wasn't Scotch. This time we both were drinking tea.

"Here's the cure," I said. "Which I once told you in different words. But then you were so angry it didn't register. There is a split between your heart/body, which wants loving and wants to give loving, and your mind/soul, which is focused on Jesus. That's it. Now you can fire your blood-sucking therapist."

"Oh, my God!" Maria exulted. "You're right. I vaguely remember hearing that. But it didn't sink in. What a great analysis. You just compressed seventeen years into one line. Why didn't my shrink see that?"

"If you paid me great wages for seventeen years, I wouldn't see that either. No wonder you don't have a bank account. Your therapist has it."

As I was saying this, she reached into her pocketbook, withdrew the therapist's little white appointment card, and ripped it into two.

"I'm just afraid of becoming a slut."

"So you need," I said, "the protection of Jesus, huh? But if you listen to me, I'll protect you from becoming a slut. Just slut me regularly and go to church on alternate Sundays and you'll be okay. This way you can pay homage to your two basic desires."

Maria didn't say Yes; she didn't say No.

Then I added: "Who's the dodo whose card you just ripped up?"

Maria put the two pieces together. "Dr. Charles Perlmutter. Do you know him?"

"Name sounds familiar. Wait a minute. I thought your shrink was a she."

"It is a she. But she's on maternity leave. He's her substitute."

Then I quickly asked the question I had been hesitating to ask. "Are you seeing anyone?" As I said this my heart constricted, from my earlobes to my feet. "I don't mean a therapist. I mean socially."

"No."

The sweetest no I had ever heard from her.

And then, with seeming disinterest, I said:

"Why don't you go out more, socialize, lead a normal life, maybe meet a man."

"Why meet a man if I have the next best thing? You." Then she added. "I'm not looking to meet a man."

"So what do you do for sex?"

"I don't."

I was going to tell her if she repressed herself so much she would explode. She would do better if she were more normal and let her physicality (her sinning, I thought) return. With me.

After some quiet moments, I leaned forward and brushed away Maria's long hair from her ear. I cupped both my hands to her ear and whispered, "I admit it. I shouldn't say it. I don't want to say it. But I miss you." She smiled a soft, compliant smile, like a Buddha accepting an offering. I took her right hand in my left and held it. She didn't pull away.

And then a wave of curiosity came over me and I did something I had never done before. I unclasped my left hand from hers and held out my five fingers in front of her. Mimicking what she had done in the car the night we drove back from Connecticut. I bent down the top half of my left ring finger until it was hidden. Now it looked more like her ring finger than mine. For what seemed like endless minutes, I held my hand out like that.

Maria looked at me. "I understand. You want to…"

"…know," I said. "Yes. Tell."

I looked at her; she stared down at her hands, silent, as if waiting for me to ask again, as if only by prompting could the memories be released.

Except for the tinkling of glasses, it was still in this section of the little pub, dark as a cocoon, like during our night drive. I hadn't realized they were playing a Haydn quartet. I had stumbled onto an upscale pub.

"Maria. I can't help thinking about your ring finger. Tell me what, how it happened. I can't believe a husband, even if he discovers what he discovers, could be so cruel. Based on what you told me in the car that night, I figured it was a punishment of some sort."

"Yes, you're absolutely right."

"So it was punishment."

"Yes. The finger that bore the ring, the wedding band, had to bear the shame, the punishment, of breaking the vow. That finger had to be broken too. By running to my lover, by being unfaithful, my marriage was no longer whole—and so the finger that had the ring could no longer be whole either. I mutilated the marriage and so..."

"How did you come to such a barbaric punishment? And who did it? Tell me. Tell. Was it your husband?"

"When I realized how barbarically I behaved, I thought it only fitting that since..."

"You still didn't answer me. Was it your husband?"

Her lips moved but I couldn't tell what she was saying.

Once again shivers ran through me.

"Then who was the sadist? Some Mafia hit man?"

"No, I didn't hire a sadist. I had my own sadist who administered Biblical justice. Eye for eye. The finger that bore the ring, that finger was beheaded."

"But who did it?"

Again an unintelligible response, as though said in a foreign tongue.

•

Katz's penciled note in the margin:

At this point, John, my brother has a variant on this scene; here too he's not sure which version he will use. This one begins with Maria initiating the telling, rather than Katz asking first. Here they're not in a cafe or a pub but riding together in Katz's car.

•

"I want to tell you about my finger," Maria said while I was driving her to a café on the outskirts of Waltham. Something stopped my heart. My mind too stopped.

"How? Who? Where?"

"You're smart, Katz. You tell me. How do you think it happened?"

"First of all, it seems to me," I said carefully, "that it's not a birth defect. You weren't born that way, right?"

"Right."

I took Maria's hand while driving. While driving, I reached out for her hand and, without looking, just feeling with my fingers, sought out her ring finger and brought it to my lips. I held it there for a few seconds between my lips, recalling how I had once kissed each of her fingers.

"Then how?" Maria insisted. She removed her hand.

I looked straight ahead as I drove. I didn't even turn to her.

"I imagine it was him, your husband. Once he discovered what you'd done, he did it in a rage....Boy am I glad I didn't see his face at the movie house that night."

"He would have to be pretty strong, don't you think," Maria countered, "to hold me while I was trying to squirm, screaming, out of his grasp? Maybe even get two other equally insane friends of his to hold me to get that finger on the chopping block?"

What is she driving at? I wondered. Did she cooperate with him in this immolation? Holding her finger down on something while turning her head and closing her eyes? The couple's own version of the Waters of Bitterness test? Was there any hint of the crucifixion in all this? Her desire to become a Christian martyr, reveling in punishment? Couldn't be. It was too absurd.

"Nevertheless, Maria, my gut feeling is that he did it. Suddenly. Without warning."

But she still didn't answer. "Is that how you imagine it?"

She was testing me, playing out the drama. Making theater out of it.

"Yes. Somehow I imagine it after breakfast...Am I right? Why do I even ask? I'm always right."

And again I cursed the bestiality of her husband, delighted that I didn't know the bastard's name.

"You're right."

"See?"

"It did happen after breakfast. But you're dead wrong about the rest."

"What?"

"I said, you're dead wrong."

I had heard what Maria said. But my "What?" was a what of shock. Surprise. Astonishment. Not a question what. But an exclamation—what! So if not the husband, then who did it? And at once my heart sank as it instinctively answered my own question. For clarity of thought, the heart always beats the mind.

Still, I couldn't help saying, "Then who?"

Maria uttered one crisp syllable and looked past me, beyond me, as she saud:

•

Another penciled comment by Katz:

= Here, once again, John, a strange, symbolic and meaningful typo. Note that my brother, instead of typing 'said,' wrote 'saud,' as if he'd been thinking of the sort of punishments meted out to this very day in Saudi Arabia.

•

Maria said:

"Me."

"You? I don't believe it."

"But it was. It was me. I did it."

"How?"

"I'm not going into that."

"Why?"

"Because."

It's her Jesus complex, I thought. She wants to be like him.

"You misunderstand, Maria. My why isn't a question as to why you're not saying how you did it. It's a question of broader dimension, a why that's thick and wide and all-encompassing. Why did you do it?"

"I'll give you three reasons. Expiation. Atonement. Punishment."

She said those words quickly, as though the answer had been well-prepared in advance.

I kept muttering, "I don't believe it, I don't believe it." I shook my head. Then I stopped asking and we stopped speaking. From both of us, like a sad melody in a canon, in alternation, antiphonally, from both of us came a deep, pent-up sigh.

I felt I was in a reverse timeline. Our being together this morning was reprising our first tram ride from Newton to Boston. But now we had a history. We had a past. A present? Nah. A future? I don't think of the future beyond the tip of my nose, the edge of my toes.

I tried not to picture the deed itself. I created a curtain and I commanded that curtain to come down over the scene. But I couldn't help thinking how she quickly bandaged the wound and rushed to the hospital. What was her explanation to the inevitable question—*How did this happen*? Her prepared reply: *I was deboning a steak with a cleaver, was distracted by a scream outside, and I brought the cleaver down on my finger.*

"You know, they had microsurgery then too. It could have been reattached."

"Do you think I would go through the charade of removing my fingertip only to have it sewn back on? As a matter of fact, the doctor suggested it to me. They asked me why I didn't bring the fingertip? I told them I didn't know that such a thing was possible. And now, Katz, that's the end of that subject. We discuss this no more. Like God says to Moses in Deuteronomy, when he pleads to go into the Land of Israel: 'Enough! Speak no more to me on this matter.' And so I too say, please, not another word on this."

Again I took Maria's hand, sought out the forlorn finger and held it in between my lips. This time she did not take it away.

"Dear, dear Maria," I said, holding the empty space of her hand. "Just one more question. One that's been bothering me. You mind?"

"No," she said, and there was a smile, a beneficence in that No.

"In fact, the word you just uttered is the subject of my question. Now you delivered it with a soft music, a Mozartean *Così fan tutte* teasing No. The one I'm referring to was hard as granite. Why did you give me such a vehement and flinty No to a shower with you? Twice, in fact."

"Did it bother you?"

"Can't you see?"

"Why do you think I said no?"

"I'll tell you what I thought. You felt that intimacy went far enough in bed. You didn't want to extend the sinning."

"Not bad," Maria said. She sounded like a teacher praising her young student. "But there was something more. Of all people, you with your rabbinic training, I'm sure you'll understand. Because it comes from the Old Testament. Your Torah. Our Torah. Like the leper purifying himself in living waters in Leviticus, I too purged myself of sin by bathing. With you in the water with me, it wouldn't have been much of a *mikva,* much of a purification, would it?"

"I see," I said with utter neutrality, then added, "So why don't we hop into bed later tonight, and then you'll take a nice long shower alone and be even purer than ever?"

"You're impossible, but cute," Maria said. "Pull over to the side of the road."

I obeyed at once.

"Close your eyes."

I did.

And then I felt her lips lightly on mine, her mouth brushing my mouth, surprising my lips with a tender little kiss.

51

WHAT HE (THOUGHT HE) HEARD

"You don't know how beautiful that kiss was, Maria," I told her.

"How beautiful? Tell me."

"Like angels' wings on my lips."

She gave me a shy smile. "You always manage to make me feel good."

Maria gave me the opening. If she hadn't given me the opening, I wouldn't have said it. But I said it because the opening was there, a vacuum waiting to be filled.

"While making love to you, I felt, do you know what I felt? I felt I became a color. One of the colors of the rainbow. The lilac band, I think."

At once Maria sat straight up, as though poked in the back.

"Oh, my God, that... is...so...beautiful."

She looked at me. She pressed my hand. I saw her lips quivering, her nose pinched. She leaned in closer to me. Maria began to cry.

"You're crying."

"I'm not."

"Why you crying?"

"Because. What you. Said. Is so. Beautiful. So. Touching. No one ever said. Anything. Like that. To me. Poetry. Ever."

I hugged her, brought her close. Stroked her hair, kissed her hair. Spread the strands and kissed her ear.

"Because you never met anyone. Like. Me. Ever."

"Do you mean it?"

"Of course I mean it." I tried to get the huff out of my voice. "Do I ever say anything I don't mean? If I didn't mean it, I wouldn't have said it."

"To become one of the colors of the rainbow. That is. Really. Something."

In the dark, with the motor still running, I kissed her salty cheeks. But I did not, no I did not kiss her lips.

"Stop crying, Maria."

"I'm not."

"Don't cry.... Please. Stop crying."

"I can't." And then, softly. Whispered. "You know what?" Her big green eyes, I swear, they widened in the dark. I saw them getting bigger, a starburst in the dark. And a soft green light, from a star long dead but still shining, a soft verdant, spring green light rayed out of her big eyes. "I guess I do love you."

My arms fell. My head lurched down to my chest.

"What? I don't believe it. Has the Messiah—someone's, either mine or yours—come?... Please repeat what you just said."

"No."

"Once more. Please. Please, once more."

"You didn't hear that."

"What?"

"What I just said. I didn't say that."

"So you do love me. So you finally said it. I knew you loved me, but I wanted to hear it from you. In person. I longed to hear it from you. Hallelujah! My little flint-heart finally says it flat out. Now I'm going to gallop them to the rainbow."

"Don't get on your high horse, Katz," Maria said as the tears trickled down her cheeks. "I love Jesus more."

I wiped the tears from her eyes.

And then did I wake? Was that a rainbow I saw vanishing slowly in the dissipating mist? I didn't believe it. I couldn't believe it. Maybe she didn't say it. Maybe it was my imagination, my fantasy, my wishing to hear those words from her that made me hear them. Maybe I had invented a new psychological phenomenon: wishful hearing. A momentary quick dream, a pleasant hallucination that lasted one second but left its punch like a long hangover. Maybe Figaro's potion, condensed love apples coming back to me again. That potent liquid talisman that Maria had not drunk but whose essence I had breathed into my lungs, that mixture made her say, and made me hear, what was not meant to be said or heard.

Never mind, I thought. I heard it. Even if I didn't hear it, I heard it. *What do you plan to do about it*? I should have said. *For you won't marry me because I'm not Christian, and I won't marry you because you're not a Jew*. Can one hear something not said? Let her love phantoms, ibises, strange gods, whatever. As long as she loves me.

52

KATZ'S CALL

A FEW DAYS LATER—I wanted to resist but I couldn't resist—I called her work number and asked to speak to Maria. Without even identifying myself, I said:

"I just want to know if you miss me as much as I miss myself."

Of course, she recognized my voice at once.

"Hi," she said quietly. "Nice to hear from you." And then she gave me that banal, enthusiastic, "How *are* you?"

"I love that soft, sexy voice of yours. So full of desire."

"I understand," she suddenly said in a flat voice, then whispered, "I have to talk softly. People nearby."

"But that doesn't mean you have to purr so erotically."

"Erratically."

"You heard me. But you still didn't answer my question. Do you miss me?"

"I think that's a very good suggestion. We'll give that idea some consideration." Then, a pitch lower, "Nice to hear from you."

"I ain't deaf. I heard that elusive..."

"Allusive..."

"Just answer."

"Sir, would you kindly call this same number tomorrow and make the last digit eight instead of seven? It's another phone and I'll pick up. I'm getting some interference on this line."

"How about your home phone?"

"Reception problems. Getting fixed," she said quickly and hung up.

Annoyed, puzzled, and impatient, I waited a full twenty-four hours and called her new number. She answered right away.

"You sounded so strange yesterday."

"There were people all around me. Because of the circumstances, I had to have a different attitude."

"Interference on the line. Humbug."

"There *was* interference. Those people next to me were interfering. Because people were all around me, I had to speak the way I spoke. Officialese. We were sitting right next to each other and they were listening in, actually grinning, leering at what I was saying, though, I was, you know, trying to sound businesslike. You know it annoys me when people invade my space. I can't stand being crowded in, having people press into me."

"Except me, of course."

"Shush. I didn't want to give the impression that I was less friendly, so I'm sorry about that. But just yesterday they gave me a private cubby with this number, and I can whisper and no one will hear me."

"You have a good whisper," I said. "A very sexy whisper…but you still didn't answer my question."

"Which one? Lately, you've been asking so many questions."

"Do you miss me?"

"Yes, of course I miss you."

I couldn't believe that either. Had she changed? I floated up to the ceiling and then, invoking gravity, sailed back down. Who says that happiness is unattainable in this world? Again, again and again, Maria surprised me. Or maybe it was a bad connection. Demonic interference.

That "Of course" passed me by. I wasn't expecting it. And then it rang, it made its mark. She had sung that "Of course" before, when I asked her long ago if it was me in her sexy dream, and she chanted "Of course" in a three-note melody. I now weighed the timbre of her just-uttered "Of course." It lacked the former tincture of eros but it did sound good.

"Remember some months ago, when you told me about your sexy dream and I asked if I was in it, and you sang out, 'Of course'?"

"Of course," she said.

"Are there any leering, sneering, profiteering perverts listening to our conversation?"

"No."

"Then I want to kiss your lips. I miss them. Your throat. I miss them."

"Them? Plural?"

"Misprint. I mean your double chins and your double breasts. Each one. The other one first and then the first second. Your thighs."

"Stop."

"How come you didn't stop me at the breasts?"

"I didn't know which one you were referring to."

"I asked if you missed me but I knew the answer. I just wanted to hear you say it."

So she actually missed me. She said it loud and clear, with no hesitation. And that lovely, open-hearted "Of course" gave me leave to say:

"I still want to buss your breasts and kiss your kitten and lie next to you on the sofa and run my hands over your clothes and feel that soaking wet patch on your crotch that shows you're hot for me."

Maria didn't say a word.

But she didn't hang up and she didn't say, *Stop it. I'm beyond that now.* She didn't say, *No revisitation rights.*

"I want to see you."

She didn't respond.

"Well?"

"In a public place."

But you said you love me, I almost cried out. *That you miss me.* But I didn't. I bided my time. Instead, I joked:

"In your apartment. With doors and windows open. Closet doors too."

"No. The closet doors remain closed." And then she added, "With windows open the New England frost chills my canary."

"Is that a code word?"

She didn't say.

"No. In a café."

My surge of heat, of enthusiasm, faded.

"Does it have private booths and doors?"

"I can't talk anymore. Gotta go back to work. Call me."

I hung up, my soul split in two. I recalled that trip to Dalton we had taken together. Those beautiful four or five hours we had spent together where she revealed her inmost self to me. She had taken off from work to keep me company. And she waited patiently for a couple of hours in the lobby of the hotel until my meeting was over. She didn't want to go to a bookstore or to a film. "Because in case you finish early, why should you wait for me? I'll wait here and read." And then the other day in the car, that confession that she loved me. Which she told me I didn't hear. And maybe I *didn't* hear it. Maybe I dreamt it. Wished it. But, in any case, she still had something for me. What that something was and what its metaphysical dimensions were, I would have to discover. Slowly. Again slowly. Always, with Maria, slowly.

And when we parted and I said I would call her, she said that double "Yes." Maria enjoyed the attention. She craved it. She enjoyed being loved. But there was a religious boundary she felt she could not compromise. She had pushed that boundary farther and farther early on and could very well do the same now. She too was no doubt split in two.

Jesus had cast a dark energy, that anti-gravity force, between us. So instead of falling toward me, she was being pulled away. I would have to find some new law of physics to undo that dark energy, maybe invoke sunlight and make it bright. Or invoke a tiny po(r)tion of dark matter, which is the glue that gluts the galaxies together.

But once we would meet a couple of times in a café and spend some time together in the intimate confines of my car, she would have to relent. Maybe the guilt liquid in the guilt flask would sink to the bottom and the old Maria would surface. Just like the druid princess Norma, heroine of Bellini's eponymous opera, breaks her vow of chastity and falls for a man, I hoped Maria would do the same.

This would be the beginning of a slow start. Remember, she said she missed me. Missed me. Her own words.

Not a misprint. Not a bad connection. No interference.

Indeed, indeed, I had heard those words: "Yes, of course I miss you."

And that phrase was topped, capped, crowned by those three magic words I was sure I had heard but didn't dare repeat for fear of her absolutely denying it.

But say those three words she did. I am sure.

She did. She did. She did.

53

WAITING IN LINE (A CHAPTER INSERTED BY JOHN)

ONE DAY, AROUND THE time Katz was away and I was reading the chapters he had given me, I changed my departure time from Trenton and had a Katz-Maria experience at the station waiting room. At that instant, I thought I was magically transported to his brother's novel, reliving the beginning of his story.

Almost the same way Katz had met Maria—before a trip to the big city—I saw a tall, fairly pretty young woman standing ahead of me in line. She was either waiting to buy a ticket or renew her weekly pass like me. Suddenly, a well-dressed man came up to her and said softly, almost apologetically:

"Excuse me, miss, but I'm in a dire situation. I know this sounds weird, but I'm on my way to New York for an important job interview and I forgot my wallet, left it in the jacket I usually wear. And it's too late for me to return home. May I ask you for a favor? Can you lend me the money for a return trip? I'll pay you back tomorrow if you take the 8:21."

I thought at once it was a scam, but I couldn't bring myself to caution her. Meanwhile, the man had told her his name and phone number.

She waved her hand. "That won't be necessary."

And at once she took out a twenty-dollar bill from her pocketbook, told the man to keep the change for the subway rides, and wished him good luck. And all with a smile on her face, as though helping out a friend, with not the slightest indication she was looking down on him.

And would you believe it, the next day I took the same train and sure enough there was the same man again. I thought he would pull his routine with someone else. But no. I saw him open his wallet, take out a twenty-dollar bill, and approach the same young woman.

"Thank you so much for trusting me," he said as he returned the money.

"How did it go?"

"I got the job. You don't know what a great deed you did. You see, I went to that interview upbeat and uplifted. Your trust gave me a spiritual boost, which affected my confidence and how I came across at the interview."

"I'm so happy for you." I thought she would hug him with joy. Then I approached her and said I had seen and admired what she had done yesterday.

"I have a beneficent nature," she said, "and faith. I sensed the poor man was, you know, in a predicament. I guess it was fated that I help him. Because I usually go in much much later, but yesterday and today I had to be in the city earlier than usual. It's very nice of you to notice."

"On the contrary. My noticing is not comparable to your beneficence and trust. Because at first glance the man's request was a classic scam."

When the train pulled in, I asked her if she would mind if I sat next to her.

"Not at all."

After we exchanged names—her name was Theresa—I asked her which train she usually takes.

"The 11:34. I usually start late and work till early evening."

The next few days I took that train instead of my usual 9:03. As I got to know Theresa, I kept thinking of Katz's Maria. Theresa also had a wide-ranging vocabulary. She seemed to be about five or so years younger than my forty. She too was an independent worker, an accountant, with an MBA from NYU, but she preferred working as a temp, which she said paid well and gave her flexibility. "And as much vacation time as I want."

I couldn't help looking at her fingers. She had no marriage band but wore three other decorative rings on other fingers. Her hair was short and brown, worn in the pageboy style.

"And you don't mind not taking full advantage of your MBA with a permanent job?" I asked.

"Well, since I don't have a family to support..."

"You don't have a family?" I wanted know, probing to see if she was married.

"No. Except for my nine cats, which is sort of family." And she rattled off all their names, which rhymed with "olly." "But my favorite is Mr. Svengali. He has two different colored eyes. One green, the other blue."

I thought of my Katz. She had nine. I have only one.

During the few mornings we sat together, I found out that she too, like Maria, didn't like to cook. Again I couldn't help thinking of Katz's heroine—but not cooking must be endemic to single working girls wherever they live. If Theresa too used her fridge as a storage unit I don't know. And she too liked to read. About sex hangups or guilt I could not (yet) comment. Also, she was slimmer than was Maria in the book and less bosomy. I didn't dare ask her if she detested botany words in the dictionary.

Since Katz's adventures took place around Boston, more than twenty years ago, I had the wild idea that perhaps Theresa was Maria's daughter. Katz's girl, when he knew her a score of years ago, was about forty. That would make Maria about sixty today. At forty she still had not had any children. Even if she gave birth—immaculately, I can hear Katz quip—a year later, her child, would have to be about twenty today. Highly unlikely, for Theresa appeared to be in her mid-thirties. So much for my fantasy.

Is it possible for stories to repeat? After all, it is said there are only three or four basic stories. The rest are just variations. Twenty or so years ago, Katz met a girl at a trolley station waiting room in Newton. Recently, same thing happened to me in Trenton before boarding a New York-bound train. Is there a transmigration of stories just as there is of souls? Katz's girl in the novel is nearly forty—and the Theresa I just met about five years younger. I suppose if I want to look for affinities I can find them, just as a scholar in doing research finds the facts to support his contentions, or just as a mean teacher can find flaws in an essay of a student he dislikes.

Katz was talking about a girl his brother, the writer, had met and was depicting in a novel. At least that's what Katz said. It could also have been someone his brother had heard about or someone he had concocted. Maybe even someone my Katz had met but, to protect his privacy, said it was his brother's story. I iterate and reiterate these possibilities because I keep thinking about them.

I didn't want to pry. That is, I wanted to pry but I didn't. As I've said before, there are certain unwritten rules in train friendships. You only explore surface, like a housemaid lazily dusting. If the other guy volunteers—fine. But there are bounds beyond which you don't encroach. But, I must say, Katz's familiarity with his brother's story was so all-encompassing it made me feel at times that it was indeed his story. Either that or he had perfectly memorized his brother's manuscript, or at least details of it which he narrated with his own variations. The fact that he occasionally read from the manuscript could have been evidence for either contention.

Storytellers are tricky that way.

Every sentence, phrase, word, syllable, letter is laden with duplicity, ambiguity, elastic veracity. And falsehoods too. And, by the way, articles are not excluded. Even "a", "and", and "the" are part of the deceptive packet of—why use an eighteen-letter word, one of the longest in the English language, one with the most vowels (seven) and the most s's (five), a highfalutin seven-syllable hissing euphemism like "disingenuousnesses"?—when a monosyllable like "lies" will do. A word that goes arrow straight to the heart.

If you, like me, hold as powerful Isaac Babel's observation—Katz had once mentioned a Babel story to me—that nothing can pierce the heart with greater force than a period properly placed, wait till you see the veil of Schweik-like innocence over the bulldozer force of a prevaricating "and" or a rattlesnake-sly "but."

Another possibility was twinning. The other Katz was yes the author but my Katz—who knows?—was perhaps editing, subtracting, changing, adding material on his own.

As I said these words to myself, it seemed to me I was rewording something I had read before. But from where? Then, bam, I got it. In one of Borges's stories, Borges and his friend are thinking of writing a "first-person novel whose narrator would omit or distort..."

Katz spoke as if he'd memorized his brother's manuscript. Only four or five times during the days we shared rides did Katz read from a few pages he held in his hand, close to his chest as if he didn't want me to look at the manuscript. And yet a couple of times he didn't hesitate, witness the chapters he'd given to me, to hand over a section of the book.

There was no way I could verify what he was saying against a script. I had told Katz from the outset that I could not read, was in no position at this time to read a manuscript, for our house had stopped publishing fiction. But, I must confess, reading the few chapters that Katz had given me made Maria come more alive for me than ever before.

Now every time I saw Theresa, I thought of Maria. And every time I thought of Maria, I pictured Theresa. Were they becoming offbeat twins in my mind?

Like Katz and his brother. Siamese Katz. Bridging the border between fiction and non-fiction. After listening to Katz's story I came to the conclusion you can no more say that this is a true fiction than you can say false biography. In the old days we had two categories of books: fiction and non-fiction. Nowadays the categories overlap. Genres play leapfrog over each other. Besides true fiction and false biography we have fictional non-fiction, non-fictional fiction, real memoir, true memoir, false memoir, fictional memoir, non-fictional memoir, memoiristic fiction, memoiristic non-fiction, non-memoiristic nonfiction.

The more the categories expand, the fewer readers we have.

The End

54

KATZ TALKS ABOUT NARRATION

Here's a problem. An ongoing conundrum.

I had to sort out—endlessly, constantly—the tale, the teller, and the reteller. Ostensibly, Katz did not know Maria, although by narrating his brother's story about Maria so faithfully and passionately my Katz had arrogated the narrator's character and fused with him.

I wasn't even going to question Katz about this. It would be a waste of time, for Katz would give me the old story: he was just Laurence Olivier to Shakespeare's Hamlet. A mere bit player. The actor. Standin.

But. Still. However. Nevertheless. There was this lingering suspicion that Katz was playing games, perhaps surreptitiously slipping in something either from his life or his own fantasy, grafting it onto his brother's tale.

Seneca wrote that each reader invents his own past. He could have said, each writer embellishes the story he's retelling. Or, better, invents his brother's past.

Which reminded me of the time I caught Katz in a contradiction. He said he took the train to New York with Maria.

= Katz, I said. = You said New York. I think you mean Boston.

= You're right. But who's writing the story, me or you?

= You or I. But actually your brother.

Katz stared at me.

= Grammar, I said. = And also a contradiction.

= It's that way in the book. Author's privilege. Call it a typo. Sometimes, to protect the identity of the innocent, wordslingers like my brother may add or subtract inches or pounds or color and length of hair, add or subtract a parent or two, change skin color. We have almost God-like freedom: change profession, move a hero from one city to another, add a sense of humor, make a teetotaler a tippler, a conservative liberal. We can remove a pimple, add wrinkles, create a lisp, enhance a bustline, make a cheapskate philanthropic. In short, turn anyone or anything inside out and upside down. We purvey make-believe. Otherwise, we are as faithful to reality as a photograph.

= Still, it's a contradiction. Doesn't a contradiction disturb you?

= I'm as much against diction as the next guy. But within limits. By the way, that's another book that Figaro sold that my brother told me about, a contradictionary, where every word was given an erroneous definition.

•

And then again, how many layers of make-believe were there? I know I've said this before, but it bugs me. Brother Katz the writer filtering a possibly true (and possibly made-up) story through his own imagination, then telling it, rather, showing his typescript to his brother who, in replaying it, relaying it, relating it, recalls, edits, tweaks, adds his own material, either real or fictional, and so we have here a quadruple mix of truth and fiction filters, not including me, who is the fifth and last—and certainly the most trustworthy—voice, for I am passing it along word for word, everything I've heard, without changing a word, a syllable, even a letter.

55

THE ESCALATOR

= Do you miss Maria? I asked Katz.

= Yes. I miss her. Ever since I began these daily re-tellings.

He stopped, but only for an eyeblink, then added: = For my brother. If you know what I mean.

If Katz was trying to palm off on his brother what could have been his own relationship with Maria, he played the game skillfully. But I must say, each pronoun change threw me off balance.

= Who does the missing? I asked. = I mean, from a philosophical point of view. You or your brother?

= True, said Katz. = Who? It's fascinating how, with constant narration, you can miss a girl from so many years ago whom you've never met. And who may not even exist at all...It's interesting how the re-telling brings you closer and closer to the subject. The actor is so bound, so enmeshed in the lines, he thinks he wrote them. The soloist for a Mozart violin concerto begins to think, especially after creating a cadenza in the Mozartean style, that he composed the entire concerto.

= I think you mentioned that analogy once.

= Only because you keep testing me on the true authorship issue, Katz said rather testily.

= Only because you interweave, interchange, he and I, me and my.

= Only because I'm the narrator, John, and narrators shift personae. Them's the rules. But, on the other hand, who says that Maria is real? She could be, and very likely is, fiction. A woman who loved Jesus too much to let anyone else into her life. But a lot of this is empty talk, for we're dancing on the precipice between fiction and reality, on the fault line between real and make-believe.

= Do you ever wish it was you who knew her? I mean, if she's based on a real person.

= In a story I once read, I think by a Spanish author, perhaps Borges, a woman is destined to meet a man named Johnny Dalton. But there are two of them, and it's really the other Johnny Dalton she must meet, but doesn't. A slight mystic error on the part of destiny.... So I made an analogy with Maria. It was destined, fated, written in the cards that she meet an M. Katz. So she met my brother. But maybe it was me she was destined for.

We sat in silence, Katz and I. He evidently had no more to say.

Were Maria's beneficent words, "Yes. Yes," the end of the story? Was that the hopeful conclusion of the narrative? Yet I felt if that were indeed the coda to the tale, Katz would have let me know.

= I may have asked you this before, Katz, but I'm curious—did you change any part of your brother's story?

= You asked and I answered. I close my eyes and I still see that indignant look on my face when I hear that question. But, in any case, I'll answer again. No, I have not.

I nodded. Just then it got dark. We had just rolled into Newark Penn Station.

Katz rose. = See you next time, he said as he ran out and made his way to the escalator.

I watched Katz slide up and away at a forty-five degree angle. Then, no more than ten seconds later, to my absolute astonishment, when he was halfway up, I saw him suddenly turn and begin to struggle against the massive uptide, attempting to make his way *down* again, evidently back to the train, which always waited here for a few minutes for the local from another line.

What had made Katz change his mind?

I watched Katz in his rebellion. He battled his way down the up escalator steps against the tight throng rushing up, pressing up, riding, moving up to get to work. Newark Penn Station doesn't have department store side-by-side up and down escalators. The platform is very narrow and there's room for only one escalator, a.m. up, p.m. down. To get down by foot at this time, you have to search at another part of the platform. Which is why Katz was laboring to come down. He seemed to hover magically in space, as if the world had been suspended. Stock still but still in motion.

Blocking now his way was a heavy black woman in a huge red coat, built like a defensive guard, like one of those concrete cylindrical pillars used to protect embassies against car bomb attacks.

Katz was fighting, elbowing, his way down the escalator as though there was a fire, as though he were being chased, his face panic-stricken, as though, as though, as though. And me, I'm standing at the open door, watching, listening, rooting for Katz.

I don't know, can't say, if that black lady was purposely blocking him, but he tried to push her aside with a loud, "Please! I've got to catch this train," which made her shout, "This train's just come in. What's to catch?", which made him say, "I've got to catch this escalator," which made her laugh, which made her teeter off balance, which gave Katz an opening and, like a clever quarterback, he sprinted forward, despite the relentless upward movement of the escalator.

Then, of a sudden, he's back up again, riding backwards.

Curiously, no one reprimands him or yells at him, no one berates, reviles, curses him, no one rages at him with words like, "You moron, this is an UP escalator!"

Then the frustrated Katz changed tactics. With a roar, he plowed down. People huddled to the side. Near the bottom, he leapt and landed on the platform, wobbly for a moment, then regained his balance and dashed to the door of my car. Seeing Katz charging toward the still-open door, I backed away to give him room. But time was up. Just as he panted, = I have a confession to make, the door slammed shut. Between "to" and "make."

Katz ran alongside the slowly accelerating train. He was trying to tell me something through the closed window. I tried to read his lips. But the combination of Katz sprinting and the train moving made this impossible. The train picked up speed. I saw he was mouthing, with exaggerated lip movements, the word

= To…mor…row, his lips out for the first syllable, as if sending a kiss, for the second mouth wide open, and then slightly pursed for the final syllable. I assumed he meant same time, same train.

What was it he wanted to confess?

That he was adding to his brother's tale, making things up from one ride to the next?

Or: that it wasn't a novel he was telling me, neither his nor his brother's, but Katz's own true story.

Or something else entirely: he wanted to reveal his real name.

56

AT THE BOOK PARTY

BUT KATZ DIDN'T SHOW up the next morning. Nor the morrow thereafter. Two weeks passed. Then three and four. Katz seemed to have disappeared. I tried taking trains at different times, earlier, later. There was no sign of him.

One day I got a call from a colleague at another small press, inviting me to a pre-publication book party for an offbeat novel, *I Love Pussycats*—a love story that he said outside readers had described as funny, touching, sexy, sad, savvy, tart, wise, and acutely observed.

"Wow!" I said. "Who's the author?"

"You haven't heard of him. It's a first novel by a guy who signs himself only as Katz...But his real name is M. Katz. And, by the way, the last syllable in the title is spelled capital K, then a...t...z."

I swallowed. It was hardly likely there were two writers with such an oddball name. My Katz too never used a first name.

"Great title. *I Love PussyKatz.*"

"You coming?"

"Sure." And he told me the date, time, and place.

So the manuscript my seatmate had read/told me over a period of many weeks had made it. I was happy for him, for the book did have the ring of a true fiction. But why was the novel under his name if it was his brother's book? Why didn't the brother get any credit?

At our last meeting, after running down the up escalator, Katz left me with that enigmatic phrase that he wanted to tell me something, confess something. He finally made it to my car just as the train door was closing, he shouting, "I have a confession to make..." as the door slammed shut with a relentless finality, clicked closed as the public address system blared out, "Next stop, New York Penn Station." So there went that unheard confession.

Of course I couldn't contact Katz. There were twenty-eight of them in the Trenton-Princeton area and I wasn't going to go through the list. And even if I did, knowing him and his penchant for privacy, he probably had an unlisted number. And I never did tell Katz which house I worked for. Even if he called several publishers and asked for John, it would do him no good. Every publisher had at least one editor named John. It was one of the requirements for the job.

Naturally, I would go to the party, if only to congratulate him. But it was, I must admit, it was more than that. It was curiosity about his aborted confession. And also to ask him why he hadn't told me about the publication of the book. That the author wanted to surprise his brother was one possible explanation. Or perhaps they had a falling-out and one Katz didn't want to tell the other.

Why hadn't I seen Katz since that day? Had he changed his mind about "confessing" and was purposely avoiding me? Or had he changed jobs and no longer had to take the train to Newark? What could he have wanted to tell me? That there was no brother? That the tale was someone else's?

I pictured Katz's surprise when I tap him on the shoulder and ask him, "What is it you wanted to confess, Katz? Now you can tell me."

I entered the party room, made my way through the crowd, and approached Katz from the rear. Three people stood in front of him listening to what he was saying. Even though I saw him only from the back, I recognized him, my Katz, at once. By his stance. The shape of his head. The little bald spot. His impeccable attire. And then, as I drew closer, I heard his resonant voice.

I tapped him on the shoulder. He turned. I saw he had shaved his beard and mustache.

"Congratulations, Katz. So it's your book after all."

Instead of greeting me, his old buddy, he said rather curtly, "So whose should it be?"

"Your brother's."

Katz let out one short bark of a laugh. "Ha! It's mine."

I had expected him to open his eyes wide and give me a big smile. Instead, he blinked at me, astonished me with his muted reaction.

"Don't you recognize me? So soon have you forgotten your riding partner, Katz?"

"I don't ride horses," he said.

"Train," I corrected. "Where did you disappear to? I've been looking for you for weeks. And why didn't you tell me your novel is coming out?"

Katz was uncomprehending. I sensed he wanted to back away, resume his conversation with his three interlocutors, two pretty women and one insipid guy, but something, the mystery of my words, kept him focused on me.

"Perhaps snipping off your beard and mustache has also affected your memory."

"I never had a beard or mustache."

"But you did, not too long ago when we rode Jersey Transit to the city three times a week."

"I've been using the Long Island Railroad for the past two years."

"Aren't you Katz?"

"I am. But I don't know you."

I stared at his face. I tried to take in his entire face, match it with my memory of Katz's, and superimpose it on the face before me. The very same face. The very one.

"You look exactly like Katz."

"I should. I am Katz. I already told you that. I'd be awfully surprised if I woke one morning and looked in the mirror and saw someone else."

"One of Figaro's specialty mirrors, huh?"

Katz looked puzzled. As if thinking: *How does this guy know about Figaro?* Then he drew me over to a quiet side of the room. Evidently, he didn't want this edgy interchange to become more public.

"You seem to know details of my book."

"I'll try just once more," I told him, "and then I'll stop. For three or more months, you read to me chapters of your brother's novel. About three times a week. How come you don't remember me? Or are you teasing me again?"

Katz stopped in mid-breath. He either flushed or paled. Maybe both. He clapped both hands to his cheeks and muttered:

"Oh, my God! Now I get it. It's Morty. My brother Mortimer. He's the one who lives in New Jersey."

"That was your brother? M. Katz. The guy I've been talking about? Your brother? And not you?"

"Yes. I'm Montmorency. He's Mortimer. I don't use my first name either."

Confusion again. Two M. Katzes.

"So it was he, not you, riding with me and telling me the story."

"Mor-ti-mer," Katz sneered. He bit off each syllable as though biting into, and spitting out, bitter horseradish root. No doubt he would have preferred Sebastian for his brother's name, for then he could have hissed it, susurrating with disdain. "That rascal. I knew I shouldn't have given him my manuscript. And right away he shares it with strangers."

"How come he's not here celebrating with you?"

"Are you kidding? I have him here and he tells everyone he wrote the book."

"But yet when he was narrating..." I made sure to say "your story" and not "the story", "when he was telling me your story, he made sure to accent repeatedly that he's just the mouthpiece. He told me not to confuse the 'I' of the narration with him. He kept saying, 'My brother the author, my brother the genius.'"

"Really?"

"Now you sound like Maria."

That made Katz smile.

"So you didn't tell him about the party."

Katz didn't answer. A vein above his left eyebrow pulsed. I know veins don't pulse. Arteries do. But this one, Katz frere's vein, pulsed. Or throbbed. Or just filled with blood and came into view. Otherwise, he was stony-faced. But his vein, his blue forehead vein gave him away.

Perhaps he thought I was being intrusive. After all, I had just met him and was asking a lot of—too many—personal questions. His silence put me on the spot. Put me down, in fact. I mumbled something about how engrossing his story was, and then a woman came up to him and freed me.

Maybe my Katz, great mimic and actor that he was, maybe he was fooling me. Maybe there was only one of them. His voice, his demeanor, his face, were the same. Perhaps this Katz was a little more acerbic than the Katz I knew, but that could be part of the act, part of the deception. This Katz sans beard was a double for the Katz I knew.

There was only one way to be sure: to see the two of them together.

I tried a different angle. "Come on, Katz. Stop pulling my leg."

But Katz disregarded me.

"You, or he, recited much of the book as if you knew the text through and through."

"Mortimer." The name came out of pressed teeth. "He's got a photographic memory. Almost total recall. Tear out a page from a phone book. He'll scan it for a few moments and remember every name, every number. He'll even recite them dramatically, like an actor. He has a camera up there, not a normal brain."

Again Katz clenched his teeth and hissed, "Giving him the manuscript was a big mistake."

I wanted to ask him why. But instead I said:

"It's amazing how much you look like your brother. You're an exact copy of each other."

"Why *shouldn't* I look like him? We're twins."

"Twins?"

"Yes. Twins. Identical twins."

"But your brother told me you're older."

"With twins, one has to be. They can't come out at the same time. In the history of twindom, it's never happened."

That edgy tone again, so unlike my Katz.

"But your brother told me you were born in one year and he the following year."

"Typical of his truth-stretching. He told you the facts, but not the truth."

I wasn't going to ask him the difference. I looked at him expectantly, chin slightly up, with a mien that said: Please continue. I'm waiting for you to explain. And sure enough, he did.

"The fact is, yes, he was born the following year. I was born during the last minutes of December 31, at 11:54 pm, and he came out during the first few minutes of Jan 1. There's your next year. Your following year. Your fact. Although with his love of vocabulary, he'll call it a prevarication."

"But isn't the hero of your book, presumably you, the liar?"

"You have to disting…" He stopped in mid-word. "What's your line of work, mister?"

"The name is John…and I happen to be a chiropractor," I said.

"Couldn't get into med school, huh?"

And with perfect equanimity, showing no reaction to his baiting, I said with a feigned supercilious air:

"I got my MD from Harvard Medical School, then went on to study chiropractry so as to combine the best of both fields."

"I see," said the now slightly ruffled Katz. "In any case, what I meant to say was you have to be able to distinguish between fact and fiction. You sort of quoted him before, when he said, Don't confuse the 'I' of the narration with me. Fiction is full of disguises. You can't take the first-person narrator to be me, the author. Just because the first-person narrator tells lies or fibs or exaggerates, it doesn't mean that it's me, the author, who is a liar. That part of the Katz personality is actually my brother, as is his wide-ranging vocabulary and love of words. But despite the name Katz in the novel, you have to view this book as a work of fiction and not as a memoir."

Which is exactly what my Katz used to say.

"If he's a liar," I told Katz, "and if he constantly said that you're the author of the book, that means he really wrote it."

"Your thought processes are too complicated for me, Mister John."

"And if he's a liar, he's a very clever one."

"The clever ones make the best liars."

I noticed that Katz did not dispute the putative "if."

Then, following my seatmate's strategy, I changed the subject.

"Interesting and unusual first names you both have. Your brother never did tell me his first name."

"Yeah. We were given those very English-sounding names like Mortimer and Montmorency, I suppose, to offset the Jewishness of Katz. But we feel like a goy who is named Moishe-Yankl Huntington, or a Jew called Christopher Luke Cohen. Totally absurd. Now you know why we both prefer being called Katz."

And then I thought: if the guy before me was really my Katz, he would have winced at my fake doctor routine. Unless his acting skills are so refined that nothing fazes him.

I figured I would test Katz again.

"I like that Thomas Mann quote," I told him.

"What Thomas Mann quote?"

"Don't you read Mann?"

"I haven't gotten around to him yet."

What kind of cultivated man, I thought, who proclaims he's a writer hasn't read Mann?

"But you quote him." I'm afraid my voice had an accusatory tone.

Katz, frowning, gave me a questioning look, then seemed to catch himself.

"It's a long book. Where?"

"When the narrator is angry at Maria after her tirade, he berates her for being 'illogical, oppressive and absurd.'"

"Oh, yeah. Forgot about that. I may have read that somewhere and threw it in."

"It's from Mann's 'Homage to Kafka,' his Introduction to *The Castle*."

"For a chiropractor you seem to be well read."

"It's the MD in me that reads. The chiropractor in me is chairman of my regional Chiropractors Love Literature Club. We meet every month and discuss bestsellers."

Katz's explanation didn't persuade me. An author should remember the writers he throws in to dazzle readers into assuming he's an all-around literati, or, to be precise, literatus—which made me change my mind again about who was the author of *I Love PussyKatz*. For a second, I thought of telling the author to insert a comma between the lower case "y" and the capital "K."

Then, looking at Katz's face, out of the blue I said:

"One more question. Is, was, your brother married?"

"That's two questions."

"Is?"

"With Katz it's hard to say. Look, if you know him so well, why don't you....?"

"Because our friendship was a train friendship. He didn't even know my last name or where I worked. We never called each other. Never socialized. I wouldn't even know how to reach him."

Then I turned away from him, looked for my editor friend again, couldn't find him. I spotted another staff member wearing a nametag.

"Hi," I said. "Tim invited me, but I haven't seen him yet. Is he around somewhere?"

"No, Tim's son came down with some sort of virus and he couldn't make it today. But he'll probably be back in the office tomorrow. Can I help you with anything?"

"Do you know Katz?"

"Not very well."

"Do you know if he has a brother?"

"No, I don't. He's sort of a secretive man, Katz is. He gave us very little about his bio. He said he's an engineer by profession but he didn't even want that on the book jacket."

I excused myself and returned to Katz.

"Before I go. I just want to wish you lots of success. I hope your book—whosoever it is—is a success. It deserves to be."

Only once I was on the subway back to Penn Station did I realize that with all the excitement, I had forgotten to ask Katz about the confession.

57

THE MEETING

AFTER THE BOOK PARTY, I was more anxious than ever to see Katz. But my Katz was gone. Was it Mortimer or Montmorency? By now I didn't know who was who. What kind of Anglophile parents saddled them with names like that? I could imagine the teasing those poor boys had from their classmates with those polysyllabic monikers—coupled with Katz.

And where was my Katz? Was he avoiding me? Maybe he knew that I knew about the book. Author Katz probably let loose a barrage of righteous indignation on his twin for sharing his story with me.

And why wasn't Katz on any of the trains I took? He had been around so long and so steadily he seemed part of the timetable. Maybe he changed jobs, left town. Moved to another country, doing surveying for Brazil. Maybe he was ill. And maybe—no, I didn't even want to think of that possibility. He wasn't an old man. Mid-fifties; sixty, tops.

Katz owed me a confession.

•

One day I left work at noon and took a 1 p.m. train back to Trenton. And there was Katz. Again a reverse. First down the up escalator and now the train *from* New York.

We stared at each other—his beard was gone—he more wary than I. I wasn't going to mention the book until he did. I looked at Katz, tried seeing him through his brother's eyes. No doubt some kind of genius lurked within him. We chatted about the coincidence of our meeting.

= Like in a Russian novel, where the characters bump into each other on the Trans-Siberian Express, Katz said. = I looked for you. I wanted to contact you, but I only knew your first name. I kept calling one publisher after another asking for an editor named John. Found loads of Johns.

= Of course. Ninety-five percent of the editors in this town are named John. If your name isn't John, you can't get a job.

A hundred questions bubbled in my mind. I wished I could ask all of them. I began with:

= First of all, Katz, I think it's about time. Let's exchange phone numbers.

After we did I said:

= Where've you been? I've been looking for you for weeks.

= The French asked me to do some surveying for them.

= In Paris?

= No. French Equatorial Africa.

I looked into his eyes, searching for some play of humor. Found none there.

= There is no such place anymore. It's long defunct.

= I know. That's why it took me so long. I had the job. The address. But no country I could fit them into.

After a period of silence, I asked quickly:

= Why didn't you tell me the novel was accepted?

= Simple. I didn't know myself. Once I found out I couldn't wait to tell you, but I didn't see you.

= Well, anyway, congratulations. Or mazel tov. By coincidence a colleague at your brother's publisher invited me to the pre-pub book party, not knowing of course that I had heard most of the novel.

= I know. My brother told me and complained about me sharing the book with a stranger. Never trust a chiropractor, he said.

= Fearful of literary heist?

= They're very quick with their hands, my brother said. I didn't know you were a chiropractor too.

= A fella's got to make a living.

= And I didn't know you were a liar. Chiropractor, my foot! And I thought lying was my brother's specialty.

Instead of reacting, I asked Katz:

= Why weren't you at the book party?

= Simple. I was in England then. In fact, I just returned a couple of days ago...By the way, the editors renamed the novel. They're going to call it *Katz or Cats*. But the bad news is they're postponing publication because of the economy.

= I'm so sorry to hear that. But it's happening more and more often.

= My brother is devastated. He waited so long...

= Tell me, Katz, does the c-a-t-s part of the title refer to the way people spell your name?

= No.

= Then what do felines have to do with the title?

= That's part of the confession, John. Remember, you asked me if I changed anything in the book I was narrating and I indignantly said no. Then, going up the escalator I thought about it.

= And that's when you changed your mind and started that gutsy run down.

= Yes. And listen to this. As I ran down the escalator, fighting the upsurging crowd, the classical music they play at the terminal to dissuade bums from hanging around—it was the "Sunrise" quartet by Haydn—this music rang backward in my ears. Instead of melody, because of the way I was traveling, I sensed the notes were being swallowed, played in reverse, with deep inhalation. It didn't make my arduous trip down the up escalator any easier, listening to backwards music.

= I still see you struggling, going down, and then sailing up again. Then charging. What a daring thing to do!

= My brother has guts.

= Wait a minute, Katz, I said. = Whoa there! You're not reading from the manuscript now, where you claim that every 'I' is really 'he.' That you're just the mouthpiece. The actor. Now you're not retelling. This time it's you, *you*, doing this. You're on the escalator. I watched, I witnessed *you* trying to go down the up escalator. What's your brother got to do with it?

Katz hesitated. = Hmm! I'm so used to using the first person for my brother's story that even when I talk about myself I attribute it to my brother...Anyway, up there on the escalator, you're right, I changed my mind. What I had told you about not changing anything wasn't exactly true. It was a prevarication. And I wanted to return and tell you the truth. You see, I can't stand cats. I have an aversion to them.

I spread my hands, shook my head in a classic expression of puzzlement.

= Maria loved cats, was crazy about them. I wish she would have been as crazy about Katz as she was about cats. To be constant, consistent, unwavering, predictable in affection, attitude, and demeanor to this Katz as she was to those cats.

I imagined him saying this in a cavernous tunnel, the words echoing, bouncing from one nonexistent wall to another. Given the experience I'd had with Theresa, a shiver, beginning with the top of my skull and ending with my toes, ran over, through and around me like an electric shock. I sat next to Katz but felt my skull was floating somewhere else, disoriented, drunk, my center of gravity displaced, just like Katz's was. Theresa loved her cats too. All nine of them.

= Remember, John, when Maria first met Katz and he told her his name, she said she just loved the name. Now you can understand why she embraced and adored it. And why after so many years she remembered the name of the author of *Travels in Bessarabia*. If you love cats, then Katz is an unforgettable name. A name to love.

I was nodding, but I was somewhere else.

Hearing Katz and cats, again I thought about Theresa, but I soon told myself: Don't make too much out of this tempting cats coincidence. There are plenty of girls who love cats. Two, maybe three, out of ten aisles in a supermarket are for cats. There's no shortage of cat lovers. And, anyway, twenty years and many miles separate the two women. And, for goodness's sake, I had to remind myself, Maria is a character in a novel.

= John, listen carefully. I'm talking for the hero of the book now. So don't get confused. When we met, I told you this already, Maria said: "Katz! I love the name. A perfect name. I just love it." At that time, of course, I had no idea why she said that. I had never before heard anyone say they loved my name. Maybe me, but not my name. Later, when I visited her apartment and saw those creatures running helter-skelter, it clicked. Then I thought that with my name I was just another cat added to her collection.

= Soon as they saw me, her furry pets scurried in all directions, those fraidy cats. That's another name I was called when I was a kid: fraidy Katz. Each of those pussycats took off like a grayhound and found a refuge, well-hidden, out of view.... So because of my aversion, in my retelling the cats were eliminated from my brother's novel. My choice.

= That's the only liberty I took with the text. Getting rid of those accursed cats. You can't imagine how when I was a kid I suffered when I was called cat names. I don't see how my brother was able to tolerate cats and include them in his novel and spend so much creative energy on them.

= Did kids make fun of your first name too?

= They sure did. With our first and last names, the kids on the block didn't need any other entertainment. They used to pronounce Mortimer nastily, stretching the three syllables with a special nasty, nasal pronunciation. Mor-de-mer.

= And Katz, of course, I said, = has its own resonances.

= Right. I told you fraidy Katz. Katz house. Pussy Katz. Will you eat my pussy, Katz? I leave the variations to your imagination. And so, with my antipathy to cats, I altered the text. On the other hand, a dog will lay down his life for you. Can be counted on. Only thing you can count on a cat for is betrayal. What do you expect? It's a pussy. A pussy betrays. So does a rooster, by the way.

I hesitated, mulling over if I should say what I wanted to say. Then I decided, yes, I will say it.

= I too have a confession, Katz. While you're narrating a fictional love affair, I met a girl too, in almost the same fashion. In a train waiting room a couple of months ago, while you were away. A well-dressed guy goes up to her and politely says he has a job interview in New York and doesn't have money for a ticket because he forgot his wallet at home. Could she lend him roundtrip fare? He'll pay her back tomorrow morning. Uh-oh, I says to myself. The world's oldest scam. But she gives him the money and subway fare too. He promises to repay the next morning. And, guess what? The next morning I saw him paying her. So I began talking to her, commending her for her good deed.

= Did she ask you if you wrote a book?

= No.

= Is she Jewish like our Maria?

= Exactly. A Christian, but she doesn't flaunt it like Maria. For instance, I didn't see her carrying a Bible. But somehow her personality, bright, idealistic, considerate, naïve, reminds me of Maria. At first I thought she might be Maria's daughter—but impossible. She's too old.

Katz went into his briefcase.

= In the hope I would meet you, I always carry with me a section of a chapter that was so full of cats I just removed it. If you don't mind, I'll read it to you.

•

How shall I articulate how much Maria loved cats? I wish I could spell that last word my way, with a "z" and not her way. In any case, I'll compare it to how much I hate dogs from Chihuahuas to Great Danes. But as much as I hated dogs, Maria loved cats. If she saw a cat on the street she'd cross over and pet it and purr ecstatically. And don't forget Maria loved Jesus. Was crazy about him. And she loved Jesus almost as much as she loved cats.

For them she had an extraordinary passion. She knew each of them by name. And I always suspect that those who expend all their love on animals don't care much for people. Which eventually was the case.

When I came into her house, all the cats vanished. Like magic. They hid in every conceivable, even inconceivable, corner. "They sense you don't like them," Maria said. Only once did one of them come out. It sprang up on the sofa where Maria and I were sitting. I relented. I put my hand out and stroked her back. She purred, made all kinds of sexy, satisfied pussy noises, arched her back, just as Maria did at the height of her pleasure. I'm stroking your pussy, I told Maria.

"Tell me you don't love her," she once declared when I petted her puss while she pressed another cat to her bosom as if it were a newborn babe.

"Okay. I don't."

"You don't what?"

"Love her."

"You don't love her? How can you not?"

"I'm just obeying. You just told me to tell you I don't love her."

"You have no feeling for animals."

"Not so. I love butterflies and fleas. But I like my cats small. Very small. Kittens. Pussycats. Pussycats, that is, with the cats removed."

"I know another Katz that should be removed. A Katz that has a one-cat mind." And she began laughing.

Then she changed the angle of the question.

"Come on. I mean, really, don't you just love her?"

"Well..." I said, trying to be honest. Then she jumped on the sofa (the cat, not Maria) and, me trying to be nice, I don't know what got into me, but I cradled her in my arms (again, the cat, not her mistress). I rocked her like a baby.

"I can't believe it. She actually likes you." Maria was actually beaming, so pleased with this reciprocal love. "Tell the truth now, don't you just love her?"

"I do," I said, false as a cat. I had absolutely no affection for that cat and let her go as soon as I felt it would be polite to disembrace her. She jumped down, her tail arched and stiff, probably ready to scratch my *falshe katz*—remember my mother's expression?—eyes out.

Maria picked up the kitty and nuzzled her face into the cat's fur, making purring, pussy happy, happy pussycat sounds. I resolved not to kiss her (that is, Maria's) face until she washed it.

"Do you love your cats?" I asked Maria.

"Yes. I do. I love my cats."

I fantasized she meant me but knew she meant hers.

"You're spelling it wrong."

It took her a while but she finally got it.

Then I added, "And I love your Katz too."

Which reminded me that once when I asked Maria if she thanked God for me, she said, "I pray to God to protect my Katz." For a moment I felt so good, so proud that my electrons and hers were buzzing back and forth on the same line, until I saw that clever little smile playing on her lips, and I immediately imagined the capital "K" shrinking into a lower case "c" and the "z" curving into an "s", the catty rascal.

And when Maria expressed her affection for one big Katz, maybe she was symbolically hugging all the cats in the world, of which this Katz was the prime example. And the opposite held true as well. When she sat in the easy chair and hugged and moozed one of her cats, maybe she really meant the real, the authentic Katz.

I have a theory about single women who love cats. Single women who love cats, and I mean lo-oh-oh-ove them, cuddle and kiss them, who fuss over felids and have lots of them indoors and strays outside, and have a cat mat in the entrance hallway, kitten carpets on the floors, meow greeting cards on their desks, books about cat culture on their shelves, magnetic kitties on the fridge, framed pussycat portraits on their walls, kittie-cat themed notepads on their writing tables, and ebony cat sculptures scattered helter-skelter—all these single women are sexually repressed. Their rooms are filled with pussycats—their own pussies unfulfilled.

•

As I replayed Katz's remarks, there came a slight echo of his words, akin to counterpoint, a kind of round. It was as if I were listening to Katz's story twice, once in its original form and the other just two or three beats thereafter—you hear that sometimes in faulty phone connections—hearing the words in harmony, the notes C and E played together, taking the flow of time and halting it, and then resuming the flow along with the moments suspended.

= So is that the confession, Katz? That's what you ran down the up escalator for?

= Yes, John, that's the confession. And I should add it wasn't a canary Maria kept. As you know by now, she kept cats.

= Which one? I said. = Montmorency or Mortimer?

= No. With a small "c". Meow! Cats. Because of my aversion to them I changed cats to canary. Don't ask me why a canary. Okay, ask me why. I still don't know. Can't answer why I changed my brother's text and made a little songbird out of Maria's pets. Usually, the cat swallows the canary. Here the canary swallowed the cat.

= How many cats did Maria have in the manuscript?

= Excluding me? Katz seemed pleased with himself.

= Yes.

= Let me answer this way. Do you know Gorki's fascinating memoir of Tolstoy? No? In it he describes Tolstoy's affection for a certain writer by using the following metaphor—or is it simile?—"Like an old maid's affection for her canary or tomcat." It's a memorable image. At once I thought of Maria's love of cats. I admired Gorki's conjunction of old maid and love of a pet. But I never, never ever, never thought of Maria as an old maid. She was too young, too vibrant for that moniker. Then, rereading Gorki, I realized I had skipped an important line, which changed the entire character of the metaphor, turned it on its head, so to speak. For Gorki actually said, "There was something faintly ridiculous about Tolstoy's affection for that writer. It was like an old maid's affection for her canary or tomcat." Hey, wait! That's where I probably got the idea of a canary, in the same phrase with a pet cat. So how much more faintly ridiculous could the love for nine pussycats be? And she knew each cat by name. And all the names rhymed.

= What? I yelled out to Katz. It wasn't a question. It was an exclamation point "what," a miniscule substitution for me clasping my heart in astonishment.

Hearing his last words was for me the equivalent of Robinson Crusoe seeing that incredible human footprint in the sand.

Twice Katz repeated what he said. My surprise obliterated his first repetition. Only with the second did the news sink in.

= Nine of them? I said.

= Yes, John. Nine.

= And with rhymed names, I said dully. = Do you remember their names?

= Yes. Rhymed, Katz said ardently. = For she was crazy about cats, and ultimately, more crazy about little cats than big Katz. The little ones don't cause problems with Jesus. The big one does.

= But do you remember their names?

= Let's see. If I excised them from the manuscript, I may have excised them from my mind. I'll try to visualize those pages.

Katz kept nodding his head, as if seeing the pages turning. Then he said:

= Their names rhymed with olly. There was Bali and Polly and Dolly. There was Jolly and Melancholy. There was By Golly and Molly and Wally. Let's see, that makes eight. There was one more.

= You're forgetting, I said, barely able to speak, = her favorite, Mr. Svengali.

= Yes. Yes. Now I remember. Mr. Svengali. With two different colored eyes. One green…

= And the other blue.

•

And then Katz and I looked at each other as though both of us had met in a different cosmos, transported to a "Wait a minute!" psychoscape.

For me, time zones melted like one of Dali's clocks and distance imploded. He threw me off balance, that prevaricating rascal. Or, rather, his writer brother did, undoing my inner clock. I couldn't tell the difference between mountain time, solar time, and daylight savings time.

My clock not only didn't stand still, it moved backwards. If it could have, it would have gone sideways. It reminded me of a watch I once had. It was so flawed it only told the right time once a day.

Katz's Yiddish expression "*falshe katz*," false cat, floated into view. Indeed, he was a stellar example of a *falshe katz*. Recalling his *falshe* phrase that he, or his brother, had known Maria "decades ago," I found myself sliding down a hill, scudding past time zones and bumping over diverse locales. Old equations tumbled. Came in new ones to pinch hit. Yesteryear=now. Tram=train. Boston=New York. Canary=cats. In this new equation, the cat didn't swallow the canary. The cat *was* the canary.

But before we parted, I managed to tell Katz:

= And I have another confession to make.

Which mitigated the force of the stun.

= Another? said Katz.

= Yes, I said.

= What is this, a Catholic chapel? What do you want to confess now, John? That you too are a twin?

= No, not me. Your manuscript. Your manuscript is a twin. Has a twin. Like you.

= How's that?

= A doppelgänger. Like the dwarf twins in Thomas Mann's *Joseph in Egypt* that we talked about months ago.

= John, I still don't know what you're talking about.

= I'm trying to tell you. Your manuscript has been cloned. Doppelgängered.

= How? Katz asked me.

= I'm not finished with synonyms. Your manuscript has been identicalized. Semi-Siamesed.

= Will you tell me already? How?

= Simple, Katz. I made a twin of your manuscript. I tape recorded all your monologues.

58

WHAT JOHN HAS DONE

Now that Katz's book, or the Katzs' book, has been postponed and postponed again—I called my friend Tim at the publishing house and he told me they were having financial problems and would probably have to eliminate fiction—I want to state that I have recorded here only what I have heard, neither adding nor subtracting a word. I have heard what I have heard and have written down word for word what I have heard, every single, even every double, word.

What I have before me is something like the book mentioned in the Jewish High Holiday prayer book for Rosh Hashana and Yom Kippur, which Katz once mentioned to me and which made a great impression on me both for its theological punch and for its mystery and imaginative imagery.

There is a crucial, memorable line that says the deeds of all men are recorded in a heavenly book and that that book "reads itself"—one of the most memorable images I have ever encountered. Can you imagine, a book that reads itself! That book records men's deeds just like I have recorded the deeds of Katz and his brother—or the deeds of Katz or his brother.

That celestial book speaks the truth and everything in it is true, for in the supernal realms there is no falseness. Nothing *falshe,* i.e., there no *falshe katz* can exist. Up there—just like in the Zuni Indian language—there is no word for "false." And here, down here too, I aver, no line is false. What I have heard you are hearing.

This book too will read itself.

You see, I am an editor, not a writer; a transcriber, not a creative artist; a meticulous court stenographer, not a concocter of tales.

So then, the only one who could be trusted—I've mentioned this before—is me, the editor, who listened carefully and is presenting the complete story to you word for word without additions, accretions, deletions, without substitutions and editorial changes, exactly, word for word, as I heard it and recorded and copied it, without the intermediary of possible changes by Mortimer Katz, the scribe, or Montmorency Katz, the writer, or vice versa, or the combined talents of Montimortimemo(i)rency Katz.

But there is one final twist to this saga, a P.S. which you will discover on the next page.

P.S.

A WHILE AFTER MY last conversation with Katz, I did something for him and then phoned him.

= Hi, it's John. Listen to this. I heard what happened to your brother's book, so I recommended it and gave it to another small house.

= Wow! That's great. My brother didn't know what to do next. With your recording the book, I thought of you as a plagiarist. But now you've come up with a solution and it's all for the good and I appreciate your help.

= But there's no guarantee, Katz. Even with my high praise.

= I know, John, I know.

= I also want to tell you that when I gave the editor a brief synopsis of your brother's book, he said, "If our firm bought the book, and there's no guarantee that will happen, we might add Jesus to the title, to reflect the contents of the book. And to catch the eye." That's what the editor said.

= That's fine with me, and it'll be fine with my brother too.

= And I'm sure you're aware, Katz, it's getting harder and harder for a first novel to be published, especially if it's by an unknown fiction writer.

= I know that too. Look, my brother is a consulting engineer. He has no pretensions to being a novelist, and I don't think he has any further literary ambitions. But with so much spiritual energy invested in this book, he just wants to see it published. He doesn't even care about a by-line. As far as he's concerned, someone else can sign it. Boccaccio, Borges, Bellow. Whoever. As long as this fun book, *Katz or Cats,* appears...By the way, can you tell me which house you gave it to?

= I can't, because this firm deals only with agents and they don't want authors calling. So you'll just have to wait for their decision. But I think it's a good omen that the first name of the editor—he's a novelist too—is one syllable like yours, Katz, and it's also spelled with four letters. What's more, his name, like the title of your brother's novel, can either be spelled with a K or with a C.